THE HISTORY OF TOM JONES

HENRY FIELDING'S

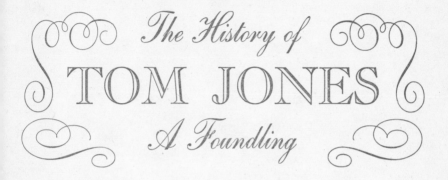

The History of
TOM JONES
A Foundling

Illustrated by Harry Diamond

10407

THE LITERARY GUILD OF AMERICA, INC.
Garden City · New York

Robert W. Arnold - 40

Henry Fielding 1707-1754

THE HISTORY OF TOM JONES

Book I

CONTAINING AS MUCH OF THE BIRTH OF THE FOUNDLING AS IS
NECESSARY OR PROPER TO ACQUAINT THE READER WITH IN THE BE-
GINNING OF THIS HISTORY

I

IN THAT part of the western division of this kingdom which is commonly called Somersetshire, there lately lived and perhaps lives still, a gentleman whose name was Allworthy, and who might well be called the favorite of both Nature and Fortune; for both of these seem to have contended which should bless and enrich him most. From the former he derived an agreeable person, a sound constitution, a sane understanding, and a benevolent heart; by the latter, he was decreed to the inheritance of one of the largest estates in the county.

This gentleman had in his youth married a very worthy and beautiful woman, of whom he had been extremely fond: by her he had three children, all of whom died in their infancy. He had likewise had the misfortune of burying this beloved wife herself, about five years before the time in which this history chooses to set out. This loss, however great, he bore like a man of sense and constancy; for he sometimes said he looked on himself as still married, and considered his wife as only gone a little before him, a journey which he should most certainly, sooner or later, take after her.

He now lived, for the most part, retired in the country, with one sister, for whom he had a very tender affection. This lady was now somewhat past the age of thirty, an era at which, in the opinion of the malicious, the title of old maid may with no impropriety be assumed. She was of that species of women whom you commend rather for good qualities than beauty; and she was so far from regretting want of beauty, that she never mentioned that perfection, if it can be called one, without contempt. Miss Bridget Allworthy (for that was the name of this lady) very rightly conceived the charms of person in a woman to be no better than snares for herself, as well as for others; and yet so discreet was she in her conduct, that her prudence was as much on the guard as if she had all the snares to apprehend which were ever laid for her whole sex. Indeed, I have observed, though it may seem unaccountable to the reader, that this guard of prudence is always readiest to go on duty where there is the least danger. It often basely and cowardly deserts those paragons for whom the men are all wishing, sighing, dying, and spreading every net in their power; and constantly attends at the heels of that higher order of women for whom the other sex have a more distant and awful respect, and whom (from despair, I suppose, of success) they never venture to attack.

II

Mr. Allworthy had been absent a full quarter of a year in London on some very particular business. He came to his house very late in the evening, and after a short supper with his sister, retired much fatigued to his chamber. Here, having spent some minutes on his knees—a custom which he never broke through on any account—he was preparing to step into bed, when, upon opening the clothes, to his great surprise he beheld an infant, wrapt up in some coarse linen, in a sweet and profound sleep, between his sheets. He stood some time lost in astonishment at this sight; but, as good-nature had always the ascendant in his mind, he soon began to be touched with sentiments of compassion for the little wretch before him. He then rang his bell, and ordered an elderly woman-servant to rise immediately, and come to him.

She no sooner opened the door, and saw her master standing by the bedside in his shirt, with a candle in his hand, than she started back in a most terrible fright, and might perhaps have swooned away, had he not now recollected his being undressed, and put an end to her terrors by desiring her to stay without the door till he had thrown some clothes over his back, and was become incapable of shocking the pure eyes of Mrs. Deborah Wilkins, who, though in the fifty-second year of her age, vowed she had never beheld a man without his coat.

When Mrs. Deborah returned into the room, and was acquainted by her master with the finding the little infant, her consternation was rather greater than his had been; nor could she refrain from crying out, with great horror of accent as well as look, "My good sir! what's to be done?" Mr. Allworthy answered, she must take care of the child that evening, and in the morning he would give orders to provide it a nurse.

"Yes, sir," says she; "and I hope your worship will send out your warrant to take up the hussy its mother, for she must be one of the neighborhood; and I should be glad to see her committed to Bride-well, and whipped at the cart's tail. Indeed, such wicked sluts cannot be too severely punished. I'll warrant 'tis not her first, by her impudence in laying it to your worship."

"In laying it to me, Deborah!" answered Allworthy: "I can't think she hath any such design. I suppose she hath only taken this method to provide for her child; and truly I am glad she hath not done worse."

"I don't know what is worse," cries Deborah, "than for such wicked strumpets to lay their sins at honest men's doors; and though your worship knows your own innocence, yet the world is censorious; and if your worship should provide for the child, it may make the people the apter to believe; besides, why should your worship provide for what the parish is obliged to maintain? If I might be so bold to give my advice, I would have it put in a basket, and sent out and laid at the churchwarden's door. It is a good night, only a little rainy and windy; and if it was well wrapt up, and put in a warm basket, it is two to one but it lives till it is found in the morning. But if it should not, we have discharged our duty in taking proper care of it."

There were some strokes in this speech which, perhaps, would have offended Mr. Allworthy had he strictly attended to it; but he had now got one of his fingers into the infant's hand, which, by its gentle pressure seeming to implore his assistance, had certainly out-pleaded the eloquence of Mrs. Deborah, had it been ten times greater than it was. He now gave Mrs. Deborah positive orders to take the child to her own bed, and that proper clothes should be procured for it early in the morning, and that it should be brought to himself as soon as he was stirring.

Such was the discernment of Mrs. Wilkins, and such the respect she bore her master, under whom she enjoyed a most excellent place, that her scruples gave way to his peremptory commands; and she took the child under her arms, without any apparent disgust at the illegality of its birth; and declaring it was a sweet little infant, walked off with it to her own chamber.

III

THE Gothic style of building could produce nothing nobler than Mr. Allworthy's house. There was an air of grandeur in it that struck you with awe, and rivaled the beauties of the best Grecian architecture; and it was as commodious within as venerable without.

It stood on the southeast side of a hill, but nearer the bottom than the top of it, so as to be sheltered from the northeast by a grove of old oaks which rose above it in a gradual ascent of near half a mile, and yet high enough to enjoy a most charming prospect of the valley beneath.

In the midst of the grove was a fine lawn, sloping down toward the house, near the summit of which rose a plentiful spring, gushing out of a rock covered with firs, and forming a constant cascade of about thirty feet, not carried down a regular flight of steps, but tumbling in a natural fall over the broken and mossy stones, till it came to the bottom of the rock; then running off in a pebbly channel, that with many lesser falls winded along, till it fell into a lake at the foot of the hill, about a quarter of a mile below the house on the south side, and which was seen from every room in the front. Out of this lake, which filled the center of a beautiful plain, embellished with groups of beeches and elms, and fed with sheep, issued a river, that for several miles was seen to meander through an amazing variety of meadows and woods, till it emptied itself into the sea, with a large arm of which, and an island beyond it, the prospect was closed.

On the right of this valley opened another of less extent, adorned with several villages, and terminated by one of the towers of an old ruined abbey, grown over with ivy, and part of the front, which remained still entire.

The left-hand scene presented the view of a very fine park, composed of very unequal ground, and agreeably varied with all the diversity that hills, lawns, wood, and water, laid out with admirable taste, but owing less to art than to Nature, could give. Beyond this the country gradually rose into a ridge of wild mountains, the tops of which were above the clouds.

It was now the middle of May, and the morning was remarkably serene, when Mr. Allworthy walked forth on the terrace, where the dawn opened every minute that lovely prospect; and now in the full blaze of his majesty rose the sun, than which one object alone in this lower creation could be more glorious, and that Mr. Allworthy himself presented—a human being replete with benevolence, meditating in what manner he might render himself most acceptable to his Creator, by doing most good to his creatures.

Reader, take care. I have unadvisedly led thee to the top of as high a hill as Mr. Allworthy's, and how to get thee down without breaking thy neck I do not well know. However, let us e'en venture to slide down together; for Miss Bridget rings her bell, and Mr. Allworthy is summoned to breakfast, where I must attend, and, if you please, shall be glad of your company.

The usual compliments having passed between Mr. Allworthy and Miss Bridget, and the tea being poured out, he summoned Mrs. Wilkins, and told his sister he had a present for her, for which she thanked him—imagining, I suppose, it had been a gown, or some ornament for her person.

But if such was her expectation, how was she disappointed when Mrs. Wilkins, according to the order she had received from her master, produced the little infant? Great surprises, as hath been observed, are apt to be silent; and so was Miss Bridget, till her brother began, and told her the whole story, which, as the reader knows it already, we shall not repeat.

Miss Bridget had always expressed so great a regard for what the ladies are pleased to call virtue, and had herself maintained such a severity of character, that it was expected, especially by Wilkins, that she would have vented much bitterness on this occasion, and would have voted for sending the child, as a kind of noxious animal, immediately out of the house; but, on the contrary, she rather took the good-natured side of the question, intimated some compassion for the helpless little creature, and commended her brother's charity in what he had done.

Perhaps the reader may account for this behavior from her

condescension to Mr. Allworthy, when we have informed him the good man had ended his narrative with owning a resolution to take care of the child, and to breed him up as his own; for, to acknowledge the truth, she was always ready to oblige her brother, and very seldom, if ever, contradicted his sentiments. She would, indeed, sometimes make a few observations, as that men were headstrong, and must have their own way, and would wish she had been blest with an independent fortune; but these were always vented in a low voice, and at the most amounted only to what is called muttering.

However, what she withheld from the infant she bestowed with the utmost profuseness on the poor unknown mother, whom she called an impudent slut, a wanton hussy, an audacious harlot, a wicked jade, a vile strumpet, with every other appellation with which the tongue of virtue never fails to lash those who bring a disgrace on the sex.

A consultation was now entered into how to proceed in order to discover the mother. A scrutiny was first made into the characters of the female servants of the house, who were all acquitted by Mrs. Wilkins, and with apparent merit; for she had collected them herself, and perhaps it would be difficult to find such another set of scarecrows.

The next step was to examine among the inhabitants of the parish; and this was referred to Mrs. Wilkins, who was to inquire with all imaginable diligence, and to make her report in the afternoon.

Matters being thus settled, Mr. Allworthy withdrew to his study, as was his custom, and left the child to his sister, who, at his desire, had undertaken the care of it.

Miss Bridget, having looked some time earnestly at the child, as it lay asleep in the lap of Mrs. Deborah, could not forbear giving it a hearty kiss, at the same time declaring herself wonderfully pleased with its beauty and innocence. Mrs. Deborah no sooner observed this than she fell to squeezing and kissing, crying out, in a shrill voice, "O, the dear little creature! The dear, sweet, pretty creature! Well, I vow it is as fine a boy as ever was seen!"

These exclamations continued till they were interrupted by the lady, who now proceeded to execute the commission given her by her brother, and gave orders for providing all necessaries for the child, appointing a very good room in the house for his nursery. Her orders were indeed so liberal, that, had it been a child of her own, she could not have exceeded them; but, lest the virtuous reader may condemn her for showing too great a regard to a base-born infant,

6

we think proper to observe that she concluded the whole with saying, "Since it was her brother's whim to adopt the little brat, she supposed little master must be treated with great tenderness. For her part, she could not help thinking it was an encouragement to vice; but that she knew too much of the obstinacy of mankind to oppose any of their ridiculous humors."

IV

Mrs. Deborah, having disposed of the child according to the will of her master, now prepared to visit those habitations which were supposed to conceal its mother.

When the approach of Mrs. Deborah was proclaimed through the street, all the inhabitants ran trembling into their houses, each matron dreading lest the visit should fall to her lot. It is the nature of such persons as Mrs. Wilkins to insult and tyrannize over little people. This being indeed the means which they use to recompense to themselves their extreme servility and condescension to their superiors; for nothing can be more reasonable, than that slaves and flatterers should exact the same taxes on all below them which they themselves pay to all above them.

Whenever Mrs. Deborah had occasion to exert any extraordinary condescension to Mrs. Bridget, and by that means had a little soured her natural disposition, it was usual with her to walk forth among these people in order to refine her temper, by venting, and, as it were, purging off all ill humors; on which account she was universally dreaded and hated by them all.

On her arrival in this place, she went immediately to the habitation of an elderly matron; to whom, as this matron had the good fortune to resemble herself in the comeliness of her person, as well as in her age, she had generally been more favorable than to any of the rest. To this woman she imparted what had happened, and these two at last fixed the strongest suspicion on one Jenny Jones.

This Jenny Jones was no very comely girl, either in her face or person; but nature had somewhat compensated the want of beauty with a very uncommon share of understanding. This gift Jenny had a good deal improved by erudition. She had lived several years a servant with a schoolmaster, and was, perhaps, as good a scholar as most of the young men of quality of the age. It is not to be wondered at that this superiority in Jenny, together with that behavior which

7

is its certain consequence, should produce among the rest some little envy and ill-will toward her; and these had, perhaps, secretly burnt in the bosoms of her neighbors ever since her return from her service.

Their envy did not, however, display itself openly, till poor Jenny, to the surprise of everybody, and to the vexation of all the young women in these parts, had publicly shone forth on a Sunday in a new silk gown, with a laced cap, and other proper appendages to these.

The flame, which had before lain in embryo, now burst forth. Jenny had, by her learning, increased her own pride, which none of her neighbors were kind enough to feed with the honor she seemed to demand; and now, instead of respect and adoration, she gained nothing but hatred and abuse by her finery. The whole parish declared she could not come honestly by such things; and parents, instead of wishing their daughters the same, felicitated themselves that their children had them not.

Jenny had lately been often at Mr. Allworthy's house. She had officiated as nurse to Miss Bridget, in a violent fit of illness, and had sat up many nights with that lady; besides which, she had been seen there the very day before Mr. Allworthy's return by Mrs. Wilkins herself, though that sagacious person had not at first conceived any suspicion of her on that account.

Jenny was now summoned to appear in person before Mrs. Deborah, which she immediately did; when Mrs. Deborah, putting on the gravity of a judge, with somewhat more than his austerity, began an oration with the words, "You audacious strumpet!" in which she proceeded rather to pass sentence on the prisoner than to accuse her.

Though Mrs. Deborah was fully satisfied of the guilt of Jenny, from the reasons above shown, it is possible Mr. Allworthy might have required some stronger evidence to have convicted her; but she saved her accusers any such trouble by freely confessing the whole fact with which she was charged.

Mrs. Deborah having succeeded beyond her hopes in her inquiry, returned with much triumph, and, at the appointed hour, made a faithful report to Mr. Allworthy, who was much surprised at the relation; for he had heard of the extraordinary parts and improvements of this girl, whom he intended to have given in marriage, together with a small living, to a neighboring curate.

Miss Bridget blessed herself, and said, "For her part, she should never hereafter entertain a good opinion of any woman." For Jenny before this had the happiness of being much in her good graces also.

The prudent housekeeper was again dispatched to bring the unhappy culprit before Mr. Allworthy, in order, not as it was hoped by some, and expected by all, to be sent to the House of Correction, but to receive wholesome admonition and reproof; which those who relish that kind of instructive writing may peruse in the next chapter.

V

WHEN Jenny appeared, Mr. Allworthy took her into his study, and spoke to her as follows: "You know, child, it is in my power as a magistrate to punish you very rigorously for what you have done; and you will, perhaps, be the more apt to fear I should execute that power, because you have in a manner laid your sins at my door.

"But, perhaps, this is one reason which hath determined me to act in a milder manner with you; for no private resentment should ever influence a magistrate. It is the other part of your offense, therefore, upon which I intend to admonish you, I mean the violation of your chastity—a crime, however lightly it may be treated by debauched persons, very heinous in itself, and very dreadful in its consequences.

"The heinous nature of this offense must be sufficiently apparent to every Christian, inasmuch as it is committed in defiance of the laws of our religion, and of the express commands of Him who founded that religion.

"There are other consequences, such as must, one would think, deter all of your sex at least from the commission of this crime.

"For by it you are rendered infamous, and driven, like lepers of old, out of society; at least, from the society of all but wicked and reprobate persons; for no others will associate with you. Thus you are often driven by necessity itself into a state of shame and misery, which unavoidably ends in the destruction of both body and soul.

"Can any pleasure compensate these evils? Can any temptation have sophistry and delusion strong enough to persuade you to so simple a bargain? Or can any carnal appetite so overpower your reason, or so totally lay it asleep, as to prevent your flying with affright and terror from a crime which carries such punishment always with it?

"For no woman, sure, will plead the passion of love for an excuse. This would be to own herself the mere tool and bubble of the man. In what light, but that of an enemy, can a reasonable woman regard the man who solicits her to entail on herself all the misery I have described to you, and who would purchase to himself a short, trivial, contemptible pleasure, so greatly at her expense! For, by the laws of custom, the whole shame, with all its dreadful consequences, falls entirely upon her. Can love, which always seeks the good of its object, attempt to betray a woman into a bargain where she is so greatly to be the loser?"

Here Jenny expressing great concern, Allworthy paused a moment, and then proceeded: "I have talked thus to you, child, not to insult you for what is past and irrevocable, but to caution and strengthen you for the future. Nor should I have taken this trouble, but from some opinion of your good sense, notwithstanding the dreadful slip you have made; I will take care to convey you from this scene of your shame, where you shall, by being unknown, avoid the punishment which, as I have said, is allotted to your crime in this world; and I hope, by repentance, you will avoid the much heavier sentence denounced against it in the other. Be a good girl the rest of your days, and want shall be no motive to your going astray; and, believe me, there is more pleasure, even in this world, in an innocent and virtuous life than in one debauched and vicious.

"As to your child, let no thoughts concerning it molest you; I will provide for it in a better manner you can ever hope. And now nothing remains but that you inform me who was the wicked man that seduced you; for my anger against him will be much greater than you have experienced on this occasion."

Jenny now lifted her eyes from the ground, and with a modest look and decent voice thus began:

"To know you, sir, and not love your goodness, would be an argument of total want of sense or goodness in anyone. My future conduct will much better declare my sentiments than any professions I can now make. But now, sir, I must on my knees entreat you not to persist in asking me to declare the father of my infant. I promise you faithfully you shall one day know; but I am under the most solemn ties and engagements of honor, as well as the most religious vows and protestations, to conceal his name at this time. And I know you too well, to think you would desire I should sacrifice either my honor or my religion."

Mr. Allworthy, whom the least mention of those sacred words was sufficient to stagger, hesitated a moment before he replied, and then told her she had done wrong to enter into such engagements to a villain; but since she had, he could not insist on her breaking them.

He said it was not from a motive of vain curiosity he had inquired, but in order to punish the fellow; at least, that he might not ignorantly confer favors on the undeserving.

As to these points Jenny satisfied him by the most solemn assurances that the man was entirely out of his reach; and was neither subject to his power, nor in any probability of becoming an object of his goodness.

The ingenuity of this behavior had gained Jenny so much credit with this worthy man, that he easily believed what she told him; for as she had disdained to excuse herself by a lie, and had hazarded his further displeasure in her present situation, rather than she would forfeit her honor or integrity by betraying another, he had but little apprehensions that she would be guilty of falsehood toward himself.

VI

JENNY returned home well pleased with the reception she had met with from Mr. Allworthy, whose indulgence to her she industriously made public; partly perhaps as a sacrifice to her own pride, and partly from the more prudent motive of reconciling her neighbors to her, and silencing their clamors.

But though this latter view, if she indeed had it, may appear reasonable enough, yet the event did not answer her expectation; for when she was convened before the justice, and it was universally apprehended that the House of Correction would have been her fate, there were many who began to pity her condition; but when it was known in what manner Mr. Allworthy had behaved, the tide turned against her. One said, "I'll assure you, madam hath had good luck." A second cried, "See what it is to be a favorite!" A third, "Ay, this comes of her learning." Every person made some malicious comment or other on the occasion, and reflected on the partiality of the justice.

Jenny was, however, by the care and goodness of Mr. Allworthy, soon removed out of the reach of reproach; when malice being no longer able to vent its rage on her, began to seek another object of its bitterness, and this was no less than Mr. Allworthy himself; for a whisper soon went abroad that he himself was the father of the foundling child.

This supposition so well reconciled his conduct to the general opinion, that it met with universal assent; and the outcry against his lenity soon began to take another turn, and was changed into an invective against his cruelty to the poor girl. Very grave and good women exclaimed against men who begot children and then disowned them. Nor were there wanting some, who, after the departure of Jenny, insinuated that she was spirited away with a design too black to be mentioned, and who gave frequent hints that a legal inquiry ought to be made into the whole matter, and that some people should be forced to produce the girl.

These calumnies might have probably produced ill consequences, at the least might have occasioned some trouble, to a person of a more doubtful and suspicious character than Mr. Allworthy was blessed with; but in his case they had no such effect; and, being heartily despised by him, they served only to afford an innocent amusement to the good gossips of the neighborhood.

Mr. Allworthy rather chose to encourage the girl; for too true I am afraid it is, that many women have become abandoned, and have sunk to the last degree of vice, by being unable to retrieve their first slip. This will be, I am afraid, always the case while they remain among their former acquaintance; it was therefore wisely done by Mr. Allworthy, to remove Jenny to a place where she might enjoy the pleasure of reputation, after having tasted the ill consequences of losing it.

To this place therefore, wherever it was, we will wish her a good journey, and for the present take leave of her, and of the little foundling her child, having matters of much higher importance to communicate to the reader.

VII

NEITHER Mr. Allworthy's house, nor his heart, were shut against any part of mankind, but they were both more particularly open to men of merit.

Among others of this kind was Dr. Blifil, a gentleman who had the misfortune of losing the advantage of great talents by the obstinacy of a father, who would breed him to a profession he disliked. In obedience to his obstinacy the doctor had in his youth been obliged to study physic, or rather to say he studied it; for in reality books of this kind were almost the only ones with which he was unacquainted; and unfortunately for him, the doctor was master of almost every other science but that by which he was to get his bread; the consequence of which was, that the doctor at the age of forty had no bread to eat.

Such a person as this was certain to find a welcome at Mr. Allworthy's table, to whom misfortunes were ever a recommendation, when they were derived from the folly or villainy of others, and not of the unfortunate person himself. Besides this negative merit, the doctor had one positive recommendation;—this was a great appearance of religion. Whether his religion was real, or consisted only in appearance, I shall not presume to say, as I am not possessed of any touchstone which can distinguish the true from the false.

If this part of his character pleased Mr. Allworthy, it delighted Miss Bridget. She engaged him in many religious controversies; on which occasions she constantly expressed great satisfaction in the doctor's knowledge, and not much less in the compliments which he frequently bestowed on her own.

As sympathies of all kinds are apt to beget love, so experience teaches us that none have a more direct tendency this way than those of a religious kind between persons of different sexes. The doctor found himself so agreeable to Miss Bridget, that he now began to lament an unfortunate accident which had happened to him about ten years before; namely, his marriage with another woman, who was not only still alive, but, what was worse, known to be so by Mr. Allworthy.

He had not long ruminated on these matters, before it occurred to his memory that he had a brother who was under no such unhappy incapacity. This brother he made no doubt would succeed; for he discerned, as he thought, an inclination to marriage in the lady; and the reader perhaps, when he hears the brother's qualifications, will not blame the confidence which he entertained of his success.

This gentleman was about thirty-five years of age. He was of a middle size, and what is called well built. He had a scar on his forehead, which did not so much injure his beauty as it denoted his valor (for he was a half-pay officer). He had good teeth, and something affable, when he pleased, in his smile; though naturally his countenance, as well as his air and voice, had much of roughness in it: yet he could at any time deposit this, and appear all gentleness and good-humor. He was not ungenteel, nor entirely devoid of wit, and in his youth had abounded in sprightliness, which, though he had lately put on a more serious character, he could, when he pleased, resume.

He had, as well as the doctor, an academic education; for his father had, with the same paternal authority we have mentioned before, decreed him for holy orders; but as the old gentleman died before he was ordained, he chose the church military, and preferred the king's commission to the bishop's.

The doctor sent for his brother, and easily found means to introduce him at Allworthy's as a person who intended only a short visit to himself. The captain had not been in the house a week before the doctor had reason to felicitate himself on his discernment. The captain was indeed as great a master of the art of love as Ovid was formerly. He had besides received proper hints from his brother, which he failed not to improve to the best advantage.

VIII

It hath been observed by wise men or women, I forget which, that all persons are doomed to be in love once in their lives. No particular season is, as I remember, assigned for this; but the age at which Miss Bridget was arrived, seems to me as proper a period as any to be fixed on for this purpose: it often, indeed, happens much earlier; but when it doth not, I have observed it seldom or never fails about this time.

Miss Bridget had not been many times in the captain's company before she was seized with this passion. Nor did she go pining and moping about the house, like a puny, foolish girl, ignorant of her distemper: she felt, she knew, and she enjoyed, the pleasing sensation, of which, as she was certain it was not only innocent but laudable, she was neither afraid nor ashamed.

And to say the truth, there is, in all points, great difference between the reasonable passion which women at this age conceive toward men, and the idle and childish liking of a girl to a boy, which is often fixed on the outside only, and on things of little value and no duration; as on cherry-cheeks, small, lily-white hands, sloe-black eyes, flowing locks, downy chins, dapper shapes; nay, sometimes on charms more worthless than these, and less the party's own; such are the outward ornaments of the person, for which men are beholden to the tailor, the lace-man, the periwig-maker, the hatter, and the milliner, and not to nature. Such a passion girls may well be ashamed, as they generally are, to own either to themselves or others.

The love of Miss Bridget was of another kind. The captain owed nothing to any of these fop-makers in his dress, nor was his person much more beholden to nature. Both his dress and person were such as, had they appeared in an assembly or a drawing-room, would have been the contempt and ridicule of all the fine ladies there. The former of these was indeed neat, but plain, coarse, ill-fancied, and out of fashion. As for the latter, we have expressly described it above. So far was the skin on his cheeks from being cherry-colored, that you could not discern what the natural color of his cheeks was, they being totally overgrown by a black beard, which ascended to his eyes. His shape and limbs were indeed exactly proportioned, but so large that they denoted the strength rather of a ploughman than any other. His shoulders were broad beyond all size, and the calves of his legs larger than those of a common chairman. In short, his whole person wanted all that elegance and beauty which is the very reverse of clumsy strength, and which so agreeably sets off most of our fine gentlemen; being partly owing to the high blood of their ancestors, viz., blood made of rich sauces and generous wines, and partly to an early town education.

Though Miss Bridget was a woman of the greatest delicacy of taste, yet such were the charms of the captain's conversation, that she totally overlooked the defects of his person. She imagined, and perhaps very wisely, that she should enjoy more agreeable minutes with the captain than with a much prettier fellow; and forewent the consideration of pleasing her eyes, in order to procure herself much more solid satisfaction.

The captain likewise very wisely preferred the more solid enjoyments he expected with this lady, to the fleeting charms of person.

To deal plainly with the reader, the captain, ever since his arrival, at least from the moment his brother had proposed the match to him, long before he had discovered any flattering symptoms in Miss Bridget, had been greatly enamored; that is to say, of Mr. Allworthy's house and gardens, and of his lands, tenements, and hereditaments; of all which the captain was so passionately fond, that he would most probably have contracted marriage with them, had he been obliged to have taken the witch of Endor into the bargain.

The satisfaction which the captain received from the kind behavior of Miss Bridget was not a little abated by his apprehensions of Mr. Allworthy; for, notwithstanding his disinterested professions, the captain imagined he would, when he came to act, follow the example of the rest of the world, and refuse his consent to a match so disadvantageous, in point of interest, to his sister. It strangely perplexed him how to regulate his conduct so as at once to convey his affection to the lady, and to conceal it from her brother. He at length resolved to take all private opportunities of making his addresses, but in the presence of Mr. Allworthy to be as reserved and as much upon his guard as was possible.

He soon found means to make his addresses, in express terms, to his mistress, from whom he received an answer in the proper form, viz.: the answer which was first made some thousands of years ago, and which hath been handed down by tradition from mother to daughter ever since. If I was to translate this into Latin, I should render it by these two words, *Nolo Espiscopari*: a phrase likewise of immemorial use on another occasion.

The captain, however he came by his knowledge, perfectly well understood the lady, and very soon after repeated his application with more warmth and earnestness than before, and was again, according to due form, rejected; but as he had increased in the eagerness of his desires, so the lady, with the same propriety, decreased in the violence of her refusal.

Not to tire the reader, by leading him through every scene of this courtship, the captain made his advances in form, the citadel was defended in form, and at length, in proper form, surrendered at discretion.

During this whole time, which filled the space of near a month, the captain preserved great distance of behavior to his lady in the presence of the brother; and the more he succeeded with her in private, the more reserved was he in public. And as for the lady, she had no sooner secured her lover than she behaved to him before company with the highest degree of indifference; so that Mr. Allworthy must have had the insight of the devil (or perhaps some of his worst qualities) to have entertained the least suspicion of what was going forward.

IX

In ALL bargains, whether to fight or to marry, or concerning any other such business, little previous ceremony is required to bring the matter to an issue when both parties are really in earnest. This was the case at present, and in less than a month the captain and his lady were man and wife.

The great concern now was to break the matter to Mr. Allworthy: and this was undertaken by the doctor.

One day, then, as Allworthy was walking in his garden, the doctor came to him, and, with great gravity of aspect, and all the concern which he could possibly affect in his countenance, said, "I am come, sir, to impart an affair to you of the utmost consequence; but how shall I mention to you what it almost distracts me to think of!" He then launched forth into the most bitter invectives both against men and women; accusing the former of having no attachment but to their interest, and the latter of being so addicted to vicious inclinations that they could never be safely trusted with one of the other sex. "Could I," said he, "sir, have suspected that a lady of such prudence, such judgment, such learning, should indulge so indiscreet a passion; or could I have imagined that my brother—why do I call him so? he is no longer a brother of mine——"

"Indeed but he is," said Allworthy, "and a brother of mine too."

"Bless me, sir!" said the doctor, "do you know the shocking affair?"

"Look'ee, Mr. Blifil," answered the good man, "it hath been my constant maxim in life to make the best of all matters which happen. My sister, though many years younger than I, is at least old enough to be at the age of discretion. Had he imposed on a child, I should have been more averse to have forgiven him; but a woman upwards of thirty must certainly be supposed to know what will make her most happy. She hath married a gentleman, though perhaps not quite her equal in fortune; and if he hath any perfections in her eye which can make up that deficiency, I see no reason why I should object to her choice of her own happiness."

The doctor acquainted his brother with what had passed between Mr. Allworthy and him, and added with a smile, "I promise you I paid you off; nay, I absolutely desired the good gentleman not to forgive you: for you know after he had made a declaration in your favor, I might with safety venture on such a request with a person of his temper; and I was willing, as well for your sake as for my own, to prevent the least possibility of a suspicion."

Captain Blifil took not the least notice of this, at that time; but he afterwards made a very notable use of it.

One of the maxims which the devil, in a late visit upon earth, left to his disciples, is, when once you are got up, to kick the stool from under you. In plain English, when you have made your fortune by the good offices of a friend, you are advised to discard him as soon as you can.

Whether the captain acted by this maxim I will not positively determine: so far we may confidently say, that no sooner was he possessed of Miss Bridget, and reconciled to Allworthy, than he began to show a coldness to his brother which increased daily, till at length it grew into rudeness, and became very visible to everyone.

The doctor remonstrated to him privately concerning this behavior, but could obtain no other satisfaction than the following plain declaration: "If you dislike anything in my brother's house, sir, you know you are at liberty to quit it." This strange, cruel, and almost unaccountable ingratitude in the captain absolutely broke the poor doctor's heart; for ingratitude never so thoroughly pierces the human breast as when it proceeds from those in whose behalf we have been guilty of transgressions.

Mr. Allworthy himself spoke to the captain in his brother's behalf, and desired to know what offense the doctor had committed; when the hard-hearted villain had the baseness to say that he should never forgive him for the injury which he had endeavored to do him in his favor; which, he said, he had pumped out of him, and was such a cruelty that it ought not to be forgiven.

Allworthy spoke in very high terms upon this declaration, which, he said, became not a human creature. He expressed, indeed, so much resentment against an unforgiving temper, that the captain at last pretended to be convinced by his arguments, and outwardly professed to be reconciled; yet the same rancor remained in his heart; and he found so many opportunities of giving him private hints of this, that the house at last grew insupportable to the poor doctor; and he chose rather to submit to any inconveniences which he might encounter in the world, than longer to bear these cruel and ungrateful insults from a brother for whom he had done so much.

He feigned, therefore, some excuse of business for his departure, and promised to return soon again; and took leave of his brother with so well-dissembled content, that, as the captain played his part to the same perfection, Allworthy remained well satisfied with the truth of the reconciliation.

The doctor went directly to London, where he died soon after of a broken heart—a distemper which kills many more than is generally imagined, and would have a fair title to a place in the bill of mortality, did it not differ in one instance from all other diseases, viz., that no physician can cure it.

Book II

CONTAINING SCENES OF MATRIMONIAL FELICITY IN DIFFERENT DE-
GREES OF LIFE; AND VARIOUS OTHER TRANSACTIONS DURING THE
FIRST TWO YEARS AFTER THE MARRIAGE BETWEEN CAPTAIN BLIFIL
AND MISS BRIDGET ALLWORTHY

I

EIGHT months after the celebration of the nuptials between Captain
Blifil and Miss Bridget Allworthy, was Miss Bridget, by reason of a
fright, delivered of a fine boy. The child was indeed to all appearances perfect; but the midwife discovered it was born a month
before its full time.

Though the birth of an heir by his beloved sister was a circumstance of great joy to Mr. Allworthy, yet it did not alienate his
affections from the little foundling, to whom he had been godfather,
had given his own name of Thomas, and whom he had hitherto
seldom failed of visiting, at least once a day, in his nursery.

He told his sister, if she pleased, the newborn infant should be
bred up together with little Tommy; to which she consented, though
with some little reluctance: for she had truly a great complacence
for her brother.

The captain could not so easily bring himself to bear what he
condemned as a fault in Mr. Allworthy. He gave him frequent hints,
that to adopt the fruits of sin was to give countenance to it.

He said, "Though the law did not positively allow the destroying such base-born children, yet it held them to be the children of nobody; that the Church considered them as the children of nobody; and that at the best, they ought to be brought up to the lowest and vilest offices of the commonwealth."

While the captain was taking all opportunities to press these and such like arguments, to remove the little foundling from Mr. Allworthy's, of whose fondness for him he began to be jealous, Mrs. Deborah had made a discovery, which, in its event, threatened at least to prove more fatal to poor Tommy than all the reasonings of the captain. She had now, as she conceived, fully detected the father of the foundling.

II

MY READER may please to remember that Jenny Jones had lived some years with a certain schoolmaster, who had, at her earnest desire, instructed her in Latin, in which, to do justice to her genius, she had so improved herself, that she was become a better scholar than her master.

Indeed, though this poor man had undertaken a profession to which learning must be allowed necessary, this was the least of his commendations. He was one of the best-natured fellows in the world, and was, at the same time, master of so much pleasantry and humor, that he was reputed the wit of the country; and all the neighboring gentlemen were so desirous of his company, that as denying was not his talent, he spent much time at their houses, which he might, with more emolument, have spent in his school.

The stipend arising hence would hardly have indulged the schoolmaster in the luxuries of life, had he not added to this office those of clerk and barber, and had not Mr. Allworthy added to the whole an annuity of ten pounds, which the poor man received every Christmas.

Among his other treasures, the pedagogue had a wife, whom he had married out of Mr. Allworthy's kitchen for her fortune, viz., twenty pounds, which she had there amassed.

This woman was not very amiable in her person. She was, besides, a professed follower of that noble sect founded by Xantippe of old; by means of which she became more formidable in the school than her husband; for to confess the truth, he was never master there, or anywhere else, in her presence.

She maintained so constant a jealousy, that he durst hardly speak to one woman in the parish; for the least degree of civility, or even correspondence, with any female, was sure to bring his wife upon her back, and his own.

In order to guard herself against matrimonial injuries in her own house, as she kept one maid-servant, she always took care to choose her out of that order of females whose faces are taken as a kind of security for their virtue; of which number Jenny Jones, as the reader hath been before informed, was one.

But it is with jealousy as with the gout: when such distempers are in the blood, there is never any security against their breaking out, and that often on the slightest occasions, and when least suspected.

Thus it happened to Mrs. Partridge, who had submitted four years to her husband's teaching this young woman, and had suffered her often to neglect her work in order to pursue her learning. For, passing by one day, as the girl was reading, and her master leaning over her, the girl, I know not for what reason, suddenly started up from her chair; and this was the first time that suspicion ever entered into the head of her mistress.

This lay lurking in her mind, and additional strength soon arrived to corroborate her suspicion; for not long after, the husband and wife being at dinner, the master said to his maid, *Da mihi aliquid potum*: upon which the poor girl smiled, perhaps at the badness of the Latin, and, when her mistress cast her eyes on her, blushed, possibly with a consciousness of having laughed at her master. Mrs. Partridge, upon this, immediately fell into a fury, and discharged the trencher on which she was eating at the head of poor Jenny, crying out, "You impudent whore, do you play tricks with my husband before my face?" and at the same instant rose from her chair with a knife in her hand, with which, most probably, she would have executed very tragical vengeance, had not the girl taken the advantage of being nearer the door than her mistress, and avoided her fury by running away; for, as to the poor husband, whether surprise had rendered him motionless, or fear (which is full as probable) had restrained him from venturing at any opposition, he sat staring and trembling in his chair; nor did he once offer to move or speak, till his wife, returning from the pursuit of Jenny, made some defensive measures necessary for his own preservation; and he likewise was obliged to retreat, after the example of the maid.

Jenny offered to make protestations of her innocence; but the tempest was too strong for her to be heard. She then betook herself to the business of packing, for which a small quantity of brown paper sufficed; and, having received her small pittance of wages, she returned home.

The schoolmaster and his consort passed their time unpleasantly enough that evening; but something or other happened before the next morning which a little abated the fury of Mrs. Partridge; and she at length admitted her husband to make his excuses: to which she gave the readier belief, as he had, instead of desiring her to recall Jenny, professed a satisfaction in her being dismissed, saying she was grown of little use as a servant, spending all her time in reading, and was become, moreover, very pert and obstinate; for, indeed, she and her master had lately had frequent disputes in literature; in which, as hath been said, she was become greatly his superior. This, however, he would by no means allow; and as he called her persisting in the right, obstinacy, he began to hate her with no small inveteracy.

III

MANKIND have always taken great delight in knowing and descanting on the actions of others. Hence there have been, in all ages and nations, certain places set apart for public rendezvous, where the curious might meet and satisfy their mutual curiosity. Among these, the barbers' shops have justly borne the preëminence.

But this serves only for the men. Now, whereas the females of this country, especially those of the lower order, do associate themselves much more than those of other nations, our polity would be highly deficient if they had not some place set apart likewise for the indulgence of their curiosity, seeing they are in this no way inferior to the other half of the species.

This place then is no other than the chandler's shop, the known seat of all the news; or, as it is vulgarly called, gossiping, in every parish in England.

Mrs. Partridge being one day at this assembly of females, was asked by one of her neighbors if she had heard no news lately of Jenny Jones? To which she answered in the negative. Upon this the other replied, with a smile, That the parish was very much obliged to her for having turned Jenny away as she did.

Mrs. Partridge, whose jealousy, as the reader well knows, was long since cured, and who had no other quarrel to her maid, answered boldly, She did not know any obligation the parish had to her on that account; for she believed Jenny had scarce left her equal behind her.

"No, truly," said the gossip, "I hope not, though I fancy we have sluts enow too. Then you have not heard, it seems, that she hath been brought to bed of two bastards? but as they are not born here, my husband and the other overseer says we shall not be obliged to keep them."

"Two bastards!" answered Mrs. Partridge hastily: "you surprise me! I don't know whether we must keep them; but I am sure they must have been begotten here, for the wench had not been nine months gone away."

Nothing can be so quick and sudden as the operations of the mind, especially when hope, or fear, or jealousy, to which the two others are but journeymen, set it to work. It occurred instantly to her that Jenny had scarce ever been out of her own house while she lived with her. The leaning over the chair, the sudden starting up, the Latin, the smile, and many other things, rushed upon her all at once. The satisfaction her husband expressed in the departure of Jenny appeared now to be only dissembled. In a word, she was convinced of her husband's guilt, and immediately left the assembly in confusion.

As fair Grimalkin, who, though the youngest of the feline family, and though inferior in strength, is equal in fierceness to the noble tiger himself, not with less fury did Mrs. Partridge fly on the poor pedagogue. Her tongue, teeth, and hands fell all upon him at once. His wig was in an instant torn from his head, his shirt from his back, and from his face descended five streams of blood, denoting the number of claws with which nature had unhappily armed the enemy.

Mr. Partridge acted for some time on the defensive only; but as he found that his antagonist abated nothing of her rage, he thought he might, at least, endeavor to disarm her.

He had, at length, the good fortune, by getting possession of her arms, to render those weapons which she wore at the ends of her fingers useless; which she no sooner perceived, than the softness of her sex prevailed over her rage, and she presently dissolved in tears, which soon after concluded in a fit.

That small share of sense which Mr. Partridge had hitherto preserved through this scene of fury, of the cause of which he was hitherto ignorant, now utterly abandoned him. He ran instantly into the street, hallooing out that his wife was in the agonies of death, and beseeching the neighbors to fly with the utmost haste to her assistance. Several good women obeyed his summons, who, entering his house, and applying the usual remedies on such occasions, Mrs. Partridge was at length, to the great joy of her husband, brought to herself.

As soon as she had a little recollected her spirits, and somewhat composed herself with a cordial, she began to inform the company of the manifold injuries she had received from her husband; who, she said, had treated her in the cruelest manner imaginable; giving her, at the same time, several blows, the marks of which she should carry to the grave.

The poor man, who bore on his face many more visible marks of the indignation of his wife, stood in silent astonishment at this accusation; which the reader will, I believe, bear witness for him, had greatly exceeded the truth; for indeed he had not struck her once; and this silence being interpreted to be a confession of the charge by the whole court, they all began at once to rebuke and revile him, repeating often, that none but a coward ever struck a woman.

Mr. Partridge bore all this patiently; but when his wife appealed to the blood on her face, as an evidence of his barbarity, he could not help laying claim to his own blood, for so it really was. To this the women made no other answer, than that it was a pity it had not come from his heart, instead of his face; all declaring, that, if their husbands should lift their hands against them, they would have their hearts' bloods out of their bodies.

After much admonition for what was past, and much good advice to Mr. Partridge for his future behavior, the company at length departed, and left the husband and wife to a personal conference together, in which Mr. Partridge soon learned the cause of all his sufferings.

IV

MRS. WILKINS, whose eyes could see objects at a distance, and who could very well look forward a few years into futurity, had perceived a strong likelihood of Captain Blifil's being hereafter her master; and as she plainly discerned that the captain bore no great goodwill to the little foundling, she fancied it would be rendering him an agreeable service if she could make any discoveries that might lessen the affection which Mr. Allworthy seemed to have contracted for this child.

Mrs. Wilkins having therefore, by accident, gotten a true scent of the above story, though long after it had happened, failed not to satisfy herself thoroughly of all the particulars; and then acquainted the captain that she had at last discovered the true father of the little bastard, which she was sorry, she said, to see her master lose his reputation in the country by taking so much notice of.

The captain chid her for the conclusion of her speech, as an improper assurance in judging of her master's actions; for if his honor, or his understanding, would have suffered the captain to make an alliance with Mrs. Wilkins, his pride would by no means have admitted it.

But though he declared no satisfaction to Mrs. Wilkins at this discovery, he enjoyed not a little from it in his own mind, and resolved to make the best use of it he was able.

He kept this matter a long time concealed within his own breast, in hopes that Mr. Allworthy might hear it from some other person; but Mrs. Wilkins, whether she resented the captain's behavior, or whether his cunning was beyond her, and she feared the discovery might displease him, never afterwards opened her lips about the matter.

I have thought it somewhat strange, upon reflection, that the housekeeper never acquainted Mrs. Blifil with this news, as women are more inclined to communicate all pieces of intelligence to their own sex than to ours. The only way, as it appears to me, of solving this difficulty, is by imputing it to that distance which was now grown between the lady and the housekeeper: whether this arose from a jealousy in Mrs. Blifil, that Wilkins showed too great a respect to the foundling; for while she was endeavoring to ruin the little infant, in order to ingratiate herself with the captain, she was every day more and more commending it before Allworthy, as his fondness for it every day increased.

The captain, therefore, finding the story in danger of perishing, at last took an opportunity to reveal it himself.

Mr. Allworthy expressed great surprise at this account, and the captain as great at his ignorance of it; for he said he had known it above a month; and at length recollected with much difficulty that he was told it by Mrs. Wilkins.

Upon this, Wilkins was immediately summoned; who having confirmed what the captain had said, was by Mr. Allworthy, by and with the captain's advice, dispatched to Little Baddington, to inform herself of the truth of the fact.

V

MRS. WILKINS, having executed her commission with great dispatch, though at fifteen miles' distance, brought back such a confirmation of the schoolmaster's guilt, that Mr. Allworthy determined to send for the criminal, and examine him *vivâ voce*. Mr. Partridge, therefore, was summoned to attend, in order to his defense (if he could make any) against this accusation.

At the time appointed, before Mr. Allworthy himself, at Paradise Hall, came as well the said Partridge, with Anne, his wife, as Mrs. Wilkins his accuser.

And now Mr. Allworthy being seated in the chair of justice, Mr. Partridge was brought before him. Having heard his accusation from the mouth of Mrs. Wilkins, he pleaded not guilty, making many vehement protestations of his innocence.

Mrs. Partridge was then examined, who, after a modest apology for being obliged to speak the truth against her husband, related all the circumstances with which the reader hath already been acquainted; and at last concluded with her husband's confession of his guilt.

Whether she had forgiven him or no, I will not venture to determine; but it is certain that she was an unwilling witness in this cause; and it is probable from certain other reasons, would never have been brought to depose as she did, had not Mrs. Wilkins, with great art, fished all out of her at her own house, and had she not indeed made promises, in Mr. Allworthy's name, that the punishment of her husband should not be such as might anywise affect his family.

Partridge still persisted in asserting his innocence, though he admitted he had made the above-mentioned confession; which he however endeavored to account for, by protesting that he was forced into it by the continued importunity she used: who vowed, that, as she was sure of his guilt, she would never leave tormenting him till he had owned it; and faithfully promised, that, in such case, she would never mention it to him more. Hence, he said, he had been induced falsely to confess himself guilty, though he was innocent; and that he believed he should have confessed a murder from the same motive.

Mrs. Partridge could not bear this imputation with patience; and having no other remedy in the present place but tears, she called forth a plentiful assistance from them, and then addressing herself to Mr. Allworthy, she said (or rather cried), "May it please your worship, there never was any poor woman so injured as I am by that base man; for this is not the only instance of his falsehood to me. I could have put up with his drunkenness and neglect of his business, if he had not broke one of the sacred commandments. Yes, you villain, you have defiled my own bed, you have; and then you have charged me with bullocking you into owning the truth. Is it very likely, an't please your worship, that I should bullock him? I have marks enow about my body to show of his cruelty to me. And since he provokes me, I am ready, an't please your worship, to take my bodily oath that I found them a-bed together. What, you have forgot, I suppose, when you beat me into a fit, and made the blood run down my forehead, because I only civilly taxed you with adultery! but I can prove it by all my neighbors. You have almost broke my heart, you have, you have."

Here Mr. Allworthy interrupted, and begged her to be pacified, promising her that she should have justice; then turning to Partridge, who stood aghast, one-half of his wits being hurried away by surprise and the other half by fear, he said he was sorry to see there was so wicked a man in the world. He assured him that his prevaricating and lying backward and forward was a great aggravation of his guilt; for which the only atonement he could make was by confession and repentance. He exhorted him, therefore, to begin by immediately confessing the fact, and not to persist in denying what was so plainly proved against him even by his own wife.

Here, reader, I beg your patience a moment, while I make a just compliment to the great wisdom and sagacity of our law, which refuses to admit the evidence of a wife for or against her husband. This, says a certain learned author, who, I believe, was never quoted before in any but a lawbook, would be the means of creating an eternal dissension between them. It would, indeed, be the means of much perjury, and of much whipping, fining, imprisoning, transporting, and hanging.

Partridge stood a while silent, till, being bid to speak, he said he had already spoken the truth, and appealed to Heaven for his innocence, and lastly to the girl herself, whom he desired his worship immediately to send for; for he was ignorant, or at least pretended to be so, that she had left that part of the country.

Mr. Allworthy, whose natural love of justice, joined to his coolness of temper, made him always a most patient magistrate in hearing all the witnesses which an accused person could produce in his defense, agreed to defer his final determination of this matter till the arrival of

Jenny, for whom he immediately dispatched a messenger; and then having recommended peace between Partridge and his wife (though he addressed himself chiefly to the wrong person), he appointed them to attend again the third day; for he had sent Jenny a whole day's journey from his own house.

At the appointed time the parties all assembled, when the messenger returning brought word that Jenny was not to be found; for that she had left her habitation a few days before in company with a recruiting officer.

Mr. Allworthy then declared that the evidence of such a slut as she appeared to be would have deserved no credit; but he said he could not help thinking that, had she been present, and would have declared the truth, she must have confirmed what so many circumstances, together with his own confession, and the declaration of his wife that she had caught her husband in the fact, did sufficiently prove. He therefore once more exhorted Partridge to confess; but he still avowing his innocence, Mr. Allworthy declared himself satisfied of his guilt, and that he was too bad a man to receive any encouragement from him. He therefore deprived him of his annuity, and recommended repentance to him on account of another world, and industry to maintain himself and his wife in this.

Whether Partridge repented or not, according to Mr. Allworthy's advice, is not so apparent. Certain it is that his wife repented heartily of the evidence she had given against him: especially when she found Mrs. Deborah had deceived her, and refused to make any application to Mr. Allworthy on her behalf.

Partridge and his wife were therefore both obliged to submit to their fate; which was indeed severe enough: for so far was he from doubling his industry on the account of his lessened income, that he did in a manner abandon himself to despair; and as he was by nature indolent, that vice now increased upon him, by which means he lost the little school he had; so that neither his wife nor himself would have had any bread to eat, had not the charity of some good Christians interposed, and provided them with what was just sufficient for their sustenance.

As this support was conveyed to them by an unknown hand, they imagined, and so, I doubt not, will the reader, that Mr. Allworthy himself was their secret benefactor; who, though he would not openly encourage vice, could yet privately relieve the distresses of the vicious themselves, when these became too exquisite and disproportionate to their demerit. In which light their wretchedness appeared now to Fortune herself; for she at length took pity on this miserable couple, and considerably lessened the wretched state of Partridge by putting a final end to that of his wife, who soon after caught the smallpox and died.

The justice which Mr. Allworthy had executed on Partridge at first met with universal approbation; but no sooner had he felt its consequences, than his neighbors began to relent and to compassionate his case; and presently after, to blame that as rigor and severity which they before called justice. They now exclaimed against punishing in cold blood, and sang forth the praises of mercy and forgiveness.

These cries were considerably increased by the death of Mrs. Partridge, which, though owing to the distemper above mentioned, which is no consequence of poverty or distress, many were not ashamed to impute to Mr. Allworthy's severity, or, as they now termed it, cruelty.

Partridge having now lost his wife, his school, and his annuity, and the unknown person having now discontinued the last-mentioned charity, resolved to change the scene, and left the country, where he was in danger of starving, with the universal compassion of all his neighbors.

VI

THOUGH the captain had effectually demolished poor Partridge, yet had he not reaped the harvest he hoped for, which was to turn the foundling out of Mr. Allworthy's house.

On the contrary, that gentleman grew every day fonder of little Tommy, as if he intended to counterbalance his severity to the father with extraordinary fondness and affection towards the son.

This a good deal soured the captain's temper, as did all the other daily instances of Mr. Allworthy's generosity; for he looked on all such largesses to be diminutions of his own wealth.

In this, we have said, he did not agree with his wife; nor, indeed, in anything else: many quarrels from time to time arose between them; which at last ended, on the side of the lady, in a sovereign contempt for her husband; and on the husband's, in an utter abhorrence of his wife.

The captain, like a well-bred man, had, before marriage, always given up his opinion to that of the lady; yet this cost him too much to be endured without some motive. Matrimony, therefore, having removed all such motives, he grew weary of this condescension, and began to treat the opinions of his wife with that haughtiness and insolence which none but those who deserve some contempt themselves can bestow, and those only who deserve no contempt can bear.

When the first torrent of tenderness was over, and when, in the calm and long interval between the fits, reason began to open the eyes of the lady, and she saw this alteration of behavior in the captain, who at length answered all her arguments only with pish and pshaw, she was far from enduring the indignity with a tame submission. Indeed, it at first so highly provoked her, that it might have produced some tragical event, had it not taken a more harmless turn, by filling her with the utmost contempt for her husband's understanding, which somewhat qualified her hatred towards him; though of this likewise she had a pretty moderate share.

The captain's hatred to her was of a purer kind: for as to any imperfections in her knowledge or understanding, he no more despised her for them than for her not being six feet high. In his opinion of the female sex he exceeded the moroseness of Aristotle himself: he looked on a woman as on an animal of domestic use, of somewhat higher consideration than a cat, since her offices were of rather more importance; but the difference between these two was, in his estimation, so small, that, in his marriage contracted with Mr. Allworthy's lands and tenements, it would have been pretty equal which of them he had taken into the bargain. And yet so tender was his pride, that it felt the contempt which his wife now began to express towards him; and this, added to the surfeit he had before taken of her love, created in him a degree of disgust and abhorrence perhaps hardly to be exceeded.

As many of my readers, I hope, know what an exquisite delight there is in conveying pleasure to a beloved object, so some few, I am afraid, may have experienced the satisfaction of tormenting one we hate. Hence the wife often puts on fits of love and jealousy, nay, even denies herself any pleasure, to disturb and prevent those of her husband; and he again, in return, puts frequent restraints on himself, and stays at home in company which he dislikes, in order to confine his wife to what she equally detests. Hence, too, must flow those tears which a widow sometimes so plentifully sheds over the ashes of a husband with whom she led a life of constant disquiet and turbulency, and whom now she can never hope to torment any more.

But if ever any couple enjoyed this pleasure, it was at present experienced by the captain and his lady. If the one proposed any amusement, the other constantly objected to it: they never loved or hated, commended or abused, the same person. And for this reason, as the captain looked with an evil eye on the little foundling, his wife began now to caress it almost equally with her own child.

VII

THE captain was made large amends for the unpleasant minutes which he passed in the conversation of his wife (and which were as few as he could contrive to make them), by the pleasant meditations he enjoyed when alone.

These meditations were entirely employed on Mr. Allworthy's fortune; for, first, he exercised much thought in calculating, as well as he could, the exact value of the whole: and, secondly and chiefly, he pleased himself with intended alterations in the house and gardens, and in projecting many other schemes, as well for the improvement of the estate as of the grandeur of the place: for this purpose he applied himself to the studies of architecture and gardening, and read over many books on both these subjects. He at last completed a most excellent plan; and very sorry we are that it is not in our power to present it to our reader, since even the luxury of the present age, I believe, would hardly match it. It had, indeed, in a superlative degree, the two principal ingredients which serve to recommend all great and noble designs of this nature; for it required an immoderate expense to execute, and a vast length of time to bring it to any sort of perfection. The former of these, the immense wealth of which the captain supposed Mr. Allworthy possessed, and which he thought himself sure of inheriting, promised very effectually to supply; and the latter, the soundness of his own constitution, and his time of life, which was only what is called middle-age, removed all apprehension of his not living to accomplish.

Nothing was wanting to enable him to enter upon the immediate execution of this plan but the death of Mr. Allworthy; in calculating which he had employed much of his own algebra, besides purchasing every book extant that treats of the value of lives, reversions, etc. From all which he satisfied himself, that as he had every day a chance of this happening, so had he more than an even chance of its happening within a few years.

But while the captain was one day busied in deep contemplations of this kind, one of the most unlucky as well as unseasonable accidents happened to him. The utmost malice of Fortune could, indeed, have contrived nothing so cruel, so malapropos, so absolutely destructive to all his schemes. In short, not to keep the reader in long suspense, just at the very instant when his heart was exulting in meditations on the happiness which would accrue to him by Mr. Allworthy's death, he himself—died of an apoplexy.

This, unfortunately, befell the captain as he was taking his evening walk by himself, so that nobody was present to lend him any assistance, if indeed any assistance could have preserved him. He took, therefore, measure of that proportion of soil which was now become adequate to all his future purposes, and he lay dead on the ground.

VIII

MR. ALLWORTHY, his sister, and another lady, were assembled at the accustomed hour in the supper-room, where, having waited a considerable time longer than usual, Mr. Allworthy first declared he began to grow uneasy at the captain's stay (for he was always most punctual at his meals); and gave orders that the bell should be rung without the doors, and especially towards those walks which the captain was wont to use.

All these summons proving ineffectual (for the captain had, by perverse accident, betaken himself to a new walk that evening), Mrs. Blifil declared she was seriously frightened. Upon which the other lady, who was one of her most intimate acquaintances, and who well knew the true state of her affections, endeavored all she could to pacify her, telling her—To be sure she could not help being uneasy; but that she should hope the best. That, perhaps, the sweetness of the evening had enticed the captain to go farther than his usual walk; or he might be detained at some neighbor's. Mrs. Blifil answered, No; she was sure some accident had befallen him; for that he would never stay out without sending her word, as he must know how uneasy it would make her.

Mr. Allworthy now returned into the parlor; for he had been himself in search after the captain. His countenance sufficiently showed the consternation he was under, which, indeed, had a good deal deprived him of speech; but as grief operates variously on different minds, so the same apprehension which depressed his voice elevated that of Mrs. Blifil. She now began to bewail herself in very bitter terms, and floods of tears accompanied her lamentations; which the lady, her companion, declared she could not blame, but at the same time dissuaded her from indulging; she said her brother's example ought to teach her patience.

"Mention not my brother," said Mrs. Blifil; "I alone am the object of your pity. What are the terrors of friendship to what a wife feels on these occasions? Oh, he is lost! Somebody hath murdered him— I shall never see him more!"

At this interval a servant came running in, out of breath, and cried out, The captain was found; and, before he could proceed further, he was followed by two more, bearing the dead body between them.

Here the curious reader may observe another diversity in the operations of grief: for as Mr. Allworthy had been before silent, from the same cause which had made his sister vociferous, so did the present sight, which drew tears from the gentleman, put an entire stop to those of the lady; who first gave a violent scream, and presently after fell into a fit.

The room was soon full of servants, some of whom, with the lady visitant, were employed in care of the wife; and others, with Mr. Allworthy, assisted in carrying off the captain to a warm bed, where every method was tried in order to restore him to life; but all experiments of bleeding, chafing, dropping, etc., proved ineffectual. Death, that inexorable judge, had passed sentence on him, and refused to grant him a reprieve, though two doctors who arrived, and were fee'd at one and the same instant, were his counsel.

The case of the lady was in the other extreme from that of her husband; for as he was past all the assistance of physic, so in reality she required none.

There is nothing more unjust than the vulgar opinion, by which physicians are misrepresented as friends to death. So little did our doctors delight in death, that they discharged the corpse after a single fee; but they were not so disgusted with their living patient; concerning whose case they immediately fell to prescribing with great diligence.

Whether, as the lady had at first persuaded her physicians to believe her ill, they had now, in return, persuaded her to believe herself so, I will not determine; but she continued a whole month with all the decorations of sickness. During this time she was visited by physicians, attended by nurses, and received constant messages from her acquaintance to inquire after her health.

At length the decent time of sickness and immoderate grief being expired, the doctors were discharged, and the lady began to see company; being altered only from what she was before, by that color of sadness in which she had dressed her person and countenance.

The captain was now interred, and might, perhaps, have already made a large progress towards oblivion, had not the friendship of Mr. Allworthy taken care to preserve his memory by the following epitaph, which was written by a man of as great genius as integrity, and one who perfectly well knew the captain.

HERE LIES,
IN EXPECTATION OF A JOYFUL RISING,
THE BODY OF

CAPTAIN JOHN BLIFIL.

LONDON
HAD THE HONOR OF HIS BIRTH,
OXFORD
OF HIS EDUCATION.
HIS PARTS
WERE AN HONOR TO HIS PROFESSION
AND TO HIS COUNTRY:
HIS LIFE, TO HIS RELIGION
AND HUMAN NATURE.
HE WAS A DUTIFUL SON,
A TENDER HUSBAND,
AN AFFECTIONATE FATHER,
A MOST KIND BROTHER,
A SINCERE FRIEND,
A DEVOUT CHRISTIAN,
AND A GOOD MAN.
HIS INCONSOLABLE WIDOW
HATH ERECTED THIS STONE,
THE MONUMENT OF
HIS VIRTUES
AND HER AFFECTION.

Book III

CONTAINING THE MOST MEMORABLE TRANSACTIONS WHICH PASSED
IN THE FAMILY OF MR. ALLWORTHY, FROM THE TIME WHEN
TOMMY JONES ARRIVED AT THE AGE OF FOURTEEN, TILL HE AT-
TAINED THE AGE OF NINETEEN. IN THIS BOOK THE READER MAY PICK
UP SOME HINTS CONCERNING THE EDUCATION OF CHILDREN

I

WHAT reader but knows that Mr. Allworthy felt, at first, for the loss of his friend, those emotions of grief which on such occasions enter into all men whose hearts are not composed of flint, or their heads of as solid materials? Again, what reader doth not know that philosophy and religion in time moderated, and at last extinguished, this grief?

Nor can the judicious reader be at a greater loss on account of Mrs. Bridget Blifil, who, he may be assured, conducted herself with the strictest regard to all the rules of custom and decency, suiting the alterations of her countenance to the several alterations of her habit: for as this changed from weeds to black, from black to gray, from gray to white, so did her countenance change from dismal to sorrowful, from sorrowful to sad, and from sad to serious, till the day came in which she was allowed to return to her former serenity.

We have mentioned these two as examples only of the task which may be imposed on readers of the lowest class. Much higher and harder exercises of judgment and penetration may reasonably be expected from the upper graduates in criticism. Many notable discoveries will, I doubt not, be made by such, of the transactions which happened in the family of our worthy man during all the years which we have thought proper to pass over.

As we are sensible that much the greatest part of our readers are very eminently possessed of this quality, we have left them a space of twelve years to exert it in; and shall now bring forth our hero, at about fourteen years of age, not questioning that many have been long impatient to be introduced to his acquaintance.

II

As we determined, when we first sat down to write this history, to flatter no man, but to guide our pen throughout by the directions of truth, we are obliged to bring our hero on the stage in a much more disadvantageous manner than we could wish; and to declare honestly, even at his first appearance, that it was the universal opinion of all Mr. Allworthy's family that he was certainly born to be hanged.

Indeed, I am sorry to say there was too much reason for this conjecture; the lad having from his earliest years discovered a propensity to many vices. He had been already convicted of three robberies, viz., of robbing an orchard, of stealing a duck out of a farmer's yard, and of picking Master Blifil's pocket of a ball.

The vices of this young man were, moreover, heightened by the disadvantageous light in which they appeared when opposed to the virtues of Master Blifil, his companion; a youth of so different a cast from little Jones, that not only the family but all the neighborhood resounded his praises. He was, indeed, a lad of a remarkable disposition; sober, discreet, and pious beyond his age; qualities which gained him the love of everyone who knew him: while Tom Jones was universally disliked; and many expressed their wonder that Mr. Allworthy would suffer such a lad to be educated with his nephew, lest the morals of the latter should be corrupted by his example.

An incident which happened about this time will set the characters of these two lads more fairly before the discerning reader than is in the power of the longest dissertation.

Tom Jones, who, bad as he is, must serve for the hero of this history, had only one friend among all the servants of the family. This friend was the gamekeeper, a fellow of a loose kind of disposition.

To say the truth, some of that atrocious wickedness in Jones, of which we have just mentioned three examples, might perhaps be derived from the encouragement he had received from this fellow, who, in two or three instances, had been what the law calls an accessory after the fact: for the whole duck, and great part of the apples, were converted to the use of the gamekeeper and his family; though, as Jones alone was discovered, the poor lad bore not only the whole smart, but the whole blame.

Contiguous to Mr. Allworthy's estate was the manor of one of those gentlemen who are called preservers of the game. This species of men, from the great severity with which they revenge the death of a hare or partridge, might be thought to cultivate the same superstition with the Bannians in India; many of whom, we are told, dedicate their whole lives to the preservation and protection of certain animals; was it not that our English Bannians, while they preserve them from other enemies, will most unmercifully slaughter whole horse-loads themselves; so that they stand clearly acquitted of any such heathenish superstition.

Little Jones went one day a-shooting with the gamekeeper; when happening to spring a covey of partridges near the border of that manor, the birds flew into it, and were marked (as it is called) by the two sportsmen, in some furze bushes, about two or three hundred paces beyond Mr. Allworthy's dominions.

Mr. Allworthy had given the fellow strict orders, on pain of forfeiting his place, never to trespass on any of his neighbors; no more on those who were less rigid in this matter than on the lord of this manor. With regard to others, indeed, these orders had not been always very scrupulously kept; but as the disposition of the gentleman with whom the partridges had taken sanctuary was well known, the gamekeeper had never yet attempted to invade his territories. Nor had he done it now, had not the younger sportsman, who was excessively eager to pursue the flying game, overpersuaded him; but Jones being very importunate, the other, who was himself keen enough after the sport, yielded to his persuasions, entered the manor, and shot one of the partridges.

The gentleman himself was at that time on horseback, at a little distance from them; and hearing the gun go off, he immediately made towards the place, and discovered poor Tom; for the gamekeeper had leaped into the thickest part of the furze-brake, where he had happily concealed himself.

The gentleman having searched the lad, and found the partridge

37

upon him, denounced great vengeance, swearing he would acquaint Mr. Allworthy. He was as good as his word; for he rode immediately to his house, and complained of the trespass on his manor in as high terms and as bitter language as if his house had been broken open, and the most valuable furniture stolen out of it. He added that some other person was in his company, though he could not discover him; for that two guns had been discharged almost in the same instant.

And, says he, "We have found only this partridge, but the Lord knows what mischief they have done."

At his return home Tom was presently convened before Mr. Allworthy. He owned the fact, and alleged no other excuse but what was really true, viz., that the covey was originally sprung in Mr. Allworthy's own manor.

Tom was then interrogated who was with him, but stoutly persisted in asserting that he was alone; yet, to say the truth, he hesitated a little at first, which would have confirmed Mr. Allworthy's belief, had what the squire and his servants said wanted any further confirmation.

The gamekeeper, being a suspected person, was now sent for, and the question put to him; but he, relying on the promise which Tom had made him, to take all upon himself, very resolutely denied being in company with the young gentleman, or indeed having seen him the whole afternoon.

Mr. Allworthy then turned towards Tom, with more than usual anger in his countenance, and advised him to confess who was with him; that he was resolved to know. The lad, however, still maintained his resolution, and was dismissed with much wrath by Mr. Allworthy, who told him he should have to the next morning to consider of it, when he should be questioned by another person, and in another manner.

Poor Jones spent a very melancholy night; and the more so, as he was without his usual companion; for Master Blifil was gone abroad on a visit with his mother. Fear of the punishment he was to suffer was on this occasion his least evil; his chief anxiety being, lest his constancy should fail him, and he should be brought to betray the gamekeeper, whose ruin he knew must now be the consequence.

In the morning, when Tom attended the reverend Mr. Thwackum, the person to whom Mr. Allworthy had committed the instruction of the two boys, he had the same questions put to him by that gentleman which he had been asked the evening before, to which he returned the same answers. The consequence of this was, so severe a whipping, that it possibly fell little short of the torture with which confessions are in some countries extorted from criminals.

Tom bore his punishment with great resolution; and though his master asked him, between every stroke, whether he would not confess, he was contented to be flayed rather than betray his friend or break the promise he had made.

The gamekeeper was now relieved from his anxiety, and Mr. Allworthy himself began to be concerned at Tom's sufferings: for besides that Mr. Thwackum, being highly enraged that he was not able to make the boy say what he himself pleased, had carried his severity much beyond the good man's intention, this latter began now to suspect that the squire had been mistaken. Now, Mr. Allworthy sent for Tom, and after many kind and friendly exhortations, said, "I am convinced, my dear child, that my suspicions have wronged you; I am sorry that you have been so severely punished on this account." And at last gave him a little horse to make him amends; again repeating his sorrow for what had passed.

Tom's guilt now flew in his face more than any severity could make it. He could more easily bear the lashes of Thwackum than the generosity of Allworthy. The tears burst from his eyes, and he fell upon his knees, crying, "Oh, sir, you are too good to me. Indeed you are. Indeed I don't deserve it." And at that very instant, from the fullness of his heart, had almost betrayed the secret; but the good genius of the gamekeeper suggested to him what might be the consequence to the poor fellow, and this consideration sealed his lips.

Thwackum did all he could to persuade Allworthy from showing any compassion or kindness to the boy, saying, "He had persisted in an untruth"; and gave some hints that a second whipping might probably bring the matter to light.

But Mr. Allworthy absolutely refused to consent to the experiment. He said the boy had suffered enough already for concealing the truth, even if he was guilty, seeing that he could have no motive but a mistaken point of honor for so doing.

"Honor!" cried Thwackum, with some warmth, "mere stubbornness and obstinacy! Can honor teach anyone to tell a lie, or can any honor exist independent of religion?"

This discourse happened at table when dinner was just ended; and there were present Mr. Allworthy, Mr. Thwackum, and a third gentleman, whom, before we proceed any further, we shall briefly introduce to our reader's acquaintance.

III

THE name of this gentleman, who had then resided some time at Mr. Allworthy's house, was Mr. Square. His natural parts were not of the first rate, but he had greatly improved them by a learned education. He was deeply read in the ancients, and a professed master of all the works of Plato and Aristotle. Upon which great models he had principally formed himself; sometimes according with the opinion of the one, and sometimes with that of the other. In morals he was a professed Platonist, and in religion he inclined to be an Aristotelian.

This gentleman and Mr. Thwackum scarce ever met without a disputation; for their tenets were indeed diametrically opposite to each other. Square held human nature to be the perfection of all virtue, and that vice was a deviation from our nature, in the same manner as deformity of body is. Thwackum, on the contrary, maintained that the human mind, since the Fall, was nothing but a sink of iniquity, till purified and redeemed by grace. The former measured all actions by the unalterable rule of right and the eternal fitness of things; the latter decided all matters by authority; but in doing this, he always used the Scriptures.

Had not Thwackum too much neglected virtue, and Square, religion, in the composition of their several systems, and had not both utterly discarded all natural goodness of heart, they had never been represented as the objects of derision in this history; in which we will now proceed.

After this short introduction, the reader will be pleased to remember that the parson had concluded his speech with a triumphant question, to which he had apprehended no answer, viz., Can any honor exist independent of religion?

To this Square answered, that it was impossible to discourse philosophically concerning words till their meaning was first established: for that there were almost as many different opinions concerning honor as concerning religion. "But," says he, "if by honor you mean the true natural beauty of virtue, I will maintain it may exist independent of any religion whatever. Nay," added he, "you yourself will allow it may exist independent of all but one: so will a Mahometan, a Jew, and all the maintainers of all the different sects in the world."

Thwackum replied, this was arguing with the usual malice of all the enemies to the true Church. He said, he doubted not but that all the infidels and heretics in the world would, if they could, confine honor to their own absurd errors and damnable deceptions; "but," says he, "when I mention religion I mean the Christian religion; and not only the Christian religion, but the Protestant religion; and not only the Protestant religion, but the Church of England. And when I mention honor, I mean that mode of Divine grace which is not only consistent with, but dependent upon, this religion; and is consistent with and dependent upon no other."

"I have asserted," says Square, "that true honor and true virtue are almost synonymous terms, and they are both founded on the unalterable rule of right and the eternal fitness of things; to which an untruth being absolutely repugnant and contrary, it is certain that true honor cannot support an untruth. In this, I think we are agreed; but that this honor can be said to be founded on religion, to which it is antecedent—"

"I agree," answered Thwackum, with great warmth, "with a man who asserts honor to be antecedent to religion! Mr. Allworthy, did I agree—?"

The matter which put an end to the debate was no other than a quarrel between Master Blifil and Tom Jones, the consequence of which had been a bloody nose to the former; for though Master Blifil, notwithstanding he was the younger, was in size above the other's match, yet Tom was much his superior at the noble art of boxing.

Tom, however, cautiously avoided all engagements with that youth; for besides that Tommy Jones was an inoffensive lad amidst all his roguery, and really loved Blifil, Mr. Thwackum being always the second of the latter, would have been sufficient to deter him.

But well says a certain author, No man is wise at all hours; it is therefore no wonder that a boy is not so. A difference arising at play between the two lads, Master Blifil called Tom a beggarly bastard. Upon which the latter, who was somewhat passionate in his disposition, immediately caused that phenomenon in the face of the former which we have above remembered.

Master Blifil now, with his blood running from his nose, and the tears galloping after from his eyes, appeared before his uncle and the tremendous Thwackum. In which court an indictment of assault, battery, and wounding, was instantly preferred against Tom; who in his excuse only pleaded the provocation, which was indeed all the matter that Master Blifil had omitted.

It is indeed possible that this circumstance might have escaped his memory; for, in his reply, he positively insisted that he had made use of no such appellation; adding, "Heaven forbid such naughty words should ever come out of his mouth!"

Tom, though against all form of law, rejoined in affirmance of the words. Upon which Master Blifil said, "It is no wonder. Those who will tell one fib, will hardly stick at another. If I had told my master such a wicked fib as you have done, I should be ashamed to show my face."

"What fib, child?" cried Thwackum pretty eagerly.

"Why, he told you that nobody was with him a-shooting when he killed the partridge; but he knows" (here he burst into a flood of tears), "yes, he knows, for he confessed it to me, that Black George the gamekeeper was there. Nay, he said—yes you did—deny it if you can, that you would not have confessed the truth though master had cut you to pieces."

At this the fire flashed from Thwackum's eyes, and he cried out in triumph, "Oh, ho! this is your mistaken notion of honor! This is the boy who was not to be whipped again!" But Mr. Allworthy, with a more gentle aspect, turned towards the lad, and said, "Is this true, child? How came you to persist so obstinately in a falsehood?"

Tom said, "He scorned a lie as much as anyone: but he thought his honor engaged him to act as he did; for he had promised the poor fellow to conceal him: which," he said, "he thought himself farther obliged to, as the gamekeeper had begged him not to go into the gentleman's manor, and had at last gone himself in compliance with his persuasions." He said, "This was the whole truth of the matter, and he would take his oath of it"; and concluded with very passionately begging Mr. Allworthy "to have compassion on the poor fellow's family, especially as he himself only had been guilty, and the other had been very difficultly prevailed on to do what he did. Indeed, sir," said he, "it could hardly be called a lie that I told, for the poor fellow was entirely innocent of the whole matter. I should have gone alone after the birds; nay, I did go at first, and he only followed me to prevent more mischief. Do, pray, sir, let me be punished; take my little horse away again; but pray, sir, forgive poor George."

Mr. Allworthy hesitated a few moments, and then dismissed the boys, advising them to live more friendly and peaceably together.

IV

IT IS probable, that by disclosing this secret, which had been communicated in the utmost confidence to him, young Blifil preserved his companion from a good lashing; for the offense of the bloody nose would have been of itself sufficient cause for Thwackum to have proceeded to correction; but now this was totally absorbed in the consideration of the other matter; and with regard to this, Mr. Allworthy declared privately, he thought the boy deserved reward rather than punishment, so that Thwackum's hand was withheld by a general pardon.

Thwackum, whose meditations were full of birch, exclaimed against this weak, and, as he said he would venture to call it, wicked lenity. To remit the punishment of such crimes was, he said, to encourage them. He enlarged much on the correction of children, and quoted many texts from Solomon, and others; which being to be found in so many other books, shall not be found here. He then applied himself to the vice of lying, on which head he was altogether as learned as he had been on the other.

Square said, he had been endeavoring to reconcile the behavior of Tom with his idea of perfect virtue, but could not. He owned there was something which at first sight appeared like fortitude in the action; but as fortitude was a virtue, and falsehood a vice, they could by no means agree or unite together.

As both these learned men concurred in censuring Jones, so were they no less unanimous in applauding Master Blifil. To bring truth to light, was by the parson asserted to be the duty of every religious man; and by the philosopher this was declared to be highly conformable with the rule of right, and the eternal and unalterable fitness of things.

All this, however, weighed very little with Mr. Allworthy. He could not be prevailed on to sign the warrant for the execution of Jones. There was something within his own breast with which the invincible fidelity which that youth had preserved, corresponded much better than it had done with the religion of Thwackum, or with the virtue of Square.

Towards the gamekeeper the good man behaved with more severity. He presently summoned that poor fellow before him, and after many bitter remonstrances, paid him his wages, and dismissed him from his service; for Mr. Allworthy rightly observed, that there was a great difference between being guilty of a falsehood to excuse yourself and to excuse another.

When this story became public, many people differed from Square and Thwackum in judging the conduct of the two lads on the occasion. Master Blifil was generally called a sneaking rascal, a poor-spirited wretch, with other epithets of the like kind; while Tom was honored with the appellations of a brave lad, a jolly dog, and an honest fellow. For all this, however, poor Tom smarted in the flesh, for though Thwackum had been inhibited to exercise his arm on the foregoing account, yet, as the proverb says, It is easy to find a stick, etc. So was it easy to find a rod; and, indeed, the not being able to find one was the only thing which could have kept Thwackum any long time from chastising poor Jones.

Had the bare delight in the sport been the only inducement to the pedagogue, it is probable Master Blifil would likewise have had his share; but though Mr. Allworthy had given him frequent orders to make no difference between the lads, yet was Thwackum altogether as kind and gentle to this youth, as he was harsh, nay even barbarous, to the other. To say the truth, Blifil had greatly gained his master's affections; partly by the profound respect he always showed his person, but much more by the decent reverence with which he received his doctrine.

Tom Jones, on the other hand, was not only deficient in outward tokens of respect, often forgetting to pull off his hat or to bow at his master's approach, but was altogether as unmindful both of his master's precepts and example. He was indeed a thoughtless, giddy youth, with little sobriety in his manners and less in his countenance; and would often very impudently and indecently laugh at his companion for his serious behavior.

Mr. Square had the same reason for his preference of the former lad; for Tom Jones showed no more regard to the learned discourses which this gentleman would sometimes throw away upon him, than to those of Thwackum. He once ventured to make a jest of the rule of right; and at another time said, he believed there was no rule in the world capable of making such a man as his father (for so Mr. Allworthy suffered himself to be called).

Master Blifil, on the contrary, had address enough at sixteen to recommend himself at one and the same time to both these opposites. With one he was all religion, with the other he was all virtue. And when both were present, he was profoundly silent, which both interpreted in his favor and in their own.

V

THOSE two learned personages, who have lately made a considerable figure on the theater of this history, had, from their first arrival at

Mr. Allworthy's house, taken so great an affection, the one to his virtue, the other to his religion, that they had meditated the closest alliance with him.

For this purpose they had cast their eyes on that fair widow, whom, though we have not for some time made any mention of her, the reader, we trust, hath not forgot. Mrs. Blifil was indeed the object to which they both aspired.

For this reason, principally, the two gentlemen concurred, as we have seen above, in their opinion concerning the two lads; this being, indeed, almost the only instance of their concurring on any point; for, beside the difference of their principles, they had both long ago strongly suspected each other's designs, and hated one another with no little degree of inveteracy.

This mutual animosity was a good deal increased by their alternate successes; for Mrs. Blifil knew what they would be at long before they imagined it; or, indeed intended she should: for they proceeded with great caution, lest she should be offended, and acquaint Mr. Allworthy. But they had no reason for any such fear; she was well enough pleased with a passion, of which she intended none should have any fruits but herself. And the only fruits she designed for herself were flattery and courtship; for which purpose she soothed them by turns, and a long time equally. She was, indeed, rather inclined to favor the parson's principles; but Square's person was more agreeable to her eye, for he was a comely man.

Whether Mrs. Blifil had been surfeited with the sweets of marriage, or disgusted by its bitters, or from what other cause it proceeded, I will not determine; but she could never be brought to listen to any second proposals. However, she at last conversed with Square with such a degree of intimacy that malicious tongues began to whisper things of her, to which, as well for the sake of the lady, as that they were highly disagreeable to the rule of right and the fitness of things, we will give no credit, and therefore shall not blot our paper with them. The pedagogue, 'tis certain, whipped on without getting a step nearer to his journey's end.

Indeed he had committed a great error, and that Square discovered much sooner than himself. Mrs. Blifil (as, perhaps, the reader may have formerly guessed) was not over and above pleased with the behavior of her husband; nay, to be honest, she absolutely hated him, till his death at last a little reconciled him to her affections. It will not be therefore greatly wondered at, if she had not the most violent regard to the offspring she had by him. And, in fact, she had so little of this regard, that in his infancy she seldom saw her son, or took any notice of him; and hence she acquiesced, after a little reluctance, in all the favors which Mr. Allworthy showered on the foundling, whom the good man called his own boy, and in all things put on an entire equality with Master Blifil. This acquiescence in Mrs. Blifil was considered by the neighbors, and by the family, as a mark of her condescension to her brother's humor, and she was imagined by all others, as well as Thwackum and Square, to hate the foundling in her heart; nay, the more civility she showed him, the more they conceived she detested him, and the surer schemes she was laying for his ruin: for as they thought it her interest to hate him, it was very difficult for her to persuade them she did not.

However, when Tom grew up, and gave tokens of that gallantry of temper which greatly recommends men to women, this disinclination which she had discovered to him when a child by degrees abated, and at last she so evidently demonstrated her affection to him to be much stronger than what she bore her own son, that it was impossible to mistake her any longer. She was so desirous of often seeing him, and discovered such satisfaction and delight in his company, that before he was eighteen years old he was become a rival to both Square and Thwackum; and what is worse, the whole country began to talk as loudly of her inclination to Tom as they had before done of that which she had shown to Square: on which account the philosopher conceived the most implacable hatred for our poor hero.

VI

THOUGH Mr. Allworthy was not of himself hasty to see things in a disadvantageous light, and was a stranger to the public voice, which seldom reaches to a brother or a husband, though it rings in the ears of all the neighborhood, yet was this affection of Mrs. Blifil to Tom, and the preference which she too visibly gave him to her own son, of the utmost disadvantage to that youth.

For such was the compassion which inhabited Mr. Allworthy's mind, that nothing but the steel of justice could ever subdue it. To be unfortunate in any respect was sufficient, if there was no demerit to counterpoise it, to turn the scale of that good man's pity, and to engage his friendship and his benefaction.

When, therefore, he plainly saw Master Blifil was absolutely detested (for that he was) by his own mother, he began, on that account only, to look with an eye of compassion upon him; and what the effects of compassion are, in good and benevolent minds, I need not here explain to most of my readers.

Henceforward he saw every appearance of virtue in the youth through the magnifying end, and viewed all his faults with the glass inverted, so that they became scarce perceptible. And this perhaps the amiable temper of pity may make commendable; but the next step the weakness of human nature alone must excuse; for he no sooner perceived that preference which Mrs. Blifil gave to Tom, than that poor youth (however innocent) began to sink in his affections as he rose in hers. This, it is true, would of itself alone never have been able to eradicate Jones from his bosom; but it was greatly injurious to him, and prepared Mr. Allworthy's mind for those impressions which afterwards produced the mighty events that will be contained hereafter in this history; and to which, it must be confessed, the unfortunate lad, by his own wantonness, wildness, and want of caution, too much contributed.

The reader may remember that Mr. Allworthy gave Tom Jones a little horse, as a kind of smart-money for the punishment which he imagined he had suffered innocently.

This horse Tom kept above half a year, and then rode him to a neighboring fair, and sold him.

At his return, being questioned by Thwackum what he had done with the money for which the horse was sold, he frankly declared he would not tell him.

"Oho!" says Thwackum, "you will not! then I will have it out of your br—h"; that being the place to which he always applied for information on every doubtful occasion.

Tom was now mounted on the back of a footman, and everything prepared for execution, when Mr. Allworthy, entering the room, gave the criminal a reprieve, and took him with him into another apartment; where, being alone with Tom, he put the same question to him which Thwackum had before asked him.

Tom answered, he could in duty refuse him nothing; but as for that tyrannical rascal, he would never make him any other answer than with a cudgel, with which he hoped soon to be able to pay him for all his barbarities.

Mr. Allworthy very severely reprimanded the lad for his indecent and disrespectful expressions concerning his master; but much more for his avowing an intention of revenge. He threatened him with the entire loss of his favor if he ever heard such another word from his mouth; for, he said, he would never support or befriend a reprobate. By these and the like declarations he extorted some compunction from Tom, in which that youth was not oversincere; for he really meditated some return for all the smarting favors he had received at the hands of the pedagogue. He was, however, brought by Mr. Allworthy to express a concern for his resentment against Thwackum; and then the good man, after some wholesome admonition, permitted him to proceed, which he did as follows:

"Indeed, my dear sir, I love and honor you more than all the world: I know the great obligations I have to you, and should detest myself if I thought my heart was capable of ingratitude. Could the little horse you gave me speak, I am sure he could tell you how fond I was of your present; nor would I have sold him upon any other account in the world than what I did. Indeed, sir, there never was any misery like theirs—"

"Like whose, child," says Allworthy: "what do you mean?"

"Oh, sir!" answered Tom, "your poor gamekeeper, with all his large family, ever since your discarding him, have been perishing with all the miseries of cold and hunger: I could not bear to see these poor wretches naked and starving, and at the same time know myself to have been the occasion of all their sufferings. I could not bear it, sir; upon my soul, I could not." [Here the tears ran down his cheeks, and he thus proceeded.] "It was to save them from absolute destruction I parted with your dear present, notwithstanding all the value I had for it: I sold the horse for them, and they have every farthing of the money."

Mr. Allworthy now stood silent for some moments, and before he spoke the tears started from his eyes. He at length dismissed Tom with a gentle rebuke, advising him for the future to apply to him in cases of distress, rather than to use extraordinary means of relieving them himself.

Soon after this, as that gentleman was walking out one evening with Master Blifil and young Jones, the latter slily drew him to the habitation of Black George, where the family of that poor wretch, namely, his wife and children, were found in all the misery with which cold, hunger, and nakedness can affect human creatures; for as to the money they had received from Jones, former debts had consumed almost the whole.

Such a scene as this could not fail of affecting the heart of Mr. Allworthy. He immediately gave the mother a couple of guineas, with which he bid her clothe her children. The poor woman burst into tears at this goodness, and while she was thanking him, could not refrain from expressing her gratitude to Tom; who had, she said, long preserved both her and hers from starving. "We have not," says she, "had a morsel to eat, nor have these poor children had a rag to put on, but what his goodness hath bestowed on us."

On their return home, Tom made use of all his eloquence to display the wretchedness of these people, and the penitence of Black George himself; and in this he succeeded so well, that Mr. Allworthy said, he thought the man had suffered enough for what was past; that he would forgive him, and think of some means of providing for him and his family.

Jones was so delighted with this news, that, though it was dark when they returned home, he could not help going back a mile, in a shower of rain, to acquaint the poor woman with the glad tidings; but, like other hasty divulgers of news, he only brought on himself the trouble of contradicting it: for the ill fortune of Black George made use of the very opportunity of his friend's absence to overturn all again.

VII

MASTER BLIFIL fell very short of his companion in the amiable quality of mercy; but he as greatly exceeded him in one of a much higher kind, namely, in justice; though he had kept silence in the presence of Jones, yet, when he had better considered the matter, could by no means endure the thought of suffering his uncle to confer favors on the undeserving. He therefore resolved immediately to acquaint him with the fact which we have above lightly hinted to the readers. The truth of which was as follows:

The gamekeeper, about a year after he was dismissed from Mr. Allworthy's service, and before Tom's selling the horse, being in want of bread, either to fill his own mouth or those of his family, as he passed through a field belonging to Mr. Western (the gentleman in whose manor the partridge was killed) espied a hare sitting in her form. This hare he had basely and barbarously knocked on the head, against the laws of the land, and no less against the laws of sportsmen.

The higgler to whom the hare was sold, being unfortunately taken many months after with a quantity of game upon him, was obliged to make his peace with the squire by becoming evidence against some poacher. And now Black George was pitched upon by him, as being a person already obnoxious to Mr. Western, and one of no good fame in the country. He was, besides, the best sacrifice the higgler could make, as he had supplied him with no game since; and by this means the witness had an opportunity of screening his better customers.

Had this fact been truly laid before Mr. Allworthy it might probably have done the gamekeeper very little mischief. But Master Blifil varied by the hasty addition of the single letter S considerably altered the story; for he said that George had wired hares. These alterations might probably have been set right, had not Master Blifil unluckily insisted on a promise of secrecy from Mr. Allworthy before he revealed the matter to him; but by that means the poor gamekeeper was condemned without having an opportunity to defend himself.

Short-lived, then, was the joy of these poor people; for Mr. Allworthy the next morning declared he had fresh reason, without assigning it, for his anger, and strictly forbade Tom to mention George any more: though as for his family, he said he would endeavor to keep them from starving; but as to the fellow himself, he would leave him to the laws, which nothing could keep him from breaking.

Tom could by no means divine what had incensed Mr. Allworthy, for of Master Blifil he had not the least suspicion. However, as his friendship was to be tired out by no disappointments, he now determined to try another method of preserving the poor gamekeeper from ruin.

Jones was lately grown very intimate with Mr. Western. He had so greatly recommended himself to that gentleman, by leaping over five-barred gates, and by other acts of sportsmanship, that the squire had declared Tom would certainly make a great man if he had but sufficient encouragement. He often wished he had himself a son with such parts; and one day very solemnly asserted at a drinking bout, that Tom should hunt a pack of hounds for a thousand pound of his money, with any huntsman in the whole country.

By such kind of talents he had so ingratiated himself with the squire, that he was a most welcome guest at his table and a favorite companion in his sport: everything which the squire held most dear, to wit, his guns, dogs, and horses, were now as much at the command of Jones as if they had been his own. He resolved, therefore, to make use of this favor on behalf of his friend Black George, whom he hoped to introduce into Mr. Western's family in the same capacity in which he had before served Mr. Allworthy.

For this purpose, then, Tom applied to Mr. Western's daughter, a young lady of about seventeen years of age, whom her father, next after those necessary implements of sport just before mentioned, loved and esteemed above all the world. Now, as she had some influence on the squire, so Tom had some little influence on her. But this being the intended heroine of this work, a lady with whom we ourselves are greatly in love, and with whom many of our readers will probably be in love too before we part, it is by no means proper she should make her appearance at the end of a book.

Book IV

CONTAINING THE TIME OF A YEAR

I

HUSHED be every ruder breath. Do thou, sweet Zephyrus, rising from thy fragrant bed, call forth the lovely Flora from her chamber, perfumed with pearly dews, when on the first of June, her birthday, the blooming maid, in loose attire, gently trips it over the verdant mead, where every flower rises to do her homage, and colors contend with sweets which shall ravish her most.

So charming may she now appear! and you the feathered choristers of nature, whose sweetest notes not even Handel can excel, tune your melodious throats to celebrate her appearance. From love proceeds your music, and to love it returns. Awaken, therefore, that gentle passion in every swain; for, lo! adorned with all the charms in which nature can array her; bedecked with beauty, youth, sprightliness, innocency, modesty, and tenderness, breathing sweetness from her rosy lips, and darting brightness from her sparkling eyes, the lovely Sophia comes!

Reader, perhaps thou hast seen the statue of the *Venus de Medicis*. Perhaps, too, thou hast seen the gallery of beauties at Hampton Court. Thou mayest remember each bright Churchill of the galaxy, and all the toasts of the Kit-cat. Or, if their reign was before thy times, at least thou hast seen their daughters, the no less dazzling beauties of the present age.

Yet is it possible, my friend, that thou mayest have seen all these without being able to form an exact idea of Sophia; for she did not exactly resemble any of them. She was most like the picture of Lady Ranelagh; and, I have heard, more still to the famous Duchess of Mazarine; but most of all she resembled one whose image never can depart from my breast, and whom, if thou dost remember, thou hast then, my friend, an adequate idea of Sophia.

But lest this should not have been thy fortune, we will endeavor with our utmost skill to describe this paragon, though we are sensible that our highest abilities are very inadequate to the task.

Sophia, then, the only daughter of Mr. Western, was a middle-sized woman; but rather inclining to tall. Her shape was not only exact, but extremely delicate; and the nice proportion of her arms promised the truest symmetry in her limbs. Her hair, which was black, was so luxuriant that it reached her middle, before she cut it to comply with the modern fashion; and it was now curled so gracefully on her neck that few could believe it to be her own. If envy could find any part of the face which demanded less commendation than the rest, it might possibly think her forehead might have been higher without prejudice to her. Her eyebrows were full, even, and arched beyond the power of art to imitate. Her black eyes had a luster in them which all her softness could not extinguish. Her nose was exactly regular, and her mouth, in which were two rows of ivory, exactly answered Sir John Suckling's description in those lines:

> Her lips were red, and one was thin,
> Compar'd to that was next her chin.
> Some bee had stung it newly.

Her cheeks were of the oval kind; and in her right she had a dimple, which the least smile discovered. Her chin had certainly its share in forming the beauty of her face; but it was difficult to say it was either large or small, though perhaps it was rather of the former kind. Her complexion had rather more of the lily than of the rose; but when exercise or modesty increased her natural color no vermilion could equal it. Her neck was long and finely turned; and here, if I was not afraid of offending her delicacy, I might justly say, the highest beauties of the famous *Venus de Medicis* were outdone. Here was whiteness which no lilies, ivory, nor alabaster could match. The finest cambric might indeed be supposed from envy to cover that bosom which was much whiter than itself.

Such was the outside of Sophia; nor was this beautiful frame disgraced by an inhabitant unworthy of it. Her mind was every way equal to her person; nay, the latter borrowed some charms from the former; for when she smiled, the sweetness of her temper diffused that glory over her countenance which no regularity of features can give.

Whatever mental accomplishments she had derived from nature, they were somewhat improved and cultivated by art; for she had been educated under the care of an aunt, who was a lady of great discretion, and was thoroughly acquainted with the world, having lived in her youth about the court, whence she had retired some years since into the country. By her conversation and instructions Sophia was perfectly well bred, though perhaps she wanted a little of that ease in her behavior which is to be acquired only by habit, and living within what is called the polite circle. But this, to say the truth, is often too dearly purchased; and though it hath charms so inexpressible, that the French, perhaps, among other qualities, mean to express this when they declare they know not what it is; yet its absence is well compensated by innocence; nor can good sense and a natural gentility ever stand in need of it.

II

The amiable Sophia was now in her eighteenth year when she is introduced into this history. Her father, as hath been said, was fonder of her than of any other human creature. To her, therefore, Tom Jones applied, in order to engage her interest on the behalf of his friend the gamekeeper.

But before we proceed to this business, a short recapitulation of some previous matters may be necessary.

Though the different tempers of Mr. Allworthy and of Mr. Western did not admit of a very intimate correspondence, yet they lived upon what is called a decent footing together; by which means the young people of both families had been acquainted from their infancy; and as they were all near of the same age, had been frequent playmates together.

The gaiety of Tom's temper suited better with Sophia than the grave and sober disposition of Master Blifil. And the preference which she gave the former of these would often appear so plainly, that a lad of a more passionate turn than Master Blifil was might have shown some displeasure at it.

Tom Jones, when very young, had presented Sophia with a little bird, which he had taken from the nest, had nursed up, and taught to sing.

Of this bird, Sophia, then about thirteen years old, was so extremely fond, that her chief business was to feed and tend it, and her chief pleasure to play with it. By these means little Tommy, for so the bird was called, was become so tame, that it would feed out of the hand of its mistress, would perch upon the finger, and lie contented in her bosom, where it seemed almost sensible of its own happiness; though she always kept a small string about its leg, nor would ever trust it with the liberty of flying away.

One day, when Mr. Allworthy and his whole family dined at Mr. Western's, Master Blifil, being in the garden with little Sophia, and observing the extreme fondness that she showed for her little bird, desired her to trust it for a moment in his hands. Sophia presently complied with the young gentleman's request, and after some previous caution, delivered him her bird; of which he was no sooner in possession, than he slipped the string from its leg and tossed it into the air.

The foolish animal no sooner perceived itself at liberty, than forgetting all the favors it had received from Sophia, it flew directly from her, and perched on a bough at some distance.

Sophia, seeing her bird gone, screamed out so loud, that Tom Jones, who was at a little distance, immediately ran to her assistance.

He was no sooner informed of what had happened, than he cursed Blifil for a pitiful malicious rascal; and then immediately stripping off his coat he applied himself to climbing the tree to which the bird escaped.

Tom had almost recovered his little namesake, when the branch on which it was perched, and that hung over a canal, broke, and the poor lad plumped over head and ears into the water.

Sophia's concern now changed its object. And as she apprehended the boy's life was in danger, she screamed ten times louder than before; and indeed Master Blifil himself now seconded her with all the vociferation in his power.

The company, who were sitting in a room next the garden, were instantly alarmed, and came all forth; but just as they reached the canal, Tom (for the water was luckily pretty shallow in that part) arrived safely on shore.

Thwackum fell violently on poor Tom, who stood drooping and shivering before him, when Mr. Allworthy desired him to have patience; and turning to Master Blifil, said, "Pray, child, what is the reason of all this disturbance?"

Master Blifil answered, "Indeed, uncle, I am very sorry for what I have done; I have been unhappily the occasion of it all. I had Miss Sophia's bird in my hand, and thinking the poor creature languished for liberty, I own I could not forbear giving it what it desired; for I always thought there was something very cruel in confining anything. It seemed to be against the law of nature, by which everything has a right to liberty; nay, it is even unchristian, for it is not doing what we would be done by; but if I had imagined Miss Sophia would have been so much concerned at it, I am sure I never would have done it; nay, if I had known what would have happened to the bird itself; for when Master Jones, who climbed up that tree after it, fell into the water, the bird took a second flight, and presently a nasty hawk carried it away."

Poor Sophia, who now first heard of her little Tommy's fate (for her concern for Jones had prevented her perceiving it when it happened), shed a shower of tears. These Mr. Allworthy endeavored to assuage, promising her a much finer bird; but she declared she would never have another. Her father chid her for crying so for a foolish bird; but could not help telling young Blifil, if he was a son of his, his backside should be well flayed.

Sophia now returned to her chamber, the two young gentlemen were sent home, and the rest of the company returned to their bottle.

III

"*Parva leves capiunt animos*"—"Small things affect light minds," was the sentiment of a great master of the passion of love. And certain it is, that from this day Sophia began to have some little kindness for Tom Jones, and no little aversion for his companion.

To say the truth, Sophia, when very young, discerned that Tom, though an idle, thoughtless, rattling rascal, was nobody's enemy but his own; and that Master Blifil, though a prudent, discreet, sober young gentleman, was at the same time strongly attached to the interest only of one single person; and who that single person was the reader will be able to divine without any assistance of ours.

Sophia had been absent upwards of three years with her aunt; dur-

This evening she played all his favorites three times over.

ing all which time she had seldom seen either of these young gentlemen. She dined, however, once, together with her aunt, at Mr. Allworthy's. This was a few days after the adventure of the partridge, before commemorated. Sophia heard the whole story at table, where she said nothing: nor indeed could her aunt get many words from her as she returned home; but her maid, when undressing her, happening to say, "Well, miss, I suppose you have seen young Master Blifil today?" she answered with much passion, "I hate the name of Master Blifil, as I do whatever is base and treacherous; and I wonder Mr. Allworthy would suffer that old barbarous schoolmaster to punish a poor boy so cruelly for what was only the effect of his goodnature." She then recounted the story to her maid, and concluded with saying, "Don't you think he is a boy of noble spirit?"

This young lady was now returned to her father; who gave her the command of his house, and placed her at the upper end of his table, where Tom (who for his great love of hunting was become a great favorite of the squire) often dined. Young men of open, generous dispositions are naturally inclined to gallantry, which, if they have good understandings, as was in reality Tom's case, exerts itself in an obliging complacent behavior to all women in general. This greatly distinguished Tom from the boisterous brutality of mere country squires on the one hand, and from the solemn and somewhat sullen deportment of Master Blifil on the other; and he began now, at twenty, to have the name of a pretty fellow among all the women in the neighborhood.

Tom behaved to Sophia with no particularity, unless perhaps by showing her a higher respect than he paid to any other. This distinction her beauty, fortune, sense, and amiable carriage seemed to demand; but as to design upon her person he had none; for which we shall at present suffer the reader to condemn him of stupidity; but perhaps we shall be able indifferently well to account for it thereafter.

Sophia, with the highest degree of innocence and modesty, had a remarkable sprightliness in her temper. This was so greatly increased whenever she was in company with Tom, that had he not been very young and thoughtless, he must have observed it; or had not Mr. Western's thoughts been generally either in the field, the stable, or the dog-kennel, it might have perhaps created some jealousy in him: but so far was the good gentleman from entertaining any such suspicion, that he gave Tom every opportunity with his daughter which any lover could have wished; and this Tom innocently improved to better advantage, by following only the dictates of his natural gallantry and good-nature, than he might perhaps have done had he had the deepest designs on the young lady.

But indeed it can occasion little wonder that this matter escaped the observation of others, since poor Sophia herself never remarked it; and her heart was irretrievably lost before she suspected it was in danger.

Matters were in this situation, when Tom, one afternoon, finding Sophia alone, began, after a short apology, with a very serious face, to acquaint her that he had a favor to ask of her which he hoped her goodness would comply with.

Though neither the young man's behavior, nor indeed his manner of opening this business, were such as could give her any just cause of suspecting he intended to make love to her; yet whether Nature whispered something into her ear, or from what cause it arose I will not determine; certain it is, some idea of that kind must have intruded itself; for her color forsook her cheeks, her limbs trembled, and her tongue would have faltered, had Tom stopped for an answer; but he soon relieved her from her perplexity, by proceeding to inform her of his request, which was to solicit her interest on behalf of the gamekeeper.

Sophia presently recovered her confusion, and, with a smile full of sweetness, said, "Is this the mighty favor you asked with so much gravity? I will do it with all my heart. I really pity the poor fellow, and no longer ago than yesterday sent a small matter to his wife." This small matter was one of her gowns, some linen, and ten shillings in money, of which Tom had heard.

"And now, Mr. Jones, I must ask you a favor."

"A favor, madam!" cried Tom: "if you knew the pleasure you have given me in the hopes of receiving a command from you, you would think by mentioning it you did confer the greatest favor on me; for by this dear hand I would sacrifice my life to oblige you."

He then snatched her hand, and eagerly kissed it, which was the first time his lips had ever touched her. The blood, which before had forsaken her cheeks, now made her sufficient amends, by rushing all over her face and neck with such violence, that they became all of a scarlet color. She now first felt a sensation to which she had been before a stranger, and which, when she had leisure to reflect on it, began to acquaint her with some secrets, which the reader, if he doth not already guess them, will know in due time.

Sophia, as soon as she could speak (which was not instantly), informed him that the favor she had to desire of him was, not to lead her father through so many dangers in hunting; for that, from what she had heard, she was terribly frightened every time they went out together, and expected some day or other to see her father brought home with broken limbs. She therefore begged him, for her sake, to be more cautious; and as he well knew Mr. Western would follow him, not to ride so madly, nor to take those dangerous leaps for the future.

Tom promised faithfully to obey her commands; and after thanking her for her kind compliance with his request, took his leave, and departed highly charmed with his success.

Poor Sophia was charmed too, but in a very different way. Her sensations, however, the reader's heart (if he or she have any) will better represent than I can.

It was Mr. Western's custom every afternoon, as soon as he was drunk, to hear his daughter play on the harpsichord; for he was a great lover of music, and perhaps, had he lived in town, might have passed for a connoisseur; for he always excepted against the finest compositions of Mr. Handel. He never relished any music but what was light and airy; and indeed his most favorite tunes were Old Sir Simon the King, St. George he was for England, Bobbing Joan, and some others.

His daughter, though she was a perfect mistress of music, and would never willingly have played any but Handel's, was so devoted to her father's pleasure, that she learned all those tunes to oblige him. However, she would now and then endeavor to lead him into her own taste; and when he required the repetition of his ballads, would answer with a "Nay, dear sir"; and would often beg him to suffer her to play something else.

This evening, however, when the gentleman was retired from his bottle, she played all his favorites three times over without any solicitation. This so pleased the good squire that he started from his couch, gave his daughter a kiss, and swore her hand was greatly improved. She took this opportunity to execute her promise to Tom; in which she succeeded so well, that the squire declared, if she would give him t'other bout of Old Sir Simon, he would give the gamekeeper his deputation the next morning. Sir Simon was played again and again, till the charms of the music soothed Mr. Western to sleep. In the morning Sophia did not fail to remind him of his engagement; and his attorney was immediately sent for, ordered to stop any further proceedings in the action, and to make out the deputation.

Tom's success in this affair soon began to ring over the country, and various were the censures passed upon it; some greatly applauding it as an act of good nature; others sneering, and saying, "No wonder that one idle fellow should love another." Young Blifil was greatly enraged at it. He represented this as flying in Mr. Allworthy's face; and declared, with great concern, that it was impossible to find any other motive for doing good to such a wretch.

Thwackum and Square likewise sung to the same tune. They were now (especially the latter) become greatly jealous of young Jones with the widow; for he now approached the age of twenty, was really a fine young fellow, and that lady, by her encouragements to him, seemed daily more and more to think him so.

Allworthy was not, however, moved with their malice. He declared himself very well satisfied with what Jones had done. He said the perseverance and integrity of his friendship was highly commendable, and he wished he could see more frequent instances of that virtue.

IV

THERE are two sorts of people, who, I am afraid, have already conceived some contempt for my hero on account of his behavior to Sophia. The former of these will blame his prudence in neglecting an opportunity to possess himself of Mr. Western's fortune; and the latter will no less despise him for his backwardness to so fine a girl, who seemed ready to fly into his arms, if he would open them to receive her.

Now, though I shall not perhaps be able absolutely to acquit him of either of these charges (for want of prudence admits of no excuse; and what I shall produce against the latter charge will, I apprehend, be scarce satisfactory); yet I shall set forth the plain matter of fact, and leave the whole to the reader's determination.

Mr. Jones had somewhat about him, which, though I think writers are not thoroughly agreed in its name, doth certainly inhabit some human breasts; whose use is not so properly to distinguish right from wrong, as to prompt and incite them to the former, and to restrain and withhold them from the latter.

It was this which taught him, that to repay the civilities and little friendships of hospitality by robbing the house where you have received them, is to be the basest and meanest of thieves. If to steal another's plate deserved death and infamy, it seemed to him difficult to assign a punishment adequate to the robbing a man of his whole fortune and of his child into the bargain. Had he been greatly enamored of Sophia, he possibly might have thought otherwise; but give me leave to say, there is great difference between running away with a man's daughter from the motive of love, and doing the same thing from the motive of theft.

Now, though this young gentleman was not insensible of the charms of Sophia, though he greatly liked her beauty, and esteemed all her other qualifications, she had made, however, no deep impression on his heart; for which, as it renders him liable to the charge of stupidity, or at least of want of taste, we shall now proceed to account. The truth then is, his heart was in the possession of another woman.

We have often mentioned the family of George Seagrim (commonly called Black George, the gamekeeper), which consisted at present of a wife and five children. The second of these children was a daughter, whose name was Molly, and who was esteemed one of the handsomest girls in the whole country.

The beauty of this girl made, however, no impression on Tom till she grew towards the age of sixteen, when Tom, who was near three years older, began first to cast the eyes of affection upon her. And this affection he had fixed on the girl long before he could bring himself to attempt the possession of her person; for though his constitution urged him greatly to this, his principles no less forcibly restrained him. To debauch a young woman, however low her condition was, appeared to him a very heinous crime; and the good will he bore the father, with the compassion he had for his family, very strongly corroborated all such sober reflections; so that he once resolved to get the better of his inclinations, and he actually abstained three whole months without ever going to Seagrim's house, or seeing his daughter.

Now, though Molly was, as we have said, generally thought a very fine girl, so little had she of modesty, that Jones had more regard for her virtue than she herself. And as most probably she liked Tom as well as he liked her, so when she perceived his backwardness she herself grew proportionately forward; and when she saw he had entirely deserted the house, she found means of throwing herself in his way, and behaved in such a manner that the youth must have had very much or very little of the hero if her endeavors had proved unsuccessful. In a word, she soon triumphed over all the virtuous resolutions of Jones; for though she behaved at least with all decent reluctance, yet I rather choose to attribute the triumph to her, since, in fact, it was her design which succeeded.

In the conduct of this matter, I say, Molly so well played her part, that Jones attributed the conquest entirely to himself, and considered the young woman as one who had yielded to the violent attacks of his passion. He likewise imputed her yielding to the ungovernable force of her love towards him; and, indeed, he was one of the handsomest young fellows in the world. He considered this poor girl as one whose happiness or misery he had caused to be dependent on himself. Her beauty was still the object of desire, though greater beauty, or a fresher object, might have been more so; but the little abatement which fruition had occasioned to this was highly overbalanced by the considerations of the affection which she visibly bore him, and of the situation into which he had brought her. The former of these created gratitude, the latter compassion; and both, together with his desire for her person, raised in him a passion which might, without any great violence to the word, be called love.

This, then, was the true reason of that insensibility which he had shown to the charms of Sophia, and that behavior in her which might have been reasonably enough interpreted as an encouragement to his addresses; for as he could not think of abandoning his Molly, poor and destitute as she was, so no more could he entertain a notion of betraying such a creature as Sophia.

V

HER mother first perceived the alteration in the shape of Molly; and in order to hide it from her neighbors, she foolishly clothed her in that sack which Sophia had sent her; though, indeed, that young lady had little apprehension that the poor woman would have been weak enough to let any of her daughters wear it in that form.

Molly was charmed with the first opportunity she ever had of showing her beauty to advantage; for though she could very well bear to contemplate herself in the glass, even when dressed in rags, and though she had in that dress conquered the heart of Jones, and perhaps of some others, yet she thought the addition of finery would much improve her charms and extend her conquests. Therefore, having dressed herself out in this sack, with a new laced cap, and some other ornaments which Tom had given her, she repairs to church with her fan in her hand the very next Sunday.

Molly had seated herself some time before she was known by her neighbors. And then a whisper ran through the whole congregation, "Who is she?" and when she was discovered, such sneering, giggling, tittering, and laughing ensued among the women, that Mr. Allworthy was obliged to exert his authority to preserve any decency among them.

Mr. Western had an estate in this parish; and as his house stood at little greater distance from this church than from his own, he very often came to Divine service here; and both he and the charming Sophia happened to be present at this time.

Sophia was much pleased with the beauty of the girl, whom she pitied for her simplicity in having dressed herself in that manner, as she saw the envy which it had occasioned among her equals. She no sooner came home than she sent for the gamekeeper, and ordered him to bring his daughter to her, saying she would provide for her in the family, and might possibly place the girl about her own person, when her own maid, who was now going away, had left her.

Poor Seagrim was thunderstruck at this; for he was no stranger to the fault in the shape of his daughter. He answered, in a stammering voice, "That he was afraid Molly would be too awkward to wait on her ladyship, as she had never been at service."

"No matter for that," says Sophia; "she will soon improve. I am pleased with the girl, and am resolved to try her."

Black George now repaired to his wife, on whose prudent counsel he depended to extricate him out of this dilemma; but when he came thither he found his house in some confusion.

VI

MOLLY had no sooner appareled herself in her accustomed rags, than her sisters began to fall violently upon her, particularly her eldest sister. "How had she the assurance to wear a gown which young Madam Western had given to mother! If one of us was to wear it, I think," says she, "I myself have the best right; but I warrant you think yourself more handsomer than any of us. You'd better have minded what the parson says," cries the eldest, "and not a hearkened after men voke."

"Indeed, child, and so she had," says the mother, sobbing: "she hath brought a disgrace upon us all. She's the vurst of the vamily that ever was a whore."

"You need not upbraid me with that, mother," cries Molly; "you yourself was brought-to-bed of sister there within a week after you was married."

"Yes, hussy," answered the enraged mother, "so I was, and what was the mighty matter of that? I was made an honest women then; and if you was to be made an honest woman, I should not be angry; but you must have to doing with a gentleman, you nasty slut; you will have a bastard, hussy, you will; and that I defy anyone to say of me."

In this situation Black George found his family, when he came home for the purpose before mentioned. As his wife and three daughters were all of them talking together, and most of them crying, it was some time before he could get an opportunity of being heard; but as soon as such an interval occurred, he acquainted the company with what Sophia had said to him.

Goody Seagrim then began to revile her daughter afresh. "Here," says she, "you have brought us into a fine quandary indeed. What will madam say to that big belly? Oh, that ever I should live to see this day!"

Molly answered with great spirit. "And what is this mighty place which you have got for me, father?" (for he had not well understood the phrase used by Sophia of being about her person). "I suppose it is to be under the cook; but I shan't wash dishes for anybody. My gentleman will provide better for me. He hath promised I shall never want money; and you sha'n't want money neither, mother, if you will hold your tongue, and know when you are well." And so saying, she pulled out several guineas, and gave her mother one of them.

The good woman no sooner felt the gold within her palm than her temper began (such is the efficacy of that panacea) to be mollified. "Why, husband," says she, "would any but such a blockhead as you not have inquired what place this was before he had accepted it? Perhaps, as Molly says, it may be in the kitchen; and truly I don't care my daughter should be a scullion wench; for, poor as I am, I am a gentlewoman. And thof I was obliged, as my father, who was a clergyman, died worse than nothing, and so could not give me a shilling of *potion*, to undervalue myself by marrying a poor man, yet I would have you to know I have a spirit above all them things. Marry come up! it would better become Madam Western to look at home, and remember who her own grandfather was. Some of my family, for aught I know, might ride in their coaches, when the grandfathers of some voke walked a-voot. I warrant she fancies she did a mighty matter, when she sent us that old gownd; some of my family would not have picked up such rags in the street; but poor people are always trampled upon. The parish need not have been in such a fluster with Molly. You might have told them, child, your grandmother wore better things new out of the shop."

"Well, but consider," cried George, "what answer shall I make to madam?"

"I don't know what answer," says she; "you are always bringing your family into one quandary or other. Do you remember when you shot the partridge, the occasion of all our misfortunes? Did I not advise you never to go into Squire Western's manor? Did not I tell you many a good year ago what would come of it? But you would have your own headstrong ways; yes, you would, you villain."

Black George was, in the main, a peaceable kind of fellow, and nothing choleric nor rash; yet did he bear about him something of what the ancients called the irascible, and which his wife, if she had been endowed with much wisdom, would have feared. He had long experienced, that when the storm grew very high, arguments were but wind, which served rather to increase than to abate it. He was therefore seldom unprovided with a small switch, a remedy of wonderful force, as he had often essayed, and which the word villain served as a hint for his applying.

No sooner, therefore, had this symptom appeared than he had immediate recourse to the said remedy, which though, as it is usual in all very efficacious medicines, it at first seemed to heighten and inflame the disease, soon produced a total calm, and restored the patient to perfect ease and tranquillity.

This is, however, a kind of horse-medicine, which requires a very robust constitution to digest, and is therefore proper only for the vulgar, unless in one single instance, viz., where superiority of birth breaks out; in which case, we should not think it very improperly applied by any husband whatever, if the application was not in itself so base, that, like certain applications of the physician kind which need not be mentioned, it so much degrades and contaminates the hand employed in it, that no gentleman should endure the thought of anything so low and detestable.

The whole family were soon reduced to a state of perfect quiet; for the virtue of this medicine, like that of electricity, is often communicated through one person to many others who are not touched by the instrument.

A council was now called, in which, after many debates, Molly still persisted that she would not go to service, it was at length resolved that Goody Seagrim herself should wait on Miss Western, and endeavor to procure the place for her eldest daughter, who declared great readiness to accept it; but Fortune, who seems to have been an enemy of this little family, afterwards put a stop to her promotion.

VII

THE next morning Tom Jones hunted with Mr. Western, and was at his return invited by that gentleman to dinner.

The lovely Sophia shone forth that day with more gaiety and sprightliness than usual. Her battery was certainly leveled at our hero; though, I believe, she herself scarce yet knew her own intention; but if she had any design of charming him, she now succeeded.

Mr. Supple, the curate of Mr. Allworthy's parish, made one of the company. He was a good-natured, worthy man, but chiefly remarkable for his great taciturnity at table, though his mouth was never shut at it. In short, he had one of the best appetites in the world. However, the cloth was no sooner taken away than he always made sufficient amends for his silence: for he was a very hearty fellow; and his conversation was often entertaining, never offensive.

When dinner was over, he began as follows: "I believe, lady, your ladyship observed a young woman at church yesterday at evensong, who was dressed in one of your outlandish garments; I think I have seen your ladyship in such a one. Such garments are rare sights in the country; and perchance, too, it was thought the more rare, respect being had to the person who wore it, who, they tell me, is the daughter of Black George, your worship's gamekeeper, whose sufferings, I should have opined, might have taught him more wit, than to dress forth his wenches in such gaudy apparel. She created so much confusion in the congregation, that if Squire Allworthy had not silenced it, it would have interrupted the service; and the wench was brought before him; when, lo! on a sudden the wench appeared (I ask your ladyship's pardon) to be, as it were, at the eve of bringing forth a bastard. The squire demanded of her who was the father? But she pertinaciously refused to make any response. So that he was about to make her mittimus to Bridewell when I departed."

"And is a wench having a bastard all your news, doctor?" cries Western; "I thought it might have been some public matter, something about the nation."

"I am afraid it is too common, indeed," answered the parson; "but I thought the whole story altogether deserved commemorating. As to national matters, your worship knows them best. My concerns extend no farther than my own parish."

"Why, ay," says the squire, "I believe I do know a little of that matter, as you say. But, come, Tommy, drink about; the bottle stands with you."

Tom begged to be excused, for that he had particular business; and getting up from table, escaped the clutches of the squire, who was rising to stop him, and went off with very little ceremony.

The squire gave him a good curse at his departure; and then turning to the parson, he cried out, "I smoke it: I smoke it. Tom is certainly the father of this bastard. Zooks, parson, you remember how he recommended the veather o' her to me. D—n un, what a sly b—ch 'tis. Ay, ay, as sure as twopence, Tom is the veather of the bastard."

"I should be very sorry for that," says the parson.

"Why sorry?" cries the squire: "Where is the mighty matter o't? What, I suppose dost pretend that thee hast never got a bastard? Pox! more good luck's thine? for I warrant hast a done a *therefore* many's the good time and often."

"Your lordship is pleased to be jocular," answered the parson; "but I do not only animadvert on the sinfulness of the action—though that surely is to be greatly deprecated—but I fear his unrighteousness may injure him with Mr. Allworthy. And truly I must say, though he hath the character of being a little wild, I never saw any harm in the young man; nor can I say I have heard any, save what your worship now mentions. I wish, indeed, he was a little more regular in his responses at church; but altogether he seems

Ingenui vultus puer ingenuique pudoris.

That is a classical line, young lady; and, being rendered into English, is, 'a lad of an ingenuous countenance, and of an ingenuous modesty'; for this was a virtue in great repute both among the Latins and Greeks. I must say, the young gentleman (for so I think I may call him, notwithstanding his birth) appears to me a very modest, civil lad, and I should be sorry that he should do himself any injury in Squire Allworthy's opinion."

"Pooh!" says the squire: "Injury, with Allworthy! Why, Allworthy loves a wench himself. Doth not all the country know whose son Tom is? You must talk to another person in that manner. I remember Allworthy at college."

67

"I thought," said the parson, "he had never been at the University."

"Yes, yes, he was," says the squire, "and many a wench have we two had together. As arrant a whore-master as any within five miles o'un. No, no. It will do'n no harm with he, assure yourself; nor with anybody else. Ask Sophy there—You have not the worse opinion of a young fellow for getting a bastard, have you, girl? No, no, the women will like un the better for't."

This was a cruel question to poor Sophia. She had observed Tom's color change at the parson's story; and that, with his hasty and abrupt departure, gave her sufficient reason to think her father's suspicion not groundless. Her heart now at once discovered the great secret to her which it had been so long disclosing by little and little; and she found herself highly interested in this matter. In such a situation, her father's malapert question rushing suddenly upon her, produced some symptoms which might have alarmed a suspicious heart; but, to do the squire justice, that was not his fault. When she rose, therefore, from her chair, and told him a hint from him was always sufficient to make her withdraw, he suffered her to leave the room, and then with great gravity of countenance remarked, "That it was better to see a daughter overmodest than overforward,"—a sentiment which was highly applauded by the parson.

VIII

Tom Jones had ridden one of Mr. Western's horses that morning in the chase; so that having no horse of his own in the squire's stable, he was obliged to go home on foot: this he did so expeditiously that he ran upwards of three miles within the half-hour.

Just as he arrived at Mr. Allworthy's outward gate he met the constable and company with Molly in their possession, whom they were conducting to that house where the inferior sort of people may learn one good lesson, viz., respect and deference to their superiors; since it must show them the wide distinction Fortune intends between those persons who are to be corrected for their faults, and those who are not; which lesson if they do not learn, I am afraid they very rarely learn any other good lesson, or improve their morals, at the House of Correction.

Tom was no sooner informed by the constable whither they were proceeding (indeed he pretty well guessed it of himself), than he caught Molly in his arms, and embracing her tenderly before them all, swore he would murder the first man who offered to lay hold of her. He bid her dry her eyes and be comforted; for, wherever she went, he would accompany her. Then turning to the constable, who stood trembling with his hat off, he desired him, in a very mild voice, to return with him for a moment only to his father (for so he now called Allworthy); for he durst, he said, be assured, that, when he had alleged what he had to say in her favor, the girl would be discharged.

The constable, who, I make no doubt, would have surrendered his prisoner had Tom demanded her, very readily consented to this request. So back they all went to Mr. Allworthy's hall; where Tom desired them to stay till his return, and then went himself in pursuit of the good man. As soon as he was found, Tom threw himself at his feet, and having begged a patient hearing, confessed himself to be the father of the child. He entreated him to have compassion on the poor girl, and to consider, if there was any guilt in the case, it lay principally at his door.

"If there is any guilt in the case!" answered Allworthy warmly: "Are you then so profligate and abandoned a libertine to doubt whether the breaking the laws of God and man, the corrupting and ruining a poor girl be guilt? I own, indeed, it doth lie principally upon you; and so heavy it is, that you ought to expect it should crush you."

"Whatever may be my fate," says Tom, "let me succeed in my intercessions for the poor girl. I confess I have corrupted her! but whether she shall be ruined depends on you. For Heaven's sake, sir, revoke your warrant, and do not send her to a place which must unavoidably prove her destruction."

Allworthy hesitated some time, and at last said, "Well, I will discharge my mittimus. You may send the constable to me." He was instantly called, discharged, and so was the girl.

Allworthy was sufficiently offended by this transgression of Jones; for, notwithstanding the assertions of Mr. Western, it is certain this worthy man had never indulged himself in any loose pleasures with women, and greatly condemned the vice of incontinence in others. Indeed, there is much reason to imagine that there was not the least truth in what Mr. Western affirmed, especially as he laid the scene of those impurities at the University, where Mr. Allworthy had never been.

But while he was angry with the incontinence of Jones, he was no less pleased with the honor and honesty of his self-accusation. He began now to form in his mind the same opinion of this young fellow, which, we hope, our reader may have conceived. And in balancing his faults with his perfections, the latter seemed rather to preponderate.

It was to no purpose, therefore, that Thwackum, who was immediately charged by Mr. Blifil with the story, unbended all his rancor against poor Tom.

But Square, who was a less violent, was a much more artful man; and as he hated Jones more perhaps than Thwackum himself did, so he contrived to do him more mischief in the mind of Mr. Allworthy.

"I am sorry, sir," said he, "to own I have been deceived as well as yourself. I could not, I confess, help being pleased with what I ascribed to the motive of friendship, though it was carried to an excess, and all excess is faulty and vicious; but in this I made allowance for youth. You now plainly see whence all the seeming generosity of this young man to the family of the gamekeeper proceeded. He supported the father in order to corrupt the daughter, and preserved the family from starving, to bring one of them to shame and ruin."

The goodness of Allworthy had prevented those considerations from occurring to himself; yet were they too plausible to be absolutely and hastily rejected, when laid before his eyes by another. They certainly stamped in the mind of Allworthy the first bad impression concerning Jones.

IX

THE reader will be pleased, I believe, to return with me to Sophia. She passed the night, after we saw her last, in no very agreeable manner. Sleep befriended her but little, and dreams less. In the morning, when Mrs. Honour, her maid, attended her at the usual hour, she was found already up and dressed.

Persons who live two or three miles' distance in the country are considered as next-door neighbors, and transactions at the one house fly with incredible celerity to the other. Mrs. Honour, therefore, had heard the whole story of Molly's shame; which she, being of a very communicative temper, had no sooner entered the apartment of her mistress, than she began to relate in the following manner:

"La, ma'am, what doth your la'ship think? the girl that your la'ship saw at church on Sunday, whom you thought so handsome; though you would not have thought her so handsome neither, if you had seen her nearer, but to be sure she hath been carried before the Justice for being big with child. She seemed to me to look like a confident slut; and to be sure she hath laid the child to young Mr. Jones. And all the parish says Mr. Allworthy is so angry with young Mr. Jones, that he won't see him. To be sure, one can't help pitying the poor young man, and yet he doth not deserve much pity neither, for demeaning himself with such kind of trumpery. Yet he is so pretty a gentleman, I should be sorry to have him turned out of doors. I dares to swear the wench was as willing as he; for she was always a forward kind of body. And when wenches are so coming, young men are not so much to be blamed neither; for to be sure they do no more than what is natural. Indeed it is beneath them to meddle with such dirty draggle-tails; and whatever happens to them, it is good enough for them. And yet, to be sure, the vile baggages are most in fault. I wishes, with all my heart, they were well to be whipped at the cart's tail; for it is pity they should be the ruin of a pretty young gentleman; and nobody can deny but that Mr. Jones is one of the most handsomest young men that ever——"

She was running on thus, when Sophia, with a more peevish voice than she had ever spoken to her in before, cried, "Prithee, why dost thou trouble me with all this stuff? What concern have I in what Mr. Jones doth? I suppose you are all alike. And you seem to me to be angry it was not your own case."

"I, ma'am!" answered Mrs. Honour, "I am sorry your ladyship should have such an opinion of me. I am sure nobody can say any such thing of me. All the young fellows in the world may go to the divil for me. Because I said he was a handsome man? Everybody says it as well as I. To be sure, I never thought as it was any harm to say a young man was handsome; but to be sure I shall never think him so any more now; for handsome is that handsome does. A beggar wench!——"

"Stop thy torrent of impertinence," cries Sophia, "and see whether my father wants me at breakfast."

Mrs. Honour then flung out of the room, muttering much to herself, of which "Marry come up, I assure you," was all that could be plainly distinguished.

Whether Mrs. Honour really deserved that suspicion, of which her mistress gave her a hint, is a matter which we cannot indulge our reader's curiosity by resolving. We will, however, make him amends in disclosing what passed in the mind of Sophia.

The reader will be pleased to recollect that a secret affection for Mr. Jones had insensibly stolen into the bosom of this young lady. That it had there grown to a pretty great height before she herself had discovered it. When she first began to perceive its symptoms, the sensations were so sweet and pleasing, that she had not resolution sufficient to check or repel them; and thus she went on cherishing a passion of which she never once considered the consequences.

This incident relating to Molly first opened her eyes. She now first perceived the weakness of which she had been guilty; and though it caused the utmost perturbation in her mind, yet it had the effect of other nauseous physic, and for the time expelled her distemper. Its operation indeed was most wonderfully quick; and in the short interval, while her maid was absent, so entirely removed all symptoms, that when Mrs. Honour returned with a summons from her father, she was become perfectly easy, and had brought herself to a thorough indifference for Mr. Jones.

Now there is no one circumstance in which the distempers of the mind bear a more exact analogy to those which are called bodily, than that aptness which both have to a relapse. Thus it happened to poor Sophia; upon whom, the very next time she saw young Jones, all the former symptoms returned, and from that time cold and hot fits alternately seized her heart.

The situation of this young lady was now very different from what it had ever been before. That passion which had formerly been so exquisitely delicious became now a scorpion in her bosom. She resisted it, therefore, with her utmost force, and summoned every argument her reason (which was surprisingly strong for her age) could suggest, to subdue and expel it. In this she so far succeeded, that she began to hope from time and absence a perfect cure. She resolved, therefore, to avoid Tom Jones as much as possible; for which purpose she began to conceive a design of visiting her aunt, to which she made no doubt of obtaining her father's consent.

But Fortune, who had other designs in her head, put an immediate stop to any such proceeding, by introducing an accident, which will be related in the next chapter.

X

MR. WESTERN grew every day fonder and fonder of Sophia, insomuch that his beloved dogs themselves almost gave place to her in his affections; but as he could not prevail on himself to abandon these, he contrived very cunningly to enjoy their company, together with that of his daughter, by insisting on her riding a-hunting with him.

Sophia, to whom her father's word was a law, readily complied with his desires, though she had not the least delight in a sport, which was of too rough and masculine a nature to suit with her disposition. She had, however, another motive, beside her obedience, to accompany the old gentleman in the chase; for by her presence she hoped in some measure to restrain his impetuosity, and to prevent him from so frequently exposing his neck to the utmost hazard.

The strongest objection was that which would have formerly been an inducement to her, namely, the frequent meeting with young Jones, whom she had determined to avoid; but as the end of the hunting season now approached, she hoped, by a short absence with her aunt, to reason herself entirely out of her unfortunate passion; and had not any doubt of being able to meet him in the field the subsequent season without the least danger.

On the second day of her hunting, as she was returning from the chase, and was arrived within a little distance from Mr. Western's house, her horse, whose mettlesome spirit required a better rider, fell suddenly to prancing and capering in such a manner that she was in the most imminent peril of falling. Tom Jones, who was at a little distance behind, saw this, and immediately galloped up to her assistance. As soon as he came up, he leapt from his own horse, and caught hold of hers by the bridle. The unruly beast presently reared himself on end on his hind legs, and threw his lovely burthen from his back, and Jones caught her in his arms.

She was so affected with the fright, that she was not immediately able to satisfy Jones, who was very solicitous to know whether she had received any hurt. She soon after, however, recovered her spirits, assured him she was safe, and thanked him for the care he had taken of her. Jones answered, "If I have preserved you, madam, I am sufficiently repaid; for I promise you, I would have secured you from the least harm at the expense of a much greater misfortune to myself than I have suffered on this occasion."

"What misfortune?" cried Sophia eagerly; "I hope you have come to no mischief?"

"Be not concerned, madam," answered Jones. "Heaven be praised you have escaped so well, considering the danger you was in. If I have broke my arm, I consider it as a trifle in comparison of what I feared upon your account."

Sophia then screamed out, "Broke your arm! Heaven forbid."

"I am afraid I have, madam," says Jones; "but I beg you will suffer me first to take care of you. I have a right hand yet at your service, to help you into the next field, whence we have but a very little walk to your father's house."

Sophia, seeing his left arm dangling by his side, while he was using the other to lead her, no longer doubted of the truth. She now grew much paler than her fears for herself had made her before. All her limbs were seized with a trembling, insomuch that Jones could scarce support her; and as her thoughts were in no less agitation, she could not refrain from giving Jones a look so full of tenderness, that it almost argued a stronger sensation in her mind than even gratitude and pity united can raise in the gentlest female bosom, without the assistance of a third more powerful passion.

Mr. Western, who was advanced at some distance when this accident happened, was now returned, as were the rest of the horsemen. Sophia immediately acquainted them with what had befallen Jones, and begged them to take care of him. Upon which Western, who had been much alarmed by meeting his daughter's horse without its rider, and was now overjoyed to find her unhurt, cried out, "I am glad it is no worse. If Tom hath broken his arm we will get a joiner to mend un again."

The squire alighted from his horse, and proceeded to his house on foot, with his daughter and Jones. An impartial spectator, who had met them on the way, would, on viewing their several countenances, have concluded Sophia alone to have been the object of compassion: for as to Jones, he exulted in having probably saved the life of the young lady, at the price only of a broken bone; and Mr. Western, though he was not unconcerned at the accident which had befallen Jones, was, however, delighted in a much higher degree with the fortunate escape of his daughter.

The generosity of Sophia's temper construed this behavior of Jones into great bravery; and it made a deep impression on her heart: for certain it is, that there is no one quality which so generally recommends men to women as this.

However this be, certain it is that the accident operated very strongly on Sophia; and, indeed, after much inquiry into the matter, I am inclined to believe, that, at this very time, the charming Sophia made no less impression on the heart of Jones; to say truth, he had for some time become sensible of the irresistible power of her charms.

XI

WHEN they arrived at Mr. Western's hall, Sophia, who had tottered along with much difficulty, sunk down in her chair; but by the assistance of hartshorn and water, she was prevented from fainting away, and had pretty well recovered her spirits, when the surgeon who was sent to for Jones appeared. Mr. Western, who imputed these symptoms in his daughter to her fall, advised her to be presently blooded by way of prevention. In this opinion he was seconded by the surgeon, who gave so many reasons for bleeding, and quoted so many cases where persons had miscarried for want of it, that the squire became very importunate, and indeed insisted peremptorily that his daughter should be blooded.

Sophia, when her arm was bound up, retired: for she was not willing (nor was it, perhaps, strictly decent) to be present at the operation on Jones. Indeed, one objection which she had to bleeding (though she did not make it) was the delay which it would occasion to setting the broken bone. For Western, when Sophia was concerned, had no consideration but for her; and as for Jones himself, he "sat like patience on a monument smiling at grief." To say the truth, when he saw the blood springing from the lovely arm of Sophia he scarce thought of what had happened to himself.

The surgeon now ordered his patient to be stripped to his shirt, and then entirely baring the arm, he began to stretch and examine it, in such a manner that the tortures he put him to caused Jones to make several wry faces; which the surgeon observing, greatly wondered at, crying, "What is the matter, sir? I am sure it is impossible I should hurt you." And then holding forth the broken arm, he began a long and very learned lecture of anatomy. Having at length finished his labored harangue, he proceeded to business, which he was more expeditious in finishing than he had been in beginning.

Jones was then ordered into a bed, which Mr. Western compelled him to accept at his own house, and sentence of water-gruel was passed upon him.

Among the good company which had attended in the hall during the bone-setting, Mrs. Honour was one; who being summoned to her mistress as soon as it was over, and asked by her how the young gentleman did, presently launched into extravagant praises on the *magnimity*, as she called it, of his behavior, which she said, "was so charming in so pretty a creature." She then burst forth into much warmer encomiums on the beauty of his person; enumerating many particulars, and ending with the whiteness of his skin.

Mrs. Honour was so entirely wrapped up in the subject that she gave her mistress time to conquer her confusion; which having done, she smiled on her maid, and told her, "she was certainly in love with this young fellow."

"I in love, madam!" answers she: "upon my word, ma'am, I assure you, ma'am, upon my soul, ma'am, I am not."

"Why, if you was," cries her mistress, "I see no reason that you should be ashamed of it; for he is certainly a pretty fellow."

"Yes, ma'am," answered the other, "that he is, the most handsomest man I ever saw in my life. Yes, to be sure, that he is, and, as your ladyship says, I don't know why I should be ashamed of loving him, though he is my betters. To be sure, gentlefolks are but flesh and blood no more than us servants. Besides, as for Mr. Jones, thof Squire Allworthy hath made a gentleman of him, he was not so good as myself by birth: for thof I am a poor body, I am an honest person's child, and my father and mother were married, which is more than some people can say, as high as they hold their heads. Marry, come up! I assure you, nobody can say that I am base born: my grandfather was a clergyman,[1] and would have been very angry, I believe, to have thought any of his family should have taken up with Molly Seagrim's dirty leavings."

Sophia now checked the torrent, as there seemed no end of its flowing.

"I wonder," says she, "at your assurance in daring to talk thus of one of my father's friends. As to the wench, I order you never to mention her name to me. And with regard to the young gentleman's birth, those who can say nothing more to his disadvantage may as well be silent on that head, as I desire you will be for the future."

"I am sorry I have offended your ladyship," answered Mrs. Honour. "I am sure I hate Molly Seagrim as much as your ladyship can; and as for abusing Squire Jones, I can call all the servants in the house to witness, that whenever any talk hath been about bastards, I have always taken his part; for which of you, says I to the footmen, would not be a bastard, if he could, to be made a gentleman of? And, says I, I am sure he is a very fine gentleman; and he hath one of the

---

[1] This is the second person of low condition whom we have recorded in this history to have sprung from the clergy. It is to be hoped such instances will, in future ages, when some provision is made for the families of the inferior clergy, appear stranger than they can be thought at present.

whitest hands in the world; for to be sure so he hath: and, says I, one of the sweetest temperedest, best naturedest men in the world he is; and, says I, all the servants and neighbors all around the country loves him. And, to be sure, I could tell your ladyship something, but that I am afraid it would offend you."

"What could you tell me, Honour?" says Sophia.

"Nay, ma'am, to be sure he meant nothing by it, therefore I would not have your ladyship be offended."

"Prithee tell me," says Sophia; "I will know it this instant."

"Why, ma'am," answered Mrs. Honour, "he came into the room one day last week when I was at work, and there lay your ladyship's muff on a chair, and to be sure he put his hands into it—that very muff your ladyship gave me but yesterday. La! says I, Mr. Jones, you will stretch my lady's muff, and spoil it: but he still kept his hands in it: and then he kissed it—to be sure I hardly ever saw such a kiss in my life as he gave it."

"I suppose he did not know it was mine," replied Sophia.

"Your ladyship shall hear, ma'am. He kissed it again and again, and said it was the prettiest muff in the world. La! sir, says I, you have seen it a hundred times. Yes, Mrs. Honour, cried he; but who can see anything beautiful in the presence of your lady but herself? Nay, that's not all neither; but I hope your ladyship won't be offended, for to be sure he meant nothing. One day, as your ladyship was playing on the harpsichord to my master, Mr. Jones was sitting in the next room, and methought he looked melancholy. La! says I, Mr. Jones, what's the matter? a penny for your thoughts, says I. Why, hussy, says he, starting up from a dream, what can I be thinking of when that angel your mistress is playing? And then squeezing me by the hand, Oh! Mrs. Honour, says he, how happy will that man be!—and then he sighed. Upon my troth, his breath is as sweet as a nosegay. But to be sure he meant no harm by it. So I hope your ladyship will not mention a word; for he gave me a crown never to mention it, and made me swear upon a book, but I believe, indeed, it was not the Bible."

Till something of a more beautiful red than vermilion be found out, I shall say nothing of Sophia's color on this occasion. "Ho—nour," says she, "I—if you will not mention this any more to me—nor to anybody else, I will not betray you—I mean, I will not be angry; but I am afraid of your tongue. Why, my girl, will you give it such liberties?"

"Nay, ma'am," answered she, "to be sure, I would sooner cut out my tongue than offend your ladyship. To be sure I shall never mention a word that your ladyship would not have me."

"Why, I would not have you mention this any more," said Sophia, "for it may come to my father's ears, and he would be angry with Mr. Jones; though I really believe, as you say, he meant nothing. I should be very angry myself, if I imagined—"

"Nay, ma'am," says Honour, "I protest I believe he meant nothing. I thought he talked as if he was out of his senses; nay, he said he believed he was beside himself when he had spoken the words. Ay, sir, says I, I believe so too. Yes, says he, Honour. But I ask your ladyship's pardon; I could tear my tongue out for offending you."

"Go on," says Sophia; "you may mention anything you have not told me before."

"Yes, Honour, says he (this was some time afterwards, when he gave me the crown), I am neither such a coxcomb, nor such a villain, as to think of her in any other delight but as my goddess; as such I will always worship and adore her while I have breath. This was all, ma'am, I will be sworn, to the best of my remembrance. I was in a passion with him myself, till I found he meant no harm."

"Indeed, Honour," says Sophia, "I believe you have a real affection for me. I was provoked the other day when I gave you warning; but if you have a desire to stay with me, you shall."

"To be sure, ma'am," answered Mrs. Honour, "I shall never desire to part with your ladyship. To be sure, I almost cried my eyes out when you gave me warning. It would be very ungrateful in me to desire to leave your ladyship; because as why, I should never get so good a place again. I am sure I would live and die with your ladyship; for, as poor Mr. Jones said, happy is the man——"

Here the dinner bell interrupted a conversation which had wrought such an effect on Sophia, that she was, perhaps, more obliged to her bleeding in the morning, than she, at the time, had apprehended she should be. As to the present situation of her mind, I shall adhere to a rule of Horace, by not attempting to describe it, from despair of success. Most of my readers will suggest it easily to themselves; and the few who cannot, would not understand the picture, or at least would deny it to be natural, if ever so well drawn.

Book V

I

Tom Jones had many visitors during his confinement, though some, perhaps, were not very agreeable to him. Mr. Allworthy saw him almost every day; but though he pitied Tom's sufferings, and greatly approved the gallant behavior which had occasioned them, yet he thought this was a favorable opportunity to bring him to a sober sense of his indiscreet conduct. Thwackum was likewise pretty assiduous in his visits; and he too considered a sick-bed to be a convenient scene for lectures. His style, however, was more severe than Mr. Allworthy's: he told his pupil "That he ought to look on his broken limb as a judgment from Heaven on his sins."

Square talked in a very different strain; he said, "Such accidents as a broken bone were below the consideration of a wise man. That it was abundantly sufficient to reconcile the mind to any of these mischances, to reflect that they are liable to befall the wisest of mankind, and are undoubtedly for the good of the whole."

Mr. Blifil visited his friend Jones but seldom, and never alone. This worthy young man, however, professed much regard for him, and as great concern at his misfortune; but cautiously avoided any intimacy, lest, as he frequently hinted, it might contaminate the sobriety of his own character.

As to Squire Western, he was seldom out of the sick-room, unless when he was engaged either in the field or over his bottle. Nay, he would sometimes retire hither to take his beer, and it was not without difficulty that he was prevented from forcing Jones to take his beer too; for no quack ever held his nostrum to be a more general panacea than he did this. From serenading his patient every hunting morning with the horn under his window it was impossible to withhold him; nor did he ever lay aside that halloo, with which he entered into all companies, when he visited Jones, without any regard to the sick person's being at time either awake or asleep.

This boisterous behavior, as it meant no harm, so happily it effected none, and was abundantly compensated to Jones, as soon as he was able to sit up, by the company of Sophia, whom the squire then brought to visit him; nor was it, indeed, long before Jones was able to attend her to the harpsichord, where she would kindly condescend, for hours together, to charm him with the most delicious music.

Notwithstanding the nicest guard which Sophia endeavored to set on her behavior, she could not avoid letting some appearances now and then slip forth: for love may again be likened to a disease in this, that when it is denied a vent in one part, it will certainly break out in another. What her lips, therefore, concealed, her eyes, her blushes, and many little involuntary actions, betrayed.

Jones, who was not without an ear any more than without eyes, made some observations; which gave him pretty strong assurances that all was not well in the tender bosom of Sophia; an opinion which many young gentlemen will, I doubt not, extremely wonder at his not having been well confirmed in long ago. In reality, as he had never once entertained any thought of possessing her, nor had ever given the least voluntary indulgence to his inclinations, he had a much stronger passion for her than he himself was acquainted with. His heart now brought forth the full secret, at the same time that it assured him the adorable object returned his affection.

The idea of lovely Molly now intruded itself before him. He had sworn eternal constancy in her arms, and she had as often vowed never to outlive his deserting her. The ruin, therefore, of the poor girl must, he foresaw, unavoidably attend his deserting her; and this thought stung him to the soul. His heart would not suffer him to destroy a human creature who, he thought, loved him, and had to that love sacrificed her innocence.

Amidst these thoughts poor Jones passed a long sleepless night, and in the morning the result of the whole was to abide by Molly, and to think no more of Sophia.

In this virtuous resolution he continued all the next day till the evening, cherishing the idea of Molly, and driving Sophia from his thoughts; but in the fatal evening, a very trifling accident set all his passions again on float.

II

THE day after Mr. Jones had that conflict with himself which we have seen in the preceding chapter, Mrs. Honour came into his room, and finding him alone, began in the following manner:

"La, sir, where do you think I have been? I warrants you, you would not guess in fifty years; but if you did guess, to be sure I must not tell you neither."

"Nay, if it be something which you must not tell me," said Jones, "I shall have the curiosity to inquire, and I know you will not be so barbarous to refuse me."

"I don't know," cries she, "why I should refuse you neither, for that matter; for to be sure you won't mention it any more. And for that matter, if you knew where I have been, unless you knew what I have been about, it would not signify much. Nay, I don't see why it should be kept a secret for my part; for to be sure she is the best lady in the world."

Upon this, Jones began to beg earnestly to be let into this secret, and faithfully promised not to divulge it. She then proceeded thus:

"Why, you must know, sir, my young lady sent me to inquire after Molly Seagrim, and to see whether the wench wanted anything; to be sure, I did not care to go, methinks; but servants must do what they are ordered. How could you undervalue yourself so, Mr. Jones? So my lady bid me go and carry her some linen, and other things. She is too good. If such forward sluts were sent to Bridewell it would be better for them. I told my lady, says I, madam, your la'ship is encouraging idleness."

"And was my Sophia so good?" says Jones.

"My Sophia! I assure you, marry come up," answered Honour. "And yet if you knew all—indeed, if I was as Mr. Jones, I should look a little higher than such trumpery as Molly Seagrim."

"What do you mean by these words," replied Jones, "if I knew all?"

"I mean what I mean," says Honour. "Don't you remember putting your hands in my lady's muff once? I vow I could almost find in my heart to tell, if I was certain my lady would never come to the hearing on't." Jones then made several solemn protestations; and Honour proceeded, "Then to be sure, my lady gave me that muff; and afterwards, upon hearing what you had done—"

"Then you told her what I had done?" interrupted Jones.

"If I did, sir," answered she, "you need not be angry with me. Many's the man would have given his head to have had my lady told, if they had known,—for, to be sure, the biggest lord in the land might be proud—but, I protest, I have a great mind not to tell you." Jones fell to entreaties, and soon prevailed on her to go on thus: "You must know then, sir, that my lady had given this muff to me; but about a day or two after I had told her the story, she quarrels with her new muff, and to be sure it is the prettiest that ever was seen. Honour, says she, this is an odious muff; it is too big for me, I can't wear it: till I can get another, you must let me have my old one again, and you may have this in the room on't—for she's a good lady, and scorns to give a thing and take a thing, I promise you that. So to be sure I fetched it her back again, and, I believe, she hath worn it upon her almost ever since, and I warrants hath given it many a kiss when nobody hath seen her."

Here the conversation was interrupted by Mr. Western himself, who came to summon Jones to the harpsichord; whither the poor young fellow went all pale and trembling. This Western observed, but, on seeing Mrs. Honour, imputed it to a wrong cause; and having given Jones a hearty curse between jest and earnest, he bid him beat abroad, and not poach up the game in his warren.

Sophia looked this evening with more than usual beauty, and we may believe it was no small addition to her charms, in the eye of Mr. Jones, that she now happened to have on her right arm this very muff.

She was playing one of her father's favorite tunes, and he was leaning on her chair, when the muff fell over her fingers, and put her out. This so disconcerted the squire, that he snatched the muff from her, and with a hearty curse threw it into the fire. Sophia instantly started up, and with the utmost eagerness recovered it from the flames.

The citadel of Jones was now taken by surprise. All those considerations of honor and prudence which our hero had lately with so much military wisdom placed as guards over the avenue of his heart ran away from their posts, and the God of Love marched in, in triumph.

III

CONCERN for what must become of poor Molly greatly disturbed and perplexed the mind of the worthy youth. The superior merit of Sophia totally eclipsed, or rather extinguished, all the beauties of the poor girl; but compassion instead of contempt succeeded to love. At length it occurred to him, that he might possibly be able to make Molly amends by giving her a sum of money. This he almost despaired of her accepting, when he recollected the frequent and vehement assurances he had received from her, that the world put in balance with him would make her no amends for his loss. However, her extreme poverty, and chiefly her egregious vanity, gave him some little hope.

One day, accordingly, when his arm was so well recovered that he could walk easily with it slung in a sash, he stole forth, at a season when the squire was engaged in his field exercises, and visited his fair one. Her mother and sisters, whom he found taking their tea, informed him first that Molly was not at home; but afterwards the eldest sister acquainted him, with a malicious smile, that she was above-stairs a-bed. Tom had no objection to this situation of his mistress, and immediately ascended the ladder which led towards her bed-chamber; but when he came to the top, he, to his great surprise, found the door fast; nor could he for some time obtain any answer from within; for Molly, as she herself afterwards informed him, was fast asleep.

It cannot be wondered at, that the unexpected sight of Mr. Jones should so strongly operate on the mind of Molly, that for some minutes she was unable to express the great raptures with which the reader will suppose she was affected on this occasion. As for Jones, he was so entirely possessed, and as it were enchanted, by the presence of his beloved object, that he for a while forgot Sophia, and consequently the principal purpose of his visit.

This, however, soon recurred to his memory; and after the first transports of their meeting were over, he found means by degrees to introduce a discourse on the fatal consequences which must attend their amour, if Mr. Allworthy, who had strictly forbidden him ever seeing her more, should discover that he still carried on this commerce.

Since therefore their hard fates had determined that they must separate, he advised her to bear it with resolution, and swore he would never omit any opportunity of providing for her in a manner beyond her utmost expectation; concluding at last, that she might soon find some man who would marry her, and who would make her much happier than she could be with him.

Molly remained a few moments in silence, and then bursting into a flood of tears, she began to upbraid him in the following words:

"And this is your love for me, to forsake me in this manner, now you have ruined me! What signifies all the riches in the world to me without you, now you have gained my heart, so you have—you have—? Why do you mention another man to me? I can never love any other man as long as I live. All other men are nothing to me. If the greatest squire in all the country would come a-suiting to me tomorrow, I would not give my company to him. No, I shall always hate and despise the whole sex for your sake."

She was proceeding thus, when an accident put a stop to her tongue before it had run out half its career. The room, or rather garret, in which Molly lay, being at the top of the house, was of a sloping figure; it was impossible to stand upright anywhere but in the middle. As this room wanted a closet, Molly had nailed up an old rug against the rafters of the house, which enclosed a little hole where her best apparel were hung up and secured from the dust.

Now, as Molly pronounced those last words, which are recorded above, the wicked rug got loose from its fastening, and discovered everything hid behind it; where among other female utensils appeared (with shame I write it, and with sorrow will it be read)—the philosopher Square, in a posture (for the place would not near admit his standing upright) as ridiculous as can possibly be conceived. He had a nightcap belonging to Molly on his head, and his two large eyes, the moment the rug fell, stared directly at Jones; so that when the idea of philosophy was added to the figure now discovered, it would have been very difficult for any spectator to have refrained from immoderate laughter.

Square no sooner made his appearance than Molly flung herself back in her bed, cried out she was undone, and abandoned herself to despair. As to the gentleman behind the arras, he was not in much less consternation. He stood for a while motionless, and seemed equally at a loss what to say, or whither to direct his eyes. Jones, though perhaps the most astonished of the three, first found his tongue; and being immediately recovered from those uneasy sensations which Molly by her upbraidings had occasioned, he burst into a loud laughter, and then saluting Mr. Square, advanced to take him by the hand, and to relieve him from his place of confinement.

Square being now arrived in the middle of the room, in which part only he could stand upright, looked at Jones with a very grave countenance, and said to him,

"Well, sir, I see you enjoy this mighty discovery, and, I dare swear, take great delight in the thoughts of exposing me; but if you will consider the matter fairly, you will find you are yourself only to blame. I am not guilty of corrupting innocence. I have done nothing for which that part of the world which judges of matters by the rule of right will condemn me. Fitness is governed by the nature of things, and not by customs, forms or municipal laws. Nothing is indeed unfit which is not unnatural."

"Well reasoned, old boy," answered Jones; "but why dost thou think that I should desire to expose thee? I promise thee, I was never better pleased with thee in my life; and unless thou hast a mind to discover it thyself, this affair may remain a profound secret for me."

"Nay, Mr. Jones," replied Square, "I would not be thought to undervalue reputation. Good fame is a species of the Kalon, and it is by no means fitting to neglect it. Besides, to murder one's own reputation is a kind of suicide, a detestable and odious vice. If you think proper, therefore, to conceal any infirmity of mine (for such I may have, since no man is perfectly perfect), I promise you I will not betray myself. Things may be fitting to be done, which are not fitting to be boasted of."

"Well," cries Jones, "it shall be your own fault, as I have promised you, if you ever hear any more of this adventure. Behave kindly to the girl, and I will never open my lips concerning the matter to any one. And, Molly, do you be faithful to your friend, and I will not only forgive your infidelity to me, but will do you all the service I can." So saying, he took a hasty leave, and, slipping down the ladder, retired with much expedition.

Square was rejoiced to find this adventure was likely to have no worse conclusion; and as for Molly, being recovered from her confusion, she began at first to upbraid Square with having been the occasion of her loss of Jones; but that gentleman soon found the means of mitigating her anger, partly by caresses, and partly by a small nostrum from his purse, of wonderful and approved efficacy in purging off the ill humors of the mind, and in restoring it to a good temper.

She then poured forth a vast profusion of tenderness towards her new lover; turned all she had said to Jones, and Jones himself, into ridicule; and vowed, though he once had the possession of her person, that none but Square had ever been master of her heart.

IV

THE infidelity of Molly, which Jones had now discovered, would, perhaps, have vindicated a much greater degree of resentment than he expressed on the occasion; and if he had abandoned her directly from that moment, very few, I believe, would have blamed him.

Certain, however, it is, that he saw her in the light of compassion and was not a little shocked on reflecting that he had himself originally corrupted her innocence.

This consideration gave him no little uneasiness, till Betty, the elder sister, was so kind, some time afterwards, entirely to cure him by a hint, that one Will Barnes, and not himself, had been the first seducer of Molly; and that the little child, which he had hitherto so certainly concluded to be his own, might very probably have an equal title, at least, to claim Barnes for its father.

Jones eagerly pursued this scent when he had first received it; and in a very short time was sufficiently assured that the girl had told him truth, not only by the confession of the fellow, but at last by that of Molly herself.

Jones was become perfectly easy by possession of this secret with regard to Molly; but as to Sophia, he was under the most violent perturbation; his heart was now, if I may use the metaphor, entirely evacuated, and Sophia took absolute possession of it. He loved her with an unbounded passion, and plainly saw the tender sentiments she had for him; yet could not this assurance lessen his despair of obtaining the consent of her father, nor the horrors which attended his pursuit of her by any base or treacherous method.

The injury which he must thus do to Mr. Western, and the concern which would accrue to Mr. Allworthy, were circumstances that tormented him all day, and haunted him on his pillow at night. He often resolved, in the absence of Sophia, to leave her father's house, and to see her no more; and as often, in her presence, forgot all those resolutions, and determined to pursue her at the hazard of his life, and at the forfeiture of what was much dearer to him.

This conflict began soon to produce very strong and visible effects: for he lost all his usual sprightliness and gaiety of temper, and became not only melancholy when alone, but dejected and absent in company. All these symptoms escaped the notice of the squire; but not so of Sophia. This highly endeared him to her, and raised in her mind two of the best affections which any lover can wish to raise in a mistress—these were, esteem and pity.

Thus his backwardness, his shunning her, his coldness, and his silence, were the forwardest, the most diligent, the warmest, and most eloquent advocates; and wrought so violently on her sensible and tender heart, that she soon felt for him all those gentle sensations which are consistent with a virtuous and elevated female mind. —In a word, she was in love with him to distraction.

One day this young couple accidentally met in the garden, at the end of the two walks which were both bounded by that canal in which Jones had formerly risked drowning to retrieve the little bird that Sophia had there lost.

This place had been of late much frequented by Sophia. Here she used to ruminate, with a mixture of pain and pleasure, on an incident which, however trifling in itself, had possibly sown the first seeds of that affection which was now arrived to such maturity in her heart.

Their conversation began, as usual, on the delicious beauty of the morning. Hence they passed to the beauty of the place, on which Jones launched forth very high encomiums. When they came to the tree whence he had formerly tumbled into the canal, Sophia could not help reminding him of that accident, and said,

"I fancy, Mr. Jones, you have some little shuddering when you see that water."

"I assure you, madam," answered Jones, "the concern you felt at the loss of your little bird will always appear to me the highest circumstance in that adventure. Poor little Tommy! there is the branch he stood upon. How could the little wretch have the folly to fly away from that state of happiness in which I had the honor to place him? His fate was a just punishment for his ingratitude."

"Upon my word, Mr. Jones," said she, "your gallantry very narrowly escaped as severe a fate. Sure the remembrance must affect you."

"Indeed, madam," answered he, "if I have any reason to reflect with sorrow on it, it is, perhaps, that the water had not been a little deeper, by which I might have escaped many bitter heartaches that Fortune seems to have in store for me."

"Fie, Mr. Jones!" replied Sophia; "I am sure you cannot be in earnest now. This affected contempt of life is only an excess of your complaisance to me. You would endeavor to lessen the obligation of having twice ventured it for my sake. Beware the third time." She spoke these last words with a smile, and a softness inexpressible.

Jones answered with a sigh, "He feared it was already too late for caution"; and then looking tenderly and steadfastly on her, he cried, "Oh, Miss Western! can you desire me to live? Can you wish me so ill?"

Sophia, looking down on the ground, answered with some hesitation, "Indeed, Mr. Jones, I do not wish you ill."

"Oh, I know too well that heavenly temper," cries Jones, "that divine goodness, which is beyond every other charm."

"Nay, now," answered she, "I understand you not. I can stay no longer."

"I—I would not be understood!" cries he; "nay, I can't be understood. I know not what I say. Meeting you here so unexpectedly, I have been unguarded: for Heaven's sake pardon me if I have said anything to offend you. I did not mean it. Indeed, I would rather have died—nay, the very thought would kill me."

"You surprise me," answered she. "How can you possibly think you have offended me?"

"Fear, madam," says he, "easily runs into madness; and there is no degree of fear like that which I feel of offending you. How can I speak then? Nay, don't look angrily at me: one frown will destroy me. I mean nothing. Blame my eyes, or blame those beauties. What am I saying? Pardon me if I have said too much. My heart overflowed. I have struggled with my love to the utmost, and have endeavored to conceal a fever which preys on my vitals, and will, I hope, soon make it impossible for me ever to offend you more."

Mr. Jones now fell a-trembling as if he had been shaken with the fit of an ague.

Sophia, who was in a situation not very different from his, answered in these words:

"Mr. Jones, I will not affect to misunderstand you; indeed, I understand you too well; but, for Heaven's sake, if you have any affection for me, let me make the best of my way into the house. I wish I may be able to support myself thither."

Jones, who was hardly able to support himself, offered her his arm, which she condescended to accept, but begged he would not mention a word more to her of this nature at present. He promised he would not; insisting only on her forgiveness of what love, without the leave of his will, had forced from him; this, she told him, he knew

Molly flung herself back in her bed, and abandoned herself to despair.

how to obtain by his future behavior; and thus this young pair tottered and trembled along, the lover not once daring to squeeze the hand of his mistress, though it was locked in his.

V

MR. WESTERN was become so fond of Jones that he was unwilling to part with him, though his arm had been long since cured; and Jones, either from the love of sport, or from some other reason, was easily persuaded to continue at his house, which he did sometimes for a fortnight together without paying a single visit at Mr. Allworthy's; nay, without ever hearing from thence.

Mr. Allworthy had been for some days indisposed with a cold, which had been attended with a little fever. This he had, however, neglected; as it was usual with him to do all manner of disorders which did not confine him to his bed. When the increase of his fever obliged him to send for assistance, the doctor at his first arrival shook his head, wished he had been sent for sooner, and intimated that he thought him in very imminent danger.

The good man gave immediate orders for all his family to be summoned round him. None of these were then abroad, but Mrs. Blifil, who had been some time in London, and Mr. Jones, whom the reader had just parted from at Mr. Western's, and who received this summons just as Sophia had left him.

The news of Mr. Allworthy's danger (for the servant told him he was dying) drove all thoughts of love out of his head. He hurried instantly into the chariot which was sent for him, and ordered the coachman to drive with all imaginable haste; nor did the idea of Sophia, I believe, once occur to him on the way.

And now the whole family, namely, Mr. Blifil, Mr. Jones, Mr. Thwackum, Mr. Square, and some of the servants (for such were Mr. Allworthy's orders) being all assembled round his bed, the good man sat up in it, and was beginning to speak, when Blifil fell to blubbering, and began to express very loud and bitter lamentations. Upon this Mr. Allworthy shook him by the hand, and said,

"Do not sorrow thus, my dear nephew, at the most ordinary of all human occurrences. When misfortunes befall our friends we are justly grieved; for those are accidents which might often have been avoided, and which may seem to render the lot of one man more peculiarly unhappy than that of others; but death is certainly unavoidable, and is that common lot in which alone the fortunes of all men agree; nor is the time when this happens to us very material. If the wisest of men hath compared life to a span, surely we may be allowed to consider it as a day. It is my fate to leave it in the evening; but those who are taken away earlier have only lost a few hours, at the best little worth lamenting, and much oftener hours of labor and fatigue, of pain and sorrow. Few men, I own, think in this manner; for, indeed, few men think of death till they are in its jaws. However gigantic and terrible an object this may appear when it approaches them, they are nevertheless incapable of seeing it at any distance; nay, though they have been ever so much alarmed and frightened when they have apprehended themselves in danger of dying, they are no sooner cleared from this apprehension than even the fears of it are erased from their minds. But, alas! he who escapes from death is not pardoned; he is only reprieved, and reprieved to a short day.

"Grieve, therefore, no more, my dear child, on this occasion: an event which may happen every hour, and which must and will most unavoidably reach us all at last, ought neither to occasion our surprise nor our lamentation.

"But I shall waste my strength too much. I intend to speak concerning my will, that I may have the comfort of perceiving you are all satisfied with the provision I have there made for you.

"Nephew Blifil, I leave you the heir to my whole estate, except only £500 a-year, which is to revert to you after the death of your mother, and except one other estate of £500 a-year, and the sum of £6000, which I have bestowed in the following manner:

"The estate of £500 a-year I have given to you, Mr. Jones; and as I know the inconvenience which attends the want of ready money, I have added £1000 in specie. In this I know not whether I have exceeded or fallen short of your expectation. Perhaps you will think I have given you too little, and the world will be as ready to condemn me for giving you too much; but the latter censure I despise; and as to the former, unless you should entertain that common error which I have often heard in my life pleaded as an excuse for a total want of charity, namely, that instead of raising gratitude by voluntary acts of bounty, we are apt to raise demands, which of all others are the most boundless and most difficult to satisfy. Pardon me the bare mention of this; I will not suspect any such thing."

Jones flung himself at his benefactor's feet, and taking eagerly hold of his hand, assured him his goodness to him, both now and all other times, had so infinitely exceeded not only his merit but his hopes, that no words could express his sense of it.

"And I assure you, sir," said he, "your present generosity hath left me no other concern than for the present melancholy occasion. Oh, my friend, my father!" Here his words choked him, and he turned away to hide a tear which was starting from his eyes.

Allworthy then gently squeezed his hand, and proceeded thus:

"I am convinced, my child, that you have much goodness, generosity, and honor, in your temper: if you will add prudence and religion to these, you must be happy; for the three former qualities, I admit, make you worthy of happiness, but the latter only will put you in possession of it.

"One thousand pound I have given to you, Mr. Thwackum; a sum, I am convinced, which greatly exceeds your desires as well as your wants. However, you will receive it as a memorial of my friendship.

"A like sum, Mr. Square, I have bequeathed to you. This, I hope, will enable you to pursue your profession with better success than hitherto. I have often observed with concern, that among men of business, poverty is understood to indicate want of ability. But the little I have been able to leave you will extricate you from those difficulties with which you have formerly struggled; and then I doubt not but you will meet with sufficient prosperity to supply what a man of your philosophical temper will require.

"I find myself growing faint, so I shall refer you to my will for my disposition of the residue. My servants will there find some tokens to remember me by; and there are a few charities which, I trust, my executors will see faithfully performed. Bless you all. I am setting out a little before you."

Here a footman came hastily into the room, and said there was an attorney from Salisbury who had a particular message, which he said he must communicate to Mr. Allworthy himself: that he seemed in a violent hurry, and protested he had so much business to do, that, if he could cut himself into four quarters, all would not be sufficient.

"Go, child," said Allworthy to Blifil, "see what the gentleman wants. I am not able to do any business now, nor can he have any with me, in which you are not at present more concerned than myself. Besides, I really am—I am incapable of seeing anyone at present, or of any longer attention."

Some of the company shed tears at their parting; and even the philosopher Square wiped his eyes, albeit unused to the melting mood. As to Mrs. Wilkins, she dropped her pearls as fast as the Arabian trees their medicinal gums; for this was a ceremonial which that gentlewoman never omitted on a proper occasion.

After this Mr. Allworthy again laid himself down on his pillow and endeavored to compose himself to rest.

VI

BESIDES grief for her master, there was another source for that briny stream which so plentifully rose above the two mountainous cheek-bones of the housekeeper. She was no sooner retired than she began to mutter to herself in the following pleasant strain: "Sure master might have made some difference, methinks, between me and the other servants. I suppose he hath left me mourning; but, i'fackins! if that be all, the devil shall wear it for him, for me. I'd have his worship know I am no beggar. I have saved five hundred pounds in his service, and after all to be used in this manner. It is a fine encouragement to servants to be honest; and to be sure, if I have taken a little something now and then, others have taken ten times as much; and now we are all put in a lump together. If so be that it be so, the legacy may go to the devil with him that gave it. No, I won't give it up neither, because that will please some folks. No, I'll buy the gayest gown I can get, and dance over the old curmudgeon's grave in it. Ay, ay, I shall remember you for huddling me among the servants. One would have thought he might have mentioned my name as well as that of Square; but he is a gentleman forsooth, though he had not clothes on his back when he came hither first." Much more of the like kind she muttered to herself.

Neither Thwackum nor Square were much better satisfied with their legacies.

About an hour after they had left the sickroom, Square met Thwackum in the hall and accosted him thus:

"Well, sir, have you heard any news of your friend since we parted from him?"

"If you mean Mr. Allworthy," answered Thwackum, "I think you might rather give him the appellation of your friend; for he seems to me to have deserved that title."

"The title is as good on your side," replied Square, "for his bounty, such as it is, hath been equal to both."

"I should not have mentioned it first," cries Thwackum, "but since you begin, I must inform you I am of a different opinion. The duty I have done in his family, and the care I have taken in the education of his two boys, are services for which some men might have expected a greater return. Though the Scriptures obliges me to remain contented, it does not restrain me from seeing when I am injured by an unjust comparison."

"Since you provoke me," returned Square, "that injury is done to me; nor did I ever imagine Mr. Allworthy had held my friendship so light as to put me in balance with one who received his wages. That pitiful memorial of our friendship which he hath thought fit to bequeath me, I despise; and nothing but the unfortunate situation of my circumstances should prevail on me to accept it."

The physician now arrived, and began to inquire of the two disputants, how we all did above-stairs? Before they came to an explanation, Mr. Blifil came to them with a most melancholy countenance, and acquainted them that he brought sad news, that his mother was dead at Salisbury; that she had been seized on the road home with the gout in her head and stomach, which had carried her off in a few hours.

"Good-lack-a-day!" says the doctor. "One cannot answer for events; but I wish I had been at hand, to have been called in. The gout is a distemper which it is difficult to treat; yet I have been remarkably successful in it."

Thwackum and Square both condoled with Mr. Blifil for the loss of his mother, which the one advised him to bear like a man, and the other like a Christian. The young gentleman said he could not help complaining a little against the peculiar severity of his fate, which brought the news of so great a calamity to him by surprise. He said, the present occasion would put to the test those excellent rudiments which he had learnt from Mr. Thwackum and Mr. Square; and it would be entirely owing to them if he was enabled to survive such misfortunes.

It was now debated whether Mr. Allworthy should be informed of the death of his sister. This the doctor violently opposed; in which, I believe, the whole College would agree with him: but Mr. Blifil said, he had received such positive and repeated orders from his uncle, never to keep any secret from him for fear of the disquietude which it might give him, that he durst not think of disobedience, whatever might be the consequence. So together moved Mr. Blifil and the doctor toward the sickroom; where the physician first entered, and approached the bed, in order to feel his patient's pulse, which he had no sooner done than he declared he was much better; that the last application had succeeded to a miracle, and had brought the fever to intermit: so that, he said, there appeared now to be little danger.

Mr. Allworthy had no sooner lifted up his eyes, and thanked Heaven for these hopes of his recovery, than Mr. Blifil drew near, with a very dejected aspect, and having applied his handkerchief to his eyes, he communicated to his uncle what the reader hath been just before acquainted with.

Allworthy received the news with concern, with patience, and with resignation. He dropped a tender tear, then composed his countenance, and at last cried, "The Lord's will be done in everything."

He now inquired for the messenger; but Blifil told him it had been impossible to detain him a moment.

VII

THE reader may perhaps wonder at hearing nothing of Mr. Jones in the last chapter. In fact, his behavior was so different from that of the persons there mentioned, that we chose not to confound his name with theirs.

When the good man had ended his speech, Jones was the last who deserted the room. Thence he retired to his own apartment to give vent to his concern; but the restlessness of his mind would not suffer him to remain long there; he slipped softly, therefore, to Allworthy's chamber-door, where he listened a considerable time without hearing any kind of motion within, unless a violent snoring, which at last his fears misrepresented as groans. This so alarmed him, that he could not forbear entering the room; where he found the good man in the bed, in a sweet composed sleep, and his nurse snoring in the above-mentioned hearty manner at the bed's feet. He immediately took the only method of silencing this thorough bass, whose music he feared might disturb Mr. Allworthy; and then sitting down by the nurse, he remained motionless till Blifil and the doctor came in.

When he first heard Blifil tell his uncle this story, Jones could hardly contain the wrath which kindled in him at the other's indiscretion, especially as the doctor shook his head, and declared his unwillingness to have the matter mentioned to his patient. But the consequences which any violent expression towards Blifil might have on the sick, stilled his rage at the present.

The physician dined that day at Mr. Allworthy's; and having after dinner visited his patient, he returned to the company, and told them, that he had now the satisfaction to say, with assurance, that his patient was out of all danger.

This account so pleased Jones, and threw him into such immoderate excess of rapture, that he might be truly said to be drunk with joy—an intoxication which greatly forwards the effects of wine; and as he was very free too with the bottle on this occasion (for he drank many bumpers to the doctor's health, as well as to other toasts) he became very soon literally drunk. He gave a loose to mirth, sang two or three amorous songs, and fell into every frantic disorder which unbridled joy is apt to inspire; but so far was he from any disposition to quarrel, that he was ten times better humored, if possible, than when he was sober.

Mr. Blifil was highly offended at a behavior which was so inconsistent with the sober and prudent reserve of his own temper. He bore it too with the greater impatience, as it appeared to him very indecent at this season; "When," as he said, "the house was a house of mourning on the account of his dear mother; and if it had pleased Heaven to give him some prospect of Mr. Allworthy's recovery, it would become them better to express the exultations of their hearts in thanksgiving than in drunkenness and riots."

Wine had not so totally overpowered Jones as to prevent his recollecting Mr. Blifil's loss, the moment it was mentioned. As no person, therefore, was more ready to confess and condemn his own errors, he offered to shake Mr. Blifil by the hand, and begged his pardon, saying, "His excessive joy for Mr. Allworthy's recovery had driven every other thought out of his mind."

Blifil scornfully rejected his hand; and with much indignation answered, "It was little to be wondered at, if tragical spectacles made no impression on the blind; but, for his part, he had the misfortune to know who his parents were, and consequently must be affected with their loss."

Jones, who, notwithstanding his good humor, had some mixture of the irascible in his constitution, leaped hastily from his chair, and catching hold of Blifil's collar, cried out, "D—n you for a rascal, do you insult me with the misfortune of my birth?" A scuffle immediately ensued, which might have produced mischief, had it not been prevented by the interposition of Thwackum and the physician; for the philosophy of Square rendered him superior to all emotions, and he very calmly smoked his pipe, as was his custom in all broils, unless when he apprehended some danger of having it broke in his mouth.

A truce was at length agreed on, by the mediation of the neutral parties, and the whole company again sat down at the table; where Jones being prevailed on to ask pardon, and Blifil to give it, peace was restored, and everything seemed *in statu quo*.

VIII

JONES retired from the company, in which we have seen him engaged, into the fields, where he intended to cool himself by a walk in the open air before he attended Mr. Allworthy. There, whilst he renewed those meditations on his dear Sophia, while his wanton fancy roamed unbounded over all her beauties, and his lively imagination painted the charming maid in various ravishing forms, his warm heart melted with tenderness; and at length, throwing himself on the ground, by the side of a gently murmuring brook, he broke forth into the following ejaculation:

"O Sophia, would Heaven give thee to my arms, how blest would be my condition! Curst be that fortune which sets a distance between us. Was I but possessed of thee, one only suit of rags thy whole estate, is there a man on earth whom I would envy! How contemptible would the brightest Circassian beauty, dressed in all the jewels of the Indies, appear to my eyes! But why do I mention another woman? Could I think my eyes capable of looking at any other with tenderness, these hands should tear them from my head. Sophia, Sophia alone shall be mine. What raptures are in that name! I will engrave it on every tree."

At these words he started up, and beheld—not his Sophia—no, nor a Circassian maid richly and elegantly attired for the grand Signior's seraglio. No; without a gown, in a shift that was somewhat of the coarsest, and none of the cleanest, bedewed likewise with some odoriferous effluvia, the produce of the day's labor, with a pitchfork in her hand, Molly Seagrim approached. Our hero had his penknife in his hand, which he had drawn for the before-mentioned purpose of carving on the bark; when the girl coming near him, cried out with a smile,

"You don't intend to kill me, squire, I hope!"

"Why should you think I would kill you?" answered Jones.

"Nay," replied she, "after your cruel usage of me when I saw you last, killing me would, perhaps, be too great kindness for me to expect."

Here ensued a parley, which, as I do not think myself obliged to relate it, I shall omit. It is sufficient that it lasted a full quarter of an hour, at the conclusion of which they retired into the thickest part of the grove.

Some of my readers may be inclined to think this event unnatural. However, the fact is true; and perhaps may be sufficiently accounted for by suggesting, that Jones probably thought one woman better than none, and Molly as probably imagined two men to be better than one. Besides the before-mentioned motive assigned to the present behavior of Jones, the reader will be likewise pleased to recollect in his favor, that he was not at this time perfect master of that wonderful power of reason, which so well enables grave and wise men to subdue their unruly passions, and to decline any of these prohibited amusements.

No sooner had our hero retired with his Dido, but the parson and the young squire, who were taking a serious walk, arrived at the stile which leads into the grove, and the latter caught a view of the lovers just as they were sinking out of sight.

Blifil knew Jones very well, though he was at above a hundred yards' distance, and he was as positive to the sex of his companion, though not to the individual person. He started, blessed himself, and uttered a very solemn ejaculation.

Thwackum expressed some surprise at these sudden emotions, and asked the reason of them. To which Blifil answered, "He was certain he had seen a fellow and wench retire together among the bushes, which he doubted not was with some wicked purpose." As to the name of Jones, he thought proper to conceal it, and why he did so much be left to the judgment of the sagacious reader; for we never choose to assign motives to the actions of men.

The parson, who was not only strictly chaste in his own person, but a great enemy to the opposite vice in all others, desired Mr. Blifil to conduct him immediately to the place. The way through which our hunters were to pass in pursuit of their game was beset with briars, that caused such a rustling that Jones had sufficient warning of their arrival before they could surprise him; nay, indeed, so incapable was Thwackum of concealing his indignation, and such vengeance did he mutter forth every step he took, that this alone must have abundantly satisfied Jones that he was (to use the language of sportsmen) found sitting.

As IN the season of *rutting* (an uncouth phrase, by which the vulgar denote that gentle dalliance, which in the well-wooded [1] forest of Hampshire, passes between lovers of the ferine kind), if, while the lofty-crested stag meditates the amorous sport, a couple of puppies, or any other beasts of hostile note, should wander so near the temple of Venus Ferina that the fair hind should shrink from the place, fierce and tremendous rushes forth the stag to the entrance of the thicket; there stands he sentinel over his love, stamps the ground with his foot, and with his horns brandished aloft in the air, proudly provokes the apprehended foe to combat.

Thus, and more terrible, when he perceived the enemy's approach, leaped forth our hero. Many a step advanced he forwards, in order to conceal the trembling hind, and, if possible, to secure her retreat. And now Thwackum, having first darted some livid lightning from his fiery eyes, began to thunder forth,

"Fie upon it! Mr. Jones. Is it possible you should be the person?"

"You see," answered Jones, "it is possible I should be here."

"And who," said Thwackum, "is that wicked slut with you?"

"If I have any wicked slut with me," cries Jones, "it is possible I shall not let you know who she is."

"I command you to tell me immediately," says Thwackum; "and I would not have you imagine, young man, that your age, though it hath somewhat abridged the purpose of tuition, hath totally taken away the authority of the master. The relation of the master and scholar is indelible; as, indeed, all other relations are; for they all derive their original from Heaven. I would have you think yourself, therefore, as much obliged to obey me now as when I taught you your first rudiments."

"I believe you would," cries Jones; "but that will not happen unless you had the same birchen argument to convince me."

"Then I must tell you plainly," said Thwackum, "I am resolved to discover the wicked wretch."

"And I must tell you plainly," returned Jones, "I am resolved you shall not."

Thwackum then offered to advance, and Jones laid hold of his arms, which Mr. Blifil endeavored to rescue, declaring "he would not see his old master insulted."

---

[1] This is an ambiguous phrase, and may mean either a forest well clothed with wood, or well stripped of it.

Jones now finding himself engaged with two, thought it necessary to rid himself of one of his antagonists as soon as possible. He therefore applied to the weakest first; and, letting the parson go, he directed a blow at the young squire's breast, which luckily taking place, reduced him to measure his length on the ground.

This parson had been a champion in his youth, and had won much honor by his fist, both at school and at the university. He had now indeed, for a great number of years, declined the practice of that noble art; yet was his courage full as strong as his faith, and his body no less strong than either. He was, moreover, as the reader may perhaps have conceived, somewhat irascible in his nature. When he saw his friend stretched out on the ground, he threw himself into a posture of offense; and collecting all his force, attacked Jones in the front with as much impetuosity as he had formerly attacked him in the rear.

Our hero received the enemy's attack with the most undaunted intrepidity. Many lusty blows were given on both sides; at last a violent fall, in which Jones had thrown his knees into Thwackum's breast, so weakened the latter, that victory had been no longer dubious, had not Blifil, who had now recovered his strength, again renewed the fight, and by engaging with Jones, given the parson a moment's time to shake his ears and to regain his breath.

And now both together attacked our hero. The victory, according to modern custom, was like to be decided by numbers, when, on a sudden, a fourth pair of fists appeared in the battle, and immediately paid their compliments to the parson; and the owner of them at the same time crying out,

"Are not you ashamed, and be d—n'd to you, to fall two of you upon one?"

The battle, which was of the kind that for distinction's sake is called royal, now raged with the utmost violence during a few minutes; till Blifil being a second time laid sprawling by Jones, Thwackum condescended to apply for quarter to his new antagonist, who was now found to be Mr. Western himself; for in the heat of the action none of the combatants had recognized him.

X

THE rest of Mr. Western's company were now come up, being just at the instant when the action was over. These were the honest clergyman, whom we have formerly seen at Mr. Western's table; Mrs. Western, the aunt of Sophia; and lastly, the lovely Sophia herself.

At this time the following was the aspect of the bloody field. In one place lay on the ground, all pale, and almost breathless, the vanquished Blifil. Near him stood the conqueror Jones, almost covered with blood, part of which was naturally his own, and part had been lately the property of the Reverend Mr. Thwackum. In a third place stood the said Thwackum, like King Porus, sullenly submitting to the conqueror. The last figure in the piece was Western the Great, most gloriously forbearing the vanquished foe.

Blifil, in whom there was little sign of life, was at first the principal object of the concern of everyone, when on a sudden the attention of the whole company was diverted. For now a more melancholy and a more lovely object lay motionless before them. This was no other than the charming Sophia herself, who, from the sight of blood, or from fear for her father, or from some other reason, had fallen down in a swoon, before anyone could get to her assistance.

Mrs. Western first saw her and screamed. Immediately two or three voices cried out, "Miss Western is dead."

Jones was rubbing Blifil's temples, for he began to fear he had given him a blow too much, when the words, Miss Western and Dead, rushed at once on his ear. He started up, left Blifil to his fate, and flew to Sophia, whom he caught up in his arms, and then ran away with her over the field to the rivulet above mentioned, where, plunging himself into the water, he contrived to besprinkle her face, head, and neck very plentifully.

Happy was it for Sophia that the confusion prevented her other friends from obstructing Jones. He had actually restored her to life before they reached the waterside. She stretched out her arms, opened her eyes, and cried, "Oh! heavens!" just as her father, aunt, and the parson came up.

Jones, who had hitherto held this lovely burthen in his arms, now relinquished his hold; but gave her at the same instant a tender caress, which, had her senses been then perfectly restored, could not have escaped her observation. As she expressed, therefore, no displeasure at this freedom, we suppose she was not sufficiently recovered from her swoon at the time.

This tragical scene was now converted into a sudden scene of joy. Mr. Western, after having once or twice embraced his daughter, fell to hugging and kissing Jones. He called him the preserver of Sophia, and declared there was nothing, except her, or his estate, which he would not give him; but upon recollection, he afterwards excepted his fox-hounds, the Chevalier, and Miss Slouch (for so he called his favorite mare).

All fears for Sophia being now removed, Jones became the object of the squire's consideration.

"Come, my lad," says Western, "d'off thy quoat and wash thy feace."

Jones immediately complied, threw off his coat, went down to the water, and washed both his face and bosom; for the latter was as much exposed and as bloody as the former. But though the water could clear off the blood, it could not remove the black and blue marks which Thwackum had imprinted on both his face and breast, and which, being discerned by Sophia, drew from her a sigh and a look full of inexpressible tenderness.

Western began now to inquire into the original rise of this quarrel. To which neither Blifil nor Jones gave any answer; but Thwackum said surlily,

"I believe the cause is not far off; if you beat the bushes well you may find her."

"Find her?" replied Western: "what! have you been fighting for a wench?"

"Ask the gentleman in his waistcoat there," said Thwackum: "he best knows."

"Nay then," cries Western, "it is a wench certainly. Ah, Tom, Tom, thou art a liquorish dog. But come, gentlemen, be all friends, and go home with me, and make final peace over a bottle."

But Blifil and Thwackum absolutely refused; the former saying, there were more reasons than he could then mention why he must decline this honor; and the latter declaring (perhaps rightly) that it was not proper for a person of his function to be seen at any place in his present condition.

Jones was incapable of refusing the pleasure of being with his Sophia; so on he marched with Squire Western and his ladies, the parson bringing up the rear.

Book VI

CONTAINING ABOUT THREE WEEKS

I

THE reader hath seen Mr. Western, his sister, and daughter, with young Jones, and the parson, going together to Mr. Western's house, where the greater part of the company spent the evening with much joy and festivity. Sophia was indeed the only grave person; for as to Jones, Mr. Allworthy's recovery, and the presence of his mistress, so elevated our hero, that he joined the mirth of the other three, who were perhaps as good-humored people as any in the world.

Sophia retained the same gravity of countenance the next morning at breakfast; whence she retired likewise earlier than usual, leaving her father and aunt together. The squire took no notice of this change in his daughter's disposition. To say the truth, though he was somewhat of a politician, and had been twice a candidate in the country interest at an election, he was a man of no great observation. His sister was a lady of a different turn. She had lived about the court, and had seen the world. Hence she was a perfect mistress of manners, customs, ceremonies, and fashions. Nor did her erudition stop here. She had considerably improved her mind by study; she had not only read all the modern plays, operas, oratorios, poems, and romances; to these she had added most of the political pamphlets and journals published within the last twenty years. She was, moreover, excellently well skilled in the doctrine of Amour, and was never diverted by any affairs of her own; for her masculine person, which was near six foot high, added to her manner and learning, possibly prevented the other sex from regarding her, notwithstanding her petticoats, in the light of a woman. However, she perfectly well knew, though she had never practiced them, all the arts which fine ladies use when they desire to give encouragement, or to conceal liking; but as to the plain simple workings of honest nature, as she had never seen any such, she could know but little of them.

By means of this wonderful sagacity, Mrs. Western had now, as she thought, made a discovery of something in the mind of Sophia. She took an opportunity, one morning, when she was alone with her brother, to interrupt one of his whistles in the following manner:

"Pray, brother, have you not observed something very extraordinary in my niece lately?"

"No, not I," answered Western; "is anything the matter with the girl?"

"I think there is," replied she; "and something of much consequence too."

"Why, she doth not complain of anything," cries Western; "and she hath had the smallpox."

"Brother," returned she, "girls are liable to other distempers besides the smallpox, and sometimes possibly to much worse."

Here Western interrupted her with much earnestness, and begged her, if anything ailed his daughter, to acquaint him immediately; adding, "she knew he loved her more than his own soul, and that he would send to the world's end for the best physician to her."

"Nay, nay," answered she, smiling, "the distemper is not so terrible; but I believe, brother, you are convinced I know the world, and I promise you I was never more deceived in my life if my niece be not most desperately in love."

"How! in love!" cries Western, in a passion; "in love, without acquainting me! I'll disinherit her; I'll turn her out of doors, stark naked, without a farthing. Is all my kindness vor 'ur, and vondness o'ur come to this, to fall in love without asking me leave?"

"But you will not," answered Mrs. Western, "turn this daughter, whom you love better than your own soul, out of doors, before you know whether you shall approve her choice. Suppose she should have fixed on the very person whom you yourself would wish, I hope you would not be angry then?"

"No, no," cries Western, "that would make a difference. If she marries the man I would ha' her, she may love whom she pleases, I sha'n't trouble my head about that."

"That is spoken," answered the sister, "like a sensible man; but I believe the very person she hath chosen would be the very person you would choose for her. What think you of Mr. Blifil? Did she not faint away on seeing him lie breathless on the ground?"

" 'Fore George!" cries the squire, "now you mind me on't, I remember it all. It is certainly so, and I am glad on't with all my heart. I knew Sophy was a good girl, and would not fall in love to make me angry. I was never more rejoiced in my life; for nothing can lie so handy together as our two estates. I had rather bate something than marry my daughter among strangers and foreigners. Besides, most o' zuch great estates be in the hands of lords, and I heate the very name of *themmun*. Well but, sister, what would you advise me to do; for I tell you women know these matters better than we do?"

"Oh, your humble servant, sir," answered the lady: "we are obliged to you for allowing us a capacity in anything. Since you are pleased, then, to ask my advice, I think you may propose the match to Allworthy yourself. There is no indecorum in the proposal's coming from the parent of either side. I need not caution so politic a person not to say that your daughter is in love; that would indeed be against all rules."

"Well," said the squire, "I will propose it; but I shall certainly lend un a flick, if he should refuse me."

"Fear not," cries Mrs. Western; "the match is too advantageous to be refused."

"I don't know that," answered the squire: "Allworthy is a queer b—ch, and money hath no effect o'un."

"Brother," said the lady, "your politics astonish me. Are you really to be imposed on by professions? Do you think Mr. Allworthy hath more contempt for money than other men because he professes more? Such credulity would better become one of us weak women."

II

MR. ALLWORTHY had been engaged to dine with Mr. Western at the time when he was taken ill. He was therefore no sooner discharged out of the custody of physic, but he thought (as was usual with him on all occasions, both the highest and the lowest) of fulfilling his engagement.

Sophia had, from certain obscure hints thrown out by her aunt, collected some apprehension that the sagacious lady suspected her passion for Jones. She now resolved to take this opportunity of wiping out all such suspicion.

First, she endeavored to conceal a throbbing melancholy heart with the utmost sprightliness in her countenance and the highest gaiety in her manner. Secondly, she addressed her whole discourse to Mr. Blifil, and took not the least notice of poor Jones the whole day.

The squire was so delighted with this conduct of his daughter that he scarce ate any dinner, and spent almost his whole time in watching opportunities of conveying signs of his approbation by winks and nods to his sister. Dinner being ended, and the company retired into the garden, Mr. Western, who was thoroughly convinced of the certainty of what his sister had told him, took Mr. Allworthy aside, and very bluntly proposed a match between Sophia and young Mr. Blifil.

Mr. Allworthy received Mr. Western's proposal without any visible emotion, or without any alteration of countenance. He said the alliance was such as he sincerely wished; then launched forth into a very just encomium on the young lady's merit; acknowledged the offer to be advantageous in point of fortune; and after thanking Mr. Western for the good opinion he had professed of his nephew, concluded, that if the young people liked each other he should be very desirous to complete the affair.

Western was a little disappointed at Mr. Allworthy's answer, which was not so warm as he expected. He treated the doubt whether the young people might like one another with great contempt, saying, "That parents were the best judges of proper matches for their children: that for his part he should insist on the most resigned obedience from his daughter: and if any young fellow could refuse such a bed-fellow, he was his humble servant, and hoped there was no harm done."

Allworthy endeavored to soften this resentment by many eulogiums on Sophia, declaring he had no doubt but that Mr. Blifil would very gladly receive the offer; but all was ineffectual; he could obtain no other answer from the squire but—"I say no more—I humbly hope there's no harm done—that's all." Which words he repeated at least a hundred times before they parted.

As soon as Mr. Allworthy returned home, he took Mr. Blifil apart, and after some preface, communicated to him the proposal which had been made by Mr. Western, and at the same time informed him how agreeable this match would be to himself.

The charms of Sophia had not made the least impression on Blifil; not that his heart was pre-engaged; neither was he totally insensible of beauty, or had any aversion to women; but his appetites were by nature moderate, and as to passion, he had not the least tincture of it in his whole composition.

Yet was he altogether as well furnished with some other passions, that promised themselves very full gratification in the young lady's fortune. He had more than once considered the possession of this fortune as a very desirable thing, and had entertained some distant views concerning it. Blifil, therefore, after a very short hesitation, answered Mr. Allworthy that matrimony was a subject on which he had not yet thought; but that he was so sensible of his friendly and fatherly care, that he should in all things submit himself to his pleasure.

Allworthy was naturally a man of spirit; he had possessed much fire in his youth, and had married a beautiful woman for love. He was not therefore greatly pleased with this cold answer of his nephew; nor could he help launching forth into the praises of Sophia, and expressing some wonder that the heart of a young man could be impregnable to the force of such charms.

Blifil then proceeded to discourse so wisely and religiously on love and marriage, that the good man was satisfied that his nephew, far from having any objections to Sophia, had that esteem for her, which in sober and virtuous minds is the sure foundation of friendship and love. With Mr. Blifil's consent, therefore, he wrote the next morning to Mr. Western, acquainting him that his nephew had very thankfully and gladly received the proposal, and would be ready to wait on the young lady, whenever she should be pleased to accept his visit.

Western was much pleased with this letter, and immediately returned an answer; in which, without having mentioned a word to his daughter, he appointed that very afternoon for opening the scene of courtship.

III

Sophia was in her chamber, reading, when her aunt came in. The moment she saw Mrs. Western, she shut the book with so much eagerness, that the good lady could not forbear asking her, What book that was which she seemed so much afraid of showing?

"Upon my word, madam," answered Sophia, "it is a book which I am neither ashamed nor afraid to own I have read. There appears to me a great deal of human nature in it; and in many parts so much true tenderness and delicacy, that it hath cost me many a tear."

"Ay, and do you love to cry then?" says the aunt.

"I love a tender sensation," answered the niece, "and would pay the price of a tear for it at any time."

"Well, but show me," said the aunt, "what was you reading when I came in; there was something very tender in that, I believe, and very loving too. You blush, my dear Sophia. Ah! child, you should read books which would teach you a little hypocrisy, which would instruct you how to hide your thoughts a little better."

"I hope, madam," answered Sophia, "I have no thoughts which I ought to be ashamed of discovering."

"Ashamed! no," cries the aunt, "I don't think you have any thoughts which you ought to be ashamed of; and yet, child, you blushed just now when I mentioned the word loving. Dear Sophy, I have seen a little too much of the world to be deceived. Nay, nay, do not blush again. I tell you it is a passion you need not be ashamed of. It is a passion I myself approve, and have already brought your father into the approbation of it."

"La, madam," says Sophia, "you come upon one so unawares, and on a sudden. To be sure, madam, I am not blind—and certainly, if it be a fault to see all human perfections assembled together—but is it possible my father and you, madam, can see with my eyes?"

"I tell you," answered the aunt, "we do entirely approve; and this very afternoon your father hath appointed for you to receive your lover."

"My father, this afternoon!" cries Sophia, with the blood starting from her face.

"Yes, child," said the aunt, "this afternoon. You know the impetuosity of my brother's temper. I acquainted him with the passion which I first discovered in you that evening when you fainted away in the field. I saw it in your fainting. I saw it immediately upon your recovery. I saw it that evening at supper, and the next morning at breakfast (you know, child, I have seen the world). Well, I no sooner acquainted my brother, but he immediately wanted to propose it to Allworthy. He proposed it yesterday, Allworthy consented (as to be sure he must with joy), and this afternoon, I tell you, you are to put on all your best airs."

"This afternoon!" cries Sophia. "Dear aunt, you frighten me out of my senses."

"O, my dear," said the aunt, "you will soon come to yourself again; for he is a charming young fellow, that's the truth on't."

"Nay, I will own," says Sophia, "I know none with such perfections. So brave, and yet so gentle; so witty, yet so inoffensive; so humane, so civil, so genteel, so handsome! What signifies his being base born, when compared with such qualifications as these?"

"Base born? What do you mean?" said the aunt, "Mr. Blifil base born?"

Sophia turned instantly pale at this name, and faintly repeated it. Upon which the aunt cried, "Mr. Blifil—ay, Mr. Blifil, of whom else have we been talking?"

"Good heavens," answered Sophia, ready to sink, "of Mr. Jones, I thought; I am sure I know no other who deserves—"

"I protest," cries the aunt, "you frighten me in your turn. Is it Mr. Jones, and not Mr. Blifil, who is the object of your affection?"

"Mr. Blifil!" repeated Sophia. "Sure it is impossible you can be in earnest; if you are, I am the most miserable woman alive."

Mrs. Western now stood a few moments silent, while sparks of fiery rage flashed from her eyes. At length, collecting all her force of voice, she thundered forth in the following articulate sounds:

"And is it possible you can think of disgracing your family by allying yourself to a bastard? Can the blood of the Westerns submit to such contamination? If you have not sense sufficient to restrain such monstrous inclinations, I thought the pride of our family would have prevented you from giving the least encouragement to so base an affection; much less did I imagine you would ever have had the assurance to own it to my face."

"Madam," answered Sophia, trembling, "what I have said you have extorted from me. I do not remember to have ever mentioned the name of Mr. Jones with approbation to anyone before; nor should I now had I not conceived he had your approbation. Whatever were my thoughts of that poor, unhappy young man, I intended to have carried them with me to my grave—to that grave where only now, I find, I am to seek repose." Here she sunk down in her chair, drowned in her tears, and, in all the moving silence of unutterable grief, presented a spectacle which must have affected almost the hardest heart.

All this tender sorrow, however, raised no compassion in her aunt. On the contrary, she now fell into the most violent rage. "And I would rather," she cried, in a most vehement voice, "follow you to your grave, than I would see you disgrace yourself and your family by such a match. O heavens! could I have ever suspected that I should live to hear a niece of mine declare a passion for such a fellow? You are the first—yes, Miss Western, you are the first of your name who ever entertained so groveling a thought. A family so noted for the prudence of its women"—here she ran on a full quarter of an hour, till, having exhausted her breath rather than her rage, she concluded with threatening to go immediately and acquaint her brother.

Sophia then threw herself at her feet, and laying hold of her hands, begged her with tears to conceal what she had drawn from her; urging the violence of her father's temper, and protesting that no inclinations of hers should ever prevail with her to do anything which might offend him.

Mrs. Western stood a moment looking at her, and then, have recollected herself said, "That on one consideration only she would keep the secret from her brother; and this was, that Sophia should promise to entertain Mr. Blifil that very afternoon as her lover, and to regard him as the person who was to be her husband."

Poor Sophia was too much in her aunt's power to deny her anything positively; she was obliged to promise that she would see Mr. Blifil, and be as civil to him as possible; but begged her aunt that the match might not be hurried on. She said, "Mr. Blifil was by no means agreeable to her, and she hoped her father would be prevailed on not to make her the most wretched of women."

Mrs. Western assured her, "That the match was entirely agreed upon, and that nothing could or should prevent it. I must own," said she, "I looked on it as on a matter of indifference; nay, perhaps, had some scruples about it before, which were actually got over by my thinking it highly agreeable to your own inclinations; but now I regard it as the most eligible thing in the world: nor shall there be, if I can prevent it, a moment of time lost on the occasion."

Sophia replied, "Delay at least, madam, I may expect from both your goodness and my father's. Surely you will give me time to endeavor to get the better of so strong a disinclination as I have at present to this person."

The aunt answered, "She knew too much of the world to be so deceived; that as she was sensible another man had her affections, she should persuade Mr. Western to hasten the match as much as possible. It would be bad politics, indeed," added she, "to protect a siege when the enemy's army is at hand, and in danger of relieving it. No, no, Sophy," said she, "as I am convinced you have a violent passion which you can never satisfy with honor, I will do all I can to put your honor out of the care of your family: for when you are married those matters will belong only to the consideration of your husband. I hope, child, you will always have prudence enough to act as becomes you; but if you should not, marriage hath saved many a woman from ruin."

Sophia well understood what her aunt meant, but did not think proper to make her an answer. However, she took a resolution to see Mr. Blifil, and to behave to him as civilly as she could, for on that condition only she obtained a promise from her aunt to keep secret the liking which her ill fortune, rather than any scheme of Mrs. Western, had unhappily drawn from her.

IV

THAT afternoon Mr. Western, for the first time, acquainted his daughter with his intention; telling her, he knew very well that she had heard it before from her aunt. Sophia looked very grave upon this, nor could she prevent a few pearls from stealing into her eyes.

"Come, come," says Western, "none of your maidenish airs; I know all; I assure you sister hath told me all."

"Is it possible," says Sophia, "that my aunt can have betrayed me already?"

"Ay, ay," says Western; "betrayed you! ay. Why, you betrayed yourself yesterday at dinner. You showed your fancy very plainly, I think. But you young girls never know what you would be at. So you cry because I am going to marry you to the man you are in love with! Your mother, I remembered, whimpered and whined just in the same manner; but it was all over within twenty-four hours after we were married: Mr. Blifil is a brisk young man, and will soon put an end to your squeamishness. Come, cheer up, cheer up; I expect un every minute."

Sophia was now convinced that her aunt had behaved honorably to her: and she determined to go through that disagreeable afternoon with as much resolution as possible, and without giving the least suspicion in the world to her father.

Mr. Blifil soon arrived; and Mr. Western soon after withdrawing, left the young couple together.

Here a long silence of near a quarter of an hour ensued; for the gentleman who was to begin the conversation had all the unbecoming modesty which consists in bashfulness. He often attempted to speak, and as often suppressed his words just at the very point of utterance. At last out they broke in a torrent of far-fetched and high-strained compliments, which were answered on her side by downcast looks, half bows, and civil monosyllables. Blifil, from his inexperience in the ways of women, and from his conceit of himself, took this behavior for a modest assent to his courtship; and when, to shorten a scene which she could no longer support, Sophia rose up and left the room, he imputed that, too, merely to bashfulness, and comforted himself that he should soon have enough of her company.

Of Jones he certainly had not even the least jealousy; and I have often thought it wonderful that he had not. Perhaps he imagined the character which Jones bore all over the country (how justly, let the reader determine), of being one of the wildest fellows in England, might render him odious to a lady of the most exemplary modesty. Blifil, moreover, thought the affair of Molly Seagrim still went on, and indeed believed it would end in marriage; for Jones really loved him from his childhood, and had kept no secret from him, till his behavior on the sickness of Mr. Allworthy had entirely alienated his heart; and it was by means of the quarrel which had ensued on this occasion, and which was not yet reconciled, that Mr. Blifil knew nothing of the alteration which had happened in the affection which Jones had formerly borne towards Molly.

From these reasons, therefore, Mr. Blifil saw no bar to his success with Sophia. He concluded her behavior was like that of all other young ladies on a first visit from a lover, and it had indeed entirely answered his expectations.

Mr. Western took care to waylay the lover at his exit from his mistress. He found him so elevated with his success, so enamored with his daughter, and so satisfied with her reception of him, that the old gentleman began to caper and dance about his hall, and by many other antic actions to express the extravagance of his joy; for he had not the least command over any of his passions; and that which had at any time the ascendant in his mind hurried him to the wildest excesses.

As soon as Blifil was departed, which was not till after many hearty kisses and embraces bestowed on him by Western, the good squire went instantly in quest of his daughter, whom he no sooner found than he poured forth the most extravagant raptures, bidding her choose what clothes and jewels she pleased; and declaring that he had no other use for fortune but to make her happy. He then caressed her again and again with the utmost profusion of fondness, called her by the most endearing names, and protested she was his only joy on earth.

Sophia perceiving her father in this bit of affection, thought she should never have a better opportunity of disclosing herself than at present, as far at least as regarded Mr. Blifil. After having thanked the squire, therefore, for all his professions of kindness, she added, with a look full of inexpressible softness, "And is it possible my papa can be so good to place all his joy in his Sophy's happiness?" which Western having confirmed by a great oath and a kiss; she then laid hold of his hand, and, falling on her knees, after many warm and passionate declarations of affection and duty, she begged him "not to make her the most miserable creature on earth by forcing her to marry a man whom she detested. This I entreat of you, dear sir," said she, "for your sake, as well as my own, since you are so very kind to tell me your happiness depends on mine."

"How! what!" says Western, staring wildly.

"Oh! sir," continued she, "not only your poor Sophy's happiness; her very life, her being, depends upon your granting her request. I cannot live with Mr. Blifil. To force me into this marriage would be killing me."

"You can't live with Mr. Blifil?" says Western.

"No, upon my soul I can't," answered Sophia.

"Then die and be d—d," cries he, spurning her from him.

"Oh! sir," cries Sophia, catching hold of the skirt of his coat, "take pity on me, I beseech you. Don't look and say such cruel——Can you be unmoved while you see your Sophy in this dreadful condition? Can the best of fathers break my heart? Will he kill me by the most painful, cruel, lingering death?"

"Pooh! pooh!" cries the squire; "all stuff and nonsense; all maidenish tricks. Kill you, indeed! Will marriage kill you?"

"Oh! sir," answered Sophia, "such a marriage is worse than death. He is not even indifferent; I hate and detest him."

"If you detest un never so much," cries Western, "you shall ha'un." This he bound by an oath too shocking to repeat; and after many violent asseverations, concluded in these words: "I am resolved upon the match, and unless you consent to it I will not give you a groat, not a single farthing; no, though I saw you expiring with famine in the street, I would not relieve you with a morsel of bread. This is my fixed resolution, and so I leave you to consider on it." He then broke from her with such violence, that her face dashed against the floor, and he burst directly out of the room, leaving poor Sophia prostrate on the ground.

When Western came into the hall, he there found Jones. The squire immediately acquainted him with the whole matter, concluding with bitter denunciations against Sophia, and very pathetic lamentations of the misery of all fathers who are so unfortunate to have daughters.

Jones, to whom all the resolutions which had been taken in favor of Blifil were yet a secret, was at first almost struck dead with this relation; but recovering his spirits a little, mere despair, as he afterwards said, inspired him to mention a matter to Mr. Western, which seemed to require more impudence than a human forehead was ever gifted with. He desired leave to go to Sophia, that he might endeavor to obtain her concurrence with her father's inclinations.

If the squire had been as quicksighted as he was remarkable for the contrary, passion might at present very well have blinded him. He thanked Jones for offering to undertake the office, and said, "Go, go, prithee, try what canst do"; and then swore many execrable oaths that he would turn her out of doors unless she consented to the match.

V

JONES departed instantly in quest of Sophia, whom he found just risen from the ground, where her father had left her, with the tears trickling from her eyes, and the blood running from her lips. He ran to her, and with a voice full at once of tenderness and terror, cried,

"O my Sophia, what means this dreadful sight?"

She looked softly at him for a moment before she spoke, and then said,

"Mr. Jones, for Heaven's sake how came you here? Leave me, I beseech you, this moment."

"Do not," says he, "impose so harsh a command upon me—my heart bleeds faster than those lips. O Sophia, how easily could I drain my veins to preserve one drop of that dear blood."

"I have too many obligations to you already," answered she, "for sure you meant them such." Here she looked at him tenderly almost a minute, and then bursting into an agony, cried, "Oh, Mr. Jones, why did you save my life? my death would have been happier for us both."

"Happier for us both!" cried he. "Could racks or wheels kill me so painfully as Sophia's—I cannot bear the dreadful sound. Do I live but for her?" Both his voice and looks were full of inexpressible tenderness when he spoke these words; and at the same time he laid gently hold on her hand, which she did not withdraw from him; to say the truth, she hardly knew what she did or suffered.

A few moments now passed in silence between these lovers, while his eyes were eagerly fixed on Sophia, and hers declining towards the ground: at last she recovered strength enough to desire him again to leave her, for that her certain ruin would be the consequence of their being found together; adding,

"Oh, Mr. Jones, you know not, you know not what hath passed this cruel afternoon."

"I know all, my Sophia," answered he; "your cruel father hath told me all, and he himself hath sent me to you to be an advocate for my odious rival, to solicit you in his favor. O speak to me, Sophia! comfort my bleeding heart. Sure no one ever loved, ever doted like me."

She stood a moment silent, and covered with confusion; then lifting up her eyes gently towards him, she cried,

"What would Mr. Jones have me say?"

"O do but promise," cried he, "that you never will give yourself to Blifil."

"Name not," answered she, "the detested sound. Be assured I never will give him what is in my power to withhold from him."

"Now then," cries he, "while you are so perfectly kind, go a little farther, and add that I may hope."

"Alas!" says she, "Mr. Jones, whither will you drive me? What hope have I to bestow? You know my father's intentions."

"But I know," answered he, "your compliance with them cannot be compelled."

"What," says she, "must be the dreadful consequence of my disobedience? My own ruin is my least concern. I cannot bear the thoughts of being the cause of my father's misery."

"He is himself the cause," cries Jones, "by exacting a power over you which Nature hath not given him. Think on the misery which I am to suffer if I am to lose you, and see on which side pity will turn the balance."

"Think of it!" replied she: "can you imagine I do not feel the ruin which I must bring on you, should I comply with your desire? It is that thought which gives me resolution to bid you fly from me forever, and avoid your own destruction."

"I fear no destruction," cries he, "but the loss of Sophia. If you would save me from the most bitter agonies, recall that cruel sentence. Indeed, I can never part with you, indeed I cannot."

The lovers now stood both silent and trembling, Sophia being unable to withdraw her hand from Jones, and he almost as unable to hold it.

VI

Soon after Jones had left Mr. Western, his sister came to him, and was informed of all that had passed between her brother and Sophia relating to Blifil.

This behavior in her niece the good lady construed to be an absolute breach of the condition on which she had engaged to keep her love for Mr. Jones a secret. She considered herself, therefore, at full liberty to reveal all she knew to the squire, which she immediately did in the most explicit terms, and without any ceremony or preface.

The idea of a marriage between Jones and his daughter had never once entered into the squire's head, either in the warmest minutes of his affection towards that young man, or from suspicion, or on any other occasion. He did indeed consider a parity of fortune and circumstances to be physically as necessary an ingredient in marriage as difference of sexes, or any other essential; and had no more apprehension of his daughter's falling in love with a poor man than with any animal of a different species.

He became, therefore, like one thunderstruck at his sister's relation. He was, at first, incapable of making any answer. The first use he made of the power of speech, after his recovery from the sudden effects of his astonishment, was to discharge a round volley of oaths and imprecations. After which he proceeded hastily to the apartment where he expected to find the lovers, and murmured, or rather indeed roared forth, intentions of revenge every step he went.

And now the squire, having burst open the door, beheld an object which instantly suspended all his fury against Jones; this was the ghastly appearance of Sophia, who had fainted away in her lover's arms. This tragical sight Mr. Western no sooner beheld than all his rage forsook him; he roared for help with his utmost violence; ran first to his daughter, then back to the door calling for water, and then back again to Sophia, never considering in whose arms she then was, nor perhaps once recollecting that there was such a person in the world as Jones.

Mrs. Western and a great number of servants soon came to the assistance of Sophia with water, cordials, and everything necessary on those occasions. These were applied with such success, that Sophia in a very few minutes began to recover, and all the symptoms of life to return. Upon which she was presently led off by her own maid and Mrs. Western.

The squire, no sooner was cured of his immediate fears for his daughter, than he relapsed into his former frenzy, which must have produced an immediate battle with Jones, had not Parson Supple, who was a very strong man, been present, and by mere force restrained the squire from acts of hostility.

The moment Sophia was departed, Jones advanced in a very suppliant manner to Mr. Western, whom the parson held in his arms, and begged him to be pacified; for that, while he continued in such a passion, it would be impossible to give him any satisfaction.

"I wull have satisfaction o' thee," answered the squire; "so doff thy clothes. *At unt* half a man, and I'll lick thee as well as wast ever licked in thy life." He then bespattered the youth with abundance of that language which passes between country gentlemen who embrace opposite sides of the question.

Jones very calmly answered, "Sir, this usage may perhaps cancel every other obligation you have conferred on me; but there is one you can never cancel; nor will I be provoked by your abuse to lift my hand against the father of Sophia."

At these words the squire grew still more outrageous than before; so that the parson begged Jones to retire. Jones accepted this advice with thanks, and immediately departed. The squire now regained so much temper as to express some satisfaction in the restraint which had been laid upon him; and declared a resolution of going the next morning early to acquaint Mr. Allworthy.

VII

MR. ALLWORTHY was retired from breakfast with his nephew, well satisfied with the report of the young gentleman's successful visit to Sophia, when Mr. Western broke abruptly in upon them, and without any ceremony began as follows:

"There, you have done a fine piece of work truly! There is a fine kettle-of-fish made on't up at our house."

"What can be the matter, Mr. Western?" said Allworthy.

"O, matter enow of all conscience: my daughter hath fallen in love with your bastard, that's all; but I won't ge her a ha'penny. It's well vor un I could not get at un: I'd a lick'd un; I'd a spoil'd his caterwauling; if she will ha un, one smock shall be her portion. I'd sooner ge my esteate to the zinking fund."

"I am heartily sorry," cries Allworthy.

"Pox o' your sorrow," says Western; "it will do me abundance of good when I have lost my only child, my poor Sophy, that was the joy of my heart, and all the hope and comfort of my age; but I am resolved I will turn her out o' doors; she shall beg, and starve, and rot in the streets."

"I am in amazement," cries Allworthy, "at what you tell me, after what passed between my nephew and the young lady no longer ago than yesterday."

"Yes, sir," answered Western, "it was after what passed between your nephew and she that the whole matter came out. Little did I think when I used to love him for a sportsman that he was all the while a poaching after my daughter."

"But was it possible," says Allworthy, "that you should never discern any symptoms of love between them, when you have seen them so often together?"

"Never in my life, as I hope to be saved," cries Western: "I never so much as zeed him kiss her in all my life; and so far from courting her, he used rather to be more silent when she was in company than at any other time; and as for the girl, she was always less civil to'n than to any young man that came to the house. As to that matter, I am not more easy to be deceived than another; I would not have you think I am, neighbor."

Allworthy could scarce refrain laughter at this; but he resolved to do a violence to himself; for he perfectly well knew mankind, and had too much good-breeding and good-nature to offend the squire in his present circumstances. He then asked Western what he would have him do upon this occasion. To which the other answered, "That he would have him keep the rascal away from his house, and that he would go and lock up the wench; for he was resolved to make her marry Mr. Blifil in spite of her teeth." He then shook Blifil by the hand, and swore he would have no other son-in-law. After which he took his leave; saying his house was in such disorder that it was necessary for him to make haste home, to take care his daughter did not give him the slip.

When Allworthy and Blifil were again left together, a long silence ensued between them; all which interval the young gentleman filled up with sighs, which proceeded partly from disappointment, but more from hatred; for the success of Jones was much more grievous to him than the loss of Sophia.

At length his uncle asked him what he was determined to do, and he answered in the following words:

"Alas! sir, reason dictates to me, to quit all thoughts of a woman who places her affections on another; my passion bids me hope she may in time change her inclinations in my favor. I shall, by so doing, promote the happiness of every party; not only that of the parent, who will thus be preserved from the highest degree of misery, but of both the others, who must be undone by this match. The lady, I am sure, will be undone in every sense; for she will be not only married to a beggar, but the little fortune which her father cannot withhold from her will be squandered on that wench with whom I know he yet converses. Nay, that is a trifle; for I know him to be one of the worst men in the world; for had my dear uncle known what I have hitherto endeavored to conceal, he must have long since abandoned so profligate a wretch."

"How!" said Allworthy; "hath he done anything worse than I already know? Tell me, I beseech you?"

"No," replied Blifil; "it is now past, and perhaps he may have repented of it."

"I command you, on your duty," said Allworthy, "to tell me what you mean."

"You know, sir," says Blifil, "I never disobeyed you; but I am sorry I mentioned it, since it may now look like revenge, whereas, I thank Heaven, no such motive ever entered my heart; and if you oblige me to discover it, I must be his petitioner to you for your forgiveness."

"I will have no conditions," answered Allworthy; "I think I have shown tenderness enough towards him, and more perhaps than you ought to thank me for."

"More, indeed, I fear, than he deserves," cries Blifil; "for in the very day of your utmost danger, when myself and all the family were in tears, he filled the house with riot and debauchery. He drank, and sung, and roared; and when I gave him a gentle hint of the indecency of his actions, he fell into a violent passion, swore many oaths, called me rascal, and struck me."

"How!" cries Allworthy; "did he dare to strike you?"

"I am sure," cries Blifil, "I have forgiven him that long ago. I wish I could so easily forget his ingratitude to the best of benefactors; and yet even that I hope you will forgive him, since he must have certainly been possessed with the devil: for that very evening, as Mr. Thwackum and myself were taking the air in the fields, and exulting in the good symptoms which then first began to discover themselves, we unluckily saw him engaged with a wench in a manner not fit to be mentioned. Mr. Thwackum, with more boldness than prudence, advanced to rebuke him, when (I am sorry to say it) he fell upon the worthy man, and beat him so outrageously that I wish he may have yet recovered the bruises. Nor was I without my share of the effects of his malice, while I endeavored to protect my tutor; but that I have long forgiven; nay, I prevailed with Mr. Thwackum to forgive him too, and not to inform you of a secret which I feared might be fatal to him. And now, sir, since I have unadvisedly dropped a hint of this matter, and your commands have obliged me to discover the whole, let me intercede with you for him."

"O child!" said Allworthy, "I know not whether I should blame or applaud your goodness, in concealing such villainy a moment: but where is Mr. Thwackum? Not that I want any confirmation of what you say; but I will examine all the evidence of this matter, to justify to the world the example I am resolved to make of such a monster."

Thwackum was now sent for, and presently appeared. He corroborated every circumstance which the other had deposed; nay, he produced the record upon his breast, where the handwriting of Mr. Jones remained very legible in black and blue. He concluded with declaring to Mr. Allworthy, that he should have long since informed him of this matter, had not Mr. Blifil, by the most earnest interpositions, prevented him.

"He is," says he, "an excellent youth: though such forgiveness of enemies is carrying the matter too far."

In reality, Blifil had taken some pains to prevail with the parson, and to prevent the discovery at that time; for which he had many reasons. He knew that the minds of men are apt to be softened and relaxed from their usual severity by sickness. Besides, he imagined that if the story was told when the fact was so recent, and the physician about the house, who might have unraveled the real truth, he should never be able to give it the malicious turn which he intended. Again, he resolved to hoard up this business till the indiscretion of Jones should afford some additional complaints; for he thought the joint weight of many facts falling upon him together would be the most likely to crush him; and he watched, therefore, some such opportunity as that with which Fortune had now kindly presented him.

Lastly, by prevailing with Thwackum to conceal the matter for a time, he knew he should confirm an opinion of his friendship to Jones, which he had greatly labored to establish in Mr. Allworthy.

VIII

IT WAS Mr. Allworthy's custom never to punish anyone, not even to turn away a servant, in a passion. He resolved, therefore, to delay passing sentence on Jones till the afternoon.

The poor young man attended at dinner, as usual; but his heart was too much loaded to suffer him to eat. His grief, too, was a good deal aggravated by the unkind looks of Mr. Allworthy; whence he concluded that Western had discovered the whole affair between him and Sophia; but as to Mr. Blifil's story, he had not the least apprehension; for of much the greater part he was entirely innocent; and for the residue, as he had forgiven and forgotten it himself; so he suspected no remembrance on the other side.

When dinner was over, and the servants departed, Mr. Allworthy began to harangue. He set forth, in a long speech, the many iniquities of which Jones had been guilty, particularly those which this day had brought to light; and concluded by telling him, "That unless he could clear himself of the charge, he was resolved to banish him his sight forever."

Many disadvantages attended poor Jones in making his defense; nay, indeed, he hardly knew his accusation; for as Mr. Allworthy, in recounting the drunkenness, etc., while he lay ill, out of modesty sunk everything that related particularly to himself, which indeed principally constituted the crime, Jones could not deny the charge. His heart was, besides, almost broken already; and his spirits were so sunk, that he could say nothing for himself; but acknowledged the whole, and, like a criminal in despair, threw himself upon mercy; concluding, "That though he must own himself guilty of many follies and inadvertencies, he hoped he had done nothing to deserve what would be to him the greatest punishment in the world."

Allworthy answered, That he had forgiven him too often already, in compassion to his youth, and in hopes of his amendment: that he now found he was an abandoned reprobate, and such as it would be criminal in anyone to support and encourage.

"Nay," said Mr. Allworthy to him, "your audacious attempt to steal away the young lady calls upon me to justify my own character in punishing you. The world who have already censured the regard

I have shown for you may think, with some color at least of justice, that I connive at so base and barbarous an action—an action of which you must have known my abhorrence; and which, had you had any concern for my ease and honor, as well as for my friendship, you would never have thought of undertaking. Fie upon it, young man! indeed there is scarce any punishment equal to your crimes, and I can scarce think myself justifiable in what I am now going to bestow on you. However, as I have educated you like a child of my own, I will not turn you naked into the world. When you open this paper, therefore, you will find something which may enable you, with industry, to get an honest livelihood; but if you employ it to worse purposes, I shall not think myself obliged to supply you farther, being resolved, from this day forward, to converse no more with you on any account. I cannot avoid saying, there is no part of your conduct which I resent more than your ill-treatment of that good young man (meaning Blifil) who hath behaved with so much tenderness and honor towards you."

These last words were a dose almost too bitter to be swallowed. A flood of tears now gushed from the eyes of Jones, and every faculty of speech and motion seemed to have deserted him. It was some time before he was able to obey Allworthy's peremptory commands of departing; which he at length did, having first kissed his hands with a passion difficult to be affected, and as difficult to be described.

The reader must be very weak, if, when he considers the light in which Jones then appeared to Mr. Allworthy, he should blame the rigor of his sentence. And yet all the neighborhood, either from this weakness, or from some worse motive, condemned this justice and severity as the highest cruelty. None ever mentioned the sum contained in the paper which Allworthy gave Jones, which was no less than five hundred pounds; but all agreed that he was sent away penniless, and some said naked, from the house of his inhuman father.

IX

JONES was commanded to leave the house immediately, and told, that his clothes and everything else should be sent to him whithersoever he should order them.

He accordingly set out, and walked above a mile, scarce knowing whither he went. At length a little brook obstructing his passage, he threw himself down by the side of it; nor could he help muttering with some little indignation, "Sure my father will not deny me this place to rest in!"

Here he presently fell into the most violent agonies, tearing his hair from his head, and using most other actions which generally accompany fits of madness, rage, and despair.

When he had in this manner vented the first emotions of passion, he began to come a little to himself. He became at last cool enough to reason with his passion, and to consider what steps were proper to be taken in his deplorable condition.

And now the great doubt was, how to act with regard to Sophia. The thoughts of leaving her almost rent his heart asunder; but the consideration of reducing her to ruin and beggary still racked him, if possible, more; and if the violent desire of possessing her person could have induced him to listen one moment to this alternative, still he was by no means certain of her resolution to indulge his wishes at so high an expense. The resentment of Mr. Allworthy, and the injury he must do to his quiet, argued strongly against this latter; and lastly, the apparent impossibility of his success, even if he would sacrifice all these considerations to it, came to his assistance; and thus honor at last backed with despair, with gratitude to his benefactor, and with real love to his mistress, got the better of burning desire, and he resolved rather to quit Sophia than pursue her to her ruin.

It is difficult for any who have not felt it, to conceive the glowing warmth which filled his breast on the first contemplation of this victory over his passion. Pride flattered him so agreeably, that his mind perhaps enjoyed perfect happiness; but this was only momentary: Sophia soon returned to his imagination, and allayed the joy of his triumph with no less bitter pangs than a good-natured general must feel, when he surveys the bleeding heaps at the price of whose blood he hath purchased his laurels; for thousands of tender ideas lay murdered before our conqueror.

Being resolved, however, to pursue the paths of honor, he determined to write a farewell letter to Sophia; and accordingly proceeded to a house not far off, where, being furnished with proper materials, he wrote as follows:

"MADAM—When you reflect on the situation in which I write, I am sure your good-nature will pardon any inconsistency or absurdity which my letter contains; for everything here flows from a heart so full, that no language can express its dictates.

"I have resolved, madam, to obey your commands, in flying forever from your dear, your lovely sight. Cruel indeed those commands are; but it is a cruelty which proceeds from fortune, not from my Sophia. Fortune hath made it necessary, necessary to your preservation, to forget there ever was such a wretch as I am.

"Believe me, I would not hint all my sufferings to you, if I imagined they could possibly escape your ears. I know the goodness and tenderness of your heart, and would avoid giving you any of those pains which you always feel for the miserable. Oh, let nothing which you shall hear of my hard fortune cause a moment's concern; for, after the loss of you, everything is to me a trifle.

"O Sophia! it is hard to leave you; it is harder still to desire you to forget me; yet the sincerest love obliges me to both. Pardon my conceiving that any remembrance of me can give you disquiet; but if I am so gloriously wretched, sacrifice me every way to your relief. Think I never loved you; or think truly how little I deserve you; and learn to scorn me for a presumption which can never be too severely punished.—I am unable to say more.—May guardian angels protect you forever!"

He was now searching his pockets for his wax, but found none, nor indeed anything else, therein; for in truth he had, in his frantic disposition, tossed everything from him, and amongst the rest, his pocket-book, which he had received from Mr. Allworthy, which he had never opened, and which now first occurred to his memory.

The house supplied him with a wafer for his present purpose, with which, having sealed his letter, he returned hastily towards the brook side, in order to search for the things which he had there lost. In his way he met his old friend Black George, who heartily condoled with him on his misfortune; for this had already reached his ears, and indeed those of all the neighborhood.

Jones acquainted the gamekeeper with his loss, and he as readily went back with him to the brook, where they searched every tuft of grass in the meadow, as well where Jones had not been as where he had been; but all to no purpose, for they found nothing; for, indeed, though the things were then in the meadow, they omitted to search the only place where they were deposited; to wit, in the pockets of the said George; for he had just before found them, and being luckily apprised of their value, had very carefully put them up for his own use.

Jones now gave over all hopes of recovering his loss, and almost all thoughts concerning it, and turning to Black George, asked him earnestly if he would do him the greatest favor in the world?

George answered with some hesitation, "Sir, you know you may command me whatever is in my power, and I heartily wish it was in my power to do you any service." In fact, the question staggered him; for he had, by selling game, amassed a pretty good sum of money in Mr. Western's service, and was afraid that Jones wanted to borrow some small matter of him; but he was presently relieved from his anxiety, by being desired to convey a letter to Sophia, which with great pleasure he promised to do.

Mrs. Honour was agreed by both to be the proper means by which this letter should pass to Sophia. They then separated; the gamekeeper returned home to Mr. Western's, and Jones walked to an alehouse at half a mile's distance, to wait for his messenger's return.

George no sooner came home to his master's house than he met with Mrs. Honour; to whom, having first sounded her with a few previous questions, he delivered the letter for her mistress, and received at the same time another from her, for Mr. Jones; which Honour told him she had carried all that day in her bosom, and began to despair of finding any means of delivering it.

The gamekeeper returned hastily and joyfully to Jones, who, having received Sophia's letter from him, instantly withdrew, and eagerly breaking it open, read as follows:

"SIR—It is impossible to express what I have felt since I saw you. Your submitting, on my account, to such cruel insults from my father, lays me under an obligation I shall ever own. As you know his temper, I beg you will, for my sake, avoid him. I wish I had any comfort to send you; but believe this, that nothing but the last violence shall ever give my hand or heart where you would be sorry to see them bestowed."

Jones read this letter a hundred times over, and kissed it a hundred times as often. His passion now brought all tender desires back into his mind. He repented that he had writ to Sophia in the manner we have seen above; but he repented more that he had made use of the interval of his messenger's absence to write and dispatch a letter to Mr. Allworthy, in which he had faithfully promised and bound himself to quit all thoughts of his love. However, when his cool reflections returned, he plainly perceived that his case was neither mended nor altered by Sophia's billet, unless to give him some little glimpse of hope, from her constancy, of some favorable accident hereafter. He therefore resumed his resolution, and taking leave of Black George, set forward to a town about five miles distant, whither he had desired Mr. Allworthy to send his things after him.

SOPHIA had passed the last twenty-four hours in no very desirable manner. During a large part of them she had been entertained by her aunt with lectures of prudence. Her father at his return from All-worthy's, which was not till past ten o'clock in the morning, went directly up to her apartment, opened the door, and seeing she was not up, cried,

"Oh! you are safe then, and I am resolved to keep you so." He then locked the door, and delivered the key to Honour, having first given her the strictest charge, with great promises of rewards for her fidelity, and most dreadful menaces of punishment in case she should betray her trust.

Honour's orders were, not to suffer her mistress to come out of her room without the authority of the squire himself, and to admit none to her but him and her aunt; but she was herself to attend her with whatever Sophia pleased, except only pen, ink, and paper, of which she was forbidden the use.

The squire ordered his daughter to dress herself and attend him at dinner; which she obeyed; and having sat the usual time, was again conducted to her prison.

In the evening the gaoler Honour brought her the letter which she received from the gamekeeper. Sophia read it very attentively twice or thrice over, and then threw herself upon the bed, burst into a flood of tears and cried,

"O Honour! I am undone."

"Marry forbid," cries Honour: "I wish the letter had been burnt before I had brought it to your la'ship. I'm sure I thought it would have comforted your la'ship, or I would have seen it at the devil be-fore I would have touched it."

"Honour," says Sophia, "you are a good girl, and it is vain to at-tempt concealing longer my weakness from you; I have thrown away my heart on a man who hath forsaken me."

"And is Mr. Jones," answered the maid, "such a perfidy man?"

"He hath taken his leave of me," says Sophia, "forever in that let-ter. Nay, he hath desired me to forget him. Could he have desired that if he had loved me? Could he have borne such a thought? Could he have written such a word?"

"No, certainly, ma'am," cries Honour; "and to be sure, if the best man in England was to desire me to forget him, I'd take him at his word. Marry, come up! I am sure you la'ship hath done him too much honor ever to think on him;—a young lady who may take her choice of all the young men in the country. And to be sure, if I may be so presumptuous as to offer my poor opinion, there is young Mr. Blifil, who, besides that he is come of honest parents, and will be one of the greatest squires all hereabouts, he is to be sure, in my poor opinion, a more handsomer and a more politer man by half."

"Name not his detested name," cries Sophia.

"Nay, ma'am," says Honour, "if your la'ship doth not like him, there be more jolly handsome young men that would court your la'ship if they had but the least encouragement."

"What a wretch dost thou imagine me," cries Sophia, "by affronting my ears with such stuff! I detest all mankind."

"Nay, to be sure, ma'am," answered Honour, "your la'ship hath had enough to give you a surfeit of them. To be used ill by such a poor, beggarly fellow."

"Hold your blasphemous tongue," cries Sophia: "how dare you mention his name with disrespect before me? He use me ill? No, his poor bleeding heart suffered more when he writ the cruel words than mine from reading them. O! he is all heroic virtue and angelic goodness. I am ashamed of the weakness of my own passion, for blaming what I ought to admire. O, Honour! it is my good only which he consults. To my interest he sacrifices both himself and me. The apprehension of ruining me hath driven him to despair."

"I am very glad," says Honour, "to hear your la'ship takes that into your consideration; for to be sure, it must be nothing less than ruin to give your mind to one that is turned out of doors, and is not worth a farthing in the world."

"Turned out of doors!" cries Sophia hastily: "how! what dost thou mean?"

"Why, to be sure, ma'am, my master no sooner told Squire Allworthy about Mr. Jones having offered to make love to your la'ship than the squire stripped him stark naked, and turned him out of doors!"

"Ha!" says Sophia, "I have been the cursed, wretched cause of his destruction! Turned naked out of doors! Here, Honour, take all the money I have; take the rings from my fingers. Here, my watch: carry them all. Go find him immediately."

"For Heaven's sake, ma'am," answered Mrs. Honour, "do but consider, if my master should miss any of these things I should be made to answer for them. Therefore let me beg your la'ship not to part with your watch and jewels. Besides, the money, I think, is enough of all conscience; and as for that, my master can never know anything of the matter."

"Here, then," cries Sophia, "take every farthing I am worth, find him out immediately, and give it him. Go, go, lose not a moment."

Mrs. Honour departed according to orders, and finding Black George below-stairs, delivered him the purse, which contained sixteen guineas, being, indeed, the whole stock of Sophia; for though her father was very liberal to her, she was too generous to be rich.

Black George having received the purse, set forward towards the alehouse; but in the way a thought occurred to him, whether he should not detain this money likewise. His conscience, however, immediately started at this suggestion, and began to upbraid him with ingratitude to his benefactor. To this his avarice answered, That his conscience should have considered the matter before, when he deprived poor Jones of his £500. Poor Conscience had certainly been defeated in the argument, had not Fear stepped in to her assistance; for secreting the £500 was a matter of very little hazard; whereas the detaining the sixteen guineas was liable to the utmost danger of discovery.

By this friendly aid of Fear, Conscience obtained a complete victory in the mind of Black George, and, after making him a few compliments on his honesty, forced him to deliver the money to Jones.

Jones, no more than Adam, had any man to whom he might resort for comfort or assistance. What course of life to pursue, or to what business to apply himself, was a second consideration; and here the prospect was all a melancholy void. Every profession, and every trade, required length of time, and what was worse, money; for matters are so constituted, that "nothing out of nothing" is not a truer maxim in physics than in politics; and every man who is greatly destitute of money, is on that account entirely excluded from all means of acquiring it.

At last the Ocean, that hospitable friend to the wretched, opened her capacious arms to receive him; and he instantly resolved to accept her kind invitation. To express myself less figuratively, he determined to go to sea.

This thought indeed no sooner suggested itself, than he eagerly embraced it; and having presently hired horses, he set out for Bristol to put it in execution.

But before we attend him on this expedition, we shall resort awhile to Mr. Western's, and see what further happened to the charming Sophia.

Book VII

CONTAINING THREE DAYS

I

The morning in which Mr. Jones departed, Mrs. Western summoned Sophia into her apartment; and having first acquainted her that she had obtained her liberty of her father, she proceeded to read her a long lecture on the subject of matrimony; which she treated not as a romantic scheme of happiness arising from love; she considered it rather as a fund in which prudent women deposit their fortunes to the best advantage, in order to receive a larger interest for them than they could have elsewhere.

When Mrs. Western had finished, Sophia answered, "That she was very incapable of arguing with a lady of her aunt's superior knowledge and experience, especially on a subject which she had so very little considered, as this of matrimony."

"Indeed, Sophy," replied the aunt, "if you have not hitherto considered of this matter I promise you it is now high time, for my brother is resolved immediately to conclude the treaty with Mr. Blifil; and indeed I am a sort of guarantee in the affair, and have promised your concurrence."

"Indeed, madam," cries Sophia, "this is the only instance in which I must disobey both yourself and my father. For this is a match which requires very little consideration in me to refuse."

"If I was not as great a philosopher as Socrates himself," returned Mrs. Western, "you would overcome my patience. What objection can you have to the young gentleman?"

"A very solid objection, in my opinion," says Sophia—"I hate him."

"Will you never learn a proper use of words?" answered the aunt. "Indeed, child, you should consult Bailey's Dictionary. It is impossible you should hate a man from whom you have received no injury. By hatred, therefore, you mean no more than dislike, which is no sufficient objection against your marrying of him. I have known many couples, who have entirely disliked each other, lead very comfortable genteel lives. Believe me, child, I know these things better than you. You will allow me, I think, to have seen the world, in which I have not an acquaintance who would not rather be thought to dislike her husband than to like him. The contrary is such out-of-fashion romantic nonsense, that the very imagination of it is shocking."

"Indeed, madam," replied Sophia, "I shall never marry a man I dislike. If I promise my father never to consent to any marriage contrary to his inclinations, I think I may hope he will never force me into that state contrary to my own."

"Inclinations!" cries the aunt, with some warmth. "Inclinations! I am astonished at your assurance. A young woman of your age, and unmarried, to talk of inclinations! But whatever your inclinations may be, my brother is resolved; nay, since you talk of inclinations, I shall advise him to hasten the treaty. Inclinations!"

Sophia then flung herself upon her knees, and tears began to trickle from her shining eyes. She entreated her aunt, "to have mercy upon her, and not to resent so cruelly her unwillingness to make herself miserable"; often urging, "that she alone was concerned, and that her happiness only was at stake."

The politic aunt answered with great impetuosity, "So far, madam, from your being concerned alone, your concern is the least, or surely the least important. It is the honor of your family which is concerned in this alliance; you are only the instrument. Do you conceive, mistress, that in an intermarriage between kingdoms, as when a daughter of France is married into Spain, the princess herself is alone considered in the match? The same happens in great families such as ours. You cannot surely complain at being used no worse than all princesses are used."

"I hope, madam," cries Sophia, with a little elevation of voice, "I shall never do anything to dishonor my family; but as for Mr. Blifil, whatever may be the consequence, I am resolved against him, and no force shall prevail in his favor."

Western, who had been within hearing during the greater part of the preceding dialogue, had now exhausted all his patience; he therefore entered the room in a violent passion, crying, "D—n me then if shatunt ha'un, d—n me if shatunt, that's all—that's all; d—n me if shatunt."

Mrs. Western had collected a sufficient quantity of wrath for the use of Sophia; but she now transferred it all to the squire.

"Brother," said she, "it is astonishing that you will interfere in a matter which you had totally left to my negotiation. It is you—it is your preposterous conduct which hath eradicated all the seeds that I had formerly sown in her tender mind. It is you yourself who have taught her disobedience."

"Blood!" cries the squire, foaming at the mouth, "you are enough to conquer the patience of the devil! Have I ever taught my daughter disobedience? Here she stands; speak honestly, girl, did ever I bid you be disobedient to me? Have not I done everything to humor and to gratify you, and to make you obedient to me? And very obedient to me she was when a little child, before you took her in hand and spoiled her, by filling her head with a pack of court notions. Why—why—why—did I not overhear you telling her she must behave like a princess? You have made a Whig of the girl; and how should her father, or anybody else, expect any obedience from her?"

"Brother," answered Mrs. Western, with an air of great disdain, "I cannot express the contempt I have for your politics of all kinds; but I will appeal likewise to the young lady herself, whether I have ever taught her any principles of disobedience. When you came first under my care, I verily believe you did not know the relation between a daughter and a father."

"'Tis a lie," answered Western. "The girl is no such fool, as to live to eleven years old without knowing that she was her father's relation."

"O! more than Gothic ignorance," answered the lady. "And as for your manners, brother, I must tell you they deserve a cane."

"Why, then you may gi' it me, if you think you are able," cries the squire; "nay, I suppose your niece there will be ready enough to help you."

"Brother," said Mrs. Western, "though I despise you beyond expression, yet I shall endure your insolence no longer; so I desire my coach may be got ready immediately, for I am resolved to leave your house this very morning." And she flew into the most violent rage, uttered phrases improper to be here related, and instantly burst out of the house.

The squire sent after his sister the same holloa which attends the departure of a hare, when she is first started before the hounds. He was indeed a great master of this kind of vociferation, and had a holloa proper for most occasions in life.

II

MR. WESTERN having finished his holloa, and taken a little breath, began to lament, in very pathetic terms, the unfortunate condition of men, who are, says he, "always whipped in by the humors of some d—n'd b—— or other. I think I was hard run enough by your mother for one man; but after giving her a dodge, here's another b—— follows me upon the foil; but curse my jacket if I will be run down in this manner by any o'um."

Sophia never had a single dispute with her father, till this unlucky affair of Blifil, on any account, except in defense of her mother, whom she had loved most tenderly, though she lost her in the eleventh year of her age. The squire, to whom that poor woman had been a faithful upper-servant all the time of their marriage, had returned that behavior by making what the world calls a good husband. He very seldom swore at her (perhaps not above once a week) and never beat her: she had not the least occasion for jealousy, and was perfect mistress of her time; for she was never interrupted by her husband, who was engaged all the morning in his field exercises, and all the evening with bottle companions. She scarce indeed ever saw him but at meals; where she had the pleasure of carving those dishes which she had before attended at the dressing. From these meals she retired about five minutes after the other servants, having only stayed to drink "the king over the water." Such were, it seems, Mr. Western's orders; for it was a maxim with him, that women should come in with the first dish, and go out after the first glass.

These, however, were the only seasons when Mr. Western saw his wife; for when he repaired to her bed, he was generally so drunk that he could not see; and in the sporting season he always rose from her before it was light. Hence, perhaps, she had contracted a little gloominess of temper. She would, moreover, sometimes interfere with matters which did not concern her, as the violent drinking of her husband, which in the gentlest terms she would take some of the few opportunities he gave her of remonstrating against. And once in her life she very earnestly entreated him to carry her for two months to London, which he peremptorily denied; nay, was angry with his wife for the request ever after, being well assured that all the husbands in London are cuckolds.

For this last, and many other good reasons, Western at length heartily hated his wife; and as he never concealed this hatred before her death, so he never forgot it afterwards; but when anything in the least soured him, as a bad scenting day, or a distemper among his hounds, or any other such misfortune, he constantly vented his spleen by invectives against the deceased, saying, "If my wife was alive now, she would be glad of this."

III

DURING the foregoing speech of her father Sophia remaining silent, he cried out, "What, art dumb? why dost unt speak? Was not thy mother a d—d b—— to me? answer me that. What, I suppose you despise your father too, and don't think him good enough to speak to?"

"For Heaven's sake, sir," answered Sophia, "do not give so cruel a turn to my silence. I am sure I would sooner die than be guilty of any disrespect towards you; but how can I venture to speak, when every word must either offend my dear papa, or convict me of the blackest ingratitude as well as impiety to the memory of the best of mothers?"

"And your aunt, I suppose, is the best of sisters too!" replied the squire.

"Indeed, sir," says Sophia, "I have great obligations to my aunt. She hath been a second mother to me."

"And a second wife to me too," returned Western; "so you will take her part too! You won't confess that she hath acted the part of the vilest sister in the world?"

"Upon my word, sir," cries Sophia, "I must belie my heart wickedly if I did. I am convinced, so far from her being the worst sister in the world, there are very few who love a brother better. If my aunt had died yesterday, I am convinced she would have left you her whole fortune."

Whether Sophia intended it or no, these last words penetrated very deep into the ears of her father. He started, staggered, and turned pale. After which he remained silent above a minute, and then began in the following hesitating manner:

"Yesterday! she would have left me her esteate yesterday! would she? Why yesterday, of all the days in the year? I suppose if she dies tomorrow she will leave it to somebody else, and perhaps out of the vamily."

"My aunt, sir," cries Sophia, "hath very violent passions, and I can't answer what she may do under their influence."

"You can't!" returned the father: "and pray who hath been the occasion of putting her into those violent passions? Was not you and she hard at it before I came into the room? I have not quarreled with sister this many years but upon your account; and now you would throw the whole blame upon me, as thof I should be the occasion of her leaving the esteate out o' the vamily."

"I beseech you then," cries Sophia, "upon my knees I beseech you, if I have been the unhappy occasion of this difference, that you will endeavor to make it up with my aunt, and not suffer her to leave your house in this violent rage of anger."

"So I must go and ask pardon for your fault, must I?" answered Western. "You have lost the hare, and I must draw every way to find her again? Indeed, if I was certain"——Here he stopped, and Sophia throwing in more entreaties, at length prevailed upon him; so that after venting two or three bitter sarcastical expressions against his daughter, he departed as fast as he could to recover his sister, before her equipage could be gotten ready.

IV

THE squire overtook his sister just as she was stepping into the coach, and partly by force, and partly by solicitations, prevailed upon her to order her horses back into their quarters. He succeeded in this attempt without much difficulty; for the lady was, as we have already hinted, of a most placable disposition, and greatly loved her brother.

Poor Sophia, who had first set on foot this reconciliation, was now made the sacrifice to it. They jointly declared war against her, and proposed not only an immediate conclusion of the treaty with Allworthy, but as immediately to carry it into execution. The squire resolved to push matters as forward as possible; and addressing himself to his intended son-in-law in the hunting phrase, he cried, after a loud holloa, "Follow her, boy, follow her; run in, run in; that's it, honeys. Dead, dead, dead. Allworthy and I can finish all matters between us this afternoon, and let us ha' the wedding tomorrow."

Blifil suffered himself to be overpowered by the forcible rhetoric of the squire; and it being agreed that Western should close with Allworthy that very afternoon, the lover departed home.

Though Mr. Blifil was not ready to eat every woman he saw, yet he was far from being destitute of that appetite which is said to be the common property of all animals. Now the agonies which affected the mind of Sophia rather augmented than impaired her beauty; for her tears added brightness to her eyes, and her breasts rose higher with her sighs. Indeed, no one hath seen beauty in its highest luster who hath never seen it in distress. Nor was his desire at all lessened by the aversion which he discovered in her to himself. On the contrary, this served rather to heighten the pleasure he proposed in rifling her charms, as it added triumph to lust. The rivaling poor Jones, and supplanting him in her affections, added another spur to his pursuit, and promised another additional rapture to his enjoyment.

For these reasons Mr. Blifil was so desirous of the match that he intended to deceive Sophia, by pretending love to her; and to deceive his uncle, by pretending he was beloved by her. When he was examined touching the inclinations of Sophia by Allworthy, who said, "He would on no account be accessory to forcing a young lady into a marriage contrary to her own will," he answered, "That the real sentiments of young ladies were very difficult to be understood; that her behavior to him was full as forward as he wished it, and that if he could believe her father, she had all the affection for him which any lover could desire. As for Jones," said he, "whom I am loth to call villain, though his behavior to you, sir, sufficiently justifies the appellation, his own vanity, or perhaps some wicked views, might make him boast of a falsehood; for if there had been any reality in Miss Western's love to him, the greatness of her fortune would never have suffered him to desert her, as you are well informed he hath. Lastly, sir, I promise you I would not for the whole world consent to marry this young lady if I was not persuaded she had all the passion for me which I desire she should have."

This excellent method of conveying a falsehood with the heart only, without making the tongue guilty of an untruth, by the means of equivocation and imposture, hath quieted the conscience of many a notable deceiver; and yet, when we consider that it is Omniscience on which these endeavor to impose, it may possibly seem that this artful and refined distinction between communicating a lie and telling one, is hardly worth the pains it costs them.

Allworthy was pretty well satisfied with what Mr. Western and Mr. Blifil told him; and the treaty was now, at the end of two days, concluded.

<h1 style="text-align:center">V</h1>

THOUGH Mrs. Honour was principally attached to her own interest, she was not without some little attachment to Sophia. To say truth, it was very difficult for anyone to know that young lady without loving her. She no sooner, therefore, heard a piece of news, which she imagined to be of great importance to her mistress, than she ran hastily to inform her of the news.

The beginning of her discourse was as abrupt as her entrance into the room.

"O dear ma'am!" says she, "what doth your la'ship think? To be sure I am frightened out of my wits; and yet I thought it my duty to tell your la'ship, though perhaps it may make you angry, for we servants don't always know what will make our ladies angry; for, to be sure, everything is always laid to the charge of a servant. When our ladies are out of humor, to be sure we must be scolded; and to be sure I should not wonder if your la'ship should be out of humor; nay, it must surprise you certainly, ay, and shock you too."

"Good Honour, let me know it without any longer preface," says Sophia; "there are few things, I promise you, which will surprise, and fewer which will shock me."

"Dear ma'am," answered Honour, "to be sure, I overheard my master talking to Parson Supple about getting a license this very afternoon; and to be sure I heard him say, your la'ship should be married tomorrow morning."

Sophia turned pale at these words, and repeated eagerly, "Tomorrow morning!"

"Yes, ma'am," replied the trusty waiting-woman, "I will take my oath I heard my master say so."

"Honour," says Sophia, "you have both surprised and shocked me to such a degree that I have scarce any breath or spirits left. What is to be done in my dreadful situation?"

"I wish I was able to advise your la'ship," says she.

"Do advise me," cries Sophia; "pray, dear Honour, advise me. Think what you would attempt if it was your own case."

"Indeed, ma'am," cries Honour, "I wish your la'ship and I could change situations; that is, I mean without hurting your la'ship; for to be sure I don't wish you so bad as to be a servant; but because that if so be it was my case, I should find no manner of difficulty in it; for, in my poor opinion, young Squire Blifil is a charming, sweet, handsome man."

"Don't mention such stuff," cries Sophia.

"Such stuff!" repeated Honour; "why, there. Well, to be sure, what's one man's meat is another man's poison, and the same is altogether as true of women."

"Honour," says Sophia, "rather than submit to be the wife of that contemptible wretch I would plunge a dagger into my heart."

"O lud! ma'am!" answered the other, "I am sure you frighten me out of my wits now. Let me beseech your la'ship not to suffer such wicked thoughts to come into your head. O lud! to be sure I tremble every inch of me. Dear ma'am, consider, that to be denied Christian burial, and to have your corpse buried in the highway, and a stake drove through you, as farmer Halfpenny was served at Ox Cross; and, to be sure, his ghost hath walked there ever since, for several people have seen him."

Sophia had been too much wrapped in contemplation to pay any great attention to the foregoing excellent discourse of her maid; interrupting her, therefore, without making any answer to it, she said.

"Honour, I am come to a resolution. I am determined to leave my father's house this very night; and if you have the friendship for me which you have often professed, you will keep me company."

"That I will, ma'am, to the world's end," answered Honour; "but I beg your la'ship to consider the consequence before you undertake any rash action. Where can your la'ship possibly go?"

"There is," replied Sophia, "a lady of quality in London, a relation of mine, who spent several months with my aunt in the country; during all which time she treated me with great kindness, and expressed so much pleasure in my company, that she earnestly desired my aunt to suffer me to go with her to London. As she is a woman of very great note, I shall easily find her out, and I make no doubt of being very well and kindly received by her."

"I would not have your la'ship too confident of that," cries Honour; "for the first lady I lived with used to invite people very earnestly to her house; but if she heard afterwards they were coming, she used to get out of the way. Besides, though this lady would be very glad to see your la'ship, yet when she hears your la'ship is run away from my master—"

"You are mistaken, Honour," says Sophia: "she looks upon the authority of a father in a much lower light than I do; for she pressed me violently to go to London with her, and when I refused to go without my father's consent, she laughed me to scorn, called me silly country girl, and said I should make a pure loving wife, since I could be so dutiful a daughter. So I have no doubt but she will both receive me and protect me too, till my father, finding me out of his power, can be brought to some reason."

"Well, but, ma'am," answered Honour, "how doth your la'ship think of making your escape? Where will you get any horses or conveyance?"

"I intend to escape," said Sophia, "by walking out of the doors when they are open. I thank Heaven my legs are very able to carry me. They have supported me many a long evening after a fiddle, with no very agreeable partner; and surely they will assist me in running from so detestable a partner for life."

"Oh, Heaven, ma'am! doth your la'ship know what you are saying?" cries Honour; "would you think of walking about the country by night and alone?"

"Not alone," answered the lady; "you have promised to bear me company."

"Yes, to be sure," cries Honour, "I will follow your la'ship through the world; but your la'ship had almost as good be alone; for I should not be able to defend you, if any robbers, or other villains, should meet with you. Besides, ma'am, consider how cold the nights are now; we shall be frozen to death."

"A good brisk pace," answered Sophia, "will preserve us from the cold; and if you cannot defend me from a villain, Honour, I will defend you; for I will take a pistol with me. There are two always charged in the hall."

"Dear ma'am, you frighten me more and more," cries Honour: "sure your la'ship would not venture to fire it off!"

"Well, well," says Sophia, "I intend to take horses at the very first town we come to, and we shall hardly be attacked in our way thither. Look'ee, Honour, I am resolved to go; and if you will attend me, I promise you I will reward you to the very utmost of my power."

This last argument had a stronger effect on Honour than all the preceding. Having applied all her oratory to dissuade her mistress from her purpose, when she found her positively determined, at last started the following expedient to remove her clothes, viz., to get herself turned out of doors that very evening. Sophia highly approved of this method, but doubted how it might be brought about.

"O, ma'am," cries Honour, "your la'ship may trust that to me; we servants very well know how to obtain this favor of our masters and mistresses; and since your la'ship is resolved upon setting out to-night, I warrant I get discharged this afternoon." It was then resolved that she should pack up some linen and a nightgown for Sophia, with her own things; and as for all her other clothes, the young lady abandoned them with no more remorse than the sailor feels when he throws over the goods of others in order to save his own life.

VI

MRS. HONOUR had scarce sooner parted from her young lady, than something suggested itself to her, that by sacrificing Sophia and all her secrets to Mr. Western, she might probably make her fortune. Many considerations urged this discovery. The fair prospect of a handsome reward for so great and acceptable a service to the squire tempted her avarice; and again, the danger of the enterprise she had undertaken; the uncertainty of its success; night, cold, robbers, all alarmed her fears. So forcibly did all these operate upon her, that she was almost determined to go directly to the squire, and to lay open the whole affair. She was, however, too upright a judge to decree on one side before she had heard the other. And here, first, a journey to London appeared very strongly in support of Sophia. She eagerly longed to see a place in which she fancied charms short only of those which a raptured saint imagines in heaven. In the next place, as she knew Sophia to have much more generosity than her master, so her fidelity promised her a greater reward than she could gain by treachery. She then cross-examined all the articles which had raised her fears on the other side, and found, on fairly sifting the matter, that there was very little in them. And now both scales being reduced to a pretty even balance, her love to her mistress being thrown into the scale of her integrity, made that rather preponderate, when a circumstance struck upon her imagination which might have had a dangerous effect, had its whole weight been fairly put into the other scale. This was the length of time which must intervene before

Sophia would be able to fulfil her promises; for though she was entitled to her mother's fortune at the death of her father, and to the sum of £3000 left her by an uncle when she came of age, yet these were distant days, and many accidents might prevent the intended generosity of the young lady; whereas the rewards she might expect from Mr. Western were immediate. But while she was pursuing this thought an accident at once preserved her fidelity, and even facilitated the intended business.

Mrs. Western's maid claimed great superiority over Mrs. Honour on several accounts. First, her birth was higher; for her great-grandmother by the mother's side was a cousin, not far removed, to an Irish peer. Secondly, her wages were greater. And lastly, she had been at London, and had of consequence seen more of the world. She had always behaved, therefore, to Mrs. Honour with that reserve, and had always exacted of her those marks of distinction, which every order of females preserves and requires in conversation with those of an inferior order. Now as Honour did not at all times agree with this doctrine, but would frequently break in upon the respect which the other demanded, Mrs. Western's maid was not at all pleased with her company.

She came into the room where Honour was debating with herself in the manner we have above related.

Honour no sooner saw her, than she addressed her in the following obliging phrase:

"Soh, madam, I find we are to have the pleasure of your company longer, which I was afraid the quarrel between my master and your lady would have robbed us of."

"I don't know, madam," answered the other, "what you mean by we and us. I assure you I do not look on any of the servants in this house to be proper company for me. I am company, I hope, for their betters every day in the week. I do not speak on your account, Mrs. Honour; for you are a civilized young woman; and when you have seen a little more of the world, I should not be ashamed to walk with you in St. James's Park."

"Hoity toity!" cries Mrs. Honour, "madam is in her airs, I protest. Mrs. Honour, forsooth! sure, madam, you might call me by my sir-name; for though my lady calls me Honour, I have a sir-name as well as other folks. Ashamed to walk with me, quotha! marry, as good as yourself, I hope."

"Since you make such a return to my civility," said the other, "I must acquaint you, Mrs. Honour, that you are not so good as me. In the country, indeed, one is obliged to take up with all kind of trumpery; but in town I visit none but the women of women of quality. Indeed, Mrs. Honour, there is some difference, I hope, between you and me."

"I hope so too," answered Honour: "there is some difference in our ages, and—I think in our persons."

Upon speaking which last words, she strutted by Mrs. Western's maid with the most provoking air of contempt; turning up her nose, tossing her head, and violently brushing the hoop of her competitor with her own. The other lady put on one of her most malicious sneers, and said,

"Creature! you are below my anger; and it is beneath me to give ill words to such an audacious saucy trollop; but, hussy, I must tell you, your breeding shows the meanness of your birth as well as of your education; and both very properly qualify you to be the mean serving-woman of a country girl."

"Don't abuse my lady," cries Honour, "I won't take that of you; she's as much better than yours as she is younger, and ten thousand times more handsomer."

Here ill luck, or rather good luck, sent Mrs. Western to see her maid in tears, which began to flow plentifully at her approach; and of which being asked the reason by her mistress, she presently acquainted her that her tears were occasioned by the rude treatment of that creature there—meaning Honour. "And, madam," continued she, "I could have despised all she said to me; but she hath had the audacity to affront your ladyship, and to call you ugly—Yes, madam, she called you ugly old cat to my face. I could not bear to hear your ladyship called ugly."

"Why do you repeat her impudence so often?" said Mrs. Western. And then turning to Mrs. Honour, she asked her "How she had the assurance to mention her name with disrespect?"

"Disrespect, madam!" answered Honour; "I never mentioned your name at all: I said somebody was not as handsome as my mistress, and to be sure you know that as well as I."

"Hussy," replied the lady, "I will make such a saucy trollop as yourself know that I am not a proper subject of your discourse. And if my brother doth not discharge you this moment I will never sleep in his house again. I will find him out, and have you discharged this moment."

"Discharged!" cries Honour; "and suppose I am: there are more places in the world than one. Thank Heaven, good servants need not want places; and if you turn away all who do not think you handsome, you will want servants very soon; let me tell you that."

Mrs. Western was a very good-natured woman, and ordinarily of a forgiving temper. She had lately remitted the trespass of a stage-coachman, who had overturned her post-chaise into a ditch; nay, she had even broken the law, in refusing to prosecute a highwayman who had robbed her, not only of a sum of money, but of her ear-rings; at the same time d—ning her, and saying "Such handsome b—s as you don't want jewels to set them off, and be d—n'd to you." But now, so uncertain are our tempers, and so much do we at different times differ from ourselves, she would hear of no mitigation; nor could all the affected penitence of Honour, nor all the entreaties of Sophia for her own servant, prevail with her to desist from earnestly desiring her brother to execute justiceship (for it was indeed a syllable more than justice) on the wench.

Honour acted her part to the utmost perfection. She laid down her place, with as much affectation of content, and indeed of contempt, as was ever practiced at the resignation of places of much greater importance. If the reader pleases, therefore, we choose rather to say she resigned—which hath, indeed, been always held a synonymous expression with being turned out, or turned away.

Mr. Western ordered her to be very expeditious in packing; for his sister declared she would not sleep another night under the same roof with so impudent a slut. To work therefore she went, and that so earnestly, that everything was ready early in the evening; when, having received her wages, away packed bag and baggage, to the great satisfaction of everyone, but of none more than of Sophia; who, having appointed her maid to meet her at a certain place not far from the house, exactly at the dreadful and ghostly hour of twelve, began to prepare for her own departure.

But first she was obliged to give two painful audiences, the one to her aunt, and the other to her father. In these Mrs. Western herself began to talk to her in a more peremptory style than before; but her father treated her in so violent and outrageous a manner, that he frightened her into an affected compliance with his will; which so highly pleased the good squire, that he changed his frowns into smiles, and his menaces into promises: he vowed his whole soul was wrapped in hers; that her consent (for so he construed the words, "You know, sir, I must not, nor can, refuse to obey any absolute command of yours") had made him the happiest of mankind. He then gave her a large bank-bill to dispose of in any trinkets she pleased, and kissed and embraced her in the fondest manner, while tears of joy trickled from those eyes which a few moments before had darted fire and rage against the dear object of all his affection.

VII

THE reader will be pleased to remember that we left Mr. Jones on his road to Bristol; being determined to seek his fortune at sea, or rather, indeed, to fly away from his fortune on shore.

It happened (a thing not very unusual), that the guide who undertook to conduct him on his way, was unluckily unacquainted with the road; so that having missed his right track, and being ashamed to ask information, he rambled about backwards and forwards till night came on, and it began to grow dark. Jones, after a little persuasion, agreed to stay till the morning in a public-house.

The landlord, who was a very civil fellow, told Jones, "He hoped he would excuse the badness of his accommodations; for that his wife was gone from home, and had locked up almost everything, and carried the keys along with her."

Jones being assured that he could have no bed, very contentedly betook himself to a great chair made with rushes, when sleep, which had lately shunned his company in much better apartments, generously paid him a visit in his humble cell.

The landlord having taken his seat directly opposite to the door of the parlor, continued still waking in his chair till a violent thundering at his outward gate called him from his seat, and obliged him to open it; which he had no sooner done, than his kitchen was immediately full of gentlemen in red coats, who all rushed upon him in as tumultuous a manner as if they intended to take his little castle by storm.

The landlord was now forced from his post to furnish his numerous guests with beer, which they called for with great eagerness; and upon his second or third return from the cellar, he saw Mr. Jones standing before the fire in the midst of the soldiers; for it may easily be believed, that the arrival of so much good company should put an end to any sleep, unless that from which we are to be awakened only by the last trumpet.

The company having pretty well satisfied their thirst, nothing remained but to pay the reckoning. A violent dispute now arose, in which every word may be said to have been deposed upon oath; for the oaths were at least equal to all the other words spoken. In this controversy the whole company spoke together, and every man seemed wholly bent to extenuate the sum which fell to his share; so that the most probable conclusion which could be foreseen was, that a large portion of the reckoning would fall to the landlord's share to pay, or (what is much the same thing) would remain unpaid.

All this while Mr. Jones was engaged in conversation with the sergeant; for that officer was entirely unconcerned in the present dispute, being privileged by immemorial custom from all contribution.

The dispute now grew so very warm that it seemed to draw towards a military decision, when Jones, stepping forward, silenced all their clamors at once, by declaring that he would pay the whole reckoning, which indeed amounted to no more than three shillings and fourpence. This declaration procured Jones the thanks and applause of the whole company. The terms honorable, noble, and worthy gentleman resounded through the room.

The sergeant had informed Mr. Jones that they were marching against the rebels, and expected to be commanded by the glorious Duke of Cumberland. By which the reader may perceive (a circumstance which we have not thought necessary to communicate before) that this was the very time when the late rebellion was at the highest; and indeed the banditti were now marched into England, intending, as it was thought, to fight the king's forces, and to attempt pushing forward to the metropolis.

Jones had some heroic ingredients in his composition, and was a hearty well-wisher to the glorious cause of liberty and of the Protestant religion. It is no wonder, therefore, that in circumstances which would have warranted a much more romantic and wild undertaking, it should occur to him to serve as a volunteer in this expedition.

Our commanding officer had said all in his power to encourage and promote this good disposition, from the first moment he had been acquainted with it. He now proclaimed the noble resolution aloud, which was received with great pleasure by the whole company, who all cried out, "God bless King George and your honor"; and then added, with many oaths "We will stand by you both to the last drops of our blood."

All that day the sergeant and the young soldier marched together; and the former, who was an arch fellow, told the latter many entertaining stories of his campaigns, though in reality he had never made any; for he was but lately come into the service, and had, by his own dexterity, so well ingratiated himself with his officers, that he had promoted himself to a halberd; chiefly indeed by his merit in recruiting, in which he was most excellently well skilled.

Much mirth and festivity passed among the soldiers during their march. In which the many occurrences that had passed at their last quarters were remembered, and everyone, with great freedom, made what jokes he pleased on his officers, some of which were of the coarser kind, and very near bordering on scandal. This brought to our hero's mind the custom which he had read of among the Greeks and Romans, of indulging, on certain festivals and solemn occasions, the liberty to slaves, of using an uncontrolled freedom of speech towards their masters.

Our little army, which consisted of two companies of foot, were now arrived at the place where they were to halt that evening.

The sergeant then acquainted his lieutenant, who could not help showing some surprise; for besides that Jones was very well dressed, and was naturally genteel, he had a remarkable air of dignity in his look, which is rarely seen among the vulgar, and is indeed not inseparably annexed to the features of their superiors.

"Sir," said the lieutenant, "my sergeant informed me that you are desirous of enlisting in the company I have at present under my command; if so, sir, we shall very gladly receive a gentleman who promises to do much honor to the company by bearing arms in it."

Jones answered: "That he had not mentioned anything of enlisting himself; that he was most zealously attached to the glorious cause for which they were going to fight, and was very desirous of serving as a volunteer"; concluding with some compliments to the lieutenant, and expressing the great satisfaction he should have in being under his command.

The lieutenant returned his civility, commended his resolution, shook him by the hand, and invited him to dine with himself and the rest of the officers.

VIII

The lieutenant, whom we mentioned in the preceding chapter, and who commanded this party, was now near sixty years of age. The other officers who marched with him were a French lieutenant, who had been long enough out of France to forget his own language, but not long enough in England to learn ours, so that he really spoke no language at all, and could barely make himself understood on the most ordinary occasions. There were likewise two ensigns, both very young fellows; one of whom had been bred under an attorney, and the other was son to the wife of a nobleman's butler.

As soon as dinner was ended, Jones informed the company of the merriment which had passed among the soldiers; "and yet," says he, "notwithstanding all their vociferation, I dare swear they will behave more like Grecians than Trojans when they come to the enemy."

"Grecians and Trojans!" says one of the ensigns, "who the devil are they? I have heard of all the troops in Europe, but never of any such as these."

"Don't pretend to more ignorance than you have, Mr. Northerton," said the worthy lieutenant. "I suppose you have heard of the Greeks and Trojans, though perhaps you never read Pope's Homer; who, I remember, now the gentleman mentions it, compares the march of the Trojans to the cackling of geese, and greatly commends the silence of the Grecians. And upon my honor there is great justice in the cadet's observation."

"D—n Homo with all my heart," says Northerton; "I have the marks of him yet. And there's Corderius, another that hath got me many a flogging."

"Then you have been at school, Mr. Northerton?" said the lieutenant.

"Ay, d—n me, have I," answered he; "the devil take my father for sending me thither! The old put wanted to make a parson of me, but d—n me, thinks I to myself, I'll nick you there, old cull; the devil a smack of your nonsense shall you ever get into me." Then turning to Jones, said to him, "I am very glad, sir, you have chosen our regiment to be a volunteer in; for if our parson should at any time take a cup too much, I find you can supply his place. I presume, sir, you have been at the University; may I crave the favor to know what college?"

"Sir," answered Jones, "so far from having been at the University, I have even had the advantage of yourself, for I was never at school."

"I presumed," cries the ensign, "only upon the information of your great learning."

"Oh! sir," answered Jones, "it is as possible for a man to know something without having been at school, as it is to have been at school and to know nothing."

"Well said, young volunteer," cries the lieutenant. "Upon my word, Northerton, you had better let him alone, for he will be too hard for you."

Northerton did not very well relish the sarcasam of Jones; but he thought the provocation was scarce sufficient to justify a blow, or a rascal, or scoundrel, which were the only repartees that suggested themselves. He was, therefore, silent at present; but resolved to take the first opportunity of returning the jest by abuse.

It now came to the turn of Mr. Jones to give a toast, as it is called; who could not refrain from mentioning his dear Sophia. This he did the more readily, as he imagined it utterly impossible that anyone present should guess the person he meant.

But the lieutenant, who was the toast-master, was not contented with Sophia only. He said he must have her sir-name; upon which Jones hesitated a little, and presently after named Miss Sophia Western. Ensign Northerton declared he would not drink her health in the same round with his own toast, unless somebody would vouch for her.

"I knew one Sophy Western," says he, "that was lain with by half the young fellows at Bath; and perhaps this is the same woman."

Jones very solemnly assured him of the contrary; asserting that the young lady he named was one of great fashion and fortune.

"Ay, ay," says the ensign, "and so she is: d—n me, it is the same woman; and I'll hold half a dozen of Burgundy, Tom French of our regiment brings her into company with us at any tavern in Bridges Street." He then proceeded to describe her person exactly (for he had seen her with her aunt), and concluded with saying, "that her father had a great estate in Somersetshire."

The tenderness of lovers can ill brook the least jesting with the names of their mistresses. However, Jones, though he had enough of the lover and of the hero too in his disposition, did not resent these slanders as hastily as, perhaps, he ought to have done. To say the truth, having seen but little of this kind of wit, he did not readily understand it, and for a long time imagined Mr. Northerton had really mistaken his charmer for some other. But now, turning to the ensign with a stern aspect, he said,

"Pray, sir, choose some other subject for your wit; for I promise you I will bear no jesting with this lady's character."

"Jesting!" cries the other, "d—n me if ever I was more in earnest in my life."

"Then I must tell you in earnest," cries Jones, "that you are one of the most impudent rascals upon earth."

He had no sooner spoken these words, than the ensign, together with a volley of curses, discharged a bottle full at the head of Jones, which hitting him a little above the right temple, brought him instantly to the ground.

The conqueror perceiving the enemy to lie motionless before him, and blood beginning to flow pretty plentifully from his wound, began now to think of quitting the field of battle, where no more honor was to be gotten; but the lieutenant interposed, by stepping before the door, and thus cut off his retreat.

Northerton was very importunate with the lieutenant for his liberty; urging the ill consequences of his stay, asking him what he could have done less?

"Zounds!" says he, "I was but in jest with the fellow. I never heard any harm of Miss Western in my life."

"Have not you?" said the lieutenant; "then you richly deserve to be hanged, as well for making such jests, as for using such a weapon: you are my prisoner, sir; nor shall you stir from hence till a proper guard comes to secure you."

Such an ascendant had our lieutenant over this ensign, that all that fervency of courage which had leveled our poor hero with the floor would scarce have animated the said ensign to have drawn his sword against the lieutenant, had he then had one dangling at his side; but all the swords being hung up in the room, were, at the very beginning of the fray, secured by the French officer. So that Mr. Northerton was obliged to attend the final issue of this affair.

The French gentleman had raised up the body of Jones, which being placed upright in a chair, soon began to discover some symptoms of life and motion. These were no sooner perceived by the company (for Jones was at first generally concluded to be dead) than they all fell at once to prescribing for him.

Bleeding was the unanimous voice of the whole room; but unluckily there was no operator at hand; everyone then cried, "Call the barber"; but none stirred a step. Several cordials were likewise prescribed in the same ineffective manner; till the landlord ordered up a tankard of strong beer, with a toast, which he said was the best cordial in England.

The person principally assistant on this occasion, indeed the only one who did any service, or seemed likely to do any, was the landlady: she cut off some of her hair, and applied it to the wound to stop the blood; she fell to chafing the youth's temples with her hand; and having expressed great contempt for her husband's prescription of beer, she despatched one of her maids to her own closet for a bottle of brandy, of which, as soon as it was brought, she prevailed on Jones, who was just returned to his senses, to drink a very large and plentiful draught.

Soon afterwards arrived the surgeon, who having viewed the wound, having shaken his head, and blamed everything which was done, ordered his patient instantly to bed; in which place we think proper to leave him some time to his repose, and shall here, therefore, put an end to this chapter.

IX

THE lieutenant having collected from the learned discourse of the surgeon that Mr. Jones was in great danger, gave orders for keeping Mr. Northerton under a very strict guard, designing in the morning to attend him to a justice of peace, and to commit the conducting the troops to Gloucester to the French lieutenant, who, though he could neither read, write, nor speak any language, was, however, a good officer.

In the evening, our commander sent a message to Mr. Jones, that if a visit would not be troublesome, he would wait on him. This civility was very kindly and thankfully received by Jones, and the lieutenant accordingly went up to his room, where he found the wounded man much better than he expected; nay, Jones assured his friend, that if he had not received express orders to the contrary from the surgeon, he should have got up long ago; for he appeared to himself to be as well as ever, and felt no other inconvenience from his wound but an extreme soreness on that side of his head.

"I should be very glad," quoth the lieutenant, "if you was as well as you fancy yourself, for then you could be able to do yourself justice immediately; for the sooner you take him out the better; but I am afraid you think yourself better than you are, and he would have too much advantage over you."

"I'll try, however," answered Jones, "if you please, and will be so kind to lend me a sword, for I have none here of my own."

"My sword is heartily at your service, my dear boy," cries the lieutenant, kissing him; "you are a brave lad, and I love your spirit; but I fear your strength; for such a blow, and so much loss of blood, must have very much weakened you; and though you feel no want of strength in your bed, yet you most probably would after a thrust or two. I can't consent to your taking him out tonight; but I hope you will be able to come up with us before we get many days' march advance; and I give you my honor you shall have satisfaction, or the man who hath injured you sha'n't stay in our regiment."

"I wish," said Jones, "it was possible to decide this matter tonight: now you have mentioned it to me, I shall not be able to rest."

"Oh, never think of it," returned the other: "a few days will make no difference. The wounds of honor are not like those in your body: they suffer nothing by the delay of cure. It will be altogether as well for you to receive satisfaction a week hence as now."

"But suppose," says Jones, "I should grow worse, and die of the consequences of my present wound?"

"Then your honor," answered the lieutenant, "will require no reparation at all. I myself will do justice to your character, and testify to the world your intention to have acted properly, if you had recovered."

"Still," replied Jones, "I am concerned at the delay. I am almost afraid to mention it to you who are a soldier; but though I have been a very wild young fellow, still in my most serious moments, and at the bottom, I am really a Christian."

"So am I too, I assure you," said the officer; "and I am a little offended with you now, young gentleman, that you should express a fear of declaring your faith before anyone."

"But how terrible must it be," cries Jones, "to anyone who is really a Christian, to cherish malice in his breast, in opposition to the command of Him who hath expressly forbid it? How can I bear to do this on a sick-bed? Or how shall I make up my account, with such an article as this in my bosom against me?"

"Why, I believe there is such a command," cries the lieutenant; "but a man of honor can't keep it. And you must be a man of honor, if you will be in the army. I remember I once put the case to our chaplain over a bowl of punch, and he confessed there was much difficulty in it; but he said, he hoped there might be a latitude granted to soldiers in this one instance; and to be sure it is our duty to hope so; for who would bear to live without his honor? No, no, my dear boy, be a good Christian as long as you live; but be a man of honor too, and never put up an affront." Here he gave Jones a hearty buss, shook him by the hand, and took his leave.

Though the lieutenant's reasoning was satisfactory to himself, it was not entirely so to Jones. Therefore, having revolved this matter in his thoughts, he at last came to a resolution.

X

JONES swallowed a large mess of chicken, or rather cock, broth with a very good appetite, as indeed he would have done the cock it was made of, with a pound of bacon into the bargain; and now, finding in himself no deficiency of either health or spirit, he resolved to get up and seek his enemy.

The clock had struck twelve, and everyone in the house were in their beds, except the sentinel who stood to guard Northerton, when Jones softly opening his door, issued forth in pursuit of his enemy. It is not easy to conceive a much more tremendous figure than he now exhibited. He had on a light-colored coat, covered with streams of blood. His face, which missed that very blood, as well as twenty ounces more drawn from him by the surgeon, was pallid. Round his head was a quantity of bandage, not unlike a turban. In the right hand he carried a sword, and in the left a candle. So that the bloody Banquo was not worthy to be compared to him. In fact, I believe a more dreadful apparition was never raised in a churchyard, nor in the imagination of any good people met in a winter evening over a Christmas fire in Somersetshire.

When the sentinel first saw our hero approach, his hair began to lift up his grenadier cap; and in the same instant his knees fell to blows with each other. Presently his whole body was seized with worse than an ague fit. He then fired his piece, and fell flat on his face.

Whether fear or courage was the occasion of his firing, or whether he took aim at the object of his terror, I cannot say. If he did, however, he had the good fortune to miss his man.

Jones seeing the fellow fall, guessed the cause of his fright, at which he could not forbear smiling, not in the least reflecting on the danger from which he had just escaped. He then passed by the fellow, who still continued in the posture in which he fell, and entered the room where Northerton, as he had heard, was confined. Here, in a solitary situation, he found—an empty quart pot standing on the table, on which some beer being spilt, it looked as if the room had lately been inhabited; but at present it was entirely vacant.

Perceiving the bird was flown, at least despairing to find him, and rightly apprehending that the report of the firelock would alarm the whole house, our hero now blew out his candle, and gently stole back again to his chamber, and to his bed. Before he could reach the door to his chamber, the hall where the sentinel had been posted was half full of people, some in their shirts, and others not half dressed, all very earnestly inquiring of each other what was the matter.

The soldier was at length got upon his legs; when candles being brought, and seeing two or three of his comrades present, he came a little to himself; but when they asked him what was the matter? he answered,

"I am a dead man, that's all, I am a dead man, I can't recover it, I have seen him."

"What hast thou seen, Jack?" says one of the soldiers.

"Why, I have seen the young volunteer that was killed yesterday." He then imprecated the most heavy curses on himself, if he had not seen the volunteer, all over blood, vomiting fire out of his mouth and nostrils, pass by him into the chamber where Ensign Northerton was, and then seizing the ensign by the throat, fly away with him in a clap of thunder.

This relation met with a gracious reception from the audience. All the women present believed it firmly, and prayed Heaven to defend them from murder. Amongst the men too, many had faith in the story; but others turned it into derision and ridicule; and a sergeant who was present answered very coolly, "Young man, you will hear more of this, for going to sleep and dreaming on your post."

The soldier replied, "You may punish me if you please; but I was as broad awake as I am now; and the devil carry me away, as he hath the ensign, if I did not see the dead man, as I tell you, with eyes as big and as fiery as two large flambeaux."

But whether Northerton was carried away in thunder or fire, or in whatever other manner he was gone, it was now certain that his body was no longer in custody.

XI

BESIDES the suspicion of sleep, the lieutenant harbored another and worse doubt against the poor sentinel, and this was, that of treachery; for as he believed not one syllable of the apparition, so he imagined the whole to be an invention formed only to impose upon him, and that the fellow had in reality been bribed by Northerton to let him escape.

That the reader, therefore, may not conceive the least ill opinion of such a person, we shall not delay a moment in rescuing his character from the imputation of this guilt.

Mr. Northerton then, as we have before observed, was fully satisfied with the glory which he had obtained from this action. He was, besides, of an active disposition, and had a great antipathy to those close quarters in the castle of Gloucester, for which a justice of peace might possibly give him a billet. Nor was he, moreover, free from some uneasy meditations on a certain wooden edifice, which I forbear to name, in conformity to the opinion of mankind, who, I think, rather ought to honor than to be ashamed of this building, as it is, or at least might be made, of more benefit to society than almost any other public erection. In a word, to hint at no more reasons for his conduct, Mr. Northerton was desirous of departing that evening, and nothing remained for him but to contrive the quomodo, which appeared to be a matter of some difficulty.

Now this young gentleman, though somewhat crooked in his morals, was perfectly straight in his person, which was extremely strong and well made. His face too was accounted handsome by the generality of women, for it was broad and ruddy, with tolerably good teeth. Such charms did not fail making an impression on my landlady, who had no little relish for this kind of beauty. Having obtained, therefore, leave to make him a visit, she proceeded to throw forth some hints, which the other readily and eagerly taking up, they soon came to a right understanding; and it was at length agreed that the ensign should, at a certain signal, ascend the chimney, which communicating very soon with that of the kitchen, he might there again let himself down; for which she would give him an opportunity by keeping the coast clear.

But lest our readers, of a different complexion, should take this occasion of too hastily condemning all compassion as a folly, and pernicious to society, we think proper to mention another particular which might possibly have some little share in this action. The ensign happened to be at this time possessed of the sum of fifty pounds, which did indeed belong to the whole company; for the captain having quarreled with his lieutenant, had entrusted the payment of his company to the ensign. This money, however, he thought proper to deposit in my landlady's hand, possibly by way of bail or security that he would hereafter appear and answer to the charge against him; but whatever were the conditions, certain it is, that she had the money and the ensign his liberty.

The lovely Sophia comes!

Book VIII

CONTAINING ABOUT TWO DAYS

I

JONES had endeavored to close his eyes, but all in vain; his spirits were too lively and wakeful to be lulled to sleep. So having amused, or rather tormented, himself with the thoughts of his Sophia till it was open daylight, he called for some tea; upon which occasion my landlady herself vouchsafed to pay him a visit.

This was indeed the first time she had seen him, or at least had taken any notice of him; but as the lieutenant had assured her that he was certainly some young gentleman of fashion, she now determined to show him all the respect in her power; for, to speak truly, this was one of those houses where gentlemen, to use the language of advertisements, meet with civil treatment for their money.

She had no sooner begun to make his tea, than she likewise began to discourse:

"La! sir," said she, "I think it is great pity that such a pretty young gentleman should undervalue himself so as to go about with these soldier fellows. They call themselves gentlemen, I warrant you; but, as my first husband used to say, they should remember it is we that pay them. Then there's such swearing among 'um, to be sure it frightens me out o' my wits: I thinks nothing can ever prosper with such wicked people. And here one of 'um has used you in so barbarous a manner. Come, come, we know very well what all the matter is; but if one won't, another will; so pretty a gentleman need never want a lady. Nay, don't blush so" (for indeed he did to a violent degree). "Why, you thought, sir, I knew nothing of the matter, I warrant you, about Madam Sophia."

"How," says Jones, starting up, "do you know my Sophia?"

"Do I! ay, marry," cries the landlady; "many's the time hath she lain in this house."

"With her aunt, I suppose," says Jones.

"Why, there it is now," cries the landlady. "Ay, ay, ay, I know the old lady very well. And a sweet young creature is Madam Sophia, that's the truth on't."

"A sweet creature," cries Jones; "O heavens!

> Angels are painted fair to look like her.
> There's in her all that we believe of heav'n.
> Amazing brightness, purity, and truth,
> Eternal joy and everlasting love.

"And could I ever have imagined that you had known my Sophia!"

"I wish," says the landlady, "you knew half so much of her. What would you have given to have sat by her bedside? What a delicious neck she hath! Her lovely limbs have stretched themselves in that very bed you now lie in."

"Here!" cries Jones; "hath Sophia ever laid here?"

"Ay, ay, here; there, in that very bed," says the landlady; "where I wish you had her this moment; and she may wish so too for anything I know to the contrary, for she hath mentioned your name to me."

"Ha!" cries he; "did she ever mention her poor Jones? You flatter me now: I can never believe so much."

"Why, then," answered she, "as I hope to be saved, and may the devil fetch me if I speak a syllable more than the truth, I have heard her mention Mr. Jones; but in a civil and modest way, I confess; yet I could perceive she thought a great deal more than she said."

"O my dear woman!" cries Jones, "her thoughts of me I shall never be worthy of. Oh, she is all gentleness, kindness, goodness! Why was such a rascal as I born, ever to give her soft bosom a moment's uneasiness? Nay, torture itself could not be misery to me, did I but know that she was happy."

"Why, look you there now," says the landlady; "I told her you was a constant lover."

"But pray, madam, tell me when or where you knew anything of me; for I never was here before, nor do I remember ever to have seen you."

"Nor is it possible you should," answered she; "for you was a little thing when I had you in my lap at the squire's."

"How, the squire's?" says Jones: "what, do you know that great and good Mr. Allworthy then?"

"Yes, marry, do I," says she: "who in the country doth not?"

"The fame of his goodness indeed," answered Jones, "must have extended farther than this; but heaven only can know him—can know that benevolence which it copied from itself, and sent upon earth as its own pattern. Mankind are as ignorant of such Divine goodness as they are unworthy of it; but none so unworthy of it as myself. I, who was raised by him to such a height; taken in, as you must well know, a poor base-born child, adopted by him, and treated as his own son, to dare by my follies to disoblige him, to draw his vengeance upon me. Yes, I deserve it all; for I will never be so ungrateful as ever to think he hath done an act of injustice by me. No, I deserve to be turned out of doors, as I am. And now, madam," says he, "I believe you will not blame me for turning soldier, especially with such a fortune as this in my pocket." At which words he shook a purse which had but very little in it, and which still appeared to the landlady to have less.

My good landlady was (according to vulgar phrase) struck all of a heap by this relation. She answered coldly, "That to be sure people were the best judges what was most proper for their circumstances. But hark," says she, "I think I hear somebody call. Coming! coming! the devil's in all our volk; nobody hath any ears. I must go downstairs; if you want any more breakfast the maid will come up. Coming!" At which words, without taking any leave, she flung out of the room; for the lowest sort of people are very tenacious of respect; and though they are contented to give this gratis to persons of quality, yet they never confer it on those of their own order without taking care to be well paid for their pains.

II

BEFORE we proceed any farther, that the reader may not be mistaken in imagining the landlady knew more than she did, nor surprised that she knew so much, it may be necessary to inform him that the lieutenant had acquainted her that the name of Sophia had been the occasion of the quarrel; and as for the rest of her knowledge, the sagacious reader will observe how she came by it in the preceding scene.

She was no sooner gone than Jones reflected that he was in the same bed which he was informed had held his dear Sophia. This occasioned a thousand fond and tender thoughts. In this situation the surgeon found him, when he came to dress his wound.

The doctor perceiving, upon examination, that his pulse was disordered, and hearing that he had not slept, declared that he was in great danger; for he apprehended a fever was coming on, which he would have prevented by bleeding, but Jones would not submit, declaring he would lose no more blood; "and, doctor," says he, "if you will be so kind only to dress my head, I have no doubt of being well in a day or two."

"I wish," answered the surgeon, "I could assure your being well in a month or two. Well, indeed! No, no, people are not so soon well of such contusions; but, sir, I am not at this time of day to be instructed in my operations by a patient, and I insist on making a revulsion before I dress you."

Jones persisted obstinately in his refusal, and the doctor at last yielded; telling him at the same time that he would not be answerable for the ill consequence, and hoped he would do him the justice to acknowledge that he had given him a contrary advice; which the patient promised he would.

The doctor retired into the kitchen, where, addressing himself to the landlady, he complained bitterly of the undutiful behavior of his patient, who would not be blooded, though he was in a fever.

"It is an eating fever then," says the landlady, "for he hath devoured two swinging buttered toasts this morning for breakfast."

"Very likely," says the doctor: "I have known people to eat in a fever; and it is very easily accounted for; because the acidity occasioned by the febrile matter may stimulate the nerves of the diaphragm, and thereby occasion a craving which will not be easily distinguishable from a natural appetite; but the aliment will not be concreted, nor assimilated into chyle, and so will corrode the vascular orifices, and thus will aggravate the febrific symptoms. Indeed, I think the gentleman in a very dangerous way, and, if he is not blooded, I am afraid will die."

"Every man must die some time or other," answered the good

woman; "it is no business of mine. I hope, doctor, you would not have me hold him while you bleed him. But, hark'ee, a word in your ear; I would advise you, before you proceed too far, to take care who is to be your paymaster."

"Paymaster!" said the doctor, staring; "why, I've a gentleman under my hands, have I not?"

"I imagined so as well as you," said the landlady; "but, as my first husband used to say, everything is not what it looks to be. He is an arrant scrub, I assure you. However, take no notice that I mentioned anything to you of the matter; but I think people in business oft always to let one another know such things."

"And have I suffered such a fellow as this," cries the doctor, in a passion, "to instruct me? Shall I hear my practice insulted by one who will not pay me? I am glad I have made this discovery in time. I will see now whether he will be blooded or no." He then immediately went upstairs, and flinging open the door of the chamber with much violence, awaked poor Jones from a very sound nap, into which he was fallen, and, what was still worse, from a delicious dream concerning Sophia.

"Will you be blooded or no?" cries the doctor, in a rage.

"I have told you my resolution already," answered Jones, "and I wish with all my heart you had taken my answer; for you have awaked me out of the sweetest sleep which I ever had in my life."

"Ay, ay," cries the doctor; "many a man hath dozed away his life. Sleep is not always good, no more than food; but remember, I demand of you for the last time, will you be blooded?"

"I answer you for the last time," said Jones, "I will not."

"Then I wash my hands of you," cries the doctor; "and I desire you to pay me for the trouble I have had already. Two journeys at five shillings each, two dressings at five shillings more, and half a crown for phlebotomy."

"I hope," said Jones, "you don't intend to leave me in this condition."

"Indeed but I shall," said the other.

"Then," said Jones, "you have used me rascally, and I will not pay you a farthing."

"Very well," cries the doctor; "the first loss is the best. What a pox did my landlady mean by sending for me to such vagabonds!" At which words he flung out of the room, and his patient turning himself about soon recovered his sleep; but his dream was unfortunately gone.

III

THE clock had now struck five when Jones awaked from a nap of seven hours, so much refreshed, and in such perfect health and spirits, that he resolved to get up and dress himself; for which purpose he unlocked his portmanteaus, and took out clean linen, and a suit of clothes; but first he slipped on a frock, and went down into the kitchen to bespeak something that might pacify certain tumults he found rising within his stomach.

Meeting the landlady, he accosted her with great civility, and asked, "What he could have for dinner?"

"For dinner!" says she; "it is an odd time a day to think about dinner. There is nothing dressed in the house, and the fire is almost out."

"Well, but," says he, "I must have something to eat, and it is almost indifferent to me what; for, to tell you the truth, I was never more hungry in my life."

"Then," says she, "I believe there is a piece of cold buttock and carrot, which will fit you."

"Nothing better," answered Jones; "but I should be obliged to you, if you would let it be fried." To which the landlady consented, and said, smiling, "she was glad to see him so well recovered"; for the sweetness of our hero's temper was almost irresistible.

Jones now returned in order to dress himself, while his dinner was preparing, and was, according to his orders, attended by the barber.

This barber, who went by the name of Little Benjamin, was a fellow of great oddity and humor, which had frequently let him into small inconveniences, such as slaps in the face, kicks in the breech, broken bones, etc. For everyone doth not understand a jest; and those who do are often displeased with being themselves the subjects of it. This vice was, however, incurable in him; and though he had often smarted for it, yet if ever he conceived a joke, he was certain to be delivered of it, without the least respect of persons, time, or place.

Jones being impatient to be dressed, for a reason which may be easily imagined, thought the shaver was very tedious in preparing his suds, and begged him to make haste; to which the other answered with much gravity, for he never discomposed his muscles on any account,

"*Festina lente* is a proverb which I learned long before I ever touched a razor."

"I find, friend, you are a scholar," replied Jones.

"A poor one," said the barber, "*non omnia possumus omnes*."

"I conjecture," says Jones, "that thou art a very comical fellow."

"You mistake me widely, sir," said the barber: "I am too much addicted to the study of philosophy; *hinc illæ lacrymæ*, sir; that's my misfortune. Too much learning hath been my ruin."

"Indeed," says Jones, "I confess, friend, you have more learning than generally belongs to your trade; but I can't see how it can have injured you."

"Alas! sir," answered the shaver, "my father disinherited me for it. He was a dancing-master; and because I could read before I could dance, he took an aversion to me, and left every farthing among his other children."

"Upon my word," cries Jones, "thou art a very odd fellow, and I shall be very glad if thou wilt come to me after dinner, and drink a glass with me; I long to be better acquainted with thee."

"O dear sir!" said the barber, "I can do you twenty times as great a favor, if you will accept of it."

"What is that, my friend?" cries Jones.

"Why, I will drink a bottle with you if you please; for I dearly love good-nature; and as you have found me out to be a comical fellow, so I have no skill in physiognomy, if you are not one of the best-natured gentlemen in the universe."

Jones now walked downstairs neatly dressed, and perhaps the fair Adonis was not a lovelier figure; and yet he had no charms for my landlady; for as that good woman did not resemble Venus at all in her person, so neither did she in her taste. Happy had it been for Nanny the chambermaid, if she had seen with the eyes of her mistress, for that poor girl fell so violently in love with Jones in five minutes, that her passion afterwards cost her many a sigh.

He was, after some time, attended by the barber, who would not indeed have suffered him to wait so long for his company had he not been listening in the kitchen to the landlady, who was entertaining a circle that she had gathered round her with the history of poor Jones, part of which she had extracted from his own lips, and the other part was her own ingenious composition; for she said "he was a poor parish boy, taken into the house of Squire Allworthy, where he was bred up as an apprentice, and now turned out of doors for his misdeeds, particularly for making love to his young mistress, and probably for robbing the house; for how else should he come by the little money he hath; and this," says she, "is your gentleman."

"A servant of Squire Allworthy!" says the barber; "what's his name?"

"Why he told me his name was Jones," says she: "perhaps he goes by a wrong name. Nay, and he told me, too, that the squire had maintained him as his own son, thof he had quarreled with him now."

"And if his name be Jones, he told you the truth," said the barber; "for I have relations who live in that country; nay, and some people say he is his son."

"Why doth he not go by the name of his father?"

"I can't tell that," said the barber; "many people's sons don't go by the name of their father."

"Nay," said the landlady, "if I thought he was a gentleman's son, thof he was a bye-blow, I should behave to him in another guess manner; for many of these bye-blows come to be great men, and, as my poor first husband used to say, never affront any customer that's a gentleman."

IV

IN THE morning Jones grew a little uneasy at the desertion of his surgeon; he inquired therefore of the drawer, what other surgeons were to be met with in that neighborhood. The drawer told him there was one not far off; "but, sir," says he, "if you will take my advice, there is not a man in the kingdom can do your business better than the barber who was with you last night."

The drawer was presently despatched for Little Benjamin, who being acquainted in what capacity he was wanted, prepared himself accordingly, and attended; but with so different an air and aspect from that which he wore when his basin was under his arm, that he could scarce be known to be the same person.

"So, tonsor," says Jones, "I find you have more trades than one; how come you not to inform me of this last night?"

"A surgeon," answered Benjamin, with great gravity, "is a profession, not a trade. The reason why I did not acquaint you last night that I professed this art, was, that I then concluded you was under the hands of another gentleman, and I never love to interfere with my brethren in their business. *Ars omnibus communis*. But now, sir, if you please, I will inspect your head, and when I see into your skull, I will give my opinion of your case."

Jones had no great faith in this new professor; however, he suffered him to open the bandage and to look at his wound; which as soon as he had done, Benjamin began to groan and shake his head violently. Upon which Jones, in a peevish manner, bid him not play the fool, but tell him in what condition he found him.

"Shall I answer you as a surgeon, or a friend?" said Benjamin.

"As a friend and seriously," said Jones.

"Why, then, upon my soul," cries Benjamin, "it would require a great deal of art to keep you from being well after a very few dressings; and if you will suffer me to apply some salve of mine, I will answer for the success." Jones gave his consent, and the plaster was applied accordingly.

"There, sir," cries Benjamin: "now I will, if you please, resume my former self; but a man is obliged to keep up some dignity in his countenance whilst he is performing these operations, or the world will not submit to be handled by him. You can't imagine, sir, of how much consequence a grave aspect is to a grave character. A barber may make you laugh, but a surgeon ought rather to make you cry."

"Mr. Barber, or Mr. Surgeon, or Mr. Barber-surgeon," said Jones, "you certainly are one of the oddest, most comical fellows I ever met with, and must have something very surprising in your story, which you must confess I have a right to hear."

"I do confess it," answered Benjamin, "and will very readily acquaint you with it; but first I will fasten the door, that none may interrupt us." He did so, and then advancing with a solemn air to Jones, said: "I must begin by telling you, sir, that you yourself have been the greatest enemy I ever had."

Jones was a little startled at this sudden declaration. "I your enemy, sir!" says he, with much amazement, and some sternness in his look.

"Nay, be not angry," said Benjamin, "for I promise you I am not. You are perfectly innocent of having intended me any wrong; for you was then an infant: but I shall, I believe, unriddle all this the moment I mention my name. Did you never hear, sir, of one Partridge, who had the honor of being reputed your father, and the misfortune of being ruined by that honor?"

"I have, indeed, heard of that Partridge," says Jones, "and have always believed myself to be his son."

"Well, sir," answered Benjamin, "I am that Partridge; but I here absolve you from all filial duty, for I do assure you, you are no son of mine."

"How!" replied Jones, "and is it possible that a false suspicion should have drawn all the ill consequences upon you, with which I am too well acquainted?"

"It is possible," cries Benjamin, "for it is so: but I am convinced, from this extraordinary meeting, that you are born to make me amends for all I have suffered on that account. Besides, I dreamt, the night before I saw you, that I stumbled over a stool without hurting myself; which plainly showed me something good was towards me: and last night I dreamt again, that I rode behind you on a milk-white mare, which is a very excellent dream, and betokens much good fortune, which I am resolved to pursue unless you have the cruelty to deny me."

"I should be very glad, Mr. Partridge," answered Jones, "to have it in my power to make you amends for your sufferings on my account, though at present I see no likelihood of it; however, I assure you I will deny you nothing which is in my power to grant."

"It is in your power sure enough," replied Benjamin; "for I desire nothing more than leave to attend you in this expedition. Nay, I have so entirely set my heart upon it, that if you should refuse me, you will kill both a barber and a surgeon in one breath."

Jones answered, smiling, that he should be very sorry to be the occasion of so much mischief to the public. He then advanced many prudential reasons, in order to dissuade Benjamin (whom we shall hereafter call Partridge) from his purpose; but all were in vain. Partridge relied strongly on his dream of the milk-white mare.

"Besides, sir," says he, "I promise you I have as good an inclination to the cause as any man can possibly have; and go I will, whether you admit me to go in your company or not."

Jones, who was as much pleased with Partridge as Partridge could be with him, and who had not consulted his own inclination but the good of the other in desiring him to stay behind, when he found his friend so resolute at last gave his consent; but then recollecting himself, he said, "Perhaps, Mr. Partridge, you think I shall be able to support you, but I really am not"; and then taking out his purse, he told out nine guineas, which he declared were his whole fortune.

Partridge answered, "That his dependence was only on his future favor; for he was thoroughly convinced he would shortly have enough in his power. At present, sir," said he, "I believe I am rather the richer man of the two; but all I have is at your service, and at your disposal. I insist upon your taking the whole, and I beg only to attend you in the quality of your servant"; but to this generous proposal concerning the money Jones, of course, would by no means submit.

It was resolved to set out the next morning, when a difficulty arose concerning the baggage; for the portmanteau of Mr. Jones was too large to be carried without a horse.

"If I may presume to give my advice," says Partridge, "this portmanteau, with everything in it, except a few shirts, should be left behind. Those I shall be easily able to carry for you, and the rest of your clothes will remain very safe locked up in my house."

This method was no sooner proposed than agreed to; and then the barber departed, in order to prepare everything for his intended expedition.

V

THOUGH Partridge was one of the most superstitious of men, he would hardly perhaps have desired to accompany Jones on his expedition merely from the omens of the joint-stool and white mare, if his prospect had been no better than to have shared the plunder gained in the field of battle. In fact, when Partridge came to ruminate on the relations he had heard from Jones, he could not reconcile to himself that Mr. Allworthy should turn his son (for so he most firmly believed him to be) out of doors, for any reason which he had heard assigned. He concluded, therefore, that the whole was a fiction, and that Jones, of whom he had often from his correspondents heard the wildest character, had in reality run away from his father. It came into his head, therefore, that if he could prevail with the young gentleman to return back to his father, he should by that means render a service to Allworthy, which would obliterate all his former anger; nay, indeed, he conceived that very anger was counterfeited, and that Allworthy had sacrificed him to his own reputation. And this suspicion indeed he well accounted for, from the tender behavior of that excellent man to the foundling child; from his great severity to Partridge, who, knowing himself to be innocent, could not conceive that any other should think him guilty; lastly, from the allowance which he had privately received long after the annuity had been publicly taken from him, and which he looked upon as a kind of smart-money, or rather by way of atonement for injustice; for it is very uncommon, I believe, for men to ascribe the benefactions they receive to pure charity, when they can possibly impute them to any other motive. If he could by any means therefore persuade the young gentleman to return home, he doubted not but that he should again be received into the favor of Allworthy, and well rewarded for his pains; nay, and should be again restored to his native country—a restoration which Ulysses himself never wished more heartily than poor Partridge.

Early in the morning Partridge appeared at the bedside of Jones, ready equipped for the journey, with his knapsack at his back. This was his own workmanship; for besides his other trades, he was no indifferent tailor. He had already put up his whole stock of linen in it, consisting of four shirts, to which he now added eight for Mr. Jones; and then packing up the portmanteau, he was departing with it towards his own house, but was stopped in his way by the landlady, who refused to suffer any removals till after the payment of the reckoning.

The landlady was, as we have said, absolute governess in these regions; it was therefore necessary to comply with her rules; so the bill was presently writ out, which amounted to a much larger sum than might have been expected, from the entertainment which Jones had met with. But here we are obliged to disclose some maxims, which publicans hold to be the grand mysteries of their trade. The first is, If they have anything good in their house (which indeed very seldom happens) to produce it only to persons who travel with great equipages. Secondly, To charge the same for the very worst provisions, as if they were the best. And, lastly, If any of their guests call but for little, to make them pay a double price for everything they have; so that the amount by the head may be much the same.

The bill being made and discharged, Jones set forward with Partridge, carrying his knapsack; nor did the landlady condescend to wish him a good journey; for this was, it seems, an inn frequented by people of fashion; and I know not whence it is, but all those who get their livelihood by people of fashion, contract as much insolence to the rest of mankind, as if they really belonged to that rank themselves.

VI

MR. JONES and Partridge, or Little Benjamin (which epithet of Little was perhaps given him ironically, he being in reality near six feet high), having left their last quarters in the manner before described, traveled on to Gloucester without meeting any adventure worth relating.

The shadows began now to descend larger from the high mountains; the feathered creation had betaken themselves to their rest.

Now the highest order of mortals were sitting down to their dinners, and the lowest order to their suppers. In a word, the clock struck five just as Mr. Jones took his leave of Gloucester; an hour at which (as it was now mid-winter), the dirty fingers of Night would have drawn her sable curtain over the universe, had not the moon forbid her, who now, with a face as broad and as red as those of some jolly mortals, who, like her, turn night into day, began to rise from her bed, where she had slumbered away the day, in order to sit up all night. Jones had not traveled far before he paid his compliments to that beautiful planet, and, turning to his companion, asked him if he had ever beheld so delicious an evening? He then told Partridge the story from the Spectator, of two lovers who had agreed to entertain themselves when they were at a great distance from each other, by repairing, at a certain fixed hour, to look at the moon; thus pleasing themselves with the thought that they were both employed in contemplating the same object at the same time.

"Those lovers," added he, "must have had souls truly capable of feeling all the tenderness of the sublimest of all human passions."

"Very probably," cries Partridge: "but I envy them more, if they had bodies incapable of feeling cold; for I am almost frozen to death."

"Fie upon it, Mr. Partridge!" says Jones, "have a better heart; consider you are going to face an enemy; and are you afraid of facing a little cold? I wish, indeed, we had a guide to advise which of these roads we should take."

"May I be so bold," says Partridge, "to offer my advice? *Interdum stultus opportuna loquitur.*"

"Why, which of them," cries Jones, "would you recommend?"

"Truly neither of them," answered Partridge. "The only road we can be certain of finding is the road we came. A good hearty pace will bring us back to Gloucester in an hour; but if we go forward, the Lord Harry knows when we shall arrive at any place; for I see at least fifty miles before me, and no house in all the way."

"You see, indeed, a very fair prospect," says Jones, "which receives great additional beauty from the extreme luster of the moon. However, if you are inclined to quit me, you may, and return back again; but for my part, I am resolved to go forward."

"It is unkind in you, sir," says Partridge, "to suspect me of any such intention. What I have advised hath been as much on your account as on my own: but since you are determined to go on, I am as much determined to follow. *I præ, sequar te.*"

They now traveled some miles without speaking to each other, during which suspense of discourse Jones often sighed, and Benjamin groaned as bitterly, though from a very different reason. At length Jones made a full stop, and turning about, cries,

"Who knows, Partridge, but the loveliest creature in the universe may have her eyes now fixed on that very moon which I behold at this instant?"

"Very likely, sir," answered Partridge; "and if my eyes were fixed on a good sirloin of roast beef, the devil might take the moon and her horns into the bargain; but I wish, sir, that the moon was a looking-glass for your sake, and that Miss Sophia Western was now placed before it."

Just as Jones and his friend came to the end of their dialogue, they arrived at the bottom of a very steep hill. Here Jones stopped short, and directing his eyes upwards, stood for a while silent. At length he called to his companion, and said,

"Partridge, I wish I was at the top of this hill; it must certainly afford a most charming prospect, especially by this light; for the solemn gloom which the moon casts on all objects is beyond expression beautiful, especially to an imagination which is desirous of cultivating melancholy ideas."

"Very probably," answered Partridge; "but if the top of the hill be properest to produce melancholy thoughts, I suppose the bottom is the likeliest to produce merry ones, and these I take to be much the better of the two. I protest you have made my blood run cold with the very mentioning the top of that mountain, which seems to me to be one of the highest in the world. No, no, if we look for anything, let it be for a place underground, to screen ourselves from the frost."

"Do so," said Jones; "let it be but within hearing of this place, and I will halloo to you at my return back."

"Pardon me, sir," cries Partridge; "I have determined to follow you wherever you go." Indeed he was now afraid to stay behind; for though he was coward enough in all respects, yet his chief fear was that of ghosts, with which the present time of night, and the wildness of the place, extremely well suited.

At this instant Partridge espied a glimmering light through some trees, which seemed very near to them. He immediately cried out in a rapture, "Oh, sir! Heaven hath at last heard my prayers, and hath brought us to a house; perhaps it may be an inn. Let me beseech you, sir, if you have any compassion either for me or yourself, do not despise the goodness of Providence, but let us go directly to yon light. Whether it be a public-house or no, I am sure if they be Christians that dwell there, they will not refuse a little house-room to persons in our miserable condition." Jones at length yielded to the earnest supplications of Partridge, and both together made directly towards the place whence the light issued.

They soon arrived at the door of this house, or cottage, for it might be called either, without much impropriety. Here Jones knocked several times without receiving any answer from within; at which Partridge, whose head was full of nothing but of ghosts, devils, witches, and such like, began to tremble, crying,

"Lord, have mercy upon us! surely the people must be all dead. I can see no light neither now, and yet I am certain I saw a candle burning but a moment before. Well! I have heard of such things."

"What hast thou heard of?" said Jones. "The people are either fast asleep, or probably, as this is a lonely place, are afraid to open their door." He then began to vociferate pretty loudly, and at last an old woman, opening an upper casement, asked, Who they were, and what they wanted? Jones answered, They were travelers who had lost their way, and having seen a light in the window, had been led thither in hopes of finding some fire to warm themselves.

"Whoever you are," cries the woman, "you have no business here; nor shall I open the door to anyone at this time of night."

Partridge, whom the sound of a human voice had recovered from his fright, fell to the most earnest supplications to be admitted for a few minutes to the fire, saying, he was almost dead with the cold; to which fear had indeed contributed equally with the frost. He assured her that the gentleman who spoke to her was one of the greatest squires in the country; and made use of every argument, save one, which Jones afterwards effectually added; and this was, the promise of half-a-crown;—a bribe too great to be resisted by such a person, especially as the genteel appearance of Jones, which the light of the moon plainly discovered to her, together with his affable behavior, had entirely subdued those apprehensions of thieves which she had at first conceived. She agreed, at last, to let them in; where Partridge, to his infinite joy, found a good fire aready for his reception.

The house was furnished in the most neat and elegant manner. To say the truth, Jones himself was not a little surprised at what he saw; for, besides the extraordinary neatness of the room, it was adorned with a great number of nicknacks and curiosities, which might have engaged the attention of a virtuoso.

While Jones was admiring these things, the old woman said, "I hope, gentlemen, you will make what haste you can; for I expect my master presently, and I would not for double the money he should find you here."

"Then you have a master?" cried Jones. "Indeed, you will excuse me, good woman, but I was surprised to see all those fine things in your house."

"Ah, sir," said she, "if the twentieth part of these things were mine, I should think myself a rich woman. But pray, sir, do not stay much longer, for I look for him in every minute."

"Why, sure he would not be angry with you," said Jones, "for doing a common act of charity?"

"Alack-a-day, sir!" said she, "he is a strange man, not at all like other people. He keeps no company with anybody, and seldom walks out except by night, for he doth not care to be seen; and all the country people are as much afraid of meeting him; for his dress is enough to frighten those who are not used to it. They call him, the Man of the Hill (for there he walks by night), and the country people are not, I believe, more afraid of the devil himself. He would be terribly angry if he found you here."

"I should imagine, by this collection of rarities," cries Jones, "that your master had been a traveler."

"Yes, sir," answered she, "he hath been a very great one: there be few gentlemen that know more of all matters than he. I fancy he hath been crossed in love, or whatever it is I know not; but I have lived with him above these thirty years, and in all that time he hath hardly spoke to six living people."

She then again solicited their departure, in which she was backed by Partridge; but Jones purposely protracted the time, for his curiosity was greatly raised to see this extraordinary person. Though the old woman, therefore, concluded every one of her answers with desiring him to be gone, and Partridge proceeded so far as to pull him by the sleeve, he still continued to invent new questions, till the old woman, with an affrighted countenance, declared she heard her master's signal; and at the same instant more than one voice was heard without the door, crying, "D—n your blood, show us your money this instant. Your money, you villain, or we will blow your brains about your ears."

"O, good heaven!" cries the old woman, "some villains, to be sure, have attacked my master. O la! what shall I do? what shall I do?"

Jones made her no answer; but snatching an old broadsword

which hung in the room, he instantly sallied out, where he found the old gentleman struggling with two ruffians, and begging for mercy. Jones asked no questions, but fell so briskly to work with his broadsword, that the fellows immediately quitted their hold; and without offering to attack our hero, betook themselves to their heels and made their escape; for he did not attempt to pursue them, being contented with having delivered the old gentleman; and indeed he concluded he had pretty well done their business, for both of them, as they ran off, cried out with bitter oaths that they were dead men.

Jones presently ran to lift up the old gentleman, who had been thrown down in the scuffle, expressing at the same time great concern lest he should have received any harm from the villains. The old man stared a moment at Jones, and then cried,

"No, sir, no, I have very little harm, I thank you. Lord have mercy upon me!"

"I see, sir," said Jones, "you are not free from apprehensions even of those who have had the happiness to be your deliverers; nor can I blame any suspicions which you may have; but indeed you have no real occasion for any; here are none but your friends present. Having missed our way this cold night, we took the liberty of warming ourselves at your fire, whence we were just departing when we heard you call for assistance, which, I must say, Providence alone seems to have sent you."

"Providence, indeed," cries the old gentleman, "if it be so."

"So it is, I assure you," cries Jones. "Here is your own sword, sir; I have used it in your defense, and I now return it into your hands."

The old man having received the sword, which was stained with the blood of his enemies, looked steadfastly at Jones during some moments, and then with a sigh cried out,

"You will pardon me, young gentleman; I was not always of a suspicious temper, nor am I a friend to ingratitude."

"Be thankful then," cries Jones, "to that Providence to which you owe your deliverance: as to my part, I have only discharged the common duties of humanity, and what I would have done for any fellow-creature in your situation."

"Let me look at you a little longer," cries the old gentleman. "You are a human creature then? Well, perhaps you are. Come pray walk into my little hut. You have been my deliverer indeed."

The old woman was distracted between the fears which she had of her master, and for him; and Partridge was, if possible, in a greater fright. To say the truth, it was an appearance which might have affected a more constant mind than that of Mr. Partridge. This person was of the tallest size, with a long beard as white as snow. His body was clothed with the skin of an ass, made something into the form of a coat. He wore likewise boots on his legs, and a cap on his head, both composed of the skin of some other animals.

"I am afraid, sir," said the old gentleman to Jones, "that I have nothing in this house which you can either eat or drink, unless you will accept a dram of brandy; of which I can give you some most excellent, and which I have had by me these thirty years." Jones declined this offer in a very civil and proper speech, and then the other asked him. "Whither he was traveling when he missed his way?" saying, "I must own myself surprised to see such a person as you appear to be journeying on foot at this time of night. I suppose, sir, you are a gentleman of these parts; for you do not look like one who is used to travel far without horses?"

"Appearances," cried Jones, "are often deceitful; men sometimes look what they are not. I assure you I am not of this country; and whither I am traveling, in reality I scarce know myself."

"Whoever you are, or whithersoever you are going," answered the old man, "I have obligations to you which I can never return."

"I once more," replied Jones, "affirm that you have none; for there can be no merit in having hazarded that in your service on which I set no value; and nothing is so contemptible in my eyes as life."

"I am sorry, young gentleman," answered the stranger, "that you have any reason to be so unhappy at your years."

"Indeed I am, sir," answered Jones, "the most unhappy of mankind."

"Perhaps you have had a friend, or a mistress?" replied the other.

"How could you," cried Jones, "mention two words sufficient to drive me to distraction?"

"Either of them are enough to drive any man to distraction," answered the old man. "I inquire no farther, sir; perhaps my curiosity hath led me too far already."

"I have not, sir," cried Jones, "the assurance to ask it of you now; but you will give me leave to wish for some further opportunity of hearing the excellent observations which a man of your sense and knowledge of the world must have made in so long a course of travels."

"Indeed, young gentleman," answered the stranger, "I will endeavor to satisfy your curiosity, as far as I am able."

IN ITALY the landlords are very silent. In France they are more talkative, but yet civil. In Germany and Holland they are generally very impertinent. And as for their honesty, I believe it is pretty equal in all those countries. The *laquais à louange* are sure to lose no opportunity of cheating you; and as for the postilions, I think they are pretty much alike all the world over. These, sir, are the observations on men which I made in my travels; for these were the only men I ever conversed with. My design, when I went abroad, was to divert myself by seeing the wondrous variety of prospects, beasts, birds, fishes, insects, and vegetables, with which God has been pleased to enrich the several parts of this globe; a variety which, as it must give great pleasure to a contemplative beholder, so doth it admirably display the power, and wisdom, and goodness of the Creator. Indeed, to say the truth, there is but one work in His whole creation that doth Him any dishonor, and with that I have long since avoided holding any conversation."

"You will pardon me," cries Jones; "but I have always imagined that there is in this very work you mention as great variety as in all the rest; for, besides the difference of inclination, customs and climates have, I am told, introduced the utmost diversity into human nature."

"Very little indeed," answered the other: "those who travel in order to acquaint themselves with the different manners of men might spare themselves much pains by going to a carnival at Venice; for there they will see at once all which they can discover in the several courts of Europe. The same hypocrisy, the same fraud; in short, the same follies and vices dressed in different habits. In Spain, these are equipped with much gravity; and in Italy, with vast splendor. In France, a knave is dressed like a fop; and in the northern countries, like a sloven. But human nature is everywhere the same, everywhere the object of detestation and scorn.

"As for my own part, I passed through all these nations as you perhaps may have done through a crowd at a show—jostling to get by them, holding my nose with one hand, and defending my pockets with the other, without speaking a word to any of them, while I was pressing on to see what I wanted to see; which, however entertaining it might be in itself, scarce made me amends for the trouble the company gave me."

"Did not you find some of the nations among which you traveled less troublesome to you than others?" said Jones.

"Oh yes," replied the old man: "the Turks were much more tolerable to me than the Christians; for they are men of profound taciturnity, and never disturb a stranger with questions. Now and then, indeed, they bestow a short curse upon him, or spit in his face as he walks the streets, but then they have done with him; and a man may live an age in their country without hearing a dozen words from them."

Jones thanked the stranger for the trouble he had taken, and then expressed some wonder how he could possibly endure a life of such solitude; "in which," says he, "you may well complain of the want of variety. Indeed I am astonished how you have filled up, or rather killed, so much of your time."

"I am not at all surprised," answered the other, "that to one whose affections and thoughts are fixed on the world my hours should appear to have wanted employment in this place: but there is one single act, for which the whole life of man is infinitely too short: what time can suffice for the contemplation and worship of that glorious, immortal, and eternal Being, among the works of whose stupendous creation not only this globe, but even those numberless luminaries which we may here behold spangling all the sky, though they should many of them be suns lighting different systems of worlds, may possibly appear but as a few atoms opposed to the whole earth which we inhabit? Shall the pace of time seem sluggish to a mind exercised in studies so high, so important, and so glorious? As no time is sufficient, so no place is improper, for this great concern. It is not necessary that the rising sun should dart his fiery glories over the eastern horizon; nor that the boisterous winds should rush from their caverns, and shake the lofty forest; nor that the opening clouds should pour their deluges on the plains: it is not necessary, I say, that any of these should proclaim His majesty: there is not an insect, not a vegetable, of so low an order in the creation as not to be honored with bearing marks of the attributes of its great Creator; marks not only of His power, but of His wisdom and goodness. Man alone, the king of this globe, the last and greatest work of the Supreme Being, below the sun—man alone hath basely dishonored his own nature; and by dishonesty, cruelty, ingratitude, and treachery, hath called his Maker's goodness in question, by puzzling us to account how a benevolent Being should form so foolish and so vile an animal. Yet this is the being from whose conversation you think, I suppose, that I have been unfortunately restrained, and without whose blessed society, life, in your opinion, must be tedious and insipid."

"In the former part of what you said," replied Jones, "I most heartily and readily concur; but I believe, as well as hope, that the abhorrence which you express for mankind in the conclusion, is much too general. Indeed, you here fall into an error, which in my little experience I have observed to be a very common one, by taking the character of mankind from the worst and basest among them; whereas, indeed, as an excellent writer observes, nothing should be esteemed as characteristical of a species, but what is to be found among the best and most perfect individuals of that species. If there was, indeed, much more wickedness in the world than there is, it would not prove such general assertions against human nature, since much of this arrives by mere accident, and many a man who commits evil is not totally bad and corrupt in his heart. In truth, none seem to have any title to assert human nature to be necessarily and universally evil, but those whose own minds afford them one instance of this natural depravity; which is not, I am convinced, your case."

"And such," said the stranger, "will be always the most backward to assert any such thing. Knaves will no more endeavor to persuade us of the baseness of mankind than a highwayman will inform you that there are thieves on the road. This would, indeed, be a method to put you on your guard, and to defeat their own purposes."

The day now began to send forth its first streams of light, when Jones made an apology to the stranger for having stayed so long, and perhaps detained him from his rest. The stranger answered, "He never wanted rest less than at present; for that day and night were indifferent seasons to him; and that he commonly made use of the former for the time of his repose and of the latter for his walks and lucubrations. However," said he, "it is now a most lovely morning, and if you can bear any longer to be without your own rest or food, I will gladly entertain you with the sight of some very fine prospects which I believe you have not yet seen."

Jones very readily embraced this offer, and they immediately set forward together from the cottage. As for Partridge, he had fallen into a profound repose. Jones therefore left him to enjoy his nap; and as the reader may perhaps be at this season glad of the same favor, we will here put an end to the eighth book of our history.

Book IX

CONTAINING TWELVE HOURS

I

THEY walked to that part of the hill which hangs over a vast and extensive wood. Here they were no sooner arrived than they heard at a distance the most violent screams of a woman, proceeding from the wood below them. Jones listened a moment, and then, without saying a word to his companion (for indeed the occasion seemed sufficiently pressing), ran or rather slid down the hill, and, without the least apprehension or concern for his own safety, made directly to the thicket whence the sound had issued.

He had not entered far into the wood before he beheld a most shocking sight indeed, a woman stripped half naked, under the hands of a ruffian, who had put his garter round her neck, and was endeavoring to draw her up to a tree. Jones asked no questions at this interval, but fell instantly upon the villain, and made such good use of his trusty oaken stick that he laid him sprawling on the ground before he could defend himself, indeed almost before he knew he was attacked; nor did he cease the prosecution of his blows till the woman herself begged him to forbear, saying, she believed he had sufficiently done his business.

The redeemed captive seemed to be at least of the middle age, nor had her face much appearance of beauty; but her clothes being torn from all the upper part of her body, her breasts, which were well formed and extremely white, attracted the eyes of her deliverer, and for a few moments they stood silent, and gazing at each other; till the ruffian on the ground beginning to move, Jones took the garter which had been intended for another purpose, and bound both his hands behind him. And now, on contemplating his face, he discovered, greatly to his surprise, and perhaps not a little to his satisfaction, this very person to be no other than Ensign Northerton.

Jones helped Northerton upon his legs, and then looking him steadfastly in the face, "I fancy, sir," said he, "you did not expect to meet me any more in this world, and I confess I had as little expectation to find you here. However, Fortune, I see, hath brought us once more together, and hath given me satisfaction for the injury I have received, even without my own knowledge."

"It is very much like a man of honor, indeed," answered Northerton, "to take satisfaction by knocking a man down behind his back. Neither am I capable of giving you satisfaction here, as I have no sword; but if you dare behave like a gentleman, let us go where I can furnish myself with one, and I will do by you as a man of honor ought."

"Doth it become such a villain as you are," cries Jones, "to contaminate the name of honor by assuming it? But I shall waste no time in discourse with you. Justice requires satisfaction of you now, and shall have it."

Then turning to the woman, he asked her if she was acquainted with any house in the neighborhood where she might procure herself some decent clothes, in order to proceed to a justice of the peace. She answered she was an entire stranger in that part of the world.

The good Man of the Hill, when our hero departed, had sat himself down on the brow, where, though he had a gun in his hand, he with great patience and unconcern had attended the issue. Jones exerted his utmost agility, and with surprising expedition ascended the hill. The old man advised him to carry the woman to Upton, which, he said, was the nearest town, and Jones, having received direction to the place, took his leave of the Man of the Hill, desiring him to direct Partridge the same way.

Our hero had considered that as the ruffian's hands were tied behind him, he was incapable of executing any wicked purposes on the poor woman. But Jones unluckily forgot, that though the hands of Northerton were tied, his legs were at liberty; nor did he lay the least injunction on the prisoner that he should not make what use of these he pleased. Northerton, therefore, having given no parole of that kind, thought he might without any breach of honor depart; not being obliged, as he imagined, by any rules, to wait for a formal discharge. He therefore took up his legs, which were at liberty, and walked off through the woods, which favored his retreat.

Jones would have spent some time in searching for Northerton, but the woman would not permit him; earnestly entreating that he would accompany her to the town.

"As to the fellow's escape," said she, "it gives me no uneasiness; for philosophy and Christianity both preach up forgiveness of injuries. But for you, sir, I am concerned at the trouble I give you; nay, indeed, my nakedness may well make me ashamed to look you in the face; and if it was not for the sake of your protection, I should wish to go alone."

Jones offered her his coat; but, I know not for what reason, she absolutely refused the most earnest solicitations to accept it. He then begged her to forget both the causes of her confusion.

"With regard to the former," says he, "I have done no more than my duty in protecting you; and as for the latter, I will entirely remove it, by walking before you all the way, for I would not have my eyes offend you."

Thus our hero and the redeemed lady walked in the same manner as Orpheus and Eurydice marched heretofore; but though I cannot believe that Jones was designedly tempted by his fair one to look behind him, yet as she frequently wanted his assistance to help her over stiles, and had besides many trips and other accidents, he was often obliged to turn about. However, he had better fortune than what attended poor Orpheus, for he brought his companion, or rather follower, safe into the famous town of Upton.

II

THOUGH the reader, we doubt not, is very eager to know who this lady was, and how she fell into the hands of Mr. Northerton, we must beg him to suspend his curiosity for a short time, as we are obliged, for some very good reasons which hereafter, perhaps, he may guess, to delay his satisfaction a little longer.

Mr. Jones and his fair companion no sooner entered the town, than they went directly to that inn which in their eyes presented the fairest appearance to the street. Here Jones, having ordered a servant to show a room above stairs, was ascending, when the disheveled fair, hastily following, was laid hold on by the master of the house, who cried, "Heyday, where is that beggar wench going? Stay below stairs, I desire you." But Jones at that instant thundered from above, "Let the lady come up," in so authoritative a voice, that the good man instantly withdrew his hands, and the lady made the best of her way to the chamber.

Here Jones wished her joy of her safe arrival, and then departed, in order, as he promised, to send the landlady up with some clothes. The poor woman thanked him heartily for all his kindness, and said, she hoped she should see him again soon, to thank him a thousand times more. During this short conversation she covered her white bosom as well as she could possibly with her arms; for Jones could not avoid stealing a sly peep or two, though he took all imaginable care to avoid giving any offense.

Our travelers had happened to take up their residence at a house of exceeding good repute, whither Irish ladies of strict virtue, and many northern lasses of the same predicament, were accustomed to resort in their way to Bath. Now it required no very blamable degree of suspicion to imagine that Mr. Jones and his ragged companion had certain purposes in their intention, which, though tolerated in some Christian countries, connived at in others, and practiced in all, are however as expressly forbidden as murder, or any other horrid vice, by that religion which is universally believed in those countries. The landlady, therefore, had no sooner received an intimation of the entrance of the above-said persons than she began to meditate the most expeditious means for their expulsion. In order to this, she had provided herself with a long and deadly instrument, with which, in times of peace, the chambermaid was wont to demolish the labors of the industrious spider. In vulgar phrase, she had taken up the broomstick, and was just about to sally from the kitchen, when Jones accosted her with a demand of a gown and other vestments to cover the half-naked woman upstairs.

Nothing can be more provoking to the human temper, nor more dangerous to that cardinal virtue, patience, than solicitations of extraordinary offices of kindness on behalf of those very persons with whom we are highly incensed. Jones had scarce ended his request when she fell upon him with a certain weapon, which, though it be neither long, nor sharp, nor hard, nor indeed threatens from its appearance with either death or wound, hath been, however, held in great dread and abhorrence by many wise men—nay, by many brave ones; insomuch, that some who have dared to look into the mouth of a loaded cannon, have not dared to look into a mouth where this weapon was brandished; and rather than run the hazard of its execution, have contented themselves with making a most pitiful and sneaking figure in the eyes of all their acquaintance.

To confess the truth, I am afraid Mr. Jones was one of these; for though he was attacked and violently belabored with the aforesaid weapon, he could not be provoked to make any resistance; he only begged her with the utmost earnestness to hear him; but before he could obtain his request, my landlord himself entered into the fray, and embraced that side of the cause which seemed to stand very little in need of assistance.

There are a sort of heroes who are supposed to be determined in their choosing or avoiding a conflict by the character and behavior of the person whom they are to engage. These are said to know their men, and Jones, I believe, knew his woman; for though he had been so submissive to her, he was no sooner attacked by her husband, than he demonstrated an immediate spirit of resentment, and enjoined him silence under a very severe penalty; no less than that, I think, of being converted into fuel for his own fire.

The husband, with great indignation, but with a mixture of pity, answered, "You must pray first to be made able. I believe I am a better man than yourself; ay, every way, that I am"; when a swinging blow from the cudgel that Jones carried in his hand assaulted him over the shoulders.

It is a question whether the landlord or the landlady was the most expeditious in returning this blow. My landlord, whose hands were empty, fell to with his fist, and the good wife, uplifting her broom and aiming at the head of Jones, had probably put an immediate end to the fray, and to Jones likewise, had not the descent of this broom been prevented—not by the miraculous intervention of any heathen deity, but by a very natural though fortunate accident, viz., by the arrival of Partridge; who entered the house at that instant and who, seeing the danger which threatened his master or companion (whichever you choose to call him), prevented so sad a catastrophe, by catching hold of the landlady's arm, as it was brandished aloft in the air.

The landlady, being unable to rescue her arm from the hands of Partridge, let fall the broom; and then leaving Jones to the discipline of her husband, she fell with the utmost fury on that poor fellow, who had already given some intimation of himself, by crying, "Zounds! do you intend to kill my friend?"

Partridge, though not much addicted to battle, returned my land-lady's blows as soon as he received them: and now the fight was obstinately maintained on all parts, when the naked lady, who had listened at the top of the stairs to the dialogue which preceded the engagement, descended suddenly from above, and without weigh-ing the unfair inequality of two to one, fell upon the poor woman who was boxing with Partridge.

Victory must now have fallen to the side of the travelers (for the bravest troops must yield to numbers) had not Susan the chamber-maid come luckily to support her mistress. This Susan was as two-handed a wench (according to the phrase) as any in the country, and would, I believe, have beat the famed Thalestris herself, or any of her subject Amazons; for her form was robust and manlike, and every way made for such encounters. As her hands and arms were formed to give blows with great mischief to an enemy, so was her face as well contrived to receive blows without any great injury to herself, her nose being already flat to her face; her lips were so large that no swelling could be perceived in them, and moreover they were so hard that a fist could hardly make any impression on them. Lastly, her cheek-bones stood out, as if nature had intended them for two bastions to defend her eyes in those encounters for which she seemed so well calculated.

Now the dogs of war being let loose, began to lick their bloody lips; now Fortune, taking her scales from her shelf, began to weigh the fates of Tom Jones, his female companion, and Partridge, against the landlord, his wife, and maid; when a good-natured accident put suddenly an end to the bloody fray. This accident was the arrival of a coach and four; upon which my landlord and landlady immedi-ately desisted from fighting, and at their entreaty obtained the same favor of their antagonists: but Susan was not so kind to Partridge; for that Amazonian fair having overthrown and bestrid her enemy, was now cuffing him lustily with both her hands, without any regard to his request of a cessation of arms, or to those loud exclamations of murder which he roared forth.

The landlord, who had no visible hurt, and the landlady, hiding her well-scratched face with her handkerchief, ran both hastily to the door to attend the coach, from which a young lady and her maid now alighted. They were obliged to pass through the field of battle, which they did with the utmost haste, covering their faces with their handkerchiefs, as desirous to avoid the notice of anyone. Indeed their caution was quite unnecessary; for the poor unfortunate Helen, the fatal cause of all the bloodshed, was entirely taken up in endeavoring to conceal her own face, and Jones was no less occupied in rescuing Partridge from the fury of Susan; which being happily effected, the poor fellow immediately departed to the pump to wash his face, and to stop that bloody torrent which Susan had plentifully set a-flowing from his nostrils.

III

A SERGEANT and a file of musketeers, with a deserter in their custody, arrived about this time. Mr. Jones was comforting the poor distressed lady, who sat down at a table in the kitchen, and leaning her head upon her arm, was bemoaning her misfortunes; but lest my fair readers should be in pain concerning a particular circumstance, I think proper here to acquaint them, that before she had quitted the room above-stairs, she had so well covered herself with a pillow-beer which she there found, that her regard to decency was not in the least violated by the presence of so many men as were now in the room.

One of the soldiers now went up to the sergeant, and whispered something in his ear; upon which he steadfastly fixed his eyes on the lady, and having looked at her for near a minute, he came up to her saying, "I ask pardon, madam; but I am certain I am not deceived; you can be no other person than Captain Waters' lady?"

The poor woman answered, "That she was indeed the unhappy person he imagined her to be"; but added, "I wonder anyone should know me in this disguise." To which the sergeant replied, "He was very much surprised to see her ladyship in such a dress and was afraid some accident had happened to her."

"An accident hath happened to me, indeed," says she, "and I am highly obliged to this gentleman" (pointing to Jones) "that it was not a fatal one, or that I am now living to mention it."

"Whatever the gentleman hath done," cries the sergeant, "I am sure the captain will make him amends for it; and if I can be of any service, your ladyship may command me, and I shall think myself very happy to have it in my power to serve your ladyship; and so indeed may anyone, for I know the captain will well reward them for it."

The landlady, who heard from the stairs all that passed between the sergeant and Mrs. Waters, came hastily down, and running directly up to her, began to asks pardon for the offenses she had committed, begging that all might be imputed to ignorance of her quality: for, "Lud! madam," says she, "how should I have imagined that a lady of your fashion would appear in such a dress? I am sure, madam, if I had once suspected that your ladyship was your ladyship, I would sooner have burnt my tongue out than have said what I have said; and I hope your ladyship will accept of a gown till you can get your own clothes."

"Prithee, woman," says Mrs. Waters, "cease your impertinence: how can you imagine I should concern myself about anything which comes from the lips of such low creatures as yourself? But I am surprised at your assurance in thinking, after what is past, that I will condescend to put on any of your dirty things. I would have you know, creature, I have a spirit above that."

Here Jones interfered, and begged Mrs. Waters to forgive the landlady, and to accept her gown: "for I must confess," cries he, "our appearance was a little suspicious when first we came in; and I am well assured all this good woman did was, as she professed, out of regard to the reputation of her house."

"Yes, upon my truly was it," says she: "the gentleman speaks very much like a gentleman, and I see very plainly is so; and to be certain the house is well known to be a house of as good reputation as any on the road, and though I say it, is frequented by gentry of the best quality, both Irish and English. I defy anybody to say black is my eye, for that matter. And, as I was saying, if I had known your ladyship to be your ladyship, I would as soon have burnt my fingers as have affronted your ladyship; but truly where gentry come and spend their money, I am not willing that they should be scandalized by a set of poor shabby vermin, that, wherever they go, leave more lice than money behind them; such folks never raise my compassion, for to be certain it is foolish to have any for them; and if our justices did as they ought, they would be all whipped out of the kingdom, for to be certain it is what is most fitting for them. But as for your ladyship, I am heartily sorry your ladyship hath had a misfortune, and if your ladyship will do me the honor to wear my clothes till you can get some of your ladyship's own, to be certain the best I have is at your ladyship's service."

Whether cold, shame, or the persuasions of Mr. Jones prevailed most on Mrs. Waters, I will not determine, but she suffered herself to be pacified by this speech of my landlady, and retired with that good woman in order to apparel herself in a decent manner.

My landlord was likewise beginning his oration to Jones, but was presently interrupted by that generous youth, who shook him heartily by the hand, and assured him of entire forgiveness, saying, "If you are satisfied, my worthy friend, I promise you I am"; and indeed, in one sense, the landlord had the better reason to be satisfied; for he had received a bellyful of drubbing, whereas Jones had scarce felt a single blow.

The good people now ranged themselves round the kitchen fire, where good-humor seemed to maintain an absolute dominion. We must, however, quit this agreeable assembly for a while, and attend Mr. Jones to Mrs. Waters' apartment, where the dinner which he had bespoke was now on the table.

IV

HEROES, notwithstanding the high ideas which, by the means of flatterers, they may entertain of themselves, or the world may conceive of them, have certainly more of mortal than divine about them. However elevated their minds may be, their bodies at least (which is much the major part of most) are liable to the worst infirmities, and subject to the vilest offices of human nature. Among these latter, the act of eating, which hath by several wise men been considered as extremely mean and derogatory from the philosophic dignity, must be in some measure performed by the greatest prince, hero, or philosopher upon earth.

Now, after this short preface, we think it no disparagement to our hero to mention the immoderate ardor with which he laid about him at this season. Three pounds at least of that flesh which formerly had contributed to the composition of an ox was now honored with becoming part of the individual Mr. Jones.

This particular we thought ourselves obliged to mention, as it may account for our hero's temporary neglect of his fair companion, who ate but very little, and was indeed employed in considerations of a very different nature, which passed unobserved by Jones, till he had entirely satisfied that appetite which a fast of twenty-four hours had procured him; but his dinner was no sooner ended than his attention to other matters revived; with these matters, therefore, we shall now proceed to acquaint the reader.

Mr. Jones, of whose personal accomplishments we have hitherto said very little, was, in reality, one of the handsomest young fellows in the world. His face, besides being the picture of health, had in it the most apparent marks of sweetness and good-nature. It was, perhaps, as much owing to this as to a very fine complexion that his face had a delicacy in it almost inexpressible, and which might have given him an air rather too effeminate, had it not been joined to a most masculine person and mien: which latter had as much in them of the Hercules as the former had of the Adonis. He was besides active, genteel, gay, and good-humored, and had a flow of animal spirits which enlivened every conversation where he was present.

When the reader hath duly reflected on these many charms which all centered in our hero, and considers at the same time the fresh obligations which Mrs. Waters had to him, it will be a mark more of prudery than candor to entertain a bad opinion of her because she conceived a very good opinion of him. Mrs. Waters had, in truth, a very great affection for him. To speak out boldly at once, she was in love, according to the present universally received sense of that phrase, by which love is applied indiscriminately to the desirable objects of all our passions, appetites, and senses, and is understood to be that preference which we give to one kind of food rather than to another.

But though the love to these several objects may possibly be one and the same in all cases, its operations, however, must be allowed to be different; for, how much soever we may be in love with an excellent sirloin of beef, or bottle of Burgundy; with a damask rose, or Cremona fiddle; yet do we never smile, nor ogle, nor dress, nor flatter, nor endeavor by any other arts or tricks to gain the affection of the said beef, etc. Sigh indeed we sometimes may; but it is generally in the absence, not in the presence, of the beloved object.

The contrary happens in that love which operates between persons of the same species, but of different sexes. Here we are no sooner in love than it becomes our principal care to engage the affection of the object beloved. For what other purpose, indeed, are our youth instructed in all the arts of rendering themselves agreeable? If it was not with a view to this love, I question whether any of those trades which deal in setting off and adorning the human person would procure a livelihood. In short, all the graces which young ladies and young gentlemen too learn from others, and the many improvements which, by the help of a looking-glass, they add of their own, are in reality the whole artillery of love.

Now Mrs. Waters and our hero had no sooner sat down together than the former began to play this artillery upon the latter. But here, as we are about to attempt a description hitherto unessayed either in prose or verse, we think proper to invoke the assistance of certain aërial beings, who will, we doubt not, come kindly to our aid on this occasion.

"Say then, ye Graces! you that inhabit the heavenly mansions of Seraphina's countenance; for you are truly divine, are always in her presence, and well know all the arts of charming; say, what were the weapons now used to captivate the heart of Mr. Jones."

"First, from two lovely blue eyes, whose bright orbs flashed lightning at their discharge, flew forth two pointed ogles; but, happily for our hero, hit only a vast piece of beef which he was then conveying into his plate, and harmless spent their force. The fair warrior perceived their miscarriage, and immediately from her fair bosom drew forth a deadly sigh. A sigh which none could have heard unmoved, and which was sufficient at once to have swept off a dozen beaus; so soft, so sweet, so tender, that the insinuating air must have found its subtle way to the heart of our hero, had it not unluckily been driven from his ears by the coarse bubbling of some bottled ale, which at that time he was pouring forth.

"The fair one, enraged at her frequent disappointments, determined on a short cessation of arms. Which interval she employed in making ready every engine of amorous warfare for the renewing of the attack when dinner should be over.

"No sooner then was the cloth removed than she again began her operations. First, having planted her right eye sidewise against Mr. Jones, she shot from its corner a most penetrating glance; which, though great part of its force was spent before it reached our hero, did not vent itself absolutely without effect. This the fair one perceiving, hastily withdrew her eyes, and leveled them downwards, as if she was concerned for what she had done; though by this means she designed only to draw him from his guard, and indeed to open his eyes, through which she intended to surprise his heart. And now, gently lifting up those two bright orbs which had already begun to make an impression on poor Jones, she discharged a volley of small charms at once from her whole countenance in a smile. Not a smile of mirth, nor of joy; but a smile of affection, which most ladies have always ready at their command, and which serves them to show at once their good-humor, their pretty dimples, and their white teeth.

"This smile our hero received full in his eyes, and was immedi-

r hero and the redeemed lady walked as Orpheus and Eurydice marched heretofore.

ately staggered with its force. He then began to see the designs of the enemy, and indeed to feel their success. A parley now was set on foot between the parties; during which the artful fair so slily and imperceptibly carried on her attack, that she had almost subdued the heart of our hero before she again repaired to acts of hostility. To confess the truth, I am afraid Mr. Jones maintained a kind of Dutch defense, and treacherously delivered up the garrison, without duly weighing his allegiance to the fair Sophia. In short, no sooner had the amorous parley ended and the lady had unmasked the royal battery, by carelessly letting her handkerchief drop from her neck, than the heart of Mr. Jones was entirely taken, and the fair conqueror enjoyed the usual fruits of her victory."

Here the Graces think proper to end their description, and here we think proper to end the chapter.

V

As Jones might very justly be called a well-bred man, he had stifled all that curiosity which the extraordinary manner in which he had found Mrs. Waters must be supposed to have occasioned. He had, indeed, at first thrown out some few hints to the lady; but, when he perceived her industriously avoiding any explanation, he was contented to remain in ignorance.

Now since it is possible that some of our readers may not so easily acquiesce under the same ignorance, and as we are very desirous to satisfy them all, we have taken uncommon pains to inform ourselves of the real fact, with the relation of which we shall conclude this book.

This lady, then, had lived some years with one Captain Waters, who was a captain in the same regiment to which Mr. Northerton belonged. She passed for that gentleman's wife, and went by his name; and yet there were some doubts concerning the reality of their marriage, which we shall not at present take upon us to resolve.

Mrs. Waters, I am sorry to say it, had for some time contracted an intimacy with the above-mentioned ensign, which did no great credit to her reputation. That she had a remarkable fondness for that young fellow is most certain; but whether she indulged this to any very criminal lengths is not so extremely clear, unless we will suppose that women never grant every favor to a man but one, without granting him that one also.

Now, it had been agreed between Mrs. Waters and the captain that she would accompany him in his march as far as Worcester, where they were to take their leave of each other, and she was thence to return to Bath, where she was to stay till the end of the winter's campaign against the rebels. Northerton no sooner obtained a release from his captivity, as we have seen, than he hasted away to overtake Mrs. Waters; which, as he was a very active, nimble fellow, he did at the last-mentioned city some few hours after Captain Waters had left her. Mrs. Waters was no sooner apprised of the danger to which her lover was exposed, than she lost every consideration besides that of his safety; and this being a matter equally agreeable to the gentleman, it became the immediate subject of debate between them.

After much consultation on this matter, it was at length agreed that the ensign should make his escape abroad. Mrs. Waters was able to furnish him with money, a very material article to Mr. Northerton, she having then in her pocket three bank-notes to the amount of £90, besides some cash, and a diamond ring of pretty considerable value on her finger. All which she, with the utmost confidence, revealed to this wicked man, little suspecting she should by these means inspire him with a design of robbing her.

The ensign proposed, and the lady presently agreed, to make their first stage on foot; for which purpose the hardness of the frost was very seasonable. Mrs. Waters was not of that delicate race of women who are obliged to the invention of vehicles for the capacity of removing themselves from one place to another, and with whom consequently a coach is reckoned among the necessaries of life. Her limbs were indeed full of strength and agility, and, as her mind was no less animated with spirit, she was perfectly able to keep pace with her nimble lover.

Whether the execrable scheme which he now attempted to execute was the effect of previous deliberation, or whether it now first came into his head, I cannot determine. But he suddenly slipped his garter from his leg, and, laying violent hands on the poor woman, endeavored to perpetrate that dreadful and detestable fact which we have before commemorated, and which the providential appearance of Jones did so fortunately prevent.

Thus, reader, we have given thee the fruits of a very painful inquiry which for thy satisfaction we have made into this matter.

Book X

IN WHICH THE HISTORY GOES FORWARD ABOUT TWELVE HOURS

I

It was now midnight; and the company at the inn were all in bed. Only Susan Chambermaid was now stirring, she being obliged to wash the kitchen before she retired.

In this posture were affairs at the inn when a gentleman arrived there, alighted from his horse, and, coming up to Susan, inquired of her, in a very abrupt and confused manner, Whether there was any lady in the house? The hour of night, and the behavior of the man, who stared very wildly all the time, a little surprised Susan, so that she hesitated before she made any answer; upon which the gentleman, with redoubled eagerness, begged her to give him a true information, saying he had lost his wife, and was come in pursuit of her.

"Upon my shoul," cries he, "I have been near catching her already in two or three places, if I had not found her gone just as I came up with her. If she be in the house, do carry me up in the dark and show her to me; and if she be gone away before me, do tell me which way I shall go after her to meet her, and, upon my shoul, I will make you the richest poor woman in the nation." He then pulled out a handful of guineas, a sight which would have bribed persons of much greater consequence than this poor wench to much worse purposes.

Susan, from the account she had received of Mrs. Waters, made not the least doubt but that she was the very identical stray whom the right owner pursued. As she concluded, therefore, with great appearance of reason, that she never could get money in an honester way than by restoring a wife to her husband, she made no scruple of assuring the gentleman that the lady he wanted was then in the house; and was presently afterwards prevailed upon (by very liberal promises, and some earnest paid into her hands) to conduct him to the bedchamber of Mrs. Waters.

It hath been a custom long established in the polite world, and that upon very solid and substantial reasons, that a husband shall never enter his wife's apartment without first knocking at the door; and lucky would it have been had the custom above mentioned been observed by our gentleman in the present instance. Knock, indeed, he did at the door, but not with one of those gentle raps which is usual on such occasions. On the contrary, when he found the door locked, he flew at it with such violence that the lock immediately gave way, the door burst open, and he fell headlong into the room.

He had no sooner recovered his legs than forth appeared our hero himself, who, with a menacing voice, demanded of the gentleman who he was, and what he meant by daring to burst open his chamber in that outrageous manner.

The gentleman at first thought he had committed a mistake, and was going to ask pardon and retreat, when, on a sudden, as the moon shone very bright, he cast his eyes on stays, gowns, petticoats, caps, ribbons, stockings, garters, shoes, clogs, etc., all which lay in a disordered manner on the floor. All these operating on the natural jealousy of his temper, so enraged him, that he lost all power of speech; and, without returning any answer to Jones, he endeavored to approach the bed.

Jones immediately interposing, a fierce contention arose, which soon proceeded to blows on both sides. And now Mrs. Waters (for we must confess she was in the bed), being, I suppose, awakened from her sleep, and seeing two men fighting in her bedchamber, began to scream in the most violent manner, crying out Murder! robbery! and more frequently Rape! which last, some, perhaps, may wonder she should mention, who do not consider that these words of exclamation are used by ladies in a fright, as fa, la, la, ra, da, etc., are in music, only as the vehicles of sound, and without any fixed ideas.

Next to the lady's chamber was deposited the body of an Irish gentleman who arrived too late at the inn to have been mentioned before. This gentleman was one of those whom the Irish call a calabalaro, or cavalier. He was a younger brother of a good family, and, having no fortune at home, was obliged to look abroad in order to get one; for which purpose he was proceeding to the Bath, to try his luck with cards and the women.

This young fellow lay in bed reading one of Mrs. Behn's novels; for he had been instructed by a friend that he would find no more effectual method of recommending himself to the ladies than the improving of his understanding, and filling his mind with good literature. He no sooner, therefore, heard the violent uproar in the next room, than he leapt from his bolster, and, taking his sword in one hand, and the candle which burnt by him in the other, he went directly to Mrs. Waters' chamber.

No sooner had the calabalaro entered the room than he cried out, "Mr. Fitzpatrick, what the devil is the maning of this?"

Upon which the other immediately answered, "Oh, Mr. Maclachlan! I am rejoiced you are here. This villain hath debauched my wife, and is got into bed with her."

"What wife?" cries Maclachlan; "do not I know Mrs. Fitzpatrick very well, and don't I see that the lady in bed is none of her?"

Fitzpatrick, now perceiving, as well by the glimpse he had of the lady, as by her voice, which might have been distinguished at a greater distance than he now stood from her, that he had made a very unfortunate mistake, began to ask many pardons of the lady; and then, turning to Jones, he said,

"I would have you take notice I do not ask your pardon, for you have bate me; for which I am resolved to have your blood in the morning."

Jones treated this menace with much contempt; and Mr. Maclachlan answered, "Indeed, Mr. Fitzpatrick, you may be ashamed of your own self, to disturb people at this time of night; if all the people in the inn were not asleep, you would have awakened them as you have me. The gentleman has served you very rightly. Upon my conscience, though I have no wife, if you had treated her so, I would have cut your throat."

Jones was so confounded with his fears for his lady's reputation, that he knew neither what to say or do; but the invention of women is, as hath been observed, much readier than that of men. She recollected that there was a communication between her chamber and that of Mr. Jones; relying, therefore, on his honor and her own assurance, she answered,

"I know not what you mean, villains! I am wife to none of you. Help! Rape! Murder! Rape!" And now, the landlady coming into the room, Mrs. Waters fell upon her with the utmost virulence, saying, "She thought herself in a sober inn, and not in a bawdy-house; but that a set of villains had broke into her room, with an intent upon her honor, if not upon her life; and both, she said, were equally dear to her."

The landlady now began to roar as loudly as the poor woman in bed had done before. She cried, "She was undone, and that the reputation of her house, which was never blown upon before, was utterly destroyed." Then, turning to the men, she cried, "What, in the devil's name, is the reason of all this disturbance in the lady's room?"

Fitzpatrick, hanging down his head, repeated, "That he had committed a mistake, for which he heartily asked pardon," and then retired with his countryman. Jones, who was too ingenious to have missed the hint given him by his fair one, boldly asserted, "That he had run to her assistance upon hearing the door broke open, with what design he could not conceive, unless of robbing the lady; which, if they intended, he said, he had the good fortune to prevent."

"I never had a robbery committed in my house since I have kept it," cries the landlady; "I would have you to know, sir, I harbor no highwaymen here; I scorn the word, thof I say it. None but honest, good gentlefolks are welcome to my house; and, I thank good luck, I have always had enow of such customers; indeed as many as I could entertain. Here hath been my Lord—" and then she repeated over a catalogue of names and titles, many of which we might, perhaps, be guilty of a breach of privilege by inserting.

When the men were all departed, Mrs. Waters, recovering from her fear, recovered likewise from her anger, and spoke in much gentler accents to the landlady; upon which the landlady, after much civility and many courtesies, took her leave.

II

THE landlady, remembering that Susan had been the only person out of bed when the door was burst open, resorted presently to her, to inquire into the first occasion of the disturbance, as well as who the strange gentleman was, and when and how he arrived.

Susan related the whole story, varying the truth only in some circumstances, as she saw convenient, and totally concealing the money which she had received. But whereas her mistress had, in the preface of her inquiry, spoken much in compassion for the lady, Susan could not help endeavoring to quiet the concern which her mistress seemed to be under, by swearing heartily she saw Jones leap out from her bed.

The landlady fell into a violent rage at these words.

"A likely story, truly," cried she, "that a woman should cry out, and endeavor to expose herself, if that was the case! I desire to know what better proof any lady can give of her virtue than her crying out, which, I believe, twenty people can witness for her she did? I beg, madam, you would spread no such scandal of any of my guests; for it will not only reflect on them, but upon the house; and I am sure no vagabonds, nor wicked beggarly people, come here."

"Well," says Susan, "then I must not believe my own eyes."

"No, indeed, must you not always," answered her mistress; "I would not have believed my own eyes against such good gentlefolks. I have not had a better supper ordered this half-year than they ordered last night; and so easy and good-humored were they, that they found no fault with my Worcestershire perry, which I sold them for champagne; and to be sure it is as well tasted and as wholesome as the best champagne in the kingdom, otherwise I would scorn to give it 'em; and they drank me two bottles. No, no, I will never believe any harm of such sober good sort of people."

Susan being thus silenced, her mistress proceeded to other matters.

"And so you tell me," continued she, "that the strange gentleman came post, and there is a footman without with the horses; why, then, he is certainly some of your great gentlefolks too. Why did not you ask him whether he'd have any supper? I think he is in the other gentleman's room; go up and ask whether he called. Open the door with, Gentlemen, d'ye call? and if they say nothing, ask what his honor will be pleased to have for supper? Don't forget his honor. Go; if you don't mind all these matters better, you'll never come to anything."

Susan departed, and soon returned with an account that the two gentlemen were got both into the same bed.

"Two gentlemen," says the landlady, "in the same bed! that's impossible; they are two arrant scrubs, I warrant them; and I believe that the fellow intended to rob her ladyship; for, if he had broke open the lady's door with any of the wicked designs of a gentleman, he would never have sneaked away to another room to save the expense of a supper and a bed to himself. They are certainly thieves, and their searching after a wife is nothing but a pretense."

In these censures my landlady did Mr. Fitzpatrick great injustice; for he was really born a gentleman, though not worth a groat; and though, perhaps, he had some few blemishes in his heart as well as in his head, yet being a sneaking or a niggardly fellow was not one of them. In reality, he was so generous a man that, whereas he had received a very handsome fortune with his wife, he had now spent every penny of it, except some little pittance which was settled upon her; and, in order to possess himself of this, he had used her with such cruelty, that, together with his jealousy, which was of the bitterest kind, it had forced the poor woman to run away from him.

This gentleman, then, being well tired with his long journey from Chester in one day, with which, and some good dry blows he had received in the scuffle, his bones were so sore, that, added to the soreness of his mind, it had quite deprived him of any appetite for eating; and being now so violently disappointed in the woman whom, at the maid's instance, he had mistaken for his wife, it never once entered into his head that she might nevertheless be in the house, though he had erred in the first person he had attacked. He therefore yielded to the dissuasions of his friend from searching any farther after her that night, and accepted the kind offer of part of his bed.

The footman and post-boy were in a different disposition. They were more ready to order than the landlady was to provide; however, after being pretty well satisfied by them of the real truth of the case, and that Mr. Fitzpatrick was no thief, she was at length prevailed on to set some cold meat before them, which they were devouring with great greediness when Partridge came into the kitchen. He had been awaked by the hurry which we have before seen; and, huddling on his clothes with great expedition, ran down to the protection of the company, whom he heard talking below in the kitchen.

And now arrived another post-boy at the gate; upon which Susan, being ordered out, returned, introducing two young women in riding habits, one of which was so very richly laced, that Partridge and the post-boy instantly started from their chairs, and my landlady fell to her courtesies, and her ladyships, with great eagerness.

The lady in the rich habit said, with a smile of great condescension, "If you will give me leave, madam, I will warm myself a few minutes at your kitchen fire, for it is really very cold; but I must insist on disturbing no one from his seat." This was spoken on account of Partridge, who had retreated to the other end of the room, struck with the utmost awe and astonishment at the splendor of the lady's dress. Indeed, she had a much better title to respect than this, for she was one of the most beautiful creatures in the world.

The lady earnestly desired Partridge to return to his seat, but could not prevail. She then pulled off her gloves, and displayed to the fire two hands, which had every property of snow in them, except that of melting.

Her companion, who was indeed her maid, likewise pulled off her gloves, and discovered what bore an exact resemblance, in cold and color, to a piece of frozen beef.

"I wish, madam," quoth the latter, "your ladyship would not think of going any farther tonight. I am terribly afraid your ladyship will not be able to bear the fatigue."

"Why, sure," cries the landlady, "her ladyship's honor can never intend it. Oh, bless me! farther tonight, indeed! let me beseech your ladyship not to think on't——But, to be sure, your ladyship can't. What will your honor be pleased to have for supper? I have mutton of all kinds, and some nice chicken."

"Upon my word, I can't eat a morsel," answered the lady; "and I shall be much obliged to you if you will please to get my apartment ready as soon as possible; for I am resolved to be on horseback again in three hours."

"Why, Susan," cries the landlady, "is there a fire lit yet in the Wild-goose? I am sorry, madam, all my best rooms are full. Several people of the first quality are now in bed. Here's a great young squire and many other great gentlefolks of quality."

Susan answered, "That the Irish gentlemen were got into the Wild-goose."

"Was ever anything like it?" says the mistress; "why the devil would you not keep some of the best rooms for the quality, when you know scarce a day passes without some calling here?——If they be gentlemen, I am certain, when they know it is for her ladyship, they will get up again."

"Not upon my account," says the lady; "I will have no person disturbed for me. If you have a room that is commonly decent it will serve me very well, though it be never so plain. I beg, madam, you will not give yourself so much trouble on my account."

"Oh, madam!" cries the other, "I have several very good rooms for that matter, but none good enough for your honor's ladyship. However, as you are so condescending to take up with the best I have, do, Susan, get a fire in the Rose this minute. Will your ladyship be pleased to go up now, or stay till the fire is lighted?"

"I think I have sufficiently warmed myself," answered the lady; "so, if you please, I will go now; I am afraid I have kept people, and particularly that gentleman (meaning Partridge), too long in the cold already. Indeed, I cannot bear to think of keeping any person from the fire this dreadful weather." She then departed with her maid, the landlady marching with two lighted candles before her.

III

The lady had no sooner laid herself on her pillow than the waiting-woman returned to the kitchen to regale with some of those dainties which her mistress had refused.

The company, at her entrance, showed her the same respect which they had before paid to her mistress, by rising; but she forgot to imitate her, by desiring them to sit down again. Indeed, it was scarce possible they should have done so, for she placed her chair in such a posture as to occupy almost the whole fire. She then ordered a chicken to be broiled that instant, declaring, if it was not ready in a quarter of an hour she would not stay for it. Now, though the said chicken was then at roost in the stable, and required the several ceremonies of catching, killing, and picking, before it was brought to the gridiron, my landlady would nevertheless have undertaken to do all within the time; but the guest, being unfortunately admitted behind the scenes, must have been witness to the *fourberie;* the poor woman was therefore obliged to confess that she had none in the house; "but, madam," said she, "I can get any kind of mutton in an instant from the butcher's."

"Do you think, then," answered the waiting-gentlewoman, "that I have the stomach of a horse, to eat mutton at this time of night? Sure you people that keep inns imagine your betters are like yourselves. Indeed, I expected to get nothing at this wretched place. I wonder my lady would stop at it. I suppose none but tradesmen and graziers ever call here."

The landlady fired at this indignity offered to her house; however, she suppressed her temper, and contented herself with saying, "Very good quality frequented it, she thanked Heaven!"

"Don't tell me," cries the other, "of quality! I believe I know more of people of quality than such as you. But, prithee, without troubling me with any of your impertinence, do tell me what I can have for supper; for, though I cannot eat horse-flesh, I am really hungry."

"Why, truly, madam," answered the landlady, "you could not take me again at such a disadvantage; for I must confess I have nothing in the house, unless a cold piece of beef, which indeed a gentleman's footman and the post-boy have almost cleared to the bone."

"Woman," said Mrs. Abigail (so for shortness we will call her), "I entreat you not to make me sick. If I had fasted a month, I could not eat what has been touched by the fingers of such fellows. Is there nothing neat or decent to be had in this horrid place?"

"What think you of some eggs and bacon, madam?" said the land-lady.

"Are your eggs new laid? are you certain they were laid today? and let me have the bacon cut very nice and thin; for I can't endure anything that's gross. Prithee try if you can do a little tolerably for once, and don't think you have a farmer's wife, or some of those creatures, in the house."

The landlady began then to handle her knife; but the other stopped her, saying, "Good woman, I must insist upon your first washing your hands; for I am extremely nice, and have been always used from my cradle to have everything in the most elegant manner."

While the supper was preparing, Mrs. Abigail began to lament she had not ordered a fire in the parlor; but, she said, that was now too late. "However," said she, "I have novelty to recommend a kitchen; for I do not believe I ever eat in one before." Then, turning to the post-boys, she asked them, "Why they were not in the stable with their horses? If I must eat my hard fare here, madam," cries she to the landlady, "I beg the kitchen may be kept clear, that I may not be surrounded with all the blackguards in town. As for you, sir," says she to Partridge, "you look somewhat like a gentleman, and may sit still if you please; I don't desire to disturb anybody but mob."

The supper being now on the table, Mrs. Abigail ate very heartily for so delicate a person; and while a second course of the same was by her order preparing, she said, "And so, madam, you tell me your house is frequented by people of great quality?"

The landlady answered in the affirmative, saying, "There were a great many very good quality and gentle-folks in it now. There's young Squire Allworthy, as that gentleman there knows."

"And pray who is this young gentlemen of quality, this young Squire Allworthy?" said Abigail.

"Who should he be," answered Partridge, "but the son and heir of the great Squire Allworthy of Somersetshire?"

"Upon my word," said she, "you tell me strange news; for I know Mr. Allworthy of Somersetshire very well, and I know he hath no son alive."

The landlady pricked up her ears at this, and Partridge looked a little confounded. However, after a short hesitation, he answered,

"Indeed, madam, it is true, everybody doth not know him to be Squire Allworthy's son; for he was never married to his mother; but his son he certainly is, and will be his heir too, as certainly as his name is Jones."

At that word Abigail let drop the bacon which she was conveying to her mouth, and cried out,

"You surprise me, sir! Is it possible Mr. Jones should be now in the house?"

"*Quare non?*" answered Partridge, "it is possible, and it is certain."

Abigail now made haste to finish the remainder of her meal, and then repaired back to her mistress, when the conversation passed which may be read in the next chapter.

IV

As IN the blooming month of April the gentle, constant dove, perched on some fair bough, sits meditating on her mate; so, looking a hundred charms and breathing as many sweets, her thoughts being fixed on her Tommy, with a heart as good and innocent as her face was beautiful, Sophia (for it was she herself) lay reclining her lovely head on her hand, when her maid entered the room, and running directly to the bed, cried,

"Madam—madam—who doth your ladyship think is in the house?"

Sophia, starting up, cried, "I hope my father hath not overtaken us."

"No, madam, it is one worth a hundred fathers; Mr. Jones himself is here at this very instant."

"Mr. Jones!" says Sophia, "it is impossible! I cannot be so fortunate." Her maid averred the fact, and was presently detached by her mistress to order him to be called; for she said she was resolved to see him immediately.

Mrs. Honour returned and discharged her commission, by bidding the landlady immediately wake Mr. Jones, and tell him a lady wanted to speak with him. The landlady referred her to Partridge, saying, "He was the squire's friend; but, for her part, she never called men-folks, especially gentlemen," and then walked sullenly out of the kitchen. Honour applied herself to Partridge; but he refused, "For my friend," cries he, "went to bed very late, and he would be very angry to be disturbed so soon." Mrs. Honour insisted still to have him called, saying, "She was sure, instead of being angry, that he would be to the highest degree delighted when he knew the occasion."

"Another time, perhaps, he might," cries Partridge; "but *non omnia possumus omnes*. One woman is enough at once for a reasonable man."

"What do you mean by one woman, fellow?" cries Honour.

"None of your fellow," answered Partridge. He then proceeded to inform her plainly that Jones was in bed with a wench, and made use of an expression too indelicate to be here inserted; which so enraged Mrs. Honour, that she called him jackanapes, and returned in a violent hurry to her mistress, whom she acquainted with the success of her errand, and with the account she had received; which, if possible, she exaggerated, being as angry with Jones as if he had pronounced all the words that came from the mouth of Partridge. She discharged a torrent of abuse on the master, and advised her mistress to quit all thoughts of a man who had never shown himself deserving of her. She then ripped us the story of Molly Seagrim, and gave the most malicious turn to his formerly quitting Sophia herself; which, I must confess, the present incident not a little countenanced.

The spirits of Sophia were too much dissipated by concern to enable her to stop the torrent of her maid. At last, however, she interrupted her, saying,

"I never can believe this; some villain hath belied him. You say you had it from his friend; but surely it is not the office of a friend to betray such secrets."

"I suppose," cries Honour, "the fellow is his pimp, for I never saw so ill-looked a villain. Besides, such profligate rakes as Mr. Jones are never ashamed of these matters."

To say the truth, this behavior of Partridge was a little inexcusable; but as he was the most inquisitive of mortals, and eternally prying into the secrets of others, so he very faithfully paid them by communicating, in return, everything within his knowledge.

While Sophia, tormented with anxiety, knew not what to believe, nor what resolution to take, Susan arrived. Mrs. Honour immediately advised her mistress, in a whisper, to pump this wench, who probably could inform her of the truth. Sophia approved it, and began as follows:

"Come hither, child; now answer me truly what I am going to ask you, and I promise you I will very well reward you. Is there a young gentleman in this house, a handsome young gentleman, that——" Here Sophia blushed and was confounded.

"A young gentleman," cries Honour, "that came hither in company with that saucy rascal who is now in the kitchen?"

Susan answered, "There was."

"Do you know anything of any lady?" continues Sophia, "any lady? I don't ask you whether she is handsome or no; perhaps she is not; that's nothing to the purpose; but do you know of any lady?"

"La, madam," cries Honour, "you will make a very bad examiner. Hark'ee, child," says she, "is not that very young gentleman now in bed with some nasty trull or other?"

Here Susan smiled, and was silent. "Answer the question, child," says Sophia, "and here's a guinea for you."

"A guinea! madam," cries Susan; "la, what's a guinea? If my mistress should know it I shall certainly lose my place that very instant."

"Here's another for you," says Sophia, "and I promise you faithfully your mistress shall never know it."

Susan, after a very short hesitation, took the money, and told the whole story, concluding with saying, "If you have any great curiosity, madam, I can steal softly into his room, and see whether he be in his own bed or no." She accordingly did this by Sophia's desire, and returned with an answer in the negative.

Sophia now trembled and turned pale. Mrs. Honour begged her to be comforted, and not to think any more of so worthless a fellow.

"Why there," says Susan, "I hope, madam, your ladyship won't be offended; but pray, madam, is not your ladyship's name Madam Sophia Western?"

"How is it possible you should know me?" answered Sophia.

"Why, that man that the gentlewoman spoke of, who is in the kitchen, told about you last night. But I hope your ladyship is not angry with me."

"Indeed, child," said she, "I am not; pray tell me all, and I promise you I'll reward you."

"Why, madam," continued Susan, "that man told us all in the kitchen that Madam Sophia Western—indeed I don't know how to bring it out." Here she stopped, till, having received encouragement from Sophia, and being vehemently pressed by Mrs. Honour, she proceeded thus: "He told us, madam, though to be sure it is all a lie, that your ladyship was dying for love of the young squire, and that he was going to the wars to get rid of you. I thought to myself then he was a false-hearted wretch; but, now, to see such a fine, rich, beautiful lady as you be, forsaken for such an ordinary woman; for to be sure so she is, and another man's wife into the bargain. It is such a strange, unnatural thing, in a manner."

Sophia gave her a third guinea, and, telling her she would certainly be her friend if she mentioned nothing of what had passed, nor informed anyone who she was, dismissed the girl, with orders to the post-boy to get the horses ready immediately.

Being now left alone with her maid, she told her trusty waiting-woman, "That she never was more easy than at present. I am now convinced," said she, "he is not only a villain, but a low despicable wretch. I can forgive all rather than his exposing my name in so barbarous a manner. That renders him the object of my contempt. Yes, Honour, I am now easy; I am indeed; I am very easy"; and then she burst into a violent flood of tears.

After a short interval spent by Sophia, chiefly in crying, and assuring her maid that she was perfectly easy, Susan arrived with an account that the horses were ready, when a very extraordinary thought suggested itself to our young heroine, by which Mr. Jones would be acquainted with her having been at the inn, in a way which, if any sparks of affection for her remained in him, would be at least some punishment for his faults.

The reader will be pleased to remember a little muff, which hath had the honor of being more than once remembered already in this history. This muff, ever since the departure of Mr. Jones, had been the constant companion of Sophia by day and her bedfellow by night; and this muff she had at this very instant upon her arm; whence she took it off with great indignation, and, having writ her name with her pencil upon a piece of paper which she pinned to it, she bribed the maid to convey it into the empty bed of Mr. Jones, in which, if he did not find it, she charged her to take some method of conveying it before his eyes in the morning.

Then, having paid for what Mrs. Honour had eaten, in which bill was included an account for what she herself might have eaten, she mounted her horse, and, once more assuring her companion that she was perfectly easy, continued her journey.

V

Mr. Jones, being now returned to his own bed (but from whence he returned we must beg to be excused from relating), summoned Partridge, who, after a ceremonious preface, having obtained leave to offer his advice, delivered himself as follows:

"I ask your honor's pardon, but to be sure it is a scandalous way of traveling, for a great gentleman like you to walk afoot. Now here are two or three good horses in the stable, which the landlord will certainly make no scruple of trusting you with; but, if he should, I can easily contrive to take them; and, let the worst come to the worst, the King would certainly pardon you, as you are going to fight in his cause."

When Mr. Jones found that Partridge was in earnest in this proposal, he very severely rebuked him, and that in such bitter terms that the other attempted to laugh it off, and presently turned the discourse to other matters, saying that he had with much ado prevented two wenches from disturbing his honor in the middle of the night.

"Heyday!" says he, "I believe they got into your chamber whether I would or no; for here lies the muff of one of them on the ground."

Indeed, as Jones returned to his bed in the dark, he had never perceived the muff. This Partridge now took up, and was going to put into his pocket, when Jones desired to see it. At the same instant he saw and read the words Sophia Western upon the paper which was pinned to it. His looks now grew frantic in a moment, and he eagerly cried out,

"Oh, Heavens! how came this muff here?"

"I know no more than your honor," cried Partridge; "but I saw it upon the arm of one of the women who would have disturbed you, if I would have suffered them."

"Where are they?" cries Jones, jumping out of bed, and laying hold of his clothes.

"Many miles off, I believe, by this time," said Partridge.

And now Jones, after many bitter execrations on Partridge, and not fewer on himself, ordered the poor fellow, who was frightened out of his wits, to run down and hire him horses at any rate; and a very few minutes afterwards, having shuffled on his clothes, he hastened downstairs to the kitchen, where, as if this had been a real chase, entered a gentleman hallooing as hunters do when the hounds are at a fault. He was just alighted from his horse, and had many attendants at his heels.

Here, reader, it may be necessary to acquaint thee with some matters, which, if thou dost know already, thou art wiser than I take thee to be. And this information thou shalt receive in the next chapter.

VI

IN THE first place, then, this gentleman just arrived was no other person than Squire Western himself, who was come hither in pursuit of his daughter; and, had he fortunately been two hours earlier, he had not only found her, but his niece into the bargain; for such was the wife of Mr. Fitzpatrick, who had run away with her five years before, out of the custody of that sage lady, Madam Western.

Now this lady had departed from the inn much about the same time with Sophia; for, having been waked by the voice of her husband, she had sent up for the landlady, and being by her apprised of the matter, had bribed the good woman, at an extravagant price, to furnish her with horses for her escape.

Mr. Western and his nephew were not known to one another; nor indeed would the former have taken any notice of the latter if he had known him; for, this being a stolen match, and consequently an unnatural one in the opinion of the good squire, he had, from the time of her committing it, abandoned the poor young creature, who was then no more than eighteen, as a monster, and had never since suffered her to be named in his presence.

The kitchen was now a scene of universal confusion, Western inquiring after his daughter, and Fitzpatrick as eagerly after his wife, when Jones entered the room, unfortunately having Sophia's muff in his hand.

As soon as Western saw Jones, he set up the same holloa as is used by sportsmen when their game is in view. He then immediately ran up and laid hold of Jones, crying,

"We have got the dog fox, I warrant the bitch is not far off."

Jones having, at length, shaken Mr. Western off, and some of the company having interfered between them, our hero protested his innocence as to knowing anything of the lady; when Parson Supple stepped up, and said,

"It is folly to deny it; for why, the marks of guilt are in thy hands. I will myself asseverate and bind it by an oath, that the muff thou bearest in thy hand belongeth unto Madam Sophia; for I have frequently observed her, of later days, to bear it about her."

"My daughter's muff!" cries the squire in a rage. "Hath he got my daughter's muff? bear witness the goods are found upon him. I'll have him before a justice of peace this instant. Where is my daughter, villain?"

"Sir," said Jones, "I beg you would be pacified. The muff, I acknowledge, is the young lady's; but, upon my honor, I have never seen her." At these words Western lost all patience, and grew inarticulate with rage.

Some of the servants had acquainted Fitzpatrick who Mr. Western was. The good Irishman, therefore, thinking he had now an opportunity to do an act of service to his uncle, and by that means might possibly obtain his favor, stepped up to Jones, and cried out,

"Upon my conscience, sir, you may be ashamed of denying your having seen the gentleman's daughter before my face, when you know I found you there upon the bed together."

Then, turning to Western, he offered to conduct him immediately to the room where his daughter was; which offer being accepted, he, the squire, the parson, and some others, ascended directly to Mrs. Waters' chamber, which they entered with no less violence than Mr. Fitzpatrick had done before.

The poor lady started from her sleep with as much amazement as terror, and beheld at her bedside a figure which might very well be supposed to have escaped out of Bedlam. Such wildness and confusion were in the looks of Mr. Western; who no sooner saw the lady than he started back, showing sufficiently by his manner, before he spoke, that this was not the person sought after.

Mr. Western now gave everyone present a hearty curse, and, immediately ordering his horses, departed in pursuit of his daughter, without taking the least notice of his nephew Fitzpatrick, or returning any answer to his claim of kindred, notwithstanding all the obligations he had just received from that gentleman. In the violence, moreover, of his hurry, and of his passion, he luckily forgot to demand the muff of Jones: I say luckily; for he would have died on the spot rather than have parted with it.

Jones likewise, with his friend Partridge, set forward the moment he had paid his reckoning, in quest of his lovely Sophia, whom he now resolved never more to abandon the pursuit of. Nor could he bring himself even to take leave of Mrs. Waters; of whom he detested the very thoughts, as she had been, though not designedly, the occasion of his missing the happiest interview with Sophia, to whom he now vowed eternal constancy.

As for Mrs. Waters, she took the opportunity of the coach which was going to Bath with the two Irish gentlemen, the landlady kindly lending her clothes; in return for which she was contented only to receive about double their value as a recompense for the loan. Upon the road she was perfectly reconciled to Mr. Fitzpatrick, who was a very handsome fellow, and indeed did all she could to console him in the absence of his wife.

Thus ended the many odd adventures which Mr. Jones encountered at his inn at Upton, where they talk, to this day, of the beauty and lovely behavior of the charming Sophia, by the name of the Somersetshire angel.

Book XI

CONTAINING ABOUT THREE DAYS

I

SOPHIA having directed her guide to travel through by-roads across the country, they now passed the Severn, and had scarce got a mile from the inn, when the young lady, looking behind her, saw several horses coming after on full speed. This greatly alarmed her fears, and she called to the guide to put on as fast as possible.

He immediately obeyed her, and away they rode a full gallop. But the faster they went, the faster were they followed; and as the horses behind were somewhat swifter than those before, so the former were at length overtaken. Sophia was now instantly relieved by a female voice, that greeted her in the softest manner, and with the utmost civility. This greeting Sophia, as soon as she could recover her breath, with like civility, and with the highest satisfaction to herself, returned.

The travelers who joined Sophia, and who had given her such terror, consisted, like her own company, of two females and a guide. The two parties proceeded three full miles together before anyone offered again to open their mouths; when our heroine, having pretty well got the better of her fear (but yet being somewhat surprised that the other still continued to attend her, as she pursued no great road, and had already passed through several turnings), accosted the strange lady in a most obliging tone, and said, "She was very happy to find they were both traveling the same way."

The other, who, like a ghost, only wanted to be spoken to, readily answered, "That the happiness was entirely hers; that she was a perfect stranger in that country, and was so overjoyed at meeting a companion of her own sex, that she had perhaps been guilty of an impertinence, which required great apology, in keeping pace with her."

More civilities passed between these two ladies; for Mrs. Honour had now given place to the fine habit of the stranger, and had fallen into the rear. But, though Sophia had great curiosity to know why the other lady continued to travel on through the same by-roads with herself, nay, though this gave her some uneasiness, yet fear, or modesty, or some other consideration, restrained her from asking the question.

Daylight at length appeared in its full luster; and now the two ladies, who were riding over a common side by side, looking steadfastly at each other, at the same moment both their eyes became fixed; both their horses stopped, and, both speaking together, with equal joy pronounced, the one the name of Sophia, the other that of Harriet.

This unexpected encounter surprised the ladies much more than I believe it will the sagacious reader, who must have imagined that the strange lady could be no other than Mrs. Fitzpatrick, the cousin of Miss Western, whom we before mentioned to have sallied from the inn a few minutes after her.

So great was the surprise and joy which these two cousins conceived at this meeting (for they had formerly been most intimate acquaintances and friends, and had long lived together with their aunt Western), that it is impossible to recount half the congratulations which passed between them, before either asked a very natural question of the other, namely, whither she was going?

This at last, however, came first from Mrs. Fitzpatrick; but, easy and natural as the question may seem, Sophia found it difficult to give it a very ready and certain answer. She begged her cousin, therefore, to suspend all curiosity till they arrived at some inn, "which I suppose," says she, "can hardly be far distant; and, believe me, Harriet, I suspend as much curiosity on my side; for, indeed, I believe our astonishment is pretty equal."

The conversation which passed between these ladies on the road was, I apprehend, little worth relating. They traveled many hours, till they came into a wide and well-beaten road, which soon brought them to a very fair promising inn, where they all alighted.

Mrs. Fitzpatrick, hearing from Mrs. Honour that Sophia had not been in bed during the two last nights, and observing her to look very pale and wan with her fatigue, earnestly entreated her to refresh herself with some sleep. She was yet a stranger to her history or her apprehensions; but, had she known both, she would have given the same advice; for rest was visibly necessary for her; and their long journey through by-roads so entirely removed all danger of pursuit, that she was herself perfectly easy on that account.

Sophia was easily prevailed on to follow the counsel of her friend, which was heartily seconded by her maid. Mrs. Fitzpatrick likewise offered to bear her cousin company, which Sophia, with much complacence, accepted.

II

THE sun (for he keeps very good hours at this time of the year) had been some time retired to rest when Sophia arose greatly refreshed by her sleep; which, short as it was, nothing but her extreme fatigue could have occasioned; for, though she had told her maid, and perhaps herself too, that she was perfectly easy when she left Upton, yet it is certain her mind was a little affected with that malady which is attended with all the restless symptoms of a fever.

Mrs. Fitzpatrick likewise left her bed at the same time; and, having summoned her maid, immediately dressed herself. She was really a very pretty woman, and, had she been in any other company but that of Sophia, might have been thought beautiful; but when Mrs. Honour of her own accord attended (for her mistress would not suffer her to be waked), and had equipped our heroine, the charms of Mrs. Fitzpatrick were totally eclipsed.

Perhaps Sophia never looked more beautiful than she did at this instant. We ought not, therefore, to condemn the maid of the inn for her hyperbole, who, when she descended, after having lighted the fire, declared, and ratified it with an oath, that if ever there was an angel upon earth she was now above-stairs.

Sophia had acquainted her cousin with her design to go to London; and Mrs. Fitzpatrick had agreed to accompany her; for the arrival of her husband at Upton had put an end to her design of going to Bath, or to her aunt Western. They had therefore no sooner finished their tea than Sophia proposed to set out, the moon then shining extremely bright, and as for the frost she defied it: nor had she any of those apprehensions which many young ladies would have felt at traveling by night; for she had, as we have before observed, some little degree of natural courage.

The disposition of Mrs. Fitzpatrick was more timorous; for, though the greater terrors had conquered the less, and the presence of her husband had driven her away at so unseasonable an hour from Upton, yet, being now arrived at a place where she thought herself safe from his pursuit, she earnestly entreated her cousin to stay till the next morning, and not expose herself to the dangers of traveling by night. Sophia, when she could neither laugh nor reason her cousin out of these apprehensions, at last gave way to them.

The two cousins began now to impart to each other their reciprocal curiosity to know what extraordinary accidents on both sides occasioned this so strange and unexpected meeting. At last Mrs. Fitzpatrick, having obtained of Sophia a promise of communicating likewise in her turn, began to relate what the reader, if he is desirous to know her history, may read in the ensuing chapter.

III

Mrs. Fitzpatrick, after a silence of a few moments, fetching a deep sigh, thus began:

"The remembrance of past pleasures affects us with a kind of tender grief; for this reason, I never reflect without sorrow on those days (the happiest far of my life) which we spent together when both were under the care of my aunt Western. Alas! why are Miss Graveairs and Miss Giddy no more? You remember, I am sure, when we knew each other by no other names. Indeed, you gave the latter appellation with too much cause. I have since experienced how much I deserved it. You, my Sophia, was always my superior in everything, and I heartily hope you will be so in your fortune. I shall never forget the wise and matronly advice you once gave me, when I lamented being disappointed of a ball, though you could not be then fourteen years old.

"Though you must have heard much of my marriage; yet I will set out from the very commencement of my unfortunate acquaintance with my present husband, which was at Bath, soon after you left my aunt and returned home to your father.

"Among the gay young fellows who were at this season at Bath,

Mr. Fitzpatrick was one. He was handsome, *dégagé*, extremely gallant, and in his dress exceeded most others. The qualifications which he then possessed so well recommended him, that, though the people of quality at that time lived separate from the rest of the company, and excluded them from all their parties, Mr. Fitzpatrick found means to gain admittance. It was perhaps no easy matter to avoid him; for he required very little or no invitation; and as, being handsome and genteel, he found it no very difficult matter to ingratiate himself with the ladies, so, he having frequently drawn his sword, the men did not care publicly to affront him. They all abused him behind his back, which might probably proceed from envy; for by the women he was well received, and very particularly distinguished by them.

"My aunt, as she had always lived about the court, was enrolled in that party; for, by whatever means you get into the polite circle, when you are once there, it is sufficient merit for you that you are there. Mr. Fitzpatrick was always one of her private parties. Nor was he backward in returning such distinction; for he soon grew so very particular in his behavior to her, that the scandal club first began to take notice of it, and the better-disposed persons made a match between them. For my own part, I confess, I made no doubt but that his designs were strictly honorable, as the phrase is; that is, to rob a lady of her fortune by way of marriage. My aunt was, I conceived, neither young enough nor handsome enough to attract much wicked inclination; but she had matrimonial charms in great abundance.

"I was the more confirmed in this opinion from the extraordinary respect which he showed to myself; and the more so, as I was the only object of such respect; for he behaved at the same time to many women of quality without any respect at all.

"Agreeable as this was to me, he soon changed it into another kind of behavior, which was perhaps more so. He now put on much softness and tenderness, and languished and sighed abundantly. He became grave, and put on the softest look imaginable the moment he approached me. Indeed he was in all things so very particular towards me, that I must have been blind not to have discovered it. And, and, and——"

"And you was more pleased still, my dear Harriet," cries Sophia; "you need not be ashamed," added she, sighing, "for sure there are irresistible charms in tenderness which too many men are able to affect."

"True," answered her cousin; "men who in all other instances want common sense, are very Machiavels in the art of loving. I wish I did not know an instance. Well, scandal now began to be as busy with me as it had before been with my aunt; and some good ladies did not scruple to affirm that Mr. Fitzpatrick had an intrigue with us both.

"But, what may seem astonishing, my aunt never saw, nor in the least seemed to suspect, that which was visible enough, I believe, from both our behaviors. One would indeed think that love quite puts out the eyes of an old woman. In fact, they so greedily swallow the addresses which are made to them, that, like an outrageous glutton, they are not at leisure to observe what passes amongst others at the same table. This I have observed in more cases than my own; and this was so strongly verified by my aunt, that, though she often found us together at her return from the Pump, the least canting word of his, pretending impatience at her absence, effectually smothered all suspicion. One artifice succeeded with her to admiration. This was his treating me like a little child, and never calling me by any other name in her presence but that of pretty Miss. This indeed did him some disservice with your humble servant; but I soon saw through it, especially as in her absence he behaved to me, as I have said, in a different manner.

"At last, my lover (for so he was) thought proper, in a most solemn manner, to disclose a secret which I had known long before. He now placed all the love which he had pretended to my aunt to my account. He lamented, in very pathetic terms, the encouragement she had given him, and made a high merit of the tedious hours in which he had undergone her conversation. What shall I tell you, my dear Sophia? Then I will confess the truth. I was pleased with my man. I was pleased with my conquest. To rival my aunt delighted me; to rival so many other women charmed me. In short, I am afraid I did not behave as I should do, even upon the very first declaration— I wish I did not almost give him positive encouragement before we parted.

"But I am afraid, my dear, I shall tire you with a detail of so many minute circumstances. To be concise, therefore, imagine me married; imagine me with my husband, at the feet of my aunt; and then imagine the maddest woman in Bedlam in a raving fit, and your imagination will suggest to you no more than what really happened.

"The very next day my aunt left the place, partly to avoid seeing Mr. Fitzpatrick or myself, and as much, perhaps, to avoid seeing any one else; for, though I am told she hath since denied everything

stoutly, I believe she was then a little confounded at her disappointment. Since that time I have written to her many letters, but never
could obtain an answer." Here she paused a moment; but, Sophia
making no answer, she proceeded as in the next chapter.

IV

"We remained at Bath no longer than a fortnight after our wedding;
for as to any reconciliation with my aunt, there were no hopes; and
of my fortune not one farthing could be touched till I was of age, of
which I now wanted more than two years. My husband therefore
was resolved to set out for Ireland; against which I remonstrated very
earnestly, but he had fixed the day, and to that day he obstinately
adhered.

"The evening before our departure, as we were disputing this
point with great eagerness on both sides, he started suddenly from
his chair, and left me abruptly, saying he was going to the rooms. He
was hardly out of the house when I saw a paper lying on the floor,
which, I suppose, he had carelessly pulled from his pocket together
with his handkerchief. This paper I took up, and, finding it to be a
letter, I made no scruple to open and read it; and indeed I read it so
often that I can repeat it to you almost word for word. This, then,
was the letter:

To Mr. Brian Fitzpatrick.

Sir,—Yours received, and am surprised you should use me in
this manner, as have never seen any of your cash, unless for one
linsey-woolsey coat, and your bill now is upwards of £150. Consider, sir, how often you have fobbed me off with your being
shortly to be married to this lady and t'other lady; but I can
neither live on hopes or promises, nor will my woolen-draper
take any such in payment. You tell me you are secure of
having either the aunt or the niece, and that you might have
married the aunt before this, whose jointure you say is immense, but that you prefer the niece on account of her ready
money. Pray, sir, take a fool's advice for once, and marry the
first you can get. You will pardon my offering my advice, as
you know I sincerely wish you well. Shall draw on you per next
post, in favor of Messieurs John Drugget and company, at fourteen days, which doubt not your honoring, and am,—Sir, your
humble servant,

Sam. Cosgrave.

"I had pretty well spent my tears before his return home; but sufficient remains of them appeared in my swollen eyes. He threw himself sullenly into his chair, and for a long time we were both silent. At length, in a haughty tone, he said,

" 'I hope, madam, your servants have packed up all your things; for the coach will be ready by six in the morning.'

"My patience was totally subdued by this provocation, and I answered,

" 'No, sir, there is a letter still remains unpacked'; and then throwing it on the table I fell to upbraiding him with the most bitter language I could invent.

"Whether guilt, or shame, or prudence restrained him I cannot say; but, though he is the most passionate of men, he exerted no rage on this occasion. He endeavored, on the contrary, to pacify me by the most gentle means. He swore the phrase in the letter to which I principally objected was not his, nor had he ever written any such. He concluded by a very fond caress, and many violent protestations of love.

"Had he been guilty of twenty times as much, half the tenderness and fondness which he used would have prevailed on me to have forgiven him. I now made no further objections to our setting out, which we did the next morning, and in a little more than a week arrived at the seat of Mr. Fitzpatrick.

"This seat is an ancient mansion-house: if I was in one of those merry humors in which you have so often seen me, I could describe it to you ridiculously enough. It looked as if it had been formerly inhabited by a gentleman. Here was room enough, and not the less room on account of the furniture; for indeed there was very little in it. An old woman, who seemed coeval with the building, received us at the gate, and in a howl scarce human, and to me unintelligible, welcomed her master home. In short, the whole scene was so gloomy and melancholy, that it threw my spirits into the lowest dejection; which my husband discerning, instead of relieving, increased by two or three malicious observations. 'There are good houses, madam,' says he, 'as you find, in other places besides England; but perhaps you had rather be in a dirty lodgings at Bath.'

"My companion, far from clearing up the gloom of solitude, soon convinced me that I must have been wretched with him in any place and in any condition. In a word, he was a surly fellow, a character, perhaps, you have never seen; for indeed no woman ever sees it exemplified but in a father, a brother, or a husband; and though you have a father, he is not of that character. This surly fellow had formerly appeared to me the very reverse, and so he did still to every other person. How shall I describe his barbarity? To my fondness he was cold and insensible. My little comical ways, which you, my Sophy, and which others have called so agreeable, he treated with contempt. In my most serious moments he sung and whistled; and whenever I was thoroughly dejected and miserable he was angry and abused me; for, though he was never pleased with my good-humor, nor ascribed it to my satisfaction in him, yet my low spirits always offended him.

"It will be easily imagined that, when I once despised my husband, as I confess to you I soon did, I must consequently dislike his company; and indeed I had the happiness of being very little troubled with it; for our house was now most elegantly furnished, our cellars well stocked, and dogs and horses provided in great abundance. As my gentleman, therefore, entertained his neighbors with great hospitality, so his neighbors resorted to him with great alacrity; and sports and drinking consumed so much of his time, that a small part of his conversation, that is to say, of his ill-humors, fell to my share.

"Happy would it have been for me if I could as easily have avoided all other disagreeable company; but, alas! I was confined to some which constantly tormented me; and the more, as I saw no prospect of being relieved from them. These companions were my own racking thoughts, which plagued and in a manner haunted me night and day. In this situation I passed through a scene, the horrors of which can neither be painted nor imagined. Think, my dear, figure, if you can, to yourself, what I must have undergone. I became a mother by the man I scorned, hated, and detested. I went through all the agonies and miseries of a lying-in (ten times more painful in such a circumstance than the worst labor can be when one endures it for a man one loves) in a desert, or rather, indeed, a scene of riot and level, without a friend, without a companion, or without any of those agreeable circumstances which often alleviate, and perhaps sometimes more than compensate, the sufferings of our sex at that season.

"I was left to my solitude, and to apply to books for my only comfort. I now read almost all day long. How many books do you think I read?"

"I can't guess, indeed, cousin," answered Sophia. "Perhaps half a score."

"Half a score! half a thousand, child!" answered the other. "I read a good deal in Daniel's English History of France; a great deal in

Plutarch's Lives, the Atalantis, Pope's Homer, Dryden's Plays, Chillingworth, the Countess D'Aulnois, and Locke's Human Understanding.

"My husband now took a second journey to England, where he continued upwards of three months. During the greater part of this time I led a life which nothing but having led a worse could make me think tolerable; for perfect solitude can never be reconciled to a social mind like mine. What added to my wretchedness was the loss of my little infant: not that I pretend to have had for it that extravagant tenderness of which I believe I might have been capable under other circumstances; but I resolved, in every instance, to discharge the duty of the tenderest mother; and this care prevented me from feeling the weight of that heaviest of all things, when it can be at all said to lie heavy on our hands.

"I had spent full ten weeks almost entirely by myself, when a young lady, a relation to my husband, came from a distant part of Ireland to visit me. Perceiving me in very low spirits, without inquiring the cause, which, indeed, she very well knew, the young lady fell to compassionating my case. She said, 'Though politeness had prevented me from complaining to my husband's relations of his behavior, yet they all were very sensible of it, and felt great concern upon that account; but none more than herself.' And after some more general discourse on this head, which I own I could not forbear countenancing, at last, after much previous precaution and enjoined concealment, she communicated to me, as a profound secret—that my husband kept a mistress.

"You will certainly imagine I heard this news with the utmost insensibility. Upon my word, if you do, your imagination will mislead you. Contempt had not so kept down my anger to my husband, but that hatred rose again on this occasion. What can be the reason of this?

"Are we so abominably selfish that we can be concerned at others having possession even of what we despise? or are we not rather abominably vain, and is not this the greatest injury done to our vanity? What think you, Sophia?"

"I don't know, indeed," answered Sophia; "I have never troubled myself with any of these deep contemplations; but I think the lady did very ill in communicating to you such a secret."

"And yet, my dear, this conduct is natural," replied Mrs. Fitzpatrick; "and, when you have seen and read as much as myself, you will acknowledge it to be so."

"I am sorry to hear it is natural," returned Sophia; "for I want neither reading nor experience to convince me that it is very dishonorable and very ill-natured: nay, it is surely as ill-bred to tell a husband or wife of the faults of each other as to tell them of their own."

"Well," continued Mrs. Fitzpatrick, "my husband at last returned; and, if I am thoroughly acquainted with my own thoughts, I hated him now more than ever; but I despised him rather less, for certainly nothing so much weakens our contempt as an injury done to our pride or our vanity.

"He now assumed a carriage to me so very different from what he had lately worn, and so nearly resembling his behavior the first week of our marriage, that, had I now had any spark of love remaining, he might possibly have rekindled my fondness for him. But, though hatred may succeed to contempt, and may perhaps get the better of it, love, I believe, cannot.

"He soon acquainted me with the motive, and taught me to account for it. In a word, then, he had spent and lost all the ready money of my fortune; and, as he could mortgage his own estate no deeper, he was now desirous to supply himself with cash for his extravagance by selling a little estate of mine, which he could not do without my assistance; and to obtain this favor was the whole and sole motive of all the fondness which he now put on.

"With this I peremptorily refused to comply. I told him, and I told him truly, that, had I been possessed of the Indies at our first marriage, he might have commanded it all; for it had been a constant maxim with me, that where a woman disposes of her heart she should always deposit her fortune; but, as he had been so kind, long ago, to restore the former into my possession, I was resolved likewise to retain what little remained of the latter.

"I will not describe to you the passion into which these words, and the resolute air in which they were spoken, threw him; nor will I trouble you with the whole scene which succeeded between us. When he found I was neither to be soothed nor bullied into compliance, he took a very violent method indeed. Perhaps you will conclude he beat me; but this, though he hath approached very near to it, he never actually did. He confined me to my room, without suffering me to have either pen, ink, paper, or book; and a servant every day made my bed, and brought me my food.

"When I had remained a week under this imprisonment he made me a visit, and, with the voice of a schoolmaster, or, what is often much the same, of a tyrant, asked me, 'if I would yet comply?' I answered, very stoutly, 'That I would die first.'—'Then so you shall, and be d—ned!' cries he; 'for you shall never go alive out of this room.'

"Here I remained a fortnight longer; and, to say the truth, my constancy was almost subdued, and I began to think of submission; when, one day, in the absence of my husband, who was gone abroad for some short time, by the greatest good fortune in the world, an accident happened. I—at a time when I began to give way to the utmost despair—everything would be excusable at such a time—at that very time I received——But it would take up an hour to tell you all particulars. In one word, then (for I will not tire you with circumstances), gold, the common key to all padlocks, opened my door and set me at liberty.

"I now made haste to Dublin, where I immediately procured a passage to England; and was proceeding to Bath, in order to throw myself into the protection of my aunt, or of your father, or of any relation who would afford it me. My husband overtook me last night at the inn where I lay, and which you left a few minutes before me; but I had the good luck to escape him and to follow you.

"And thus, my dear, ends my history: a tragical one, I am sure, it is to myself; but, perhaps, I ought rather to apologize to you for its dullness."

Sophia heaved a deep sigh, and answered,

"Indeed, Harriet, I pity you from my soul!——But what could you expect? Why, why, would you marry an Irishman?"

"Upon my word," replied her cousin, "your censure is unjust. There are, among the Irish, men of as much worth and honor as any among the English; nay, to speak the truth, generosity of spirit is rather more common among them. I have known some examples there, too, of good husbands; and I believe these are not very plenty in England. Ask me, rather, what I could expect when I married a fool; and I will tell you a solemn truth: I did not know him to be so."

"Can no man," said Sophia, in a very low and altered voice, "do you think, make a bad husband who is not a fool?"

"That," answered the other, "is too general a negative; but none, I believe, is so likely as a fool to prove so. Among my acquaintance the silliest fellows are the worst husbands; and I will venture to assert, as a fact, that a man of sense rarely behaves very ill to a wife who deserves very well."

V

SOPHIA now, at the desire of her cousin, related—not what follows, but what hath gone before in this history; for which reason the reader will, I suppose, excuse me for not repeating it over again.

One remark, however, I cannot forbear making on her narrative, namely, that she made no more mention of Jones, from the beginning to the end, than if there had been no such person alive. This I will neither endeavor to account for nor to excuse. Indeed, if this may be called a kind of dishonesty, it seems the more inexcusable, from the apparent openness and explicit sincerity of the other lady. But so it was.

The landlord now ascended, and acquainted our fair travelers that a great gentleman below desired to do them the honor of waiting on them. Sophia turned pale and trembled at this message, though the reader will conclude it was too civil to have come from her father; but fear hath the common fault of a justice of peace, and is apt to conclude hastily from every slight circumstance without examining the evidence on both sides.

To ease the reader's curiosity, therefore, rather than his apprehensions, we proceed to inform him that an Irish peer had arrived very late that evening at the inn, in his way to London. This nobleman had seen the attendant of Mrs. Fitzpatrick, and, upon a short inquiry, was informed that her lady, with whom he was very particularly acquainted, was above. This information he had no sooner received than he addressed himself to the landlord, and sent him upstairs with compliments.

Sophia was very soon eased of her causeless fright by the entry of the noble peer, who was not only an intimate acquaintance of Mrs. Fitzpatrick, but in reality a very particular friend of that lady.

This nobleman had an estate in the neighborhood of Fitzpatrick, and had been for some time acquainted with the lady. No sooner, therefore, did he hear of her confinement than he earnestly applied himself to procure her liberty; which he presently effected, not by storming the castle, according to the example of ancient heroes, but by corrupting the governor, in conformity with the modern art of war, in which craft is held to be preferable to valor, and gold is found to be more irresistible than either lead or steel.

This circumstance, however, as the lady did not think it material enough to relate to her friend, we would not at that time impart it to the reader. We rather chose to leave him a while under a supposition

Tom Jones laid violent hands on the collar of poor Partridge.

that she had found, or coined, or, by some very extraordinary, perhaps supernatural means, had possessed herself of the money with which she had bribed her keeper, than to interrupt her narrative by giving a hint of what seemed to her of too little importance to be mentioned.

The peer, after a short conversation, could not forbear expressing some surprise at meeting the lady in that place; nor could he refrain from telling her he imagined she had been gone to Bath. Mrs. Fitzpatrick very freely answered, "That she had been prevented in her purpose by the arrival of a person she need not mention. In short," says she, "I was overtaken by my husband (for I need not affect to conceal what the world knows too well already). I had the good fortune to escape in a most surprising manner, and am now going to London with this young lady, who is a near relation of mine, and who hath escaped from as great a tyrant as my own."

His lordship, concluding that this tyrant was likewise a husband, made a speech full of compliments to both the ladies, and as full of invectives against his own sex; nor, indeed, did he avoid some oblique glances at the matrimonial institution itself, and at the unjust powers given by it to man over the more sensible and more meritorious part of the species. He ended his oration with an offer of his protection, and of his coach-and-six, which was instantly accepted by Mrs. Fitzpatrick, and at last, upon her persuasions, by Sophia.

Matters being thus adjusted, his lordship took his leave, and the ladies retired to rest, where Mrs. Fitzpatrick entertained her cousin with many high encomiums on the character of the noble peer, and enlarged very particularly on his great fondness for his wife; saying, she believed he was almost the only person of high rank who was entirely constant to the marriage bed.

"Indeed," added she, "my dear Sophy, that is a very rare virtue amongst men of condition. Never expect it when you marry; for, believe me, if you do, you will certainly be deceived."

A gentle sigh stole from Sophia at these words, which perhaps contributed to form a dream of no very pleasant kind; but, as she never revealed this dream to anyone, so the reader cannot expect to see it related here.

VI

THOSE members of society who are born to furnish the blessings of life now began to light their candles, in order to pursue their daily labors for the use of those who are born to enjoy these blessings. Now the bonny housemaid begins to repair the disordered drum-room, while the riotous authors of that disorder, in broken, inter-rupted slumbers, tumble and toss, as if the hardness of down dis-quieted their repose.

In simple phrase, the clock had so sooner struck seven than the ladies were ready for their journey; and, at their desire, his lordship and his equipage were prepared to attend them.

Everything being settled at the inn, the ladies discharged their for-mer guides, and Sophia made a present to the landlord. And now Sophia first discovered a loss which gave her some uneasiness; and this was of the hundred-pound bank-bill which her father had given her at their last meeting; and which, within a very inconsiderable trifle, was all the treasure she was at present worth. She searched everywhere, and shook and tumbled all her things to no purpose, the bill was not to be found; and she was at last fully persuaded that she had lost it from her pocket in the dark lane; as she now recollected some discomposure in her pockets, and the great difficulty with which she had drawn forth her handkerchief.

Misfortunes of this kind, whatever inconveniences they may be at-tended with, are incapable of subduing a mind in which there is any strength, without the assistance of avarice. Sophia, therefore, though nothing could be worse timed than this accident at such a season, im-mediately got the better of her concern, and with her wonted seren-ity and cheerfulness of countenance, returned to her company.

The coach, now having received its company, began to move for-wards, and made such good expedition that they performed a journey of ninety miles in two days, and on the second evening arrived in London without having encountered any one adventure on the road worthy the dignity of this history to relate.

Our company, being arrived at London, were set down at his lord-ship's house, where, while they refreshed themselves after the fatigue of their journey, servants were despatched to provide a lodging for the two ladies; for, as her ladyship was not then in town, Mrs. Fitz-patrick would by no means consent to accept a bed in the mansion of the peer.

Some readers will perhaps condemn this extraordinary delicacy, as I may call it, of virtue, as too nice and scrupulous, but we must make allowances for her situation, which must be owned to have been very ticklish; and, when we consider the malice of censorious tongues, we must allow, if it was a fault, the fault was an excess on the right side,

and which every woman who is in the selfsame situation will do well
to imitate. The most formal appearance of virtue, when it is only an
appearance, may, perhaps, in very abstracted considerations, seem to
be rather less commendable than virtue itself without this formality;
but it will, however, be always more commended; and this, I believe,
will be granted by all, that it is necessary, unless in some very particular cases, for every woman to support either the one or the other.

A lodging being prepared, Sophia accompanied her cousin for that
evening; but resolved early in the morning to inquire after the lady
into whose protection, as we have formerly mentioned, she had determined to throw herself when she quitted her father's house. And
this she was the more eager in doing from some observations she had
made during her journey in the coach.

The case, it seems, was this: Mrs. Fitzpatrick wisely considered
that the virtue of a young lady is, in the world, in the same situation
with a poor hare, which is certain, whenever it ventures abroad, to
meet its enemies; for it can hardly meet any other. No sooner, therefore, was she determined to take the first opportunity of quitting the
protection of her husband, than she resolved to cast herself under the
protection of some other man; and whom could she so properly
choose to be her guardian as a person of quality, of fortune, of honor;
and who, besides a gallant disposition which inclines men to knight-
errantry, that is, to be the champions of ladies in distress, had often
declared a violent attachment to herself, and had already given her all
the instances of it in his power?

But, as the law hath foolishly omitted this office of vice-husband,
or guardian to an eloped lady, and as malice is apt to denominate him
by a more disagreeable appellation, it was concluded that his lordship
should perform all such kind offices to the lady in secret, and without
publicly assuming the character of her protector. Nay, to prevent
any other person from seeing him in this light, it was agreed that the
lady should proceed to Bath, and that his lordship should first go to
London, and thence should go down to that place by the advice of
his physicians.

Now all this Sophia very plainly understood, not from the lips or
behavior of Mrs. Fitzpatrick, but from the peer, who was infinitely
less expert at retaining a secret than was the good lady; and perhaps
the exact secrecy which Mrs. Fitzpatrick had observed on this head
in her narrative served not a little to heighten those suspicions which
were now risen in the mind of her cousin.

Sophia very easily found out the lady she sought; for indeed there was not a chairman in town to whom her house was not perfectly well known; and, as she received, in return of her first message, a most pressing invitation, she immediately accepted it. Mrs. Fitzpatrick, indeed, did not desire her cousin to stay with her with more earnestness than civility required. Whether she had discerned and resented the suspicion above mentioned, or from what other motives it arose, I cannot say; but certain it is, she was full as desirous of parting with Sophia as Sophia herself could be of going.

The young lady, when she came to take leave of her cousin, could not avoid giving her a short hint of advice. She begged her, for Heaven's sake, to take care of herself, and to consider in how dangerous a situation she stood; adding, she hoped some method would be found of reconciling her to her husband.

"You must remember, my dear," says she, "the maxim which my aunt Western hath so often repeated to us both: That whenever the matrimonial alliance is broke, and war declared between husband and wife, she can hardly make a disadvantageous peace for herself on any conditions. These are my aunt's very words, and she hath had a great deal of experience in the world."

Mrs. Fitzpatrick answered, with a contemptuous smile,

"Never fear me, child; take care of yourself, for you are younger than I. I will come and visit you in a few days; but, dear Sophy, let me give you one piece of advice: leave the character of Graveairs in the country, for, believe me, it will sit very awkwardly upon you in this town."

Thus the two cousins parted, and Sophia repaired directly to Lady Bellaston, where she found a most hearty, as well as most polite, welcome. The lady had taken a great fancy to her when she had seen her formerly with her aunt Western. She was indeed extremely glad to see her, and was no sooner acquainted with the reasons which induced her to leave the squire and to fly to London than she highly applauded her sense and resolution; and, after expressing the highest satisfaction in the opinion which Sophia had declared she entertained of her ladyship, by choosing her house for an asylum, she promised her all the protection which it was in her power to give.

As we have now brought Sophia into safe hands, the reader will, I apprehend, be contented to deposit her there a while, and to look a little after other personages, and particularly poor Jones, whom we have left long enough to do penance for his past offenses, which, as is the nature of vice, brought sufficient punishment upon him themselves.

Book XII

CONTAINING·THE SAME INDIVIDUAL TIME WITH THE FORMER

I

THE history now returns to the inn at Upton, whence we shall first trace the footsteps of Squire Western.

The reader may be pleased to remember that the said squire departed from the inn in great fury, and rode full speed, vowing the utmost vengeance against poor Sophia if he should but overtake her. He proceeded about two miles, when he began to bemoan himself most bitterly, frequently crying out, "What pity is it! Sure never was so unlucky a dog as myself!" And then burst forth a volley of oaths and execrations.

The parson attempted to administer comfort to him. "Sorrow not, sir," says he. "Howbeit we have not yet been able to overtake young madam, peradventure she will soon be fatigued with her journey, and will tarry in some inn; and in that case, in all moral certainty, you will very briefly be *compos voti*."

"Pogh! d—n the slut!" answered the squire, "I am lamenting the loss of so fine a morning for hunting. It is confounded hard to lose one of the best scenting days, in all appearance, which hath been this season, and especially after so long a frost."

He had hardly uttered the words, and two or three oaths at their heels, when a pack of hounds began to open their melodious throats at a small distance from them, which the squire's horses and his rider both perceiving, both immediately pricked up their ears, and the squire, crying, "She's gone, she's gone! Damn me if she is not gone!" instantly clapped spurs to the beast, who little needed it, having indeed the same inclination with his master; and now the whole company, crossing into a corn-field, rode directly towards the hounds, with much hallooing and whooping, while the poor parson, blessing himself, brought up the rear.

Thus fable reports that the fair Grimalkin, whom Venus, at the desire of a passionate lover, converted from a cat into a fine woman, no sooner perceived a mouse than she leaped from the bed of her husband to pursue the little animal.

What are we to understand by this? Not that the bride was displeased with the embraces of her amorous bridegroom; for, though some have remarked that cats are subject to ingratitude, yet women and cats too will be pleased and purr on certain occasions. The truth is, that, "if we shut Nature out at the door, she will come in at the window." We are not to arraign the squire of any want of love for his daughter, for in reality he had a great deal; we are only to consider that he was a squire and a sportsman.

The hounds ran very hard, as it is called, and the squire pursued with all his usual vociferation, nor did the thoughts of Sophia ever once intrude themselves to allay the satisfaction he enjoyed in the chase.

As soon as the sport was ended by the death of the little animal which had occasioned it, the two squires met, and in all squire-like greeting saluted each other. The conversation was concluded with a second chase, and that with an invitation to dinner. This being accepted, was following by a hearty bout of drinking, which ended in as hearty a nap on the part of Squire Western.

No sooner had the good squire shaken off his draught, and summoned his horses in order to renew his pursuit, than Mr. Supple began his dissuasives, which at length prevailed, and Mr. Western agreed to return home; being principally moved by one argument, viz., that he knew not which way to go, and might probably be riding farther from his daughter instead of towards her. He then took leave of his brother sportsman, and expressing great joy that the frost was broken (which might perhaps be no small motive to his hastening home), set forwards, or rather backwards, for Somersetshire; but not before he had first despatched part of his retinue in quest of his daughter.

Mr. Jones and his companion Partridge left the inn a few minutes after the departure of Squire Western, and pursued the same road on foot, for the hostler told them that no horses were by any means to be at that time procured at Upton. On they marched with heavy hearts; for though their disquiet proceeded from very different reasons, yet displeased they were both; and if Jones sighed bitterly, Partridge grunted altogether as sadly at every step.

When they came to the cross-roads where the squire had stopped to take counsel, Jones stopped likewise, and turning to Partridge, asked his opinion which track they should pursue.

"Ah, sir," answered Partridge, "I wish your honor would follow my advice."

"Why should I not?" replied Jones; "for it is now indifferent to me whither I go or what becomes of me."

"My advice, then," said Partridge, "is, that you immediately face about and return home; for who that hath such a home to return to as your honor would travel thus about the country like a vagabond?"

"Alas!" cried Jones, "I have no home to return to;—but if my friend, my father, would receive me, could I bear the country from which Sophia is flown? Cruel Sophia! Cruel! No; let me blame myself! No; let me blame thee. D—nation seize thee—fool—blockhead! thou hast undone me, and I will tear thy soul from thy body." At which words he laid violent hands on the collar of poor Partridge, and shook him more heartily than an ague-fit.

Partridge fell trembling on his knees, and begged for mercy, vowing he had meant no harm—when Jones, after having played the part of a madman for many minutes, came by degrees to himself; which no sooner happened, than, turning to Partridge, he very earnestly begged his pardon for the attack he had made on him in the violence of his passion; but concluded by desiring him never to mention his return again.

Partridge easily forgave, and faithfully promised to obey the injunction now laid upon him. And then Jones very briskly cried out,

"Since it is absolutely impossible for me to pursue any farther the steps of my angel—I will pursue those of glory. Come on, my brave lad, now for the army:—it is a glorious cause, and I would willingly sacrifice my life in it, even though it was worth my preserving."

And so saying, he immediately struck into the different road from that which the squire had taken, and, by mere chance, pursued the very same through which Sophia had before passed.

Our travelers now marched a full mile without speaking a syllable to each other, though Jones indeed muttered many things to himself. As to Partridge, he was profoundly silent; for he had apprehensions of provoking his friend to a second fit of wrath, especially as he began now to suspect that Jones was absolutely out of his senses.

At length, Jones, being weary of soliloquy, addressed himself to his companion, and blamed him for his taciturnity; and now Partridge again took the bridle from his tongue.

"Certainly, sir," says he, "I dreamt of nothing all last night but of fighting; and methought the blood ran out of my nose as liquor out of a tap."

"Nothing can be more likely to happen than death to men who go into battle," answered Jones, "Perhaps we shall both fall in it—and what then?"

"What then?" replied Partridge; "why, then there is an end of us, is there not? What matters the cause to me, or who gets the victory, if I am killed? There will be an end of poor Partridge."

"And an end of poor Partridge," cries Jones, "there must be, one time or other."

"That's very certain," cries Partridge. "But there is a great difference between dying in one's bed a great many years hence, like a good Christian, with all our friends crying about us, and being shot today or tomorrow like a mad dog; or, perhaps, hacked in twenty pieces with the sword, and that too before we have repented of all our sins. Besides, for my part, I understand nothing of it. I never fired off a gun above ten times in my life; and then it was not charged with bullets. And for the sword, I never learned to fence, and know nothing of the matter. And then there are those cannons, which certainly it must be thought the highest presumption to go in the way of; and nobody but a madman—I ask pardon; upon my soul I meant no harm; I beg I may not throw your honor into another passion."

"Be under no apprehension, Partridge," cries Jones; "I am now so well convinced of thy cowardice, that thou couldst not provoke me on any account."

"Your honor," answered he, "may call me coward, or anything else you please. I never read in my grammar that a man can't be a good man without fighting; and I am sure the Scripture is so much against it, that a man shall never persuade me he is a good Christian while he sheds Christian blood."

JUST as Partridge had uttered that good and pious doctrine with which the last chapter concluded, they arrived at another cross-way, when a lame fellow in rags asked them for alms; upon which Partridge gave him a severe rebuke, saying, "Every parish ought to keep their own poor."

Jones then fell a-laughing, and asked Partridge "if he was not ashamed, with so much charity in his mouth, to have no charity in his heart. Your religion," says he, "serves you only for an excuse for your faults, but is no incentive to your virtue. Can any man who is really a Christian abstain from relieving one of his brethren in such a miserable condition?" And at the same time, putting his hand in his pocket, he gave the poor object a shilling.

"Master," cries the fellow, after thanking him, "I have a curious thing here in my pocket, which I found about two miles off, if your worship will please to buy it. I should not venture to pull it out to everyone; but, as you are so good a gentleman, and so kind to the poor, you won't suspect a man of being a thief only because he is poor." He then pulled out a little gilt pocket-book, and delivered it into the hands of Jones.

Jones opened it, and (guess, reader, what he felt) saw in the first page the words, Sophia Western, written by her own fair hand. He no sooner read the name than he pressed it close to his lips; nor could he avoid falling into some very frantic raptures, notwithstanding his company.

While Jones was kissing and mumbling the book, as if he had an excellent brown buttered crust in his mouth, or as if he had really been a book-worm, or an author who had nothing to eat but his own works, a piece of paper fell from its leaves to the ground, which Partridge took up, and delivered to Jones, who presently perceived it to be a bank-bill. It was indeed the very bill which Western had given his daughter the night before her departure; £100.

The eyes of Partridge sparkled at this news, which Jones now proclaimed aloud; and so did those of the poor fellow who had found the book, and who (I hope from a principle of honesty) had never opened it; but we should not deal honestly by the reader if we omitted to inform him that the fellow could not read.

Jones, who had felt nothing but pure joy and transport from the finding the book, was affected with a mixture of concern at this new discovery; for his imagination instantly suggested to him that the owner of the bill might possibly want it before he should be able to convey it to her. He then acquainted the finder that he knew the lady to whom the book belonged, and would endeavor to find her out as soon as possible, and return it to her.

The pocket-book was a late present from Mrs. Western to her niece; it had cost five-and-twenty shillings, having been bought of a celebrated toyman; but the real value of the silver which it contained in its clasp was about eighteen-pence; and that price the said toyman, as it was altogether as good as when it first issued from his shop, would now have given for it. Jones, on the contrary, without any hesitation gave a guinea in exchange for the book. The poor man, who had not for a long time before been possessed of so much treasure, gave Mr. Jones a thousand thanks.

The fellow very readily agreed to attend our travelers to the place where he had found the pocket-book. Together, therefore, they proceeded directly thither; but not so fast as Mr. Jones desired; for his guide unfortunately happened to be lame, and could not possibly travel faster than a mile an hour. At this place, therefore, was at above three miles' distance, though the fellow had said otherwise, the reader need not be acquainted how long they were in walking it.

At length they arrived at the very spot where Sophia unhappily dropped the pocket-book. Here Jones offered to take leave of his guide; but the fellow, who had now had sufficient time to recollect himself, put on a discontented look, and, scratching his head, said "He hoped his worship would give him something more. Your worship," said he, "will, I hope, take it into your consideration that if I had not been honest I might have kept the whole." And indeed this the reader must confess to have been true. "If the paper there," said he, "be worth £100, I am sure the finding it deserves more than a guinea. Besides, suppose your worship should never see the lady, nor give it her—it is but reasonable I should have my share."

"I promise thee, upon my honor," cries Jones, "that I know the right owner, and will restore it her."

"Nay, your worship," answered the fellow, "may do as you please as to that; if you will but give me my share, that is, one-half of the money, your honor may keep the rest yourself if you please"; and concluded with swearing, by a very vehement oath, "that he would never mention a syllable of it to any man living."

"Lookee, friend," cries Jones, "the right owner shall certainly have again all that she lost; and as for any farther gratuity, I really cannot give it you at present; but let me know your name, and where you live, and it is more than possible you may hereafter have further reason to rejoice at this morning's adventure."

"I don't know what you mean by venture," cries the fellow; "it seems I must venture whether you will return the lady her money or no; but I hope your worship will consider—"

"Come, come," said Partridge, "tell his honor your name, and where you may be found; I warrant you will never repent having put the money into his hands."

The fellow, seeing no hopes of recovering the possession of the pocket-book, at last complied in giving in his name and place of abode, which Jones writ in the same page where she had writ her name; and then he cried out,

"There, friend, you are the happiest man alive; I have joined your name to that of an angel."

"I don't know anything about angels," answered the fellow; "but I wish you would give me a little more money, or else return me the pocket-book."

Partridge now waxed wroth: he called the poor cripple by several vile and opprobrious names, and was absolutely proceeding to beat him, but Jones would not suffer any such thing; and now Mr. Jones departed and Partridge followed, while the man, who was obliged to stay behind, fell to cursing them both, as well as his parents; "for had they," says he, "sent me to charity-school to learn to write and read and cast accounts, I should have known the value of these matters as well as other people."

IV

Our travelers now walked so fast that they had very little time or breath for conversation; Jones meditating all the way on Sophia, and Partridge on the bank-bill. They had proceeded above three miles, when Partridge, being unable any longer to keep up with Jones, called to him, and begged him a little to slacken his pace: with this he was the more ready to comply, as he had for some time lost the footsteps of the horses, which the thaw had enabled him to trace for several miles.

They now arrived at an inn, or indeed an ale-house, where Jones was prevailed upon to stop, the rather as he had no longer any assurance of being in the road he desired. They walked both directly into the kitchen, where Jones began to inquire if no ladies had passed that way in the morning, and Partridge as eagerly examined into the state of their provisions; and indeed his inquiry met with the better success; for Jones could not hear news of Sophia; but Partridge, to his great satisfaction, found good reason to expect very shortly the agreeable sight of an excellent smoking dish of eggs and bacon.

In strong and healthy constitutions love hath a very different effect from what it causes in the puny part of the species. In the latter it generally destroys all appetite; in the former, though it often induces forgetfulness and a neglect of food, yet place a good piece of well-powdered buttock before a hungry lover, and he seldom fails very handsomely to play his part. Thus it happened in the present case; for though Jones perhaps wanted a prompter, and might have traveled much farther, had he been alone, with an empty stomach, yet no sooner did he sit down to the bacon and eggs, than he fell to as heartily and voraciously as Partridge himself.

Now the moon beginning to put forth her silver light, as the poets call it (though she looked at that time more like a piece of copper), Jones called for his reckoning, and ordered Partridge to prepare for his journey; but Partridge, having lately carried two points, as my reader hath seen before, was emboldened to attempt a third, which was to prevail with Jones to take up a lodging that evening in the house where he then was. He insisted strongly that unless Jones knew which way the lady was gone, every step he took might very possibly lead him the farther from her; "how much better, therefore, would it be to stay till the morning, when we may expect to meet with somebody to inquire of?"

This last argument had indeed some effect on Jones, and he was at last prevailed on to stay and refresh himself with a few hours' rest, which indeed he very much wanted, for he had hardly shut his eyes since he had left the inn where the accident of the broken head had happened.

As soon as Jones had taken a resolution to proceed no farther that night, he retired to rest with his two bedfellows, the pocket-book and the muff, but Partridge, who at several times had refreshed himself with several naps, was more inclined to eating than to sleeping, and more to drinking than to either.

Though the pride of Partridge did not submit to acknowledge himself a servant, yet he condescended in most particulars to imitate the manners of that rank. One instance of this was his greatly magnifying the fortune of his companion, as he called Jones: such is a general custom with all servants among strangers, as none of them would willingly be thought the attendant on a beggar; for, the higher the situation of the master is, the higher, consequently, is that of the man in his own opinion; the truth of which observation appears from the behavior of all the footmen of the nobility.

But, though they would be ashamed to be the footman of a beggar, they are not so to attend upon a rogue, or a blockhead; and do consequently make no scruple to spread the fame of the iniquities and follies of their said masters as far as possible, and this often with great humor and merriment.

After Partridge, therefore, had enlarged greatly on the vast fortune to which Mr. Jones was heir, he very freely communicated an apprehension which he had begun to conceive the day before. In short, he was now pretty well confirmed in an opinion that his master was out of his wits, with which opinion he very bluntly acquainted the good company round the fire.

The landlord agreed, and likewise claimed the sagacity of having observed it. "And certainly," added he, "it must be so; for no one but a madman would have thought of leaving so good a house to ramble about the country at that time of night."

An exciseman, pulling his pipe from his mouth, said, "He thought the gentleman looked and talked a little wildly"; and then turning to Partridge, "If he be a madman," says he, "he should not be suffered to travel thus about the country; for possibly he may do some mischief. It is a pity he was not secured and sent home to his relations."

Now as Partridge was persuaded that Jones had run away from Mr. Allworthy, he promised himself the highest rewards if he could by any means convey him back. But fear of Jones had discouraged him from applying himself to form any regular plan for the purpose. But no sooner did he hear the sentiments of the exciseman than he expressed a hearty wish that such a matter could be brought about.

"Could be brought about!" says the exciseman; "why, there is nothing easier."

"Ah, sir," answered Partridge, "you don't know what a devil of a fellow he is. He can take me up with one hand, and throw me out at window; and he would, too, if he did but imagine——"

"Pogh!" says the exciseman, "I believe I am as good a man as he. Besides, here are five of us."

"I don't know what five," cries the landlady; "my husband shall have nothing to do in it. The young gentleman is as pretty a young gentleman as ever I saw in my life, and I believe he is no more mad than any of us. What do you tell of his having a wild look with his eyes? they are the prettiest eyes I ever saw, and he hath the prettiest look with them; and a very modest, civil young man he is."

Healths were afterwards pledged by all present, and the bumpers which were swallowed on this occasion soon put an end to the conversation. Here, therefore, we will put an end to the chapter.

V

As THERE is no wholesomer, so perhaps there are few stronger sleeping potions than fatigue. Jones slept nine hours, and it was almost eight of the clock before all matters could be got ready for his departure.

They had not gone above two miles when a violent storm of rain overtook them; and, as they happened to be at the same time in sight of an ale-house, Partridge, with much earnest entreaty, prevailed with Jones to enter and weather the storm. The consequence of this was an excellent cold chine being produced on the table, upon which not only Partridge, but Jones himself, made a very hearty breakfast, though the latter began to grow uneasy, as the people of the house could give him no fresh information concerning Sophia.

Their meal being over, Jones was again preparing to sally, notwithstanding the violence of the storm still continued; but Partridge begged heartily for another mug; and at last casting his eyes on a lad at the fire, who had entered into the kitchen, and who at that instant was looking as earnestly at him, he turned suddenly to Jones, and cried,

"Master, give me your hand, here's more news of Madam Sophia come to town. The boy there standing by the fire is the very lad that rode before her."

At these words Jones started from his chair, and, bidding the boy follow him immediately, departed from the kitchen into a private apartment; for, so delicate was he with regard to Sophia, that he never willingly mentioned her name in the presence of many people; and though he had, as it were, from the overflowings of his heart, given Sophia as a toast among the officers, where he thought it was impossible she should be known, yet, even there, the reader may remember how difficultly he was prevailed upon to mention her surname.

Hard therefore was it, that he should principally owe his present misfortune to the supposed want of that delicacy with which he so abounded; for, in reality, Sophia was much more offended at the freedoms which she thought (and not without good reason) he had taken with her name and character than at any freedoms in which, under his present circumstances, he had indulged himself with another woman.

But however unhappily Sophia had erred in her opinion of Jones, she had sufficient reason for her opinion. Nay, had she followed her lover at this very time, and had entered this very ale-house the moment he was departed from it, she would have found the landlord as well acquainted with her name and person as the wench at Upton had appeared to be. For while Jones was examining his boy in whispers in an inner room, Partridge had no such delicacy in his disposition.

Jones had been absent a full half-hour, when he returned into the kitchen in a hurry, desiring the landlord to let him know that instant what was to pay. And now Partridge was somewhat compensated by hearing that he was to proceed no farther on foot, for Jones, by golden arguments, had prevailed with the boy to attend him back to the inn whither he had before conducted Sophia.

The horses being now produced, Jones directly leapt into the side-saddle on which his dear Sophia had ridden. The lad, indeed, very civilly offered him the use of his; but he chose the side-saddle, probably because it was softer. Partridge, however, though full as effeminate as Jones, could not bear the thoughts of degrading his manhood; he therefore accepted the boy's offer; and now, Jones being mounted on the side-saddle of his Sophia, the boy on that of Mrs. Honour, and Partridge bestriding the third horse, they set forwards on their journey, and within four hours arrived at the inn where the reader hath already spent so much time.

VI

JONES now traveled post; we will follow him, therefore, according to our custom, and to the rules of Longinus, in the same manner. From Coventry he arrived at Daventry, from Daventry at Stratford, and from Stratford at Dunstable, whither he came the next day a little after noon, and within a few hours after Sophia had left it; and though he was obliged to stay here longer than he wished, while a smith, with great deliberation, shoed the post-horse he was to ride, he doubted not but to overtake his Sophia before she should set out from St. Albans; at which place he concluded, and very reasonably, that his lordship would stop and dine.

And had he been right in this conjecture, he most probably would have overtaken his angel at the aforesaid place; but, unluckily, my lord had appointed a dinner to be prepared for him at his own house in London, and, in order to enable him to reach that place in proper time, he had ordered a relay of horses to meet him at St. Albans. When Jones therefore arrived there he was informed that the coach-and-six had set out two hours before.

If fresh post-horses had been now ready, as they were not, it seemed so apparently impossible to overtake the coach before it reached London, that Partridge thought he had now a proper opportunity to remind his friend of a matter which he seemed entirely to have forgotten; what this was the reader will guess, when we inform him that Jones had eaten nothing more than one poached egg since he had left the ale-house where he had first met the guide returning from Sophia.

The landlord so entirely agreed with the opinion of Mr. Partridge, that Jones was at length prevailed on; and now a joint of mutton was put down to the fire. While this was preparing, Partridge, being admitted to the same apartment with his friend or master, began to harangue in the following manner:

"Certainly, sir, if ever man deserved a young lady, you deserve young Madam Western; for what a vast quantity of love must a man have, to be able to live upon it without any other food, as you do! And yet your honor is seemingly in perfect good health, and you never looked better nor fresher in your life. It must be certainly love that you live upon."

"And a very rich diet too, Partridge," answered Jones. "But did not fortune send me an excellent dainty yesterday? Dost thou imagine I cannot live more than twenty-four hours on this dear pocket-book?"

"Undoubtedly," cries Partridge, "there is enough in that pocket-book to purchase many a good meal. Fortune sent it to your honor very opportunely for present use, as your honor's money must be almost out by this time."

"What do you mean?" answered Jones; "I hope you don't imagine that I should be dishonest enough, even if it belonged to any other person, besides Miss Western——"

"Dishonest!" replied Partridge; "Heaven forbid I should wrong your honor so much! but where's the dishonesty in borrowing a little for present spending, since you will be so well able to pay the lady hereafter? You will do as you please, notwithstanding all I say; but for my part, I would be hanged before I mentioned a word of the matter."

"By what I can see, Partridge," cries Jones, "hanging is a matter *non longe alienum à Scævolæ studiis.*"

"You should say *alienus,*" says Partridge. "I remember the passage; it is an example under *communis, alienus, immunis, variis casibus serviunt.*"

"If you do remember it," cries Jones, "I find you don't understand it; but I tell thee, friend, in plain English, that he who finds another's property, and willfully detains it from the known owner, deserves to be hanged, no less than if he had stolen it. And as for this very identical bill, which is the property of my angel, and was once in her dear possession, I will not deliver it into any hands but her own—no, though I was as hungry as thou art. I charge thee, if thou wouldst not incur my displeasure forever, not to shock me any more by the bare mention of such detestable baseness."

"I should not have mentioned it now," cries Partridge, "if it had appeared so to me, for I'm sure I scorn any wickedness as much as another; but it seems we are all to live and learn. I remember my old schoolmaster, who was a prodigious great scholar, used often to say, *Polly matete cry town is my daskalon.* The English of which, he told us, was, That a child may sometimes teach his grandmother to suck eggs. I have lived to a fine purpose, truly, if I am to be taught my grammar at this time of day. Perhaps, young gentleman, you may change your opinion if you live to my years; for I remember I thought myself as wise when I was a stripling of one or two-and-twenty as I am now. I am sure I always taught *alienus,* and my master read it so before me."

There were not many instances in which Partridge could provoke Jones, nor were there many in which Partridge himself could have been hurried out of his respect. Unluckily, however, they had both hit on one of these. Jones now, looking upon his companion with a contemptuous and disdainful air (a thing not usual with him), cried,

"Partridge, I see thou art a conceited old fool, and I wish thou art not likewise an old rogue. Indeed, if I was as well convinced of the latter as I am of the former, thou shouldst travel no farther in my company."

The sage pedagogue was contented with the vent which he had already given to his indignation; and, as the vulgar phrase is, immediately drew in his horns. He said he was sorry he had uttered anything which might give offense, for that he had never intended it.

As Jones had the vices of a warm disposition, he was entirely free from those of a cold one. He instantly accepted the submission of Partridge, shook him by the hand, and with the most benign aspect imaginable, said twenty kind things, and at the same time very severely condemned himself, though not half so severely as he will most probably be condemned by many of our good readers.

Partridge was now highly comforted, as his fears of having offended were at once abolished, and his pride completely satisfied by Jones having owned himself in the wrong, which submission he instantly applied to what had principally nettled him, and repeated in a muttering voice, "To be sure, sir, your knowledge may be superior to mine in some things; but as to the grammar, I think I may challenge any man living. I think, at least, I have that at my finger's end."

If anything could add to the satisfaction which the poor man now enjoyed, he received this addition by the arrival of an excellent shoulder of mutton that at this instant came smoking to the table. On which having both plentifully feasted, they again mounted their horses, and set forward for London.

VII

THEY were got about two miles beyond Barnet, and it was now the dusk of the evening, when a genteel-looking man, but upon a very shabby horse, rode up to Jones, and asked him whether he was going to London; to which Jones answered in the affirmative. The gentleman replied,

"I should be obliged to you, sir, if you will accept of my company; for it is very late, and I am a stranger to the road."

Jones readily complied with the request; and on they traveled together, holding that sort of discourse which is usual on such occasions.

Of this, indeed, robbery was the principal topic; upon which subject the stranger expressed great apprehensions; but Jones declared he had very little to lose, and consequently as little to fear. Here Partridge could not forbear putting in his word.

"Your honor," said he, "may think it a little, but, I am sure, if I had a hundred-pound bank-note in my pocket, as you have, I should be very sorry to lose it; but, for my part, I never was less afraid in my life; for if we all stand by one another, the best man in England can't rob us. Suppose he should have a pistol, he can kill but one of us, and a man can die but once. That's my comfort, a man can die but once."

Our company were now arrived within a mile of Highgate, when the stranger turned short upon Jones, and pulling out a pistol, demanded that little bank-note which Partridge had mentioned.

Jones was at first somewhat shocked at this unexpected demand; however, he presently recollected himself, and told the highwayman all the money he had in his pocket was entirely at his service; and so saying, he pulled out upwards of three guineas, and offered to deliver it; but the other answered with an oath, that would not do. Jones answered coolly, he was very sorry for it, and returned the money into his pocket.

The highwayman then threatened, if he did not deliver the bank-note that moment, he must shoot him—holding his pistol at the same time very near to his breast. Jones instantly caught hold of the fellow's hand, which trembled so that he could scarce hold the pistol in it, and turned the muzzle from him. A struggle then ensued, in which the former wrested the pistol from the hand of his antagonist, and both came from their horses on the ground together, the highwayman upon his back, and the victorious Jones upon him.

The poor fellow now began to implore mercy of the conqueror; for, to say the truth, he was in strength by no means a match for Jones.

"Indeed, sir," says he, "I could have had no intention to shoot you; for you will find the pistol was not loaded. This is the first robbery I ever attempted, and I have been driven by distress to this."

At this instant, at about a hundred and fifty yards' distance, lay another person on the ground, roaring for mercy in a much louder voice than the highwayman. This was no other than Partridge himself, who, endeavoring to make his escape from the engagement, had been thrown from his horse, and lay flat on his face, not daring to look up, and expecting every minute to be shot.

In this posture he lay, till the guide, who was no otherwise concerned than for his horses, having secured the stumbling beast, came up to him, and told him his master had got the better of the highwayman.

Partridge leapt up at this news, and ran back to the place where Jones stood with his sword drawn in his hand to guard the poor fellow; which Partridge no sooner saw than he cried out,

"Kill the villain, sir, run him through the body, kill him this instant!"

Luckily, however, for the poor wretch, he had fallen into more merciful hands; for Jones having examined the pistol, and found it to be really unloaded, began to believe all the man had told him before Partridge came up, namely, that he was a novice in the trade, and that he had been driven to it by the distress he mentioned, the greatest indeed imaginable, that of five hungry children, and a wife lying in of the sixth, in the utmost want and misery. The truth of all which the highwayman most vehemently asserted, and offered to convince Mr. Jones of it, if he would take the trouble to go to his house, which was not above two miles off; saying, "that he desired no favor, but upon condition of proving all he had alleged."

Jones at first pretended that he would take the fellow at his word, and go with him, declaring that his fate should depend entirely on the truth of his story. Upon this the poor fellow immediately expressed so much alacrity that Jones was perfectly satisfied with his veracity, and began now to entertain sentiments of compassion for him. He returned the fellow his empty pistol, advised him to think of honester means of relieving his distress, and gave him a couple of guineas for the immediate support of his wife and his family; adding, "he wished he had more for his sake, for the hundred pound that had been mentioned was not his own."

Our readers will probably be divided in their opinions concerning this action; some may applaud it perhaps as an act of extraordinary humanity, while those of a more saturnine temper will consider it as a want of regard to that justice which every man owes his country.

The highwayman was full of expressions of thankfulness and gratitude. He actually dropped tears, or pretended so to do. He vowed he would immediately return home, and would never afterwards commit such a transgression: whether he kept his word or no, perhaps may appear hereafter.

Our travelers, having remounted their horses, arrived in town without encountering any new mishap. On the road much pleasant discourse passed between Jones and Partridge on the subject of their last adventure: in which Jones expressed a great compassion for those highwaymen who are, by unavoidable distress, driven, as it were, to such illegal courses as generally bring them to a shameful death:

"I mean," said he, "those only whose highest guilt extends no farther than to robbery, and who are never guilty of cruelty nor insult to any person, which is a circumstance that, I must say, to the honor of our country, distinguishes the robbers of England from those of all other nations."

"No doubt," answered Partridge, "it is better to take away one's money than one's life; and yet what right hath any man to take sixpence from me unless I give it him? Is there any honesty in such a man?"

"No, surely," cries Jones, "no more than there is in him who takes the horses out of another man's stable, or who applies to his own use the money which he finds, when he knows the right owner."

These hints stopped the mouth of Partridge; nor did he open it again till Jones having thrown some sarcastical jokes on his cowardice, he offered to excuse himself on the inequality of fire-arms, saying, "A thousand naked men are nothing to one pistol; for though it is true it will kill but one at a single discharge, yet who can tell but that one may be himself?"

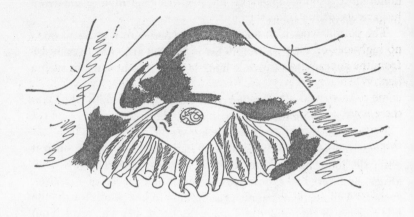

Book XIII

CONTAINING THE SPACE OF TWELVE DAYS

I

FROM that figure which the Irish peer, who brought Sophia to town, hath already made in this history, the reader will conclude, doubtless, it must have been an easy matter to have discovered his house in London without knowing the particular street or square which he inhabited, since he must have been one *whom everybody knows*. To say the truth, so it would have been to any of those tradesmen who are accustomed to attend the regions of the great; for the doors of the great are generally no less easy to find than it is difficult to get entrance into them. But Jones, as well as Partridge, was an entire stranger in London; and the peer unluckily quitted his former house when he went for Ireland. As he was just entered into a new one, the fame of his equipage had not yet sufficiently blazed in the neighborhood; so that, after a successless inquiry till the clock had struck eleven, Jones at last yielded to the advice of Partridge, and retreated to the Bull and Gate in Holborn, that being the inn where he had first alighted, and where he retired to enjoy that kind of repose which usually attends persons in his circumstances.

Early in the morning he again set forth in pursuit of Sophia; and many a weary step he took to no better purpose than before. At last, whether it was that Fortune relented, or whether it was no longer in her power to disappoint him, he came into the very street which was honored by his lordship's residence; and being directed to the house, he gave one gentle rap at the door.

The porter, who, from the modesty of the knock, had conceived no high idea of the person approaching, conceived but little better from the appearance of Mr. Jones, who was dressed in a suit of fustian. When Jones, therefore, inquired after the young lady who had come to town with his lordship, this fellow answered surlily, "That there were no ladies there."

Jones then desired to see the master of the house, but was informed that his lordship would see nobody that morning. And, upon growing more pressing, the porter said, "He had positive orders to let no person in; but if you think proper," said he, "to leave your name, I will acquaint his lordship; and if you call another time you shall know when he will see you."

Jones now declared, "That he had very particular business with the young lady, and could not depart without seeing her." Upon which the porter, with no very agreeable voice or aspect, affirmed, "That there was no young lady in that house, and consequently none could he see"; adding, "sure you are the strangest man I ever met with, for you will not take an answer."

I have often thought that, by the particular description of Cerberus, the porter of hell, in the 6th Æneid, Virgil might possibly intend to satirize the porters of the great men in his time; the porter in his lodge answers exactly to Cerberus in his den, and, like him, must be appeased by a sop before access can be gained to his master. Jones, in like manner, now began to offer a bribe to the human Cerberus, which a footman, overhearing, instantly advanced, and declared, "If Mr. Jones would give him the sum proposed, he would conduct him to the lady." Jones instantly agreed, and was forthwith conducted to the lodging of Mrs. Fitzpatrick by the very fellow who had attended the ladies thither the day before.

Nothing more aggravates ill success than the near approach to good. The gamester who loses his party at piquet by a single point laments his bad luck ten times as much as he who never came within a prospect of the game. So in a lottery, the proprietors of the next numbers to that which wins the great prize are apt to account themselves much more unfortunate than their fellow-sufferers. In short, these kind of hair-breadth missings of happiness look like the insults of Fortune, who may be considered as thus wantonly diverting herself at our expense.

Jones was now doomed to be tantalized in the like manner; for he arrived at the door of Mrs. Fitzpatrick about ten minutes after the departure of Sophia. He now addressed himself to the waiting-woman belonging to Mrs. Fitzpatrick; who told him the disagreeable news that the lady was gone, but could not tell him whither.

Though Jones had never seen Mrs. Fitzpatrick, yet he had heard that a cousin of Sophia was married to a gentleman of that name; and as he was presently convinced that this was the same woman, he very earnestly desired leave to wait on the lady herself; but she as positively refused him that honor.

Jones, who, though he had never seen a court, was better bred than most who frequent it, was incapable of any rude or abrupt behavior to a lady. When he had received, therefore a peremptory denial, he retired for the present, saying to the waiting-woman, "That if this was an improper hour to wait on her lady, he would return in the afternoon; and that he then hoped to have the honor of seeing her." The civility with which he uttered this, added to the great comeliness of his person, made an impression on the waiting-woman, and she could not help answering, "Perhaps, sir, you may"; and, indeed, she afterwards said everything to her mistress which she thought most likely to prevail on her to admit a visit from the handsome young gentleman; for so she called him.

Jones very shrewdly suspected that Sophia herself was now with her cousin, and was denied to him; which he imputed to her resentment of what had happened at Upton. Having, therefore, despatched Partridge to procure him lodgings, he remained all day in the street, watching the door where he thought his angel lay concealed; but no person did he see issue forth, except a servant of the house, and in the evening he returned to pay his visit to Mrs. Fitzpatrick, which that good lady at last condescended to admit.

There is a certain air of natural gentility which it is neither in the power of dress to give nor to conceal. Mr. Jones, as hath been before hinted, was possessed of this in a very eminent degree. He met, therefore, with a reception from the lady somewhat different from what his apparel seemed to demand; and, after he had paid her his proper respects, was desired to sit down.

This conversation ended very little to the satisfaction of poor Jones. For though Mrs. Fitzpatrick soon discovered the lover (as all women have the eyes of hawks in those matters), yet she thought it was such a lover as a generous friend of the lady should not betray her to. In short, she suspected this was the very Mr. Blifil from whom

Sophia had flown; and all the answers which she artfully drew from Jones concerning Mr. Allworthy's family confirmed her in this opinion. She therefore strictly denied any knowledge concerning the place whither Sophia was gone; nor could Jones obtain more than a permission to wait on her again the next evening.

When Jones was departed, Mrs. Fitzpatrick communicated her suspicion concerning Mr. Blifil to her maid; who answered,

"Sure, madam, he is too pretty a man, in my opinion, for any woman in the world to run away from. I had rather fancy it is Mr. Jones."

"Mr. Jones!" said the lady; "what Jones?" For Sophia had not given the least hint of any such person in all their conversation; but Mrs. Honour had been much more communicative, and had acquainted her sister Abigail with the whole history of Jones, which this now again related to her mistress.

Mrs. Fitzpatrick no sooner received this information than she immediately agreed with the opinion of her maid; and, what is very unaccountable, saw charms in the gallant, happy lover, which she had overlooked in the slighted squire.

"Betty," says she, "you are certainly in the right: he is a very pretty fellow, and I don't wonder that my cousin's maid should tell you so many women are fond of him. I am sorry now I did not inform him where my cousin was; and yet, if he be so terrible a rake as you tell me, it is a pity she should ever see him any more; for what but her ruin can happen from marrying a rake and a beggar against her father's consent? I protest, if he be such a man as the wench described him to you, it is but an office of charity to keep her from him; and I am sure it would be unpardonable in me to do otherwise, who have tasted so bitterly of the misfortunes attending such marriages."

Here she was interrupted by the arrival of a visitor, which was no other than his lordship; and as nothing passed at this visit either new or extraordinary, or any ways material to this history, we shall here put an end to this chapter.

II

WHEN Mrs. Fitzpatrick retired to rest, her thoughts were entirely taken up by her cousin Sophia and Mr. Jones. She was, indeed, a little offended with the former, for the disingenuity which she now discovered. In which meditation she had not long exercised her imagination before the following conceit suggested itself: that could she possibly become the means of preserving Sophia from this man, and of restoring her to her father, she should, in all human probability, by so great a service to the family, reconcile to herself both her uncle and her aunt Western.

As this was one of her most favorite wishes, so the hope of success seemed so reasonable that nothing remained but to consider of proper methods to accomplish her scheme. To attempt to reason the case with Sophia did not appear to her one of those methods; for Betty had reported from Mrs. Honour that Sophia had a violent inclination to Jones.

Accordingly, the next morning, before the sun, she huddled on her clothes, and at a very unfashionable, unseasonable, unvisitable hour, went to Lady Bellaston, to whom she got access, without the least knowledge or suspicion of Sophia, who, though not asleep, lay at that time awake in her bed, with Honour snoring by her side.

Mrs. Fitzpatrick made many apologies for an early, abrupt visit, at an hour when, she said, "she should not have thought of disturbing her ladyship but upon business of the utmost consequence." She then opened the whole affair, told all she had heard from Betty; and did not forget the visit which Jones had paid to herself the preceding evening.

Lady Bellaston answered with a smile, "Then you have seen this terrible man, madam; pray, is he so very fine a figure as he is represented? for Etoff entertained me last night almost two hours with him. The wench, I believe, is in love with him by reputation." Here the reader will be apt to wonder; but the truth is, that Mrs. Etoff, who had the honor to pin and unpin the Lady Bellaston, had received complete information concerning the said Mr. Jones, and had faithfully conveyed the same to her lady last night (or rather that morning) while she was undressing; on which accounts she had been detained in her office above the space of an hour and a half.

The lady, indeed, though generally well enough pleased with the narratives of Mrs. Etoff at those seasons, gave an extraordinary attention to her account of Jones; for Honour had described him as a very handsome fellow, and Mrs. Etoff, in her hurry, added so much to the beauty of his person to her report that Lady Bellaston began to conceive him to be a kind of miracle in nature.

The curiosity which her woman had inspired was now greatly increased by Mrs. Fitzpatrick, who spoke as much in favor of the person of Jones as she had before spoken in dispraise of his birth, character, and fortune.

When Lady Bellaston had heard the whole, she answered gravely, "Indeed, madam, this is a matter of great consequence. Nothing can certainly be more commendable than the part you act; and I shall be very glad to have my share in the preservation of a young lady of so much merit, and for whom I have so much esteem."

"Doth not your ladyship think," says Mrs. Fitzpatrick eagerly, "that it would be the best way to write immediately to my uncle, and acquaint him where my cousin is?"

The lady pondered a little upon this, and thus answered, "Why, no, madam, I think not. Di Western hath described her brother to me to be such a brute, that I cannot consent to put any woman under his power who hath escaped from it. I have heard he behaved like a monster to his own wife, for he is one of those wretches who think they have a right to tyrannize over us, and from such I shall ever esteem it the cause of my sex to rescue any woman who is so unfortunate to be under their power. The business, dear cousin, will be only to keep Miss Western from seeing this young fellow, till the good company, which she will have an opportunity of meeting here, give her a properer turn."

"If he should find her out, madam," answered the other, "your ladyship may be assured he will leave nothing unattempted to come at her."

"But, madam," replied the lady, "it is impossible he should come here—though indeed it is possible he may get some intelligence where she is, and then may lurk about the house—I wish therefore I knew his person. Is there no way, madam, by which I could have a sight of him? for, otherwise, you know, cousin, she may contrive to see him here without my knowledge."

Mrs. Fitzpatrick answered, "That he had threatened her with another visit that afternoon, and that, if her ladyship pleased to do her the honor of calling upon her then, she would hardly fail of seeing him between six and seven; and if he came earlier she would, by some means or other, detain him till her ladyship's arrival."

Lady Bellaston replied, "She would come the moment she could get from dinner, which she supposed would be by seven at farthest; for that it was absolutely necessary she should be acquainted with his person. Upon my word, madam," says she, "it was very good to take this care of Miss Western; but common humanity, as well as regard to our family, requires it of us both; for it would be a dreadful match, indeed."

Mrs. Fitzpatrick failed not to make a proper return to the

compliment which Lady Bellaston had bestowed on her cousin, and, after some little immaterial conversation, withdrew; and, getting as fast as she could into her chair, unseen by Sophia or Honour, returned home.

III

MR. JONES had walked within sight of a certain door during the whole day, which, though one of the shortest, appeared to him to be one of the longest in the whole year. At length, the clock having struck five, he returned to Mrs. Fitzpatrick, who, though it was a full hour earlier than the decent time of visiting, received him very civilly, but still persisted in her ignorance concerning Sophia.

Jones, in asking for his angel, had dropped the word cousin, upon which Mrs. Fitzpatrick said, "Then, sir, you know we are related; and, as we are, you will permit me the right of inquiring into the particulars of your business with my cousin."

Here Jones hesitated a good while, and at last answered, "He had a considerable sum of money of hers in his hands, which he desired to deliver to her." He then produced the pocket-book, and acquainted Mrs. Fitzpatrick with the contents, and with the method in which they came into his hands.

He had scarce finished his story when a most violent noise shook the whole house. To attempt to describe this noise to those who have heard it would be in vain; and to aim at giving any idea of it to those who have never heard the like, would be still more vain. In short, a footman knocked, or rather thundered, at the door. Jones was a little surprised at the sound, having never heard it before; but Mrs. Fitzpatrick very calmly said, that, as some company were coming, she could not make him any answer now; but if he pleased to stay till they were gone, she intimated she had something to say to him.

The door of the room now flew open, and, after pushing in her hoop sideways before her, entered Lady Bellaston, who having first made a very low courtesy to Mrs. Fitzpatrick, and as low a one to Mr. Jones, was ushered to the upper end of the room.

We mention these minute matters for the sake of some country ladies of our acquaintance, who think it contrary to the rules of modesty to bend their knees to a man.

The company were hardly well settled, before the arrival of the peer lately mentioned caused a fresh disturbance, and a repetition of ceremonials.

These being over, the conversation began to be, as the phrase is, extremely brilliant. Poor Jones was rather a spectator of this elegant scene than an actor in it; for though, in the short interval before the peer's arrival, Lady Bellaston first, and afterwards Mrs. Fitzpatrick, had addressed some of their discourse to him, yet no sooner was the noble lord entered than he engrossed the whole attention of the two ladies to himself; and as he took no more notice of Jones than if no such person had been present, unless by now and then staring at him, the ladies followed his example.

The company had now stayed so long, that Mrs. Fitzpatrick plainly perceived they all designed to stay out each other. She therefore resolved to rid herself of Jones, he being the visitant to whom she thought the least ceremony was due. Taking therefore an opportunity of a cessation of chat, she addressed herself gravely to him, and said,

"Sir, I shall not possibly be able to give you an answer tonight as to that business; but if you please to leave word where I may send to you tomorrow——"

Jones had natural, but not artificial good-breeding. Instead, therefore, of communicating the secret of his lodgings to a servant, he acquainted the lady herself with it particularly, and soon after very ceremoniously withdrew.

He was no sooner gone than the great personages, who had taken no notice of him present, began to take much notice of him in his absence; but if the reader hath already excused us from relating the more brilliant part of this conversation, he will surely be very ready to excuse the repetition of what may be called vulgar abuse; though, perhaps, it may be material to our history to mention an observation of Lady Bellaston, who took her leave in a few minutes after him, and then said to Mrs. Fitzpatrick, at her departure, "I am satisfied on the account of my cousin; she can be in no danger from this fellow."

IV

THE next morning, as early as it was decent, Jones attended at Mrs. Fitzpatrick's door, where he was answered that the lady was not at home—an answer which surprised him the more, as he had walked backwards and forwards in the street from break of day; and if she had gone out, he must have seen her. This answer, however, he was obliged to receive, and not only now, but to five several visits which he made her that day.

To be plain with the reader, the noble peer had from some reason or other, perhaps from a regard for the lady's honor, insisted that she should not see Mr. Jones, whom he looked on as a scrub, any more; and the lady had complied in making that promise to which we now see her so strictly adhere.

The young gentleman, during his unhappy separation from Sophia, took up his residence in a very reputable house, and in a very good part of the town.

Mr. Jones had often heard Mr. Allworthy mention the gentle-woman at whose house he used to lodge when he was in town. This person, who, as Jones likewise knew, lived in Bond Street, was the widow of a clergyman, and was left by him, at his decease, in possession of two daughters, and of a complete set of manuscript sermons.

Of these two daughters, Nancy, the elder, was now arrived at the age of seventeen, and Betty, the younger, at that of ten.

Hither Jones had despatched Partridge, and in this house he was provided with a room for himself in the second floor, and with one for Partridge in the fourth. The first floor was inhabited by one of those young gentlemen, who, in the last age, were called men of wit and pleasure about town, and properly enough; for as men are usually denominated from their business or profession, so pleasure may be said to have been the only business or profession of those gentlemen to whom fortune had made all useful occupations unnecessary. Play-houses, coffee-houses, and taverns were the scenes of their rendez-vous. Wit and humor were the entertainment of their looser hours, and love was the business of their more serious moments. Wine and the Muses conspired to kindle the brightest flames in their breasts.

When Jones had returned to his apartment he heard a violent up-roar below-stairs; and soon after a female voice begged him for Heaven's sake to come and prevent murder. Jones, who was never backward on any occasion to help the distressed, immediately ran downstairs; when stepping into the dining-room, whence all the noise issued, he beheld the young gentleman just before mentioned pinned close to the wall by his footman, and a young woman standing by, wringing her hands, and crying out, "He will be murdered! he will be murdered!" and, indeed, the poor gentleman seemed in some danger of being choked, when Jones flew hastily to his assistance, and rescued him, just as he was breathing his last, from the unmerciful clutches of the enemy. Now ensued a combat between Jones and the footman, which was very fierce, but short; for this fellow was no more able to contend with Jones than his master had before been to contend with him. The former victor lay breathless on the ground, and the vanquished gentleman had recovered breath enough to thank Mr. Jones for his seasonable assistance; he received likewise the hearty thanks of the young woman present, who was indeed no other than Miss Nancy, the eldest daughter of the house.

The footman, having now recovered his legs, shook his head at Jones, and, with a sagacious look, cried, "O d—n me, I'll have nothing more to do with you; you have been upon the stage, or I'm d—nably mistaken." And indeed we may forgive this his suspicion; for such was the agility and strength of our hero, that he was, perhaps, a match for one of the first-rate boxers. The master, foaming with wrath, ordered his man immediately to strip, and the fellow was discharged.

And now the young gentleman, whose name was Nightingale, began to relate the occasion of the preceding disturbance.

"I hope, sir," said he to Jones, "you will not from this accident conclude that I make a custom of striking my servants, for I assure you this is the first time I have been guilty of it, but when you hear what hath happened this evening, you will, I believe, think me excusable. The rascal had the insolence to——In short, he cast a reflection——He mentioned the name of a young lady, in a manner—in such a manner that incensed me beyond all patience, and, in my passion, I struck him."

Jones answered, "That he believed no person living would blame him; for my part," said he, "I confess I should, on that provocation, have done the same thing."

Our company had not sat long before they were joined by the mother and daughter at their return from the play. And now they all spent a very cheerful evening together. Notwithstanding the heaviness of his heart, so agreeable did Jones make himself on the present occasion, that, at their breaking up, the young gentleman earnestly desired his further acquaintance. Miss Nancy was well pleased with him; and the widow, quite charmed with her new lodger, invited him, with the other, next morning to breakfast.

V

Our company brought together in the morning the same good inclinations towards each other with which they had separated the evening before; but poor Jones was extremely disconsolate; for he had just received information from Partridge that Mrs. Fitzpatrick had left her lodging, and that he could not learn whither she was gone.

The discourse turned at present on love; and Mr. Nightingale expressed many of those warm, generous, and disinterested sentiments upon this subject which wise and sober men call romantic, but which wise and sober women generally regard in a better light. Mrs. Miller (for so the mistress of the house was called) greatly approved these sentiments; but when the young gentleman appealed to Miss Nancy, she answered only, "That she believed the gentleman who had spoke the least was capable of feeling most."

This compliment was so apparently directed to Jones, that we should have been sorry had he passed it by unregarded. He made her, indeed, a very polite answer, and concluded with an oblique hint that her own silence subjected her to a suspicion of the same kind; for indeed she had scarce opened her lips either now or the last evening.

"I am glad, Nanny," said Mrs. Miller, "the gentleman has made the observation; I protest I am almost of his opinion. What can be the matter with you, child? I never saw such an alteration. What is become of all your gaiety? Would you think, sir, I used to call her my little prattler? She hath not spoke twenty words this week."

Here their conversation was interrupted by the entrance of a maidservant, who brought a bundle in her hand, which, she said, "was delivered by a porter for Mr. Jones." She added, "That the man immediately went away, saying it required no answer."

Jones expressed some surprise on this occasion, and declared it must be some mistake; but the maid persisting that she was certain of the name, all the women were desirous of having the bundle immediately opened; which operation was at length performed by little Betsy, with the consent of Mr. Jones; and the contents were found to be a domino, a mask, and a masquerade ticket.

Jones was now more positive than ever in asserting that these things must have been delivered by mistake; and Mrs. Miller herself expressed some doubt, and said, "She knew not what to think." But when Mr. Nightingale was asked, he delivered a very different opinion. "All I can conclude from it, sir," said he, "is that you are a very happy man; for I make no doubt but these were sent you by some lady whom you will have the happiness of meeting at the masquerade."

Jones had not a sufficient degree of vanity to entertain any such flattering imagination; nor did Mrs. Miller herself give much assent to what Mr. Nightingale had said, till Miss Nancy having lifted up the domino, a card dropped from the sleeve, in which was written as follows:

TO MR. JONES.

The queen of the fairies sends you this;
Use her favors not amiss.

Mrs. Miller and Miss Nancy now both agreed with Mr. Nightingale; nay, Jones himself was almost persuaded to be of the same opinion. And as no other lady but Mrs. Fitzpatrick, he thought, knew his lodging, he began to flatter himself with some hopes that it came from her, and that he might possibly see his Sophia.

Mr. Jones having now determined to go to the masquerade that evening, Mr. Nightingale offered to conduct him thither. The young gentleman, at the same time, offered tickets to Miss Nancy and her mother; but the good woman would not accept them. She said, "She did not conceive the harm which some people imagined in a masquerade; but that such extravagant diversions were proper only for persons of quality and fortune, and not for young women who were to get their living, and could, at best, hope to be married to a good tradesman."

"A tradesman!" cries Nightingale; "you shan't undervalue my Nancy. There is not a nobleman upon earth above her merit."

"O fie! Mr. Nightingale," answered Mrs. Miller, "you must not fill the girl's head with such fancies; but if it was her good luck" (says the mother with a simper) "to find a gentleman of your generous way of thinking, I hope she would make a better return to his generosity than to give her mind up to extravagant pleasures.——I beg, therefore, I may hear of no more masquerades. Nancy is, I am certain, too good a girl to desire to go; for she must remember when you carried her thither last year it almost turned her head, and she did not return to herself, or to her needle, in a month afterwards."

Though a gentle sigh, which stole from the bosom of Nancy, seemed to argue some secret disapprobation of these sentiments, she did not dare openly to oppose them.

Mr. Nightingale, who grew every minute fonder of Jones, was very desirous of his company that day to dinner at the tavern, where he offered to introduce him to some of his acquaintance; but Jones begged to be excused, "as his clothes," he said, "were not yet come to town."

To confess the truth, Mr. Jones was now in a situation which sometimes happens to be the case of young gentlemen of much better figure than himself. In short, he had not one penny in his pocket. Notwithstanding, therefore, all the delicacies which love had set before him, namely, the hopes of seeing Sophia at the masquerade—on which, however ill-founded his imagination might be, he had voluptuously feasted during the whole day—the evening no sooner came than Mr. Jones began to languish for some food of a grosser kind. Partridge discovered this by intuition, and took the occasion to give some oblique hints concerning the bank-bill; and, when these were rejected with disdain, he collected courage enough once more to mention a return to Mr. Allworthy.

"Partridge," cries Jones, "you cannot see my fortune in a more desperate light than I see it myself; and I begin heartily to repent that I suffered you to leave a place where you was settled, and to follow me. However, I insist now on your returning home; and for the expense and trouble which you have so kindly put yourself to on my account, all the clothes I left behind in your care I desire you would take as your own. I am sorry I can make you no other acknowledgment."

He spoke these words with so pathetic an accent, that Partridge, among whose vices ill-nature or hardness of heart were not numbered, burst into tears; and, after swearing he would not quit him in his distress, he began with the most earnest entreaties to urge his return home.

"For Heaven's sake, sir," says he, "do but consider; what can your honor do?—how is it possible you can live in this town without money? Do what you will, sir, or go wherever you please, I am resolved not to desert you. But pray, sir, consider—do, pray, sir, for your own sake, take it into your consideration; and I'm sure," says he, "that your own good sense will bid you return home."

"How often shall I tell thee," answered Jones, "that I have no home to return to? Had I any hopes that Mr. Allworthy's doors would be open to receive me, I want no distress to urge me—but, alas! that I am forever banished from. His last words were—oh, Partridge, they still ring in my ears—his last words were, when he gave me a sum of money—what it was I know not, but considerable I'm sure it was—his last words were, 'I am resolved from this day forward on no account to converse with you any more.'"

Here passion stopped the mouth of Jones, as surprise for a moment did that of Partridge; but he soon recovered the use of speech, and after a short preface, in which he declared he had no inquisitiveness in his temper, inquired what Jones meant by a considerable sum—he knew not how much—and what was become of the money.

In both these points he now received full satisfaction; on which he was proceeding to comment, when he was interrupted by a message from Mr. Nightingale, who desired his master's company in his apartment.

When the two gentlemen were both attired for the masquerade, and Mr. Nightingale had given orders for chairs to be sent for, a circumstance of distress occurred to Jones, which will appear very ridiculous to many of my readers. This was how to procure a shilling; but if such readers will reflect a little on what they have themselves felt from the want of a thousand pounds, or, perhaps, of ten or twenty, to execute a favorite scheme, they will have a perfect idea of what Mr. Jones felt on this occasion. For this sum, therefore, he applied to Partridge, which was the first he had permitted him to advance, and was the last he intended that poor fellow should advance in his service. To say the truth, Partridge had lately made no offer of this kind. Whether it was that he desired to see the bank-bill broke in upon, or that distress should prevail on Jones to return home, or from what other motive it proceeded, I will not determine.

VI

OUR cavaliers now arrived at that temple where Heydegger, the great high-priest of pleasure, presides; and Mr. Nightingale, having taken a turn or two with his companion, soon left him, and walked off with a female, saying, "Now you are here, sir, you must beat about for your own game."

Jones now accosted every woman he saw whose stature, shape, or air bore any resemblance to his angel. Some of these answered by a question, in a squeaking voice, "Do you know me?" Much the greater number said, "I don't know you, sir," and nothing more. Some called him an impertinent fellow; some made him no answer at all; and many gave him as kind answers as he could wish, but not in the voice he desired to hear.

Whilst he was talking with one of these last (who was in the habit of a shepherdess) a lady in a domino came up to him, and slapping him on the shoulder, whispered him, at the same time, in the ear, "If you talk any longer with that trollop I will acquaint Miss Western."

"Is she here, then, madam?" replied Jones, with some vehemence. Upon which the lady cried,

"Hush, sir, you will be observed. I promise you, upon my honor, Miss Western is not here."

Jones, now taking the mask by the hand, fell to entreating her in the most earnest manner to acquaint him where he might find Sophia; and when he could obtain no direct answer, he began to upbraid her gently for having disappointed him the day before; and concluded, saying, "Indeed, my good fairy queen, I know your majesty very well, notwithstanding the affected disguise of your voice. Indeed, Mrs. Fitzpatrick, it is a little cruel to divert yourself at the expense of my torments."

The mask answered, "Though you have so ingeniously discovered me, I must still speak in the same voice, lest I should be known by others. And do you think, good sir, that I have no greater regard for my cousin than to assist in carrying on an affair between you two which must end in her ruin as well as your own?"

Jones vowed he had no such design on Sophia, "That he would rather suffer the most violent of deaths than sacrifice her interest." He said, "He knew how unworthy he was of her, every way; that he had long ago resolved to quit all such aspiring thoughts, but that some strange accidents had made him desirous to see her once more, when he promised he would take leave of her forever. No, madam," concluded he, "my love is not of that base kind which seeks its own satisfaction at the expense of what is most dear to its object. I would sacrifice everything to the possession of my Sophia, but Sophia herself."

The lady now, after silence of a few moments, said, "She did not see his pretensions to Sophia in the light of presumption. Young fellows," says she, "can never have too aspiring thoughts. Perhaps you may succeed with those who are infinitely superior in fortune; nay, I am convinced there are women——but don't you think me a strange creature, Mr. Jones, to be thus giving advice to a man with whom I am so little acquainted, and one with whose behavior to me I have so little reason to be pleased?"

Here Jones began to apologize, and to hope he had not offended in anything he had said of her cousin. To which the mask answered, "And are you so little versed in the sex, to imagine you can well affront a lady more than by entertaining her with your passion for another woman? If the fairy queen had conceived no better opinion of your gallantry, she would scarce have appointed you to meet her at the masquerade."

Jones had never less inclination to an amour than at present; but gallantry to the ladies was among his principles of honor, and he held it as much incumbent on him to accept a challenge to love as if it had been a challenge to fight. He began, therefore, to make a very warm answer to her last speech.

While Jones and his mask were walking together about the room, he observed his lady speak to several masks with the same freedom of acquaintance as if they had been barefaced. He could not help expressing his surprise at this, to which the lady answered,

"You cannot conceive anything more insipid and childish than a masquerade to the people of fashion, who know one another as well here as when they meet in an assembly or a drawing room, and generally retire from hence more tired than from the longest sermon. If I have any faculty at guessing, you are not much better pleased. I protest it would be almost charity in me to go home for your sake."

"I know but one charity equal to it," cries Jones, "and that is to suffer me to wait on you home."

"Sure," answered the lady, "you have a strange opinion of me, to imagine that upon such an acquaintance I would let you into my doors at this time of night. Are you used, Mr. Jones, to make these sudden conquests?"

"I am not used, madam," said Jones, "to submit to such sudden conquests; but as you have taken my heart by surprise, the rest of my body hath a right to follow; so you must pardon me if I resolve to attend you wherever you go."

He accompanied these words with some proper actions; upon which the lady, after a gentle rebuke, and saying their familiarity would be observed, told him, "She was going to sup with an acquaintance, whither she hoped he would not follow her."

The lady presently after quitted the masquerade, and Jones, notwithstanding the severe prohibition he had received, presumed to attend her. He was now reduced to the same dilemma we have mentioned before, namely, the want of a shilling, and could not relieve it by borrowing as before. He therefore walked boldly on after the chair in which his lady rode, pursued by a grand huzza from all the chairmen present, who wisely take the best care they can to discountenance all walking afoot by their betters.

The lady was set down in a street not far from Hanover Square, where the door being presently opened, she was carried in, and the gentleman, without any ceremony, walked in after her.

Jones and his companion were now together in a very well-furnished and well-warmed room; when the female, still speaking in her masquerade voice, said she was surprised at her friend, who must absolutely have forgot her appointment; at which, after venting much resentment, she suddenly expressed some apprehension from Jones, and asked him what the world would think of their having been alone together in a house at that time of night? But instead of a direct answer to so important a question, Jones began to be very importunate with the lady to unmask; and at length having prevailed, there appeared not Mrs. Fitzpatrick, but the Lady Bellaston herself.

It would be tedious to give the particular conversation, which consisted of very common and ordinary occurrences, and which lasted from two till six o'clock in the morning. It is sufficient to mention all of it that is anywise material to this history. And this was a promise that the lady would endeavor to find out Sophia, and in a few days bring him to an interview with her, on condition that he would then take his leave of her. When this was thoroughly settled, and a second meeting in the evening appointed at the same place, they separated; the lady returned to her house, and Jones to his lodgings.

VII

Jones, having refreshed himself with a few hours' sleep, summoned Partridge to his presence; and delivering him a bank-note of fifty pounds, ordered him to go and change it. Partridge received this with sparkling eyes, though the only way he could possibly find to account for the possession of this note was by robbery; and, to confess the truth, the reader, unless he should suspect it was owing to the generosity of Lady Bellaston, can hardly imagine any other.

To clear, therefore, the honor of Mr. Jones, and to do justice to the liberality of the lady, he had really received this present from her, who, though she did not give much into the hackney charities of the age, such as building hospitals, etc., was not, however, entirely void of that Christian virtue; and conceived (very rightly, I think) that a young fellow of merit without a shilling in the world, was no improper object of this virtue.

Mr. Jones and Mr. Nightingale had been invited to dine this day with Mrs. Miller. At the appointed hour, therefore, the two young gentlemen, with the two girls, attended in the parlor, where they waited from three till almost five before the good woman appeared. She had been out of town to visit a relation, of whom, at her return, she gave the following account:

"I hope, gentlemen, you will pardon my making you wait; I am sure if you knew the occasion—I have been to see a cousin of mine, about six miles off, who now lies in. It should be a warning to all persons" (says she, looking at her daughters) "how they marry indiscreetly. Oh, Nancy! how shall I describe the wretched condition in which I found your poor cousin? there was she, this dreadful weather, in a cold room, without any curtains to her bed, and not a bushel of coals in her house to supply her with fire. This was a love-match, as they call it, on both sides; that is, a match between two beggars. I must, indeed, say I never saw a fonder couple; but what is their fondness good for, but to torment each other?"

"I never saw the least sign of misery at her house," replied Nancy; "I am sure my heart bleeds for what you now tell me."

"Oh, child," answered the mother, "she hath always endeavored to make the best of everything. Indeed, this absolute ruin hath been brought upon them by others. The poor man was bail for the villain his brother; and about a week ago, the very day before her lying-in, their goods were all carried away and sold by an execution."

It was not with dry eyes that Jones heard this narrative; when it was ended he took Mrs. Miller apart with him into another room, and, delivering her his purse, in which was the sum of £50, desired her to send as much of it as she thought proper to these poor people. She burst into a kind of agony of transport, and cried out,

"Good heavens! is there such a man in the world?" But recollecting herself, she said, "Indeed I know one such; but can there be another?"

"I hope, madam," cries Jones, "there are many who have common humanity; for to relieve such distresses in our fellow creatures can hardly be called more."

Mrs. Miller then took ten guineas, which were the utmost he could prevail with her to accept. They then returned to the parlor, where Nightingale expressed much concern at the dreadful situation of these wretches. "Suppose, madam," said he, "you should recommend them to Mr. Allworthy? Or what think you of a collection? I will give them a guinea with all my heart."

Mrs. Miller made no answer; and Nancy, to whom her mother

had whispered the generosity of Jones, turned pale upon the occasion; though, if either of them was angry with Nightingale, it was surely without reason. For there are thousands who would not have contributed a single halfpenny, as indeed he did not in effect, for as the others thought proper to make no demand, he kept his money in his pocket.

VIII

JONES grew still more and more impatient to see Sophia; and finding, after repeated interviews with Lady Bellaston, no likelihood of obtaining this by her means (for, on the contrary, the lady began to treat even the mention of the name of Sophia with resentment), he resolved to try some other method. He made no doubt but that Lady Bellaston knew where his angel was, so he thought it most likely that some of her servants should be acquainted with the same secret. Partridge, therefore, was employed to get acquainted with those servants in order to fish this secret out of them.

Few situations can be imagined more uneasy than that to which his poor master was at present reduced; for besides the difficulties he met with in discovering Sophia, besides the fears he had of having disobliged her, he had still a difficulty to combat which it was not in the power of his mistress to remove, however kind her inclination might have been. This was the exposing of her to be disinherited of all her father's estate.

Add to all these the many obligations which Lady Bellaston, whose violent fondness we can no longer conceal, had heaped upon him; so that by her means he was now become one of the best-dressed men about town, and was not only relieved from those ridiculous distresses we have before mentioned, but was actually raised to a state of affluence beyond what he had ever known.

Such was the unhappy case of Jones; for he could never have been able to have made any adequate return to the generous passion of this lady, who had indeed been once an object of desire, but was now entered at least into the autumn of life, though she wore all the gaiety of youth, both in her dress and manner; nay, she contrived still to maintain the roses in her cheeks; but these, like flowers forced out of season by art, had none of that lively blooming freshness with which Nature, at the proper time, bedecks her own productions.

Though Jones saw all these discouragements on the one side, he knew the tacit consideration upon which all her favors were conferred; and as his necessity obliged him to accept them, so his honor, he concluded, forced him to pay the price.

While he was meditating on these matters he received the following note from the lady:

"A very foolish, but a very perverse accident hath happened since our last meeting, which makes it improper I should see you any more at the usual place. I will, if possible, contrive some other place by tomorrow. In the meantime, adieu."

This disappointment, perhaps, the reader may conclude was not very great; but if it was, he was quickly relieved; for in less than an hour afterwards another note was brought him from the same hand, which contained as follows:

"I have altered my mind since I wrote; a change which, if you are no stranger to the tenderest of all passions, you will not wonder at. I am now resolved to see you this evening at my own house, whatever may be the consequence. Come to me exactly at seven; I dine abroad, but will be at home by that time. A day, I find, to those that sincerely love seems longer than I imagined.

"If you should accidentally be a few moments before me, bid them show you into the drawing-room."

Before we attend him to this intended interview with the lady, we think proper to account for both the preceding notes.

First, then, the mistress of the house where these lovers had hitherto met, had that very morning waited upon her ladyship, and had positively declared that she would, on no account, be instrumental in carrying on any of her affairs for the future.

Luckily it came into her head to propose to Sophia to go to the play, which was immediately consented to, and a proper lady provided for her companion. Mrs. Honour was likewise despatched with Mrs. Etoff on the same errand of pleasure; and thus her own house was left free for the safe reception of Mr. Jones.

IX

Mr. Jones was just dressed to wait on Lady Bellaston, when Mrs. Miller rapped at his door; and, being admitted, very earnestly desired his company below-stairs, to drink tea in the parlor.

Upon his entrance into the room she presently introduced a person to him, saying, "This, sir, is my cousin, who hath been so greatly beholden to your goodness, for which he begs to return you his sincerest thanks."

The man had scarce entered upon that speech which Mrs. Miller had so kindly prefaced, when both Jones and he, looking steadfastly at each other, showed at once the utmost tokens of surprise. The voice of the latter began instantly to falter; and, instead of finishing his speech, he sunk down into a chair, crying, "It is so, I am convinced it is so!"

"Bless me! what's the meaning of this?" cries Mrs. Miller; "you are not ill, I hope, cousin? Some water, a dram this instant."

"Be not frighted, madam," cries Jones, "I have almost as much need of a dram as your cousin. We are equally surprised at this unexpected meeting. Your cousin is an acquaintance of mine, Mrs. Miller."

"An acquaintance!" cries the man.——"Oh, Heaven!"

"Ay, an acquaintance," repeated Jones, "and an honored acquaintance too. When I do not love and honor the man who dares venture everything to preserve his wife and children from instant destruction, may I have a friend capable of disowning me in adversity!"

"Cousin," cries the man, who had now pretty well recovered himself, "this is the angel from heaven whom I meant. He is, indeed, the worthiest, bravest, noblest of all human beings. Oh, cousin, I have obligations to this gentleman of such a nature!"

"Mention nothing of obligations," cries Jones eagerly; "not a word, I insist upon it, not a word" (meaning, I suppose, that he would not have him betray the affair of the robbery to any person).

Here Jones attempted to prevent the poor man from proceeding; but indeed the overflowing of his own heart would of itself have stopped his words.

And now Mrs. Miller likewise began to pour forth thanksgivings, as well in her own name as in that of her cousin, and concluded with saying, "She doubted not but such goodness would meet a glorious reward."

Jones answered, "He had been sufficiently rewarded already. If there are men who cannot feel the delight of giving happiness to others, I sincerely pity them."

The hour of appointment being now come, Jones was forced to take a hasty leave, but not before he had heartily shaken his friend by the hand.

X

Mr. Jones was rather earlier than the time appointed, and earlier than the lady, whose arrival was hindered. He was accordingly shown into the drawing-room, where he had not been many minutes before the door opened, and in came—no other than Sophia herself, who had left the play before the end of the first act; for a violent uproar had so terrified our heroine, that she was glad to put herself under the protection of a young gentleman who safely conveyed her to her chair.

Sophia, expecting to find no one in the room, came hastily in, and went directly to a glass which almost fronted her, without once looking towards the upper end of the room, where the statue of Jones now stood motionless. In this glass it was, after contemplating her own lovely face, that she first discovered the said statue; when, instantly turning about, she perceived the reality of the vision; upon which she gave a violent scream, and scarce preserved herself from fainting, till Jones was able to move to her, and support her in his arms. After a short pause, Jones, with faltering accents said,

"I see, madam, you are surprised."

"Surprised!" answered she; "oh, heavens! Indeed, I am surprised. I almost doubt whether you are the person you seem."

"Indeed," cries he, "my Sophia—pardon me, madam, for this once calling you so—I am that very wretched Jones, whom Fortune, after so many disappointments, hath, at last, kindly conducted to you. Oh, my Sophia; did you know the thousand torments I have suffered in this long, fruitless pursuit."

"Pursuit of whom?" said Sophia, a little recollecting herself, and assuming a reserved air.

"Can you be so cruel to ask that question?" cries Jones; "need I say, of you?"

"Of me!" answered Sophia: "hath Mr. Jones, then, any such important business with me?"

"To some, madam," cried Jones, "this might seem an important business" (giving her the pocket-book). "I hope, madam, you will find it of the same value as when it was lost." Sophia took the pocket-book, and was going to speak, when he interrupted her thus: "Let us not, I beseech you, lose one of these precious moments which Fortune hath so kindly sent us. Oh, my Sophia! I have business of a much superior kind. Thus, on my knees, let me ask your pardon."

"My pardon!" cries she; "sure, sir, after what is past, you cannot expect, after what I have heard."

"I scarce know what I say," answered Jones. "By heavens! I scarce wish you should pardon me. Oh, my Sophia! henceforth never cast away a thought on such a wretch as I am. If any remembrance of me should ever intrude to give a moment's uneasiness to that tender bosom, think of my unworthiness; and let the remembrance of what passed at Upton blot me forever from your mind."

Sophia stood trembling all this while. Her face was whiter than snow, and her heart was throbbing through her stays. But, at the mention of Upton, a blush arose in her cheeks, and her eyes, which before she had scarce lifted up, were turned upon Jones with a glance of disdain. He understood this silent reproach, and replied to it thus:

"Oh, my Sophia! my only love! you cannot hate or despise me more for what happened there than I do myself; but yet do me the justice to think that my heart was never unfaithful to you. Believe me, my angel, I never have seen her from that day to this, and never intend or desire to see her again."

Sophia, in her heart, was very glad to hear this; but forcing into her face an air of more coldness than she had yet assumed, "Why," said she, "Mr. Jones, do you take the trouble to make a defense where you are not accused? If I thought it worth while to accuse you, I have a charge of unpardonable nature indeed."

"What is it, for heaven's sake?" answered Jones, trembling and pale, expecting to hear of his amour with Lady Bellaston.

"Oh," said she, "how is it possible! can everything noble and everything base be lodged together in the same bosom?" Lady Bellaston, and the ignominious circumstance of having been kept, rose again in his mind, and stopped his mouth from any reply. "Could I have expected," proceeded Sophia, "such treatment from you? Nay, from any gentleman, from any man of honor? To have my name traduced in public; in inns, among the meanest vulgar! to have any little favors that my unguarded heart may have too lightly betrayed me to grant, boasted of there; nay, even to hear that you had been forced to fly from my love!"

Nothing could equal Jones's surprise at these words of Sophia; but yet, not being guilty, he was much less embarrassed how to defend himself than if she had touched that tender string at which his conscience had been alarmed. By some examination he presently found, that her supposing him guilty of so shocking an outrage against his love and her reputation was entirely owing to Partridge's talk at the inns before landlords and servants; for Sophia confessed to him it was from them that she received her intelligence. He had no very great difficulty to make her believe that he was entirely innocent of an offense so foreign to his character; but she had a great deal to hinder him from going instantly home and putting Partridge to death, which he more than once swore he would do.

This point being cleared up, they soon found themselves so well pleased with each other that Jones quite forgot he had begun the conversation with conjuring her to give up all thoughts of him; and she was in a temper to have given ear to a petition of a very different nature; for before they were aware they had both gone so far that he let fall some words that sounded like a proposal of marriage. To which she replied, "That, did not her duty to her father forbid her to follow her own inclinations, ruin with him would be more welcome to her than the most affluent fortune with another man."

At the mention of the word ruin he started, let drop her hand, which he had held for some time, and striking his breast with his own, cried out, "Oh, Sophia! can I then ruin thee? No; by heavens, no! My love I will ever retain, but it shall be in silence; it shall be at a distance from you; it shall be in some foreign land, from whence no voice, no sigh of my despair, shall ever reach and disturb your ears. And when I am dead"—he would have gone on, but was stopped by a flood of tears which Sophia let fall in his bosom, upon which she leaned, without being able to speak one word. He kissed them off, which, for some moments, she allowed him to do without any resistance; but then recollecting herself, gently withdrew out of his arms; and, to turn the discourse from a subject too tender, bethought herself to ask him a question she never had time to put to him before, "How he came into that room?"

He began to stammer, when the door opened and in came Lady Bellaston.

Having advanced a few steps, and seeing Jones and Sophia together, she suddenly stopped; when, after a pause of a few moments, recollecting herself with admirable presence of mind, she said— though with sufficient indications of surprise both in voice and countenance—"I thought, Miss Western, you had been at the play?"

Sophia had not the least suspicion that Jones and Lady Bellaston were acquainted, so with very little hesitation she went through the story of what had happened at the playhouse, and the cause of her hasty return. This narrative gave Lady Bellaston an opportunity of rallying her spirits, and of considering in what manner to act. And as the behavior of Sophia gave her hopes that Jones had not betrayed her, she put on an air of good-humor, and said, "I should not have broke in so abruptly upon you, Miss Western, if I had known you had company."

Lady Bellaston fixed her eyes on Sophia whilst she spoke these words. To which that poor young lady, having her face overspread with blushes and confusion, answered, in a stammering voice,

"I am sure, madam, I shall always think the honor of your ladyship's company——"

"I hope, at least," cries Lady Bellaston, "I interrupt no business."

"No, madam," answered Sophia, "our business was at an end. Your ladyship may be pleased to remember I have often mentioned the loss of my pocket-book, which this gentleman, having very luckily found, was so kind to return it to me with the bill in it."

Jones, ever since the arrival of Lady Bellaston, had been ready to sink with fear. He began, however, now to recover himself; and taking a hint from the behavior of Lady Bellaston, who, he saw, did not intend to claim any acquaintance with him, he said, "Ever since he had the pocket-book in his possession he had used great diligence in inquiring out the lady whose name was writ in it, but never till that day could be so fortunate to discover her."

Lady Bellaston believed not one syllable of what Sophia now said, and wonderfully admired the extreme quickness of the young lady in inventing such an excuse. Though she could not account for the meeting between these two lovers, she was firmly persuaded it was not accidental.

"That was very fortunate, indeed," cries the lady. "And it was no less so, that you heard Miss Western was at my house; for she is very little known."

"Why, madam," answered he, "it was by the luckiest chance imaginable I made this discovery. I was mentioning what I had found, and the name of the owner, the other night to a lady at the masquerade, who directed me to your ladyship's house."

Upon his mentioning the masquerade he looked very slily at Lady Bellaston. This hint a little alarmed the lady, and she was silent; when Jones, who saw the agitation of Sophia's mind, resolved to take the only method of relieving her, which was by retiring; but, before he did this, he said,

"I believe, madam, it is customary to give some reward on these occasions;—I must insist on a very high one for my honesty,—it is, madam, no less than the honor of being permitted to pay another visit here."

"Sir," replied the lady, "I make no doubt that you are a gentleman, and my doors are never shut to people of fashion."

Upon the stairs Jones met his old acquaintance, Mrs. Honour. This meeting proved a lucky circumstance, as he communicated to her the house where he lodged, with which Sophia was unacquainted.

XI

JONES had not been long gone before Lady Bellaston cried, "Upon my word, a good pretty young fellow; I wonder who he is; for I don't remember ever to have seen his face before."

"Nor I neither, madam," cries Sophia. "I must say he behaved very handsomely in relation to my note."

"Yes; and he is a very handsome fellow," said the lady: "don't you think so?"

"I did not take much notice of him," answered Sophia, "but I thought he seemed rather awkward and ungenteel than otherwise."

"You are extremely right," cries Lady Bellaston: "you may see, by his manner, that he hath not kept good company. Nay, notwithstanding his returning your note and refusing the reward, I almost question whether he is a gentleman.——I have always observed there is a something in persons well born which others can never acquire. ——I think I will give orders not to be at home to him."

"Nay, sure, madam," answered Sophia, "one can't suspect after what he hath done; besides, if your ladyship observed him, there was an elegance in his discourse, a delicacy, a prettiness of expression that, that——"

"I confess," said Lady Bellaston, "the fellow hath words—— And indeed, Sophia, you must forgive me, indeed you must."

"I forgive your ladyship!" said Sophia.

"Yes, indeed, you must," answered she, laughing; "for I had a horrible suspicion when I first came into the room——I vow you must forgive it; but I suspected it was Mr. Jones himself."

"Did your ladyship, indeed?" cries Sophia, blushing, and affecting a laugh.

"Yes, I vow I did," answered she. "I can't imagine what put it into my head; for, give the fellow his due, he was genteelly dressed;

which, I think, dear Sophy, is not commonly the case with your friend."

"This raillery," cries Sophia, "is a little cruel, Lady Bellaston, after my promise to your ladyship."

"Not at all, child," said the lady;——"It would have been cruel before; but after you have promised me never to marry without your father's consent, in which you know is implied your giving up Jones, sure you can bear a little raillery on a passion which was pardonable enough in a young girl in the country, and of which you tell me you have so entirely got the better. What must I think, my dear Sophy, if you cannot bear a little ridicule even on his dress? I shall begin to fear you are very far gone indeed; and almost question whether you have dealt ingenuously with me."

"Indeed, madam," cries Sophia, "your ladyship mistakes me if you imagine I had any concern on his account."

"On his account!" answered the lady: "you must have mistaken me; I went no farther than his dress;——for I would not injure your taste by any other comparison—I don't imagine, my dear Sophy, if your Mr. Jones had been such a fellow as this——"

"I thought," says Sophia, "your ladyship had allowed him to be handsome——"

"Whom, pray?" cried the lady hastily.

"Mr. Jones," answered Sophia;—and immediately recollecting herself, "Mr. Jones!—no, no; I ask your pardon;—I mean the gentleman who was just now here."

"Oh, Sophy! Sophy!" cries the lady; "this Mr. Jones, I am afraid, still runs in your head."

"Then, upon my honor, madam," said Sophia, "Mr. Jones is as entirely indifferent to me as the gentleman who just now left us."

"Upon my honor," said Lady Bellaston, "I believe it. Forgive me, therefore, a little innocent raillery; but I promise you I will never mention his name any more."

And now the two ladies separated, infinitely more to the delight of Sophia than of Lady Bellaston, who would willingly have tormented her rival a little longer, had not business of more importance called her away.

Book XIV

CONTAINING TWO DAYS

I

Jones had not been long at home before he received the following letter:

"I was never more surprised than when I found you was gone. When you left the room I little imagined you intended to have left the house without seeing me again. Your behavior is all of a piece, and convinces me how much I ought to despise a heart which can doat upon an idiot; though I know not whether I should not admire her cunning more than her simplicity: wonderful both! For though she understood not a word of what passed between us, yet she had the skill, the assurance, the——what shall I call it? to deny to my face that she knows you, or ever saw you before.——Was this a scheme laid between you, and have you been base enough to betray me?——Oh, how I despise her, you, and all the world, but chiefly myself! for—— I dare not write what I should afterwards run mad to read; but remember, I can detest as violently as I have loved."

Jones had but little time given him to reflect on this letter, before a second was brought him from the same hand; and this likewise we shall set down in the precise words:

"When you consider the hurry of spirits in which I must have writ, you cannot be surprised at any expressions in my former note. Yet, perhaps, on reflection, they were rather too warm. At least I would, if possible, think all owing to the odious play-house, and to the impertinence of a fool, which detained me beyond my appointment.——How easy it is to think well of those we love!—Perhaps you desire I should think so. I have resolved to see you tonight; so come to me immediately.

"P.S.—I have ordered to be at home to none but yourself.

"P.S.—Mr. Jones will imagine I shall assist him in his defense; for I believe he cannot desire to impose on me more than I desire to impose on myself.

"P.S.—Come immediately."

To the men of intrigue I refer the determination, whether the angry or the tender letter gave the greatest uneasiness to Jones. Certain it is, he had no violent inclination to pay any more visits that evening. However, he thought his honor engaged, and after some discontented walks about the room, he was preparing to depart, when the lady kindly prevented him, by her own presence. She entered the room very disordered in her dress, and very discomposed in her looks, and threw herself into a chair, where, having recovered her breath, she said,

"You see, sir, when women have gone one length too far, they will stop at none. If any person would have sworn this to me a week ago, I would not have believed it of myself."

"Pardon me, my dear angel," said he, "if, after the letters I have received, the terrors of your anger, though I know not how I have deserved it——"

"And have I then," says she, with a smile, "so angry a countenance? Have I really brought a chiding face with me?"

"If there be honor in man," said he, "I have done nothing to merit your anger. You remember the appointment you sent me; I went in pursuance."

"I beseech you," cried she, "do not run through the odious recital. Answer me but one question, and I shall be easy. Have you not betrayed my honor to her?"

Jones fell upon his knees, and began to utter the most violent protestations, when Partridge came dancing and capering into the room, like one drunk with joy, crying out, "She's found! she's found! Here, sir, here, she's here—Mrs. Honour is upon the stairs."

"Stop her a moment," cries Jones. "Here, madam, step behind the bed, I have no other room nor closet, nor place on earth to hide you in; sure never was so damned an accident."

"D—ned indeed!" said the lady, as she went to her place of concealment; and presently afterwards in came Mrs. Honour.

"Heyday!" says she, "Mr. Jones, what's the matter? That impudent rascal your servant would scarce let me come upstairs. I hope he hath not the same reason to keep me from you as he had at Upton. I suppose you hardly expected to see me; but you have certainly bewitched my lady. Poor dear young lady!"

Jones begged her only to whisper, for that there was a lady dying in the next room.

"A lady!" cries she; "ay, I suppose one of your ladies. Oh, Mr. Jones, there are too many of them in the world; I believe we are got into the house of one, for my Lady Bellaston, I darst to say, is no better than she should be."

"Hush! hush!" cries Jones, "every word is overheard in the next room."

"I don't care a farthing," cries Honour, "I speaks no scandal of anyone; but, to be sure, the servants make no scruple of saying as how her ladyship meets men at another place."

"The servants are villains," cries Jones, "and abuse their lady unjustly."

"Ay, to be sure, servants are always villains, and so my lady says, and won't hear a word of it."

"No, I am convinced," says Jones, "my Sophia is above listening to such base scandal. I can't hear all this of a lady of such honor, and a relation of Sophia; besides, you will distract the poor lady in the next room. Let me entreat you to walk with me downstairs."

"Nay, sir, if you won't let me speak, I have done. Here, sir, is a letter from my young lady. But, Mr. Jones, I think you are not over and above generous, and yet I have heard some servants say——but I am sure you will do me the justice to own I never saw the color of your money." Here Jones hastily took the letter, and presently after slipped five pieces into her hand. He then returned a thousand thanks to his dear Sophia in a whisper, and she departed, not without expressing much grateful sense of his generosity.

Lady Bellaston now came from behind the curtain. How shall I describe her rage? Her tongue was at first incapable of utterance; but streams of fire darted from her eyes, and well indeed they might, for her heart was all in a flame. And now, as soon as her voice found way, instead of expressing any indignation against Honour or her own servants, she began to attack poor Jones. "You see," said she, "what I have sacrificed to you; my reputation, my honor—gone forever! And what return have I found? Neglected, slighted for a country girl, for an idiot."

"What neglect, madam, or what slight," cries Jones, "have I been guilty of?"

"Mr. Jones," said she, "it is in vain to dissemble; if you will make me easy, you must entirely give her up; and, as a proof of your intention, show me the letter."

"And can your ladyship," cries he, "ask of me what I must part with my honor before I grant? What security could you have that I should not act the same part by yourself?"

"Very well," said she, "I need not insist on your becoming this contemptible wretch in your own opinion; for the inside of the letter could inform me of nothing more than I know already."

Here ensued a long conversation, which the reader, who is not too curious, will thank me for not inserting at length. It shall suffice, therefore, to inform him that Lady Bellaston grew more and more pacified, and at length believed, or affected to believe, his protestations. She was, indeed, well convinced that Sophia possessed the first place in Jones's affections; and yet, haughty and amorous as this lady was, she submitted at last to bear the second place; or, to express it more properly in a legal phrase, was contented with the possession of that of which another woman had the reversion.

It was at length agreed that Jones should for the future visit at the house; for that Sophia, her maid, and all the servants would place these visits to the account of Sophia.

The next day was appointed for the first visit, and then, after proper ceremonials, the Lady Bellaston returned home.

II

JONES was no sooner alone than he eagerly broke open his letter, and read as follows:

"Sir—It is impossible to express what I have suffered since you left this house; and as I have reason to think you intend coming here again, I have sent Honour, though so late at night, as she tells me she knows your lodgings, to prevent you. I charge you, by all the regard you have for me, not to think of visiting here; for it will certainly be discovered; nay, I almost doubt, from some things which have dropped from her ladyship, that she is not already without some suspicion. Something favorable perhaps may happen; we must wait with patience; but I once more entreat you, if you have any concern for my ease, do not think of returning hither."

This letter administered the same kind of consolation to poor Jones which Job formerly received from his friends. At length, after much deliberation, he determined to feign himself sick; for this suggested itself as the only means of failing the appointed visit, without incensing Lady Bellaston.

The first thing, however, which he did in the morning was to write an answer to Sophia, which he enclosed in one to Honour. He then despatched another to Lady Bellaston, containing the above-mentioned excuse.

Mr. Jones now received a visit from Mrs. Miller, who, after some formal introduction, began the following speech:

"I am very sorry, sir, to wait upon you on such an occasion; but I hope you will consider the ill consequence which it must be to the reputation of my poor girls if my house should once be talked of as a house of ill-fame. I hope you won't think me, therefore, guilty of impertinence if I beg you not to bring any more ladies in at that time of night. The clock had struck two before one of them went away."

"I do assure you, madam," said Jones, "the lady who was here last night is a woman of very great fashion, and my near relation."

"I don't know what fashion she is of," answered Mrs. Miller; "but her chairmen did nothing but make jests all the evening in the entry, and asked Mr. Partridge, in the hearing of my own maid, if madam intended to stay with his master all night. I have really a great respect for you, Mr. Jones; nay, I have a very high obligation to you for your generosity to my cousin. Oh, heavens! what goodness have you shown! The character which Mr. Allworthy hath formerly given me of you was, I find, strictly true. Nay, believe me, dear Mr. Jones, if my daughters' and my own reputation were out of the case, I should, for your own sake, be sorry that so pretty a young gentleman should converse with these women: but if you are resolved to do it, I must beg you to take another lodging; especially upon the account of my girls, who have little, Heaven knows, besides their character, to recommend them."

Jones started and changed color at the name of Allworthy. "Indeed, Mrs. Miller," answered he, a little warmly, "I do not take this at all kind. I will never bring any slander on your house; but I must insist on seeing what company I please in my own room; and if that gives you any offense, I shall, as soon as I am able, look for another lodging."

"I am sorry we must part, then, sir," said she; "but I am convinced Mr. Allworthy himself would never come within my doors if he had the least suspicion of my keeping an ill house."

"Very well, madam," said Jones, "but I beg you will send Partridge up to me immediately"; which she promised to do, and then with a very low curtsy retired.

As soon as Partridge arrived, Jones fell upon him in the most out-rageous manner.

"How often," said he, "am I to suffer for your folly, or rather for my own in keeping you? is that tongue of yours resolved upon my destruction?"

"What have I done, sir?" answered affrighted Partridge.

"How durst you, after all the precautions I gave you, mention the name of Mr. Allworthy in this house?"

Partridge denied that he ever had, with many oaths. "Oh, Lord, sir," said Partridge, "hear me but out, and you will own how wrong-fully you have accused me. When Mrs. Honour came downstairs last night she met me in the entry, and asked me when my master had heard from Mr. Allworthy; and, to be sure, Mrs. Miller heard the very words; and the moment Madam Honour was gone, she called me into the parlor to her. 'Mr. Partridge,' says she, 'what Mr. Allworthy is it that the gentlewoman mentioned? is it the great Mr. Allworthy of Somersetshire?' 'Upon my word, madam,' says I, 'I know nothing of the matter.' 'Sure,' says she, 'your master is not the Mr. Jones I have heard Mr. Allworthy talk of?' 'Upon my word, madam,' says I, 'I know nothing of the matter.' Nay, sir, so far was I from telling her anything about Mr. Allworthy, that I told her the very direct contrary; for, though I did not contradict it at that moment, yet, as second thoughts, they say, are best, so when I came to consider that somebody must have informed her, thinks I to my-self, I will put an end to the story; and so I went back again into the parlor some time afterwards, and says I, upon my word, says I, whoever, says I, told you that this gentleman was Mr. Jones; that is, says I, that this Mr. Jones was that Mr. Jones, told you a confounded lie: and I beg, says I, you will never mention any such matter, says I; for my master, says I, will think I must have told you so; and I defy anybody in the house ever to say I mentioned any such word."

The simplicity of Partridge set Jones a-laughing, and put a final end to his anger, which had indeed seldom any long duration in his mind; and, instead of commenting on his defense, he told him he intended to leave those lodgings, and ordered him to go and endeavor to get him others.

III

PARTRIDGE had no sooner left Mr. Jones than Mr. Nightingale, with whom he had now contracted a great intimacy, came to him, and, after a short salutation, said,

"So, Tom, I hear you had company very late last night." He then ran on with much commonplace raillery till Jones interrupted him, saying,

"I suppose you have received all this information from Mrs. Miller, who hath been up here a little while ago to give me warning. Nay, upon my honor, I think she's in the right of it. However, I have taken her at her word, and have sent Partridge to look for another lodging."

"If you will," says Nightingale, "we may, I believe, be again together; for, to tell you a secret, which I desire you won't mention in the family, I intend to quit the house today."

"And do you intend to make a secret of your going away?" said Jones.

"I promise you," answered Nightingale, "I don't intend to bilk my lodgings; but I have a private reason for not taking a formal leave."

"Not so private," answered Jones; "I promise you, I have seen it ever since the second day of my coming to the house. Here will be some wet eyes on your departure. Poor Nancy, I pity her, faith! Indeed, Jack, you have played the fool with that girl. You have given her a longing which I am afraid nothing will ever cure her of."

Nightingale answered, "What the devil would you have me do? would you have me marry her to cure her?"

"No," answered Jones; "I would not have had you make love to her, as you have often done in my presence. I have been astonished at the blindness of her mother in never seeing it."

"Pugh, see it!" cries Nightingale. "What the devil should she see?"

"Why, see," said Jones, "that you have made her daughter distractedly in love with you."

"If I have," said Nightingale, "I am sorry for it; but time and absence will soon wear off such impressions. It is a receipt I must take myself; for, to confess the truth to you—I never liked any girl half so much in my whole life; but I must let you into the whole secret,

Tom. My father hath provided a match for me with a woman I never saw; and she is now coming to town, in order for me to make my addresses to her."

At these words Jones burst into a loud fit of laughter; when Nightingale cried—"Nay, prithee, don't turn me into ridicule. The devil take me if I am not half mad about this matter! my poor Nancy! Oh! Jones, Jones, I wish I had a fortune in my own possession."

"I heartily wish you had," cries Jones; "for, if this be the case, I sincerely pity you both; but surely you don't intend to go away without taking your leave of her?"

"I would not," answered Nightingale, "undergo the pain of taking leave, for ten thousand pounds; besides, I am convinced, instead of answering any good purpose, it would only serve to inflame my poor Nancy the more. I beg, therefore, you would not mention a word of it today, and in the evening, or tomorrow morning, I intend to depart."

Jones promised he would not; and said, upon reflection, he thought, as he had determined and was obliged to leave her, he took the most prudent method. He then told Nightingale he should be very glad to lodge in the same house with him; and it was accordingly agreed between them, that Nightingale should procure him either the ground floor, or the two pair of stairs; for the young gentleman himself was to occupy that which was between them.

IV

MR. JONES slept till eleven the next morning, and would perhaps have continued in the same quiet situation much longer, had not a violent uproar awakened him.

Partridge was now summoned, who, being asked what was the matter, answered, "That there was a dreadful hurricane belowstairs; that Miss Nancy was in fits; and that the other sister and the mother were both crying and lamenting over her."

Jones expressed much concern at this news; which Partridge endeavored to relieve, by saying, with a smile, "He fancied the young lady was in no danger of death; for that Susan" (which was the name of the maid) "had given him to understand, it was nothing more than a common affair. In short," said he, "Miss Nancy hath had a mind to be as wise as her mother; that's all; she was a little hungry, it seems, and so sat down to dinner before grace was said; and so there is a child coming for the Foundling Hospital."

"Prithee, leave thy stupid jesting," cries Jones. "Is the misery of these poor wretches a subject of mirth? Go immediately to Mrs. Miller, and tell her I beg leave—Stay, you will make some blunder; I will go myself; for she desired me to breakfast with her." The maid presently brought a message to Mr. Jones, "That her mistress hoped he would excuse the disappointment, but an accident had happened, which made it impossible for her to have the pleasure of his company at breakfast that day." Jones desired, "She would give herself no trouble about anything so trifling as his disappointment; that ne was heartily sorry for the occasion; and that if he could be of any service to her, she might command him."

He had scarce spoke these words, when Mrs. Miller, who heard them all, coming out to him in a flood of tears, said,

"Oh, Mr. Jones! you are certainly one of the best young men alive. I give you a thousand thanks for your kind offer of your service; but, alas! sir, it is out of your power to preserve my poor girl. That Nightingale, that barbarous villain, hath undone my daughter. She is—she is—oh! Mr. Jones, my girl is with child by him; and in that condition he hath deserted her. Here! here, sir, is his cruel letter: read it, Mr. Jones, and tell me if such another monster lives."

The letter was as follows:

"DEAR NANCY—As I found it impossible to mention to you what, I am afraid, will be no less shocking to you than it is to me, I have taken this method to inform you, that my father insists upon my immediately paying my addresses to a young lady of fortune, whom he hath provided for my—I need not write the detested word. Your own good understanding will make you sensible how entirely I am obliged to an obedience by which I shall be forever excluded from your dear arms. The fondness of your mother may encourage you to trust her with the unhappy consequence of our love, which may be easily kept a secret from the world, and for which I will take care to provide, as I will for you. I wish you may feel less on this account than I have suffered; but summon all your fortitude to your assistance, and forgive and forget the man whom nothing but the prospect of certain ruin could have forced to write this letter. I bid you forget me, I mean only as a lover; but the best of friends you shall ever find in your faithful, though unhappy,

"J. N."

When Jones had read this letter, they both stood silent during a minute, looking at each other; at last he began thus: "I cannot express, madam, how much I am shocked at what I have read; yet let me beg you, in one particular, to take the writer's advice. Consider the reputation of your daughter."

"It is gone, it is lost, Mr. Jones," cried she, "as well as her innocence. She received the letter in a room full of company, and immediately swooning away upon opening it, the contents were known to everyone present. But the loss of her reputation, bad as it is, is not the worst: I shall lose my child; she hath attempted twice to destroy herself already; and, though she hath been hitherto prevented, vows she will not outlive it." She then turned to Jones, and began to renew her apologies for having disappointed him of his breakfast.

"I hope, madam," said Jones, "I shall have a more exquisite repast than any you could have provided for me, if I can do any service to this little family of love. I am very much deceived in Mr. Nightingale, if, notwithstanding what hath happened, he hath not much goodness of heart at the bottom, as well as a very violent affection for your daughter. If this be the case, I think the picture which I shall lay before him will affect him. Endeavor, madam, to comfort yourself and Miss Nancy as well as you can. I will go instantly in quest of Mr. Nightingale; and I hope to bring you good news."

V

MR. NIGHTINGALE, Jones found in his new lodgings, sitting melancholy by the fire, and silently lamenting the unhappy situation in which he had placed poor Nancy. He no sooner saw his friend appear than he arose hastily to meet him; and after much congratulation said, "Nothing could be more opportune than this kind visit; for I was never more in the spleen in my life."

"I am sorry," answered Jones, "that I bring news very unlikely to relieve you: nay, what I am convinced must, of all other, shock you the most. However, it is necessary you should know it. Without further preface, then, I come to you, Mr. Nightingale, from a worthy family, which you have involved in misery and ruin." Jones proceeded, in the liveliest manner, to paint the tragical story.

Nightingale never once interrupted the narration, but when it was concluded, after fetching a deep sigh, he said, "What you tell me, my friend, affects me in the tenderest manner. Sure there never was so cursed an accident as the poor girl's betraying my letter. Her reputation might otherwise have been safe, and the affair might have remained a profound secret."

"Indeed, my friend," answered Jones, "You have so entirely gained her affections, that it is the loss of you, and not of her reputation, which afflicts her."

"Nay, for that matter, I promise you," cries Nightingale, "she hath my affections so absolutely, that my wife, whoever she is to be, will have very little share in them."

"And is it possible, then," said Jones, "you can think of deserting her?"

"Why, what can I do?" answered the other.

"If you ask me what you shall do, what can you do less," cries Jones, "than fulfil the expectations of her family, and her own? Nay, I sincerely tell you, they were mine too, ever since I first saw you together. Though there may have been no direct promise of marriage in the case, I will leave to your own good understanding, how far you are bound to proceed."

"Nay, I must not only confess what you have hinted," said Nightingale; "but I am afraid even that very promise you mention I have given."

"And can you, after owning that," said Jones, "hesitate a moment?"

"Consider, my friend," answered the other; "I know you are a man of honor, and would advise no one to act contrary to its rules: if there were no other objection, can I, after this publication of her disgrace, think of such an alliance with honor?"

"Undoubtedly," replied Jones, "and the very best and truest honor, which is goodness, requires it of you. As you mention a scruple of this kind, you will give me leave to examine it. Can you, with honor, be guilty of having under false pretenses deceived a young woman and her family, and of having by these means treacherously robbed her of her innocence? Can you, with honor, be the knowing, the wilful occasion, nay, the artful contriver, of the ruin of a human being?"

"Common sense, indeed," said Nightingale, "warrants all you say; but yet you well know the opinion of the world is so contrary to it, that, was I to marry a whore, though my own, I should be ashamed of ever showing my face again."

"Fie upon it, Mr. Nightingale!" said Jones; "do not call her by so ungenerous a name: when you promised to marry her she became your wife; and she hath sinned more against prudence than virtue."

"Oh, my dear friend!" cries Nightingale, "I pity poor Nancy from my soul, and if I had no inclinations to consult but my own,

I would marry her tomorrow morning: I would, by Heaven! but you will easily imagine how impossible it would be to prevail on my father to consent to such a match; besides, he hath provided another for me, and tomorrow, by his express command, I am to wait on the lady."

"I have not the honor to know your father," said Jones; "but, suppose he could be persuaded, would you yourself consent to the only means of preserving these poor people?"

"As eagerly as I would pursue my happiness," answered Nightingale; "for I never shall find it in any other woman."

"Then I am resolved to undertake it," said Jones. "If you will therefore tell me where I may find the old gentleman, I will not lose a moment in the business; which, while I pursue, you cannot do a more generous action than by paying a visit to the poor girl. You will find I have not exaggerated in the account I have given of the wretchedness of the family."

Nightingale immediately consented to the proposal; and now, having acquainted Jones with his father's lodging, and the coffee-house where he would most probably find him, he hesitated a moment, and then said, "Suppose you told him I was already married, it might be easier to reconcile him to the fact after it was done; and, upon my honor, I am so affected with what you have said, and I love my Nancy so passionately, I almost wish it was done, whatever might be the consequence."

Jones greatly approved the hint, and promised to pursue it. They then separated, Nightingale to visit his Nancy, and Jones in quest of the old gentleman.

VI

This gentleman, whom Mr. Jones now visited, was what they call a man of the world; that is to say, a man who directs his conduct in this world as one who, being fully persuaded there is no other, is resolved to make the most of this. In his early years he had been bred to trade; but, having acquired a very good fortune, he had lately declined his business; or, to speak more properly, had changed it from dealing in goods to dealing only in money, of which he had always a plentiful fund at command. He had indeed conversed so entirely with money, that it may be almost doubted whether he imagined there was any other thing really existing in the world.

As money, then, was always uppermost in this gentleman's thoughts, so the moment he saw a stranger within his doors it immediately occurred to his imagination, that such stranger was either come to bring him money, or to fetch it from him. And according as one or other of these thoughts prevailed, he conceived a favorable or unfavorable idea of the person who approached him.

Unluckily for Jones, as a young gentleman had visited him the day before, with a bill from his son for a play debt, he apprehended, at the first sight of Jones, that he was come on such another errand. Jones therefore had no sooner told him that he was come on his son's account than the old gentleman, being confirmed in his suspicion, burst forth into an exclamation, "That he would lose his labor."

"Is it then possible, sir," answered Jones, "that you can guess my business?"

"If I do guess it," replied the other, "I repeat again to you, you will lose your labor. What, I suppose you are one of those sparks who lead my son into all those scenes of riot and debauchery, which will be his destruction? but I shall pay no more of his bills, I promise you. I expect he will quit all such company for the future. If I had imagined otherwise, I should not have provided a wife for him."

"How, sir," said Jones, "and was this lady of your providing?"

"Pray, sir," answered the old gentleman, "how comes it to be any concern of yours?"

"Nay, dear sir," replied Jones, "be not offended that I interest myself in what regards your son's happiness, for whom I have so great an honor and value. It was upon that very account I came to wait upon you. Nay, sir, it is not easy to express the esteem I have for you, who could be so generous, so good, so kind, so indulgent, to provide such a match for your son; a woman who, I dare swear, will make him one of the happiest men upon earth."

Nightingale no sooner found that Jones had no demand on him, than he began to be pleased with his presence.

"Pray, good sir," said he, "be pleased to sit down. If you are a friend of my son, and have anything to say concerning this young lady, I shall be glad to hear you. As to her making him happy, it will be his own fault if she doth not. She will bring him a fortune capable of making any reasonable, prudent, sober man happy."

"Undoubtedly," cries Jones, "for she is in herself a fortune; so beautiful, so genteel, so sweet-tempered, and so well educated; she is indeed a most accomplished young lady; sings admirably well, and hath a most delicate hand at the harpsichord."

"I did not know any of these matters," answered the old gentleman, "for I never saw the lady; but I do not like her the worse for what you tell me."

"I do assure you, sir," cries Jones, "she hath them all in the most eminent degree. For my part, I own I was afraid you might have been a little backward, a little less inclined to the match; therefore I came, sir, to entreat you, to conjure you, as you value the happiness of your son, not to be averse to his match."

"If that was your business, sir," said the old gentleman, "we are both obliged to you; and you may be perfectly easy; for I give you my word I was very well satisfied with her fortune."

"Sir," answered Jones, "I honor you every moment more and more. To be so easily satisfied, so very moderate on that account, is a proof of the soundness of your understanding, as well as the nobleness of your mind."

"Not so very moderate, young gentleman, not so very moderate," answered the father. "Why, pray, what fortune do you imagine this lady to have?"

"What fortune?" cries Jones; "why, too contemptible a one to be named for your son."

"Well, well, well," said the other, "perhaps he might have done better."

"That I deny," said Jones, "for she is one of the best of women."

"Ay, ay, but in point of fortune I mean," answered the other. "And yet, as to that now, how much do you imagine your friend is to have?"

"How much?" cries Jones, "how much? Why, at the utmost, perhaps £200."

"Do you mean to banter me, young gentleman?" said the father, a little angry.

"No, upon my soul," answered Jones, "I am in earnest: nay, I believe I have gone to the utmost farthing. If I do the lady an injury, I ask her pardon."

"Indeed you do," cries the father; "I am certain she hath fifty times that sum, and she shall produce fifty to that before I consent that she shall marry my son."

"Nay," said Jones, "it is too late to talk of consent now; if she had not fifty farthings your son is married."

"My son married!" answered the old gentleman, with surprise. "My son married to Miss Harris!"

"To Miss Harris!" said Jones; "no, sir; to Miss Nancy Miller, the daughter of Mrs. Miller, at whose house he lodged; a young lady, who, though her mother is reduced to let lodgings——"

"Are you bantering, or are you in earnest?" cries the father, with a most solemn voice.

"Indeed, sir," answered Jones, "I scorn the character of a banterer. I came to you in most serious earnest, imagining, as I find true, that your son had never dared acquaint you with a match so much inferior to him in point of fortune, though the reputation of the lady will suffer it no longer to remain a secret."

While the father stood like one struck suddenly dumb at this news, a gentleman came into the room, and saluted him by the name of brother.

The young lady whom Mr. Nightingale had intended for his son was a near neighbor of his brother, and in reality it was upon the account of his projected match that he was now come to town; not, indeed, to forward, but to dissuade his brother from a purpose which he conceived would inevitably ruin his nephew; for he foresaw no other event from a union with Miss Harris, notwithstanding the largeness of her fortune, as she was very tall, very thin, very ugly, very affected, very silly, and very ill-natured.

His brother, therefore, no sooner mentioned the marriage of his nephew with Miss Miller than he expressed the utmost satisfaction; and when the father had very bitterly reviled his son, and pronounced sentence of beggary upon him, the uncle began in the following manner:

"If you was a little cooler, brother, I would ask you whether you love your son for his sake or for your own. You would answer, I suppose, and so I suppose you think, for his sake; and doubtless it is his happiness which you intended in the marriage you proposed for him.

"Now, brother, to prescribe rules of happiness to others hath always appeared to me very absurd, and to assist on doing this very tyrannical. And if this be absurd in other things, it is mostly so in the affair of marriage, the happiness of which depends entirely on the affection which subsists between the parties.

"I own my nephew in a fault; but surely it is not an unpardonable fault. Will you increase the ill consequences of his simple choice? In a word, brother, because he hath put it out of your power to make his circumstances as affluent as you would, will you distress them as much as you can?"

By the force of the true Catholic faith St. Anthony won upon the fishes. Orpheus and Amphion went a little farther, and by the charms of music enchanted things merely inanimate. Wonderful, both! but neither history nor fable have ever yet ventured to record an instance of anyone who, by force of argument and reason, hath triumphed over habitual avarice.

Jones fell into raptures with this good gentleman; and when, after much persuasion, they found the father grew still more and more irritated, instead of appeased, Jones conducted the uncle to his nephew at the house of Mrs. Miller.

VII

THE mother, the two daughters, and young Mr. Nightingale were now sat down to supper together, when the uncle was, at his own desire, introduced without any ceremony into the company.

The old gentleman immediately walked up to Miss Nancy, saluted and wished her joy, as he did afterwards the mother and the other sister; and lastly, he paid the proper compliments to his nephew.

Miss Nancy and her supposed husband looked rather foolish than otherwise upon the occasion; but Mrs. Miller took the first opportunity of withdrawing; and, having sent for Jones into the dining-room, she threw herself at his feet, and, in a most passionate flood of tears, called him her good angel, with many other respectful and endearing appellations.

After the first gust of her passion was a little over, she proceeded to inform Mr. Jones that all matters were settled between Mr. Nightingale and her daughter, and that they were to be married the next morning; at which Mr. Jones having expressed much pleasure, the poor woman fell again into a fit of joy and thanksgiving, which he at length with difficulty silenced, and prevailed on her to return with him back to the company.

This little society now passed two or three very agreeable hours together, when the maid of the house informed Jones that a gentle-woman desired to speak with him.——He went immediately out, ushered his visitant upstairs, who, in the person of Mrs. Honour, acquainted him with such dreadful news concerning his Sophia, that he immediately lost all consideration for every other person.

What this dreadful matter was, the reader will be informed, after we have first related the many preceding steps which produced it, and those will be the subject of the following book.

Mr. Jones and Mr. Nightingale discuss poor Nancy's plight.

Book XV

IN WHICH THE HISTORY ADVANCES ABOUT TWO DAYS

I

I REMEMBER a wise old gentleman who used to say, "When children are doing nothing, they are doing mischief." When the effects of female jealousy do not appear openly in their proper colors of rage and fury, we may suspect that mischievous passion to be at work privately, and attempting to undermine what it doth not attack aboveground.

This was exemplified in the conduct of Lady Bellaston, who, under all the smiles which she wore in her countenance, concealed much indignation against Sophia, and resolved to get rid of her by some means or other; nor was it long before a very favorable opportunity of accomplishing this presented itself to her.

The reader may be pleased to remember, that Sophia at the playhouse, had put herself under the protection of a young nobleman. As beauty never looks more amiable than in distress, he might now, without any great impropriety, be said to be actually in love with her.

The next morning, therefore, after this accident, he waited on Sophia, with the usual compliments, and hopes that she had received no harm from her last night's adventure. Time now flew away unperceived, and the noble lord had been two hours in company with the lady, before it entered into his head that he had made too long a visit. Though this circumstance alone would have alarmed Sophia, she had indeed much more pregnant evidence from the eyes of her lover of what passed within his bosom; nay, though he did not make any open declaration of his passion, yet many of his expressions were rather too warm, and too tender, to have been imputed to complaisance.

Lady Bellaston therefore ordered her servants, that when my lord was going, they should tell him she desired to speak with him. Lord Fellamar (for that was the title of this young nobleman) was no sooner introduced to her ladyship than she attacked him in the following strain:

"Bless me, my lord, are you here yet?"

"Indeed, Lady Bellaston," said he, "I don't wonder you are astonished at the length of my visit; for I have stayed above two hours, and I did not think I had stayed above half a one."

"What am I to conclude from thence, my lord?" said she. "The company must be very agreeable which can make time slide away so very deceitfully."

"Upon my honor," said he, "the most agreeable I ever saw. Pray tell me, Lady Bellaston, who is this blazing star which you have produced among us all of a sudden?"

"Oh, my cousin Western!" said she; "why, that blazing star, my lord, is the daughter of a country booby squire, and hath been in town about a fortnight, for the first time."

"Upon my soul," said he, "I should swear she had been bred up in a court; for besides her beauty, I never saw anything so genteel, so sensible, so polite."

"Oh, brave!" cries the lady, "my cousin hath you, I find."

"Upon my honor," answered he, "I wish she had; for I am in love with her to distraction."

"Nay, my lord," said she, "it is not wishing yourself very ill neither, for she is a very great fortune: I assure you she is an only child, and her father's estate is a good £3000 a year."

"Then I can assure you, madam," answered the lord, "I think her the best match in England."

"Indeed, my lord," replied she, "if you like her, I heartily wish you had her."

"If you think so kindly of me, madam," said he, "as she is a relation of yours, will you do me the honor to propose it to her father?"

"Indeed, then," said the lady, "I will most readily propose your lordship to her father; and I can, I believe, assure you of his joyful acceptance of the proposal. But there is a bar, which I am almost ashamed to mention. You have a rival, my lord, and a rival who, though I blush to name him, neither you, nor all the world, will ever be able to conquer."

"I promise you, madam," answered he, "there are very few things I would not undertake for your charming cousin; but pray, who is this happy man?"

"Why, he is," said she, "one of the lowest fellows in the world. He is a beggar, a bastard, a foundling, a fellow in meaner circumstances than one of your lordship's footmen."

"Indeed, madam," replied my lord, "your cousin is of too immense a value to be thrown away; such ruin as this must be prevented."

"Alas!" cries she, "my lord, how can it be prevented? The family have already done all in their power; but the girl is, I think, intoxicated, and nothing less than ruin will content her. And to deal more openly with you, I expect every day to hear she is run away with him."

"What you tell me, Lady Bellaston," answered his lordship, "affects me most tenderly, and only raises my compassion, instead of lessening my adoration of your cousin. Some means must be found to preserve so inestimable a jewel. Hath your ladyship endeavored to reason with her?"

Here the lady affected a laugh, and cried, "My dear lord, sure you know us better than to talk of reasoning a young woman out of her inclinations? Nothing but violent methods will do."

"What is to be done?" cries my lord; "what methods are to be taken? Is there any method upon earth? Oh! Lady Bellaston! there is nothing which I would not undertake for such a reward."

"Nay, my lord," answered she, "I am so far from doubting you, I am much more inclined to doubt my own courage; for I must run a monstrous risk. I must place such a confidence in your honor as a wise woman will scarce ever place in a man on any consideration." In this point likewise my lord very well satisfied her; for common fame did him no more than justice, in speaking well of him.

"Well, then," said she, "my lord,—I—I vow, I can't bear the apprehension of it. No, it must not be.——At least every other method shall be tried. Can you get rid of your engagements, and dine here today? Your lordship will have an opportunity of seeing a little more of Miss Western. I promise you we have no time to lose. Here will be nobody but Lady Betty, and Miss Eagle, and Colonel Hampsted, and

Tom Edwards; they will all go soon—and I shall be at home to nobody. Then your lordship may be a little more explicit. Nay, I will contrive some method to convince you of her attachment to this fellow."

My lord made proper compliments, accepted the invitation, and then they parted.

II

THOUGH the reader may have long since concluded Lady Bellaston to be a member (and no inconsiderable one) of the great world; she was in reality a very considerable member of the little world; by which appellation was distinguished a very worthy and honorable society which not long since flourished in this kingdom.

Among other good principles upon which this society was founded, there was one very remarkable; that every member should, within the twenty-four hours, tell at least one merry fib.

Edwards was likewise a member of this comical society. To him, therefore, Lady Bellaston applied as a proper instrument for her purpose, and furnished him with a fib, which he was to vent whenever the lady gave him her cue; and this was not to be till the evening, when all the company but Lord Fellamar and himself were gone, and while they were engaged in a rubber at whist.

To this time, then, which was between seven and eight in the evening, we will convey our reader; when Lady Bellaston, Lord Fellamar, Miss Western, and Tom, being engaged at whist, Tom received his cue from Lady Bellaston, which was, "I protest, Tom, you are grown intolerable lately; you used to tell us all the news of the town, and now you know no more of the world than if you lived out of it."

Mr. Edwards then began as follows: "The fault is not mine, madam: it lies in the dullness of the age, that doth nothing worth talking of.——Oh, la! though now I think on't there hath a terrible accident befallen poor Colonel Wilcox.——Poor Ned.——You know him, my lord, everybody knows him; faith! I am very much concerned for him."

"What is it, pray?" says Lady Bellaston.

"Why, he hath killed a man this morning in a duel, that's all."

His lordship, who was not in the secret, asked gravely, whom he had killed? To which Edwards answered, "A young fellow we none of us know; a Somersetshire lad just come to town, one Jones his name is; a near relation of one Mr. Allworthy, of whom your lordship, I believe, hath heard. I saw the lad lie dead in a coffee-house. Upon my soul, he is one of the finest corpses I ever saw in my life!"

Sophia, who had just begun to deal as Tom had mentioned that a man was killed, stopped her hand, and listened with attention (for all stories of that kind affected her); but no sooner had he arrived at the latter part of the story than she began to deal again; and having dealt three cards to one, and seven to another, and ten to a third, at last dropped the rest from her hand, and fell back in her chair.

The company behaved as usually on these occasions. The usual disturbance ensued, the usual assistance was summoned, and Sophia at last, as it is usual, returned again to life, and was soon after, at her earnest desire, led to her own apartment; where, at my lord's request, Lady Bellaston acquainted her with the truth, attempted to carry it off as a jest of her own, and comforted her with repeated assurances, that neither his lordship nor Tom, though she had taught him the story, were in the true secret of the affair.

There was no further evidence necessary to convince Lord Fella-mar how justly the case had been represented to him by Lady Bellaston; and now, at her return into the room, a scheme was laid between these two noble persons, though it appeared in very heinous light to his lordship.

The next evening at seven was appointed for the fatal purpose, when Lady Bellaston undertook that Sophia should be alone, and his lordship should be introduced to her. The whole family were to be regulated for the purpose, most of the servants despatched out of the house; and for Mrs. Honour, who, to prevent suspicion, was to be left with her mistress till his lordship's arrival, Lady Bellaston herself was to engage her in an apartment as distant as possible from the scene of the intended mischief, and out of the hearing of Sophia.

The young lord's scruples, she treated with disdain. "My dear lord," said she, "you certainly want a cordial. Fie upon it! have more resolution. Are you frightened by the word rape? Or are you apprehensive——? All women love a man of spirit."

"Nay, dear Lady Bellaston," cried he, "don't ridicule me in this manner."

"Why, my good lord," answered she, "you force me to use a strange kind of language, and to betray my sex most abominably; but I am contented with knowing my intentions are good, and that I am endeavoring to serve my cousin; for I think you will make her a husband notwithstanding this; or, upon my soul, I would not even persuade her to fling herself away upon an empty title. She should not upbraid me hereafter with having lost a man of spirit; for that his enemies allow this poor young fellow to be."

Lady Bellaston, perceiving she had fired the young lord's pride, began now, like a true orator, to rouse other passions to its assistance.

"My lord," says she, in a graver voice, "you will be pleased to remember, you mentioned this matter to me first; for I would not appear to you in the light of one who is endeavoring to put off my cousin upon you. Fourscore thousand pounds do not stand in need of an advocate to recommend them."

"Nor doth Miss Western," said he, "require any recommendation from her fortune; for, in my opinion, no woman ever had half her charms."

"Yes, yes, my lord," replied the lady, looking in the glass, "there have been women with more than half her charms, I assure you; not that I need lessen her on that account: she is a most delicious girl, that's certain; and within these few hours she will be in the arms of one who surely doth not deserve her, though I will give him his due, I believe he is truly a man of spirit."

"I hope so, madam," said my lord; "though I must own he doth not deserve her; for, unless Heaven or your ladyship disappoint me, she shall within that time be in mine."

"Well spoken, my lord, answered the lady; "I promise you no disappointment shall happen from my side; and within this week I am convinced I shall call your lordship my cousin in public."

Here we shall put an end to this dialogue, and hasten to the fatal hour when everything was prepared for the destruction of poor Sophia.

III

THE clock had now struck seven, and poor Sophia, alone and melancholy, sat reading a tragedy, when the door opened, and in came Lord Fellamar. Sophia started from her chair at his entrance; and his lordship advancing forwards, and making a low bow, said, "I am afraid, Miss Western, I break in upon you abruptly."

"Indeed, my lord," says she, "I must own myself a little surprised at this unexpected visit."

"If this visit be unexpected, madam," answered Lord Fellamar, "my eyes must have been very faithless interpreters of my heart, for surely you could not otherwise have hoped to detain my heart in your possession, without receiving a visit from its owner."

Sophia, confused as she was, answered this bombast (and very properly I think) with a look of inconceivable disdain. My lord then made another and a longer speech of the same sort. Upon which Sophia, trembling, said,

"Am I really to conceive your lordship to be out of your senses?"

"I am, indeed, madam," cries his lordship; "and sure you will pardon the effects of a frenzy which you yourself have occasioned; for love hath so totally deprived me of reason, that I am scarce accountable for any of my actions." Then fetching a deep sigh, and laying hold of her hand, he ran on for some minutes in a strain which would be little more pleasing to the reader than it was to the lady; and at last concluded with a declaration, "That if he was master of the world, he would lay it at her feet."

Sophia then, forcibly pulling away her hand from his, answered with much spirit, "I promise you, sir, your world and its master I should spurn from me with equal contempt." She then offered to go; and Lord Fellamar, again laying hold of her hand, said, "Pardon me, my beloved angel, freedoms which nothing but despair could have tempted me to take.——Believe me, could I have had any hope that my title and fortune, neither of them inconsiderable, unless when compared with your worth, would have been accepted, I had, in the humblest manner, presented them to your acceptance.——But I cannot lose you. By Heaven, I will sooner part with my soul! You are, you must, you shall be only mine."

"My lord," says she, "I entreat you to desist from a vain pursuit; for, upon my honor, I will never hear you on this subject. Let go my hand, my lord; for I am resolved to go from you this moment; nor will I ever see you more."

"Then, madam," cries his lordship, "I must make the best use of this moment; for I cannot live, nor will I live without you."

"What do you mean, my lord?" said Sophia. "I will raise the family."

"I have no fear, madam," answered he, "but of losing you and that I am resolved to prevent, the only way which despair points to me." He then caught her in his arms: upon which she screamed so loud, that she must have alarmed someone to her assistance, had not Lady Bellaston taken care to remove all ears.

But a more lucky circumstance happened for poor Sophia: another noise now broke forth, which almost drowned her cries; for now the whole house rang with, "Where is she? D—n me, I'll unkennel her this instant. Show me her chamber, I say. Where is my daughter? I know she's in the house, and I'll see her if she's above-ground. Show me where she is." At which last words the door flew open, and in came Squire Western, with his parson and a set of myrmidons at his heels.

Sophia, notwithstanding her fright, knew her father's voice; and his lordship, notwithstanding his passion, knew the voice of reason, which peremptorily assured him it was not now a time for the perpetration of his villainy. Hearing, therefore, the voice approach, he thought proper to relinquish his prey, having only disordered her handkerchief, and with his rude lips committed violence on her lovely neck.

If the reader's imagination doth not assist me, I shall never be able to describe the situation of these two persons when Western came into the room. Sophia tottered into a chair, where she sat disordered, pale, breathless, bursting with indignation at Lord Fellamar; affrighted, and yet more rejoiced, at the arrival of her father.

His lordship sat down near her, with the bag of his wig hanging over one of his shoulders, the rest of his dress being somewhat disordered, and rather a greater proportion of linen than is usual appearing at his bosom. As to the rest, he was amazed, affrighted, vexed, and ashamed.

Squire Western, was, literally speaking, drunk; which circumstance, together with his natural impetuosity, could produce no other effect than his running immediately up to his daughter, upon whom he fell foul with his tongue in the most inveterate manner; nay, he had probably committed violence with his hands, had not the parson interposed, saying, "Let me beg you to mitigate your wrath; I stand assured, if you will forgive her, she will repent her of all past offenses, and return unto her duty."

The strength of the parson's arms had at first been of more service than the strength of his rhetoric. However, his last words wrought some effect, and the squire answered, "I'll forgee her if she wull ha un. If wot ha un, Sophy, I'll forgee thee all. Why dost unt speak? Shat ha un! d—n me, shat ha un! Why dost unt answer? Was ever such a stubborn tuoad?"

"Let me entreat you, sir, to be a little more moderate," said the parson; "you frighten the young lady so, that you deprive her of all power of utterance."

"Power of mine a——," answered the squire. "You take her part, then, you do? A pretty parson, truly, to side with an unmindful child! Yes, yes, I will gee you a living with a pox. I'll gee un to the devil sooner."

"I humbly crave your pardon," said the parson; "I assure your worship I meant no such matter."

My Lady Bellaston now entered the room, and came up to the squire, who no sooner saw her, than, resolving to follow the instructions of his sister, he made her a very civil bow, in the rural manner, and paid her some of his best compliments. He then immediately proceeded to his complaints, and said, "There, my lady cousin; there stands the most undutiful child in the world; she hankers after a beggarly rascal, and won't marry one of the greatest matches in all England, that we have provided for her."

"Indeed, cousin Western," answered the lady, "I am persuaded you wrong my cousin. I am sure she hath a better understanding. I am convinced she will not refuse what she must be sensible is so much to her advantage."

This was a wilful mistake in Lady Bellaston, for she well knew whom Mr. Western meant; though perhaps she thought he would easily be reconciled to his lordship's proposals.

"Do you hear there," quoth the squire, "what her ladyship says? All your family are for the match. Come, Sophy, be a good girl, and be dutiful, and make your father happy."

"If my death will make you happy, sir," answered Sophia, "you will shortly be so."

"It's a lie, Sophy; it's a d—n'd lie, and you know it," said the squire.

"Let me give him your hand, cousin," said the lady. "It is the fashion nowadays to dispense with time and long courtships."

As Lord Fellamar was very well assured that he was meant by Lady Bellaston, so, never having heard nor suspected a word of Blifil, he made no doubt of his being meant by the father. Coming up, therefore, to the squire, he said,

"Though I have not the honor, sir, of being personally known to you, yet, as I find I have the happiness to have my proposals accepted, let me intercede, sir, in behalf of the young lady, that she may not be more solicited at this time."

"You intercede, sir!" said the squire; "why, who the devil are you?"

"Sir, I am Lord Fellamar," answered he, "and am the happy man whom I hope you have done the honor of accepting for a son-in-law."

"You are a son of a b———," replied the squire, "for all your laced coat. You my son-in-law, and be d—n'd to you!"

"I shall take more from you, sir, than from any man," answered the lord; "but I must inform you that I am not used to hear such language without resentment."

"Resent my a—," quoth the squire. "Don't think I am afraid of such a fellow as thee art! because hast got a spit there dangling at thy side. Lay by your spit, and I'll give thee enough of meddling with what doth not belong to thee. I'll teach you to father-in-law me. I'll lick thy jacket."

"It's very well, sir," said my lord, "I shall make no disturbance before the ladies. I am very well satisfied. Your humble servant, sir; Lady Bellaston, your most obedient."

His lordship was no sooner gone, than Lady Bellaston, coming up to Mr. Western, said, "Bless me, sir, what have you done? You know not whom you have affronted; he is a nobleman of the first rank and fortune, and yesterday made proposals to your daughter; and such as I am sure you must accept with the highest pleasure."

"Answer for yourself, lady cousin," said the squire, "I will have nothing to do with any of your lords. My daughter shall have an honest country gentleman. Come, madam, you must go along with me by fair means, or I'll have you carried down to the coach."

Sophia said she would attend him without force; but begged to go in a chair, for she said she should not be able to ride any other way.

"Prithee," cries the squire, "wout unt persuade me canst not ride in a coach, wouldst? That's a pretty thing, surely! No, no, I'll never let thee out of my sight any more till art married, that I promise thee." Sophia told him, she saw he was resolved to break her heart. "Oh, break thy heart and be d—n'd," quoth he, "if a good husband will break it. I don't value a brass varden, not a halfpenny, of any undutiful b— upon earth." He then took violent hold of her hand.

Mrs. Honour appeared below-stairs, and with a low curtsey to the squire offered to attend her mistress; but he pushed her away, saying,

"Hold, madam, hold, you come no more near my house."

"And will you take my maid away from me?" said Sophia.

"Yes, indeed, madam, will I," cries the squire: "you need not fear being without a servant; I will get you another maid. No, no, Sophy, she shall contrive no more escapes, I promise you." He then packed up his daughter and the parson into the hackney coach, after which he mounted himself, and ordered it to drive to his lodgings. In the way thither he suffered Sophia to be quiet, and entertained himself with reading a lecture to the parson on good manners, and a proper behavior to his betters.

It is possible he might not so easily have carried off his daughter from Lady Bellaston, had that good lady desired to have detained her; but, in reality, she was not a little pleased with the confinement into which Sophia was going; and as her project with Lord Fellamar had failed of success, she was well contented that other violent methods were now going to be used in favor of another man.

IV

THOUGH the reader, in many histories, is obliged to digest much more unaccountable appearances than this of Mr. Western, without any satisfaction at all; yet, as we dearly love to oblige him whenever it is in our power, we shall now proceed to show by what method the squire discovered where his daughter was.

Mrs. Fitzpatrick, who was very desirous of reconciling her uncle and aunt Western, thought she had a probable opportunity, by the service of preserving Sophia from committing the same crime which had drawn on herself the anger of her family. After much deliberation, therefore, she writ the following letter:

"HONORED MADAM—The occasion of my writing this will perhaps make a letter of mine agreeable to my dear aunt, for the sake of one of her nieces.

As I was coming to throw my unhappy self at your feet, I met, by the strangest accident in the world, my cousin Sophy, whose history you are better acquainted with than myself, though, alas! I know enough indeed to satisfy me, that unless she is immediately prevented, she is in danger of running into the same fatal mischief which, by foolishly and ignorantly refusing your most wise and prudent advice, I have unfortunately brought on myself.

"In short, I have seen the man, nay, I was most part of yesterday in his company, and a charming young fellow I promise you he is. He doth not yet know where she is, and it is advisable he should not, till my uncle hath secured her.——No time, therefore, is to be lost; and I need only inform you, that she is now with Lady Bellaston, whom I have seen, and who hath, I find, a design of concealing her from her family.

"I hope, madam, the care which I have shown on this occasion for the good of my family will recommend me again to the favor of a lady who hath always exerted so much zeal for the honor and true interest of us all. I am, with the utmost respect, honored madam, your most dutiful obliged niece, and most obedient humble servant,

"HARRIET FITZPATRICK."

Mrs. Western was now at her brother's house, where she had resided ever since the flight of Sophia, in order to administer comfort to the poor squire in his affliction. The above letter she had no sooner read than she delivered it to him, saying, "There, sir, there is an account of your lost sheep. Fortune hath again restored her to you, and if you will be governed by my advice, it is possible you may yet preserve her."

The squire had no sooner read the letter than he leaped from his chair, threw his pipe into the fire, and gave a loud huzza for joy. He then summoned his servants, called for his boots, and ordered the Chevalier and several other horses to be saddled, and that parson Supple should be immediately sent for. Having done this, he turned to his sister, caught her in his arms, and gave her a close embrace, saying,

"Zounds! you don't seem pleased; one would imagine you was sorry I have found the girl."

"I protest," cries she, "you make me tremble for the event of this matter. Do you really imagine, brother, that the house of a woman of figure is to be attacked by brutal justices of the peace? I will inform you how to proceed. As soon as you arrive in town, and have got yourself into a decent dress (for indeed, brother, you have none at present fit to appear in), you must send your compliments to Lady Bellaston, and desire leave to wait on her. When you are admitted to her presence, as you certainly will be, and have told her your story, I am confident she will withdraw her protection from my niece, who hath certainly imposed upon her."

Here then a league was struck between the contending parties; and now the parson arriving, and the horses being ready, the squire departed, having promised his sister to follow her advice, and she prepared to follow him the next day.

But having communicated these matters to the parson on the road, they both agreed that the prescribed formalities might very well be dispensed with; and the squire, having changed his mind, proceeded in the manner we have already seen.

V

AFFAIRS were in the aforesaid situation when Mrs. Honour arrived at Mrs. Miller's, and called Jones out from the company, with whom, when she found herself alone, she began as follows:

"Oh, my dear sir! how shall I get spirits to tell you; you are undone, sir, and my poor lady's undone, and I am undone."

"Hath anything happened to Sophia?" cries Jones, staring like a madman.

"All that is bad," cries Honour. "Oh I shall never get such another lady! Oh, that I should ever live to see this day!" At these words Jones turned pale as ashes, trembled, and stammered; but Honour went on—"Oh! Mr. Jones, I have lost my lady forever."

"D—n your place!" cries Jones; "where is—what—what is become of my Sophia?"

"Ay, to be sure," cries she, "servants may be d—n'd. It signifies nothing what becomes of them, though they are turned away, and ruined ever so much. To be sure, they are not flesh and blood like other people. No, to be sure, it signifies nothing what becomes of them."

"If you have any pity, any compassion," cries Jones, "I beg you will instantly tell me what hath happened to Sophia?"

"To be sure, I have more pity for you than you have for me," answered Honour; "I don't d—n you because you have lost the sweetest lady in the world. To be sure, you are worthy to be pitied, and I am worthy to be pitied too; for, to be sure, if ever there was a good mistress——"

"What hath happened?" cries Jones, in almost a raving fit.

"What?—what?" said Honour. "Why, the worst that could have happened both for you and for me. Her father is come to town, and hath carried her away from us both." Here Jones fell on his knees in thanksgiving that it was no worse. "No worse!" repeated Honour; "what could be worse for either of us? He carried her off, swearing she should marry Mr. Blifil; that's for your comfort; and, for poor me, I am turned out of doors."

"Indeed, Mrs. Honour," answered Jones, "you frightened me out of my wits. I imagined some most dreadful sudden accident had happened to Sophia—something compared to which even seeing her married to Blifil would be a trifle; but while there is life there are hopes, my dear Honour. Women in this land of liberty cannot be married by actual brutal force."

"To be sure, sir," said she, "that's true. There may be some hopes for you; but alack-a-day! what hopes are there for poor me?"

"Indeed, Mrs. Honour," answered he, "I will leave nothing in my power undone to make you amends."

"Alas! sir," said she, "what can make a servant amends for the loss of one place but the getting another altogether as good?"

"Do not despair, Mrs. Honour," said Jones, "I hope to reinstate you again in the same."

"Alack-a-day, sir," said she, "how can I flatter myself with such hopes when I know it is a thing impossible? for the squire is so set against me: and yet, if you should ever have my lady, as, to be sure, I now hopes heartily you will; for you are a generous, good-natured gentleman; and I am sure you loves her, and, to be sure, she loves you as dearly as her own soul; it is a matter in vain to deny it; because as why everybody that is in the least acquainted with my lady must see it; for, poor dear lady, she can't dissemble: and if two people who loves one another a'n't happy, why, who should be so? It is pity, me-thinks, she had not a little of my courage. If I was in love with a young man, and my father offered to lock me up, I'd tear his eyes out but I'd come at him; but then there's a great fortune in the case, which it is in her father's power either to give her or not; that, to be sure, may make some difference."

Whether Jones gave strict attention to all the foregoing harangue, I cannot determine; but he never once attempted to answer, till Partridge came running into the room, and informed him that the great lady was upon the stairs.

Nothing could equal the dilemma to which Jones was now reduced. Honour knew nothing of any acquaintance that subsisted between him and Lady Bellaston, and she was almost the last person in the world to whom he would have communicated it. In this hurry and distress, he took (as is common enough) the worst course, and, instead of exposing her to the lady, which would have been of little consequence, he chose to expose the lady to her; he therefore resolved to hide Honour, whom he had but just time to convey behind the bed and to draw the curtains.

The hurry, the terrors occasioned by Mrs. Honour, and the confusion into which he was thrown by the sudden arrival of Lady Bellaston, had altogether driven former thoughts out of his head; so that it never once occurred to his memory to act the part of a sick man; which, indeed, neither the gaiety of his dress, nor the freshness of his countenance, would have at all supported.

Lady Bellaston no sooner entered the room than she squatted herself down on the bed:

"So, my dear Jones," said she, "you find nothing can detain me long from you. Perhaps I ought to be angry with you, that I have neither seen nor heard from you all day; for I perceive your distemper would have suffered you to come abroad. But don't think I intend to scold you; for I never will give you an excuse for the cold behavior of a husband by putting on the ill-humor of a wife."

Jones was certainly at this instant in one of the most disagreeable and distressed situations imaginable; for Jones could not receive satisfaction, nor so much as offer to ask it, in the presence of a third person. As this objection did not occur to Lady Bellaston, who was ignorant of any other woman being there but herself, she waited some time in great astonishment for an answer from Jones, who, not daring to give the proper answer, gave none at all. Nothing can be imagined more comic, nor yet more tragical than this scene would have been if it had lasted much longer. The lady had already changed color two or three times, while Jones was wishing the ground to sink under him, when an odd accident freed him from embarrassment.

This was no other than the arrival of young Nightingale, dead drunk, or rather in that state of drunkenness which deprives men of the use of their reason without depriving them of the use of their limbs.

Mrs. Miller and her daughters were in bed, and Partridge was smoking his pipe by the kitchen fire; so that he arrived at Mr. Jones's chamber-door without any interruption. This he burst open, and was entering without any ceremony, when Jones started from his seat and ran to oppose him, which he did so effectually that Nightingale never came far enough within the door to see who was sitting on the bed.

Nightingale had in reality mistaken Jones's apartment for that in which himself had lodged; he therefore strongly insisted on coming in, often swearing that he would not be kept from his own bed. Jones, however, prevailed over him, and delivered him into the hands of Partridge, whom the noise on the stairs soon summoned to his master's assistance.

And now Jones was unwillingly obliged to return to his own apartment, where at the very instant of his entrance he heard Lady Bellaston venting an exclamation, though not a very loud one; and at the same time saw her flinging herself into a chair in a vast agitation, which in a lady of a tender constitution would have been an hysteric fit.

In reality the lady, frightened with the struggle between the two men, attempted to retire to her known place of hiding, which to her great confusion she found already occupied by another.

"Is this usage to be borne, Mr. Jones?" cries the lady. "Basest of men?——What wretch is this to whom you have exposed me?"

"Wretch!" cries Honour, bursting in a violent rage from her place of concealment——"Marry come up!——Wretch, forsooth?——as poor a wretch as I am, I am honest; this is more than some folks who are richer can say."

Jones fell to cursing his stars, and lamenting himself as the most unfortunate man in the world; and presently after, addressing himself to Lady Bellaston, he fell to some very absurd protestations of innocence. By this time the lady, having recovered the use of her reason, which she had as ready as any woman in the world, especially on such occasions, calmly replied: "Sir, you need make no apologies, I see now who the person is: I did not at first know Mrs. Honour; but now I do, I can suspect nothing wrong between her and you; and I am sure she is a woman of too good sense to put any wrong constructions upon my visit to you. I have been always her friend, and it may be in my power to be much more hereafter."

Mrs. Honour was altogether as placable as she was passionate. Hearing, therefore, Lady Bellaston assume the soft tone, she likewise softened hers.

"I'm sure, madam," says she, "I have been always ready to acknowledge your ladyship's friendships to me; sure I never had so good a friend as your ladyship——and, to be sure, now I see it is your ladyship that I spoke to, I could almost bite my tongue off for very mad. To be sure, it doth not become a servant, as I am, to think about such a great lady—I mean I was a servant; for indeed I am nobody's servant now, the more miserable wretch is me. I have lost the best mistress——" Here Honour thought fit to produce a shower of tears.

"Don't cry, child," says the good lady; "ways perhaps may be found to make you amends. Come to me tomorrow morning." She then took up her fan, which lay on the ground, and, without even looking at Jones, walked very majestically out of the room; there being a kind of dignity in the impudence of women of quality, which their inferiors vainly aspire to attain to in circumstances of this nature.

Jones followed her downstairs, often offering her his hand, which she absolutely refused him, and got into her chair without taking any notice of him as he stood bowing before her.

At his return upstairs, a long dialogue passed between him and Mrs. Honour. The subject of this was his infidelity to her young lady, on which she enlarged with great bitterness; but Jones at last found means to reconcile her, and not only so, but to obtain a promise of most inviolable secrecy. Thus ended this unfortunate adventure to the satisfaction only of Mrs. Honour.

VI

NOTWITHSTANDING all the obligations she had received from Jones, Mrs. Miller could not forbear in the morning some gentle remonstrances for the hurricane which had happened the preceding night in his chamber. These were, however, so gentle and so friendly, professing, and indeed truly, to aim at nothing more than the real good of Mr. Jones himself, that he, far from being offended, thankfully received the admonition of the good woman, expressed much concern for what had passed, excused it as well as he could, and promised never more to bring the same disturbances into the house.

But though Mrs. Miller did not refrain from a short expostulation in private at their first meeting, yet the occasion of his being summoned downstairs that morning was of a much more agreeable kind, being indeed to perform the office of a father to Miss Nancy, and to give her in wedlock to Mr. Nightingale, who was now ready dressed, and full as sober as many of my readers will think a man ought to be who receives a wife in so imprudent a manner.

All parties being quickly ready, the mother, Mr. Jones, Mr. Nightingale, and his love stepped into a hackney-coach, which conveyed them to Doctors' Commons; where Miss Nancy was, in vulgar language, soon made an honest woman, and the poor mother became, in the purest sense of the word, one of the happiest of all human beings.

And now Mr. Jones, having seen his good offices to that poor woman and her family brought to a happy conclusion, began to apply himself to his own concerns; but here we think proper to assure our reader, that he was so far from being unconcerned in this matter, that he had indeed a very considerable interest in bringing it to that final consummation. He was never an indifferent spectator of the misery or happiness of anyone; and he felt either the one or the other in great proportion as he himself contributed to either. He could not, therefore, be the instrument of raising a whole family from the lowest state of wretchedness to the highest pitch of joy without conveying great felicity to himself.

Those readers who are of the same complexion with him will perhaps think this short chapter contains abundance of matter; while others may probably wish, short as it is, that it had been totally spared as impertinent to the main design, which I suppose they conclude is to bring Mr. Jones to the gallows, or, if possible, to a more deplorable catastrophe.

VII

MR. JONES, at his return home, found the following letters lying on his table, which he luckily opened in the order they were sent.

LETTER I

"Surely I am under some strange infatuation; I cannot keep my resolutions a moment, however strongly made or justly founded. Last night I resolved never to see you more; this morning I am willing to hear if you can, as you say, clear up this affair. And yet I know that to be impossible, I have said everything to myself which you can invent.——Perhaps not. Perhaps your invention is stronger. Come to me, therefore, the moment you receive this. If you can forge an excuse I almost promise you to believe it. Betrayed too——I will think no more. ——Come to me directly.——This is the third letter I have writ, the two former are burnt——I am almost inclined to burn this too——I wish I may preserve my senses—Come to me presently."

LETTER II

"If you ever expect to be forgiven, or even suffered within my doors, come to me this instant."

LETTER III

"I now find you was not at home when my notes came to your lodgings. The moment you receive this let me see you;—— I shall not stir out; nor shall anybody be let in but yourself. Sure nothing can detain you long."

Jones had just read over these three billets when Mr. Nightingale came into the room. "Well, Tom," said he, "any news from Lady Bellaston, after last night's adventure?"

"The Lady Bellaston?" answered Jones, very gravely.

"Nay, dear Tom," cries Nightingale, "don't be so reserved to your friends. Though I was too drunk to see her last night, I saw her at the masquerade. Do you think I am ignorant who the queen of the fairies is?"

"And did you really then know the lady at the masquerade?" said Jones.

"Yes, upon my soul, did I," said Nightingale, "and have given you twenty hints of it since, though you seemed always so tender on that point that I would not speak plainly. I fancy, my friend, by your extreme nicety in this matter, you are not so well acquainted with the character of the lady as with her person. Don't be angry, Tom, but, upon my honor you are not the first young fellow she hath debauched. Her reputation is in no danger, believe me."

Jones, having very attentively heard all that Nightingale had to say, fetched a deep sigh; which the other, observing cried, "Heyday! why, thou art not in love, I hope!"

"Oh, my dear friend!" cries Jones, "I am so entangled with this woman, that I know not how to extricate myself. In love, indeed! no, my friend, but I am under obligations to her, and very great ones."

"Pooh!" answered the other, "you are not the first upon whom she hath conferred obligations of this kind. She is remarkably liberal where she likes; though, let me tell you, her favors are so prudently bestowed that they should rather raise a man's vanity than his gratitude." Nightingale proceeded so far on this head, and told his friend so many stories of the lady, which he swore to the truth of, that he entirely removed all esteem for her from the breast of Jones; and his gratitude was lessened in proportion. Indeed he began to look on all the favors he had received rather as wages than benefits, which depreciated not only her, but himself too in his own conceit, and put him quite out of humor with both. The result of all was, that, he determined to quit her, if he could but find a handsome pretense: which being communicated to his friend, Nightingale considered a little, and then said:

"I have it, my boy! I have found out a sure method: propose marriage to her, and I would venture hanging upon the success."

"Marriage?" cries Jones.

"Ay, propose marriage," answered Nightingale, "and she will declare off in a moment. I knew a young fellow whom she kept formerly, who made the offer to her in earnest, and was presently turned off for his pains."

Jones declared he could not venture the experiment. "Perhaps," said he, "she may be less shocked at this proposal from one man than from another. And if she should take me at my word, where am I then? caught in my own trap, and undone for ever."

"No," answered Nightingale, "not if I can give you an expedient by which you may at any time get out of the trap."

"What expedient can that be?" replied Jones.

"This," answered Nightingale. "The young fellow I mentioned, who is one of the most intimate acquaintances I have in the world, is so angry with her for some ill offices she hath since done him, that I am sure he would, without any difficulty, give you a sight of her letters; upon which you may decently break with her, and declare off before the knot is tied, if she should really be willing to tie it, which I am convinced she will not."

After some hesitation, Jones, upon the strength of this assurance, consented; but, as he swore he wanted the confidence to propose the matter to her face, he wrote the following letter, which Nightingale dictated:

"MADAM—I am extremely concerned that, by an unfortunate engagement abroad, I should have missed receiving the honor of your ladyship's commands the moment they came; and the delay which I must now suffer of vindicating myself to your ladyship greatly adds to this misfortune. Oh, Lady Bellaston! what a terror have I been in for fear your reputation should be exposed by these perverse accidents! There is one only way to secure it. I need not name what that is. Only permit me to say, that as your honor is as dear to me as my own, so my sole ambition is to have the glory of laying my liberty at your feet; and believe me when I assure you, I can never be made completely happy without you generously bestow on me a legal right of calling you mine forever.—I am, madam, with most profound respect, your ladyship's most obliged, obedient, humble servant,
"THOMAS JONES."

To this she presently returned the following answer:

"SIR—When I read over your serious epistle, I could, from its coldness and formality, have sworn that you already had the legal right you mention; nay, that we had for many years composed that monstrous animal a husband and wife. Do you really then imagine me a fool? or do you fancy yourself capable of so entirely persuading me out of my senses, that I should deliver my whole fortune into your power, in order to enable you to support your pleasures at my expense? Are these the proofs of love which I expected? Is this the return for——? but I scorn to upbraid you, and am in great admiration of your profound respect.
"P.S.—I am prevented from revising:——Perhaps I have said more than I meant.——Come to me at eight this evening."

Jones, by the advice of his privy council, replied:

"MADAM—It is impossible to express how much I am shocked at the suspicion you entertain of me. Can Lady Bellaston have

300

conferred favors on a man whom she could believe capable of so base a design? or can she treat the most solemn tie of love with contempt? Can you imagine, madam, that if the violence of my passion, in an unguarded moment, overcame the tenderness which I have for your honor, I would think of indulging myself in the continuance of an intercourse which could not possibly escape long the notice of the world, and which, when discovered, must prove so fatal to your reputation? If such be your opinion of me, I must pray for a sudden opportunity of returning those pecuniary obligations which I have been so unfortunate to receive at your hands; and for those of a more tender kind, I shall ever remain, etc."

And so concluded in the very words with which he had concluded the former letter. The lady answered as follows:

"I see you are a villain! and I despise you from my soul. If you come here I shall not be at home."

Though Jones was well satisfied with his deliverance from a thraldom which those who have ever experienced it will, I apprehend, allow to be none of the lightest, he was not, however, perfectly easy in his mind. There was in this scheme too much of fallacy to satisfy one who utterly detested every species of falsehood or dishonesty: nor would he, indeed, have submitted to put it in practice, had he not been obliged to be guilty of some dishonor, either to the one lady or the other.

The two gentlemen were now summoned down to dinner, where Mrs. Miller, who performed herself the office of cook, had exerted her best talents to celebrate the wedding of her daughter.

Dinner was just ended when Mrs. Miller received a letter; but, as we have had letters enow in this chapter, we shall communicate its contents in our next.

VIII

THE letter, then, which arrived at the end of the preceding chapter was from Mr. Allworthy, and the purport of it was, his intention to come immediately to town, with his nephew Blifil, and a desire to be accommodated with his usual lodgings, which were the first floor for himself, and the second for his nephew.

Mrs. Miller could not conceal her uneasiness at this letter; with the contents of which she had no sooner acquainted the company, and given some hints of her distress, than Jones, her good angel, presently relieved her anxiety.

"As for myself, madam," said he, "my lodging is at your service at a moment's warning; and Mr. Nightingale, I am sure, as he cannot yet prepare a house fit to receive his lady, will consent to return to his new lodging, whither Mrs. Nightingale will certainly consent to go." With which proposal both husband and wife instantly agreed.

The reader will easily believe that the cheeks of Mrs. Miller began again to glow with additional gratitude to Jones; but perhaps it may be more difficult to persuade him that Mr. Jones, having in his last speech called her daughter Mrs. Nightingale (it being the first time that agreeable sound had ever reached her ears), gave the fond mother more satisfaction, and warmed her heart more towards Jones, than his having dissipated her present anxiety.

The next day was then appointed for the removal of the new-married couple, and of Mr. Jones, who was likewise to be provided for in the same house with his friend. And now the serenity of the company was again restored, and they passed the day in the utmost cheerfulness, all except Jones, who, though he outwardly accompanied the rest in their mirth, felt many a bitter pang on the account of his Sophia, which were not a little heightened by the news of Mr. Blifil's coming to town (for he clearly saw the intention of his journey).

IX

PARTRIDGE came capering into the room, as was his custom when he brought, or fancied he brought, any good tidings. "I have seen, sir," says he, "Black George, the gamekeeper, who is one of the servants whom the squire hath brought with him to town.

"Well, but what is your good news?" cried Jones; "what do you know of my Sophia?"

"Nay, sir," answered Partridge, "I know nothing more of Madam Sophia than what I am going to tell you; and I should have told you all before this if you had not interrupted me; but if you look so angry at me you will frighten all of it out of my head, or, to use a purer phrase, out of my memory. I never saw you look so angry since the day we left Upton, which I shall remember if I was to live a thousand years."

"Well, pray go on your own way," said Jones: "you are resolved to make me mad, I find."

"Not for the world," answered Partridge, "I have suffered enough for that already; which, as I said, I shall bear in my remembrance the longest day I have to live."

"Well, but Black George?" cries Jones.

"Well, sir, where was I?——Oh—well, we no sooner knew each other, than, after many hearty shakes by the hand, we agreed to go to an ale-house and take a pot, and by good luck the beer was some of the best I have met with since I have been in town. Now, sir, I am coming to the point; for no sooner did I name you, and told him that you and I came to town together, and had lived together ever since, than he called for another pot, and swore he would drink to your health; and indeed he drank your health so heartily that I was over-joyed to see there was so much gratitude left in the world; and after we had emptied that pot I said I would buy my pot too, and so we drank another to your health; and then I made haste home to tell you the news."

"What news?" cries Jones, "you have not mentioned a word of my Sophia!"

"Bless me! I had like to have forgot that. Indeed we mentioned a great deal about young Madam Western, and George told me all; that Mr. Blifil is coming to town in order to be married to her. He had best make haste then, says I, or somebody will have her before he comes; and indeed, says I, Mr. Seagrim, it is a thousand pities somebody should not have her; for he certainly loves her above all the women in the world. I would have both you and she know, that it is not for her fortune he follows her; for I can assure you, as to matter of that, there is another lady, one of much greater quality and fortune than she can pretend to, who is so fond of somebody that she comes after him day and night."

Here Jones fell into a passion with Partridge, for having, as he said, betrayed him; but the poor fellow answered, he had mentioned no name: "Besides, sir," said he, "I can assure you, George is sincerely your friend, and wished Mr. Blifil at the devil more than once; nay, he said he would do anything in his power upon earth to serve you; and so I am convinced he will. Betray you, indeed! why, I question whether you have a better friend than George upon earth, except myself, or one that would go farther to serve you."

"Well," says Jones, a little pacified, "you say this fellow, who, I believe, indeed, is enough inclined to be my friend, lives in the same house with Sophia?"

"In the same house!" answered Partridge; "why, sir, he is one of the servants of the family, and very well dressed I promise you he is; if it was not for his black beard you would hardly know him."

"One service, then, at least he may do me," says Jones: "sure he can certainly convey a letter to my Sophia."

"You have hit the nail *ad unguem*," cries Partridge; "I will engage he shall do it upon the very first mentioning."

"Well, then," said Jones, "do you leave me at present, and I will write a letter, which you shall deliver to him tomorrow morning; for I suppose you know where to find him."

"Oh yes, sir," answered Partridge, "I shall certainly find him again; there is no fear of that. The liquor is too good for him to stay away long. I make no doubt but he will be there every day he stays in town."

And now, having dismissed the sagacious Partridge, Mr. Jones sat himself down to write, in which employment we shall leave him for a time.

Book XVI

CONTAINING THE SPACE OF FIVE DAYS

I

WE MUST now convey the reader to Mr. Western's lodgings, which were in Piccadilly; for at the inn which was the first he saw on his arrival in town, he placed his horses, and in those lodgings, which were the first he heard of, he deposited himself.

While Sophia was left with no other company than what attend the closest state prisoner, namely, fire and candle, the squire sat down to regale himself over a bottle of wine. All this time Sophia passed by herself; for her father swore she should never come out of her chamber alive, unless she first consented to marry Blifil; nor did he ever suffer the door to be unlocked, unless to convey her food, on which occasions he always attended himself.

The second morning after his arrival, while he and the parson were at breakfast together on a toast and tankard, he was informed that a gentleman was below to wait on him.

"A gentleman!" quoth the squire; "who the devil can he be? Mr. Blifil can hardly be come to town yet. Go down, do, and know what his business is."

The doctor returned with an account that it was a very well-dressed man, and by the ribbon in his hat he took him for an officer of the army; that he said he had some particular business, which he could deliver to none but Mr. Western himself.

A very genteel man now entered the room; who, having made his compliments to the squire, and desired the favor of being alone with him, delivered himself as follows:

"Sir, I come to wait upon you by the command of my Lord Fellamar; but with a very different message from what I suppose you expect, after what passed the other night."

"My lord who?" cries the squire; "I never heard the name o' un."

"His lordship," said the gentleman, "is willing to impute everything to the effect of liquor, and the most trifling acknowledgment of that kind will set everything right; for, as he hath the most violent attachment to your daughter, you, sir, are the last person upon earth from whom he would resent an affront; and happy is it for you both that he hath given such public demonstrations of his courage as to be able to put up an affair of this kind without danger of any imputation on his honor. All he desires, therefore, is, that you will before me make some acknowledgment; the slightest in the world will be sufficient; and he intends this afternoon to pay his respects to you, in order to obtain your leave of visiting the young lady on the footing of a lover."

"I don't understand much of what you say, sir," said the squire; "but I suppose, by what you talk about my daughter, that this is the lord which my cousin, Lady Bellaston, mentioned to me, and said something about his courting my daughter. You may give my service to his lordship, and tell un the girl is disposed of already."

"Perhaps, sir," said the gentleman, "you are not sufficiently apprised of the greatness of this offer. I believe such a person, title, and fortune would be nowhere refused."

"Lookee, sir," answered the squire; "to be very plain, my daughter is bespoke already; but if she was not, I would not marry her to a lord upon any account; I hate all lords; and I will have nothing to do with them."

"Well, sir," said the gentleman ,"if that is your resolution, the message I am to deliver to you is that my lord desires the favor of your company this morning in Hyde Park."

"You may tell my lord," answered the squire, "that I am busy and cannot come. I have enough to look after at home, and can't stir abroad on any account."

"I am sure, sir," quoth the other, "you are too much a gentleman to send such a message. His lordship would have been willing to have made up matters in another way; but unless he is to look on you as a father, his honor will not suffer his putting up such an indignity as you must be sensible you offered him."

"I offered him!" cries the squire; "it is a d—n'd lie! I never offered him anything."

Upon these words the gentleman returned a very short verbal rebuke, and this he accompanied at the same time with some manual remonstrances, which no sooner reached the ears of Mr. Western, than that worthy squire began to caper very briskly about the room bellowing at the same time with all his might, as if desirous to summon a greater number of spectators to behold his agility.

The parson, who had left great part of the tankard unfinished, was not retired far; he immediately attended, therefore, on the squire's vociferation, crying, "Bless me! sir, what's the matter?"

"Matter!" quoth the squire, "here's a highwayman, I believe, who wants to rob and murder me—for he hath fallen upon me with that stick there in his hand, when I wish I may be d—n'd if I gid un the least provocation."

"How, sir," said the captain, "did you not tell me I lied?"

"No, as I hope to be saved," answered the squire, "—I believe I might say, 'Twas a lie that I had offered any affront to my lord—but I never said the word, you lie. If I had a stick in my hand, you would not have dared strike me. I'd have knocked thy lantern jaws about thy ears. Come down into yard this minute, and I'll take a bout with thee at single-stick for a broken head, that I will; or I will go into naked room and box thee for a bellyful. At unt half a man, at unt, I'm sure."

The captain, with some indignation, replied, "I see, sir, you are below my notice, and I shall inform his lordship you are below his. I am sorry I have dirtied my fingers with you." At which words he withdrew, the parson interposing to prevent the squire from stopping him, in which he easily prevailed.

Poor Sophia who, in her prison, heard all her father's outcries from first to last, began now first to thunder with her foot, and afterwards to scream as loudly as the old gentleman himself had done before, though in a much sweeter voice. These screams soon turned all his consideration towards his daughter, whom he loved so tenderly, that the least apprehension of any harm happening to her threw him into agonies.

Having ended his rage against the captain, with swearing he would take the law of him, the squire now mounted upstairs to Sophia, whom, as soon as he had unlocked and opened the door, he found all pale and breathless. The moment, however, that she saw her father, she collected all her spirits, and, catching him hold by the hand, she cried passionately,

"Oh, my dear sir, I am almost frightened to death! I hope to Heaven no harm hath happened to you."

"No, no," cries the squire, "no great harm. The rascal hath not hurt me much."

"But, dear sir," cries she, "what was the occasion of your quarrel?"

"What should it be," answered the squire, "but about you, Sophy? All my misfortunes are about you; you will be the death of your poor father at last. Here's a varlet of a lord, the Lord knows who, forsooth! who hath a taan a liking to you, and because I would not gi un my consent he sent me a kallenge. Come, do be a good girl, Sophy, and put an end to all your father's troubles; come, do consent to ha un; he will be in town within this day or two; do but promise me to marry un as soon as he comes, and you will make me the happiest man in the world, and I will make you the happiest woman; you shall have the finest clothes in London, and the finest jewels, and a coach and six at your command. I promised Allworthy already to give up half my estate—odrabbet it! I should hardly stick at giving up the whole."

"Will my papa be so kind," says she, "as to hear me speak?"

"Why wout ask, Sophy?" cries he, "when dost know I had rather hear thy voice than the music of the best pack of dogs in England."

Sophia, observing, begged to be heard out, and then proceeded: "If my father's life, his health, or any real happiness of his was at stake, here stands your resolved daughter; may Heaven blast me if there is a misery I would not suffer to preserve you!—No, that most detested, most loathsome of all lots would I embrace. I would give my hand to Blifil for your sake."

"I tell thee, it will preserve me," answers the father; "it will give me health, happiness, life, everything. Upon my soul I shall die if dost refuse me; I shall break my heart, I shall, upon my soul."

"Is it possible," says she, "you can have such a desire to make me miserable?"

"I tell thee noa," answered he loudly, "d—n me if there is a thing upon earth I would not do to see thee happy."

"And will not my dear papa allow me to have the least knowledge of what will make me so? What must be my condition when I shall think myself the most miserable of all wretches upon earth?"

"Better think yourself so," said he, "than know it by being married to a poor bastardly vagabond."

"If it will content you, sir," said Sophia, "I will give you the most solemn promise never to marry him, nor any other, while my papa lives, without his consent. Let me dedicate my whole life to your service; let me be again your poor Sophy, and my whole business and pleasure be, as it hath been, to please and divert you."

"Lookee, Sophy," answered the squire, "I am not to be choused in this manner. No, no, Sophy, I'd have you to know I have a got more wisdom, and know more of the world, than to take the word of a woman in a matter where a man is concerned."

"How, sir, have I deserved this want of confidence?" said she; "have I ever broke a single promise to you? or have I ever been found guilty of a falsehood from my cradle?"

"Lookee, Sophy," cries he; "that's neither here nor there. I am determined upon this match, and have him you shall, d—n me if shat unt. D—n me if shat unt, though dost hang thyself the next morning." At repeating which words he clinched his fist, knit his brows, bit his lips, and thundered so loud, that the poor, afflicted, terrified Sophia sunk trembling into her chair, and, had not a flood of tears come immediately to her relief, perhaps worse had followed.

In this condition he left his poor Sophia, and, departing with a very vulgar observation on the effect of tears, he locked the room, and returned to the parson, who said everything he durst in behalf of the young lady, which, though perhaps it was not quite so much as his duty required, yet was it sufficient to throw the squire into a violent rage, and into many indecent reflections on the whole body of the clergy, which we have too great an honor for that sacred function to commit to paper.

II

In the evening, while Sophia was meditating, a violent noise from below disturbed her. This noise was no other than a round bout at altercation between two persons. One of the combatants, by his voice, she immediately distinguished to be her father; but she did not so soon discover the shriller pipes to belong to the organ of her aunt Western, who was just arrived in town.

The squire and the parson (for the landlord was now otherwise engaged) were smoking their pipes together, when the arrival of the lady was first signified. The squire no sooner heard her name, than he immediately ran down to usher her upstairs; for he was a great observer of such ceremonials, especially to his sister, of whom he stood more in awe than of any other human creature, though he never would own this, nor did he perhaps know it himself.

"Well, and where's my niece?" says the lady. "Have you been to wait upon Lady Bellaston yet?"

"Ay, ay," cries the squire, "your niece is safe enough; she is upstairs in chamber."

"How!" answered the lady; "is my niece in this house, and does she not know of my being here?"

"No, nobody can well get to her," says the squire, "for she is under lock and key."

"Good Heaven!" returned Mrs. Western, "what do I hear? Did not you promise me, brother, that you would take none of these headstrong measures? Was it not by these headstrong measures that you forced my niece to run away from you in the country? Have you a mind to oblige her to take such another step?"

"Z——ds and the devil!" cries the squire, dashing his pipe on the ground; "did ever mortal hear the like? when I expected you would have commended me for all I have done, to be fallen upon in this manner!"

"How, brother!" said the lady; "have I ever given you the least reason to imagine I should commend you for locking up your daughter? If you expect I should stay a moment longer in this wretched house, I insist upon it that my niece be set at liberty this instant." This she spoke with so commanding an air, standing with her back to the fire, with one hand behind her, and a pinch of snuff in the other, that I question whether Thalestris, at the head of her Amazons, ever made a more tremendous figure. It is no wonder, therefore, that the poor squire was not proof against the awe which she inspired.

"There," he cried, throwing down the key, "there it is, do whatever you please. I intended only to have her kept up till Blifil came to town, which can't be long; and now if any harm happens in the meantime, remember who is to be blamed for it."

"I will answer it with my life," cried Mrs. Western; "but I shall not intermeddle at all, unless upon one condition, and that is, that you will commit the whole entirely to my care, without taking any one measure yourself."

And now having summoned a servant to show her to Sophia, she departed, bearing the key with her.

She was no sooner gone, than the squire (having first shut the door) ejaculated twenty bitches, and as many hearty curses against her, not sparing himself for having ever thought of her estate; but added, "Now one hath been a slave so long, it would be pity to lose it at last, for want of holding out a little longer. The bitch can't live forever, and I know I am down for it upon the will."

The parson greatly commended this resolution: and now the squire, having ordered in another bottle, which was his usual method when anything either pleased or vexed him, did, by drinking plentifully of this medicinal julep, so totally wash away his choler, that his temper was become perfectly placid and serene when Mrs. Western returned with Sophia into the room. The young lady had on her hat and capuchin, and the aunt acquainted Mr. Western, "that she intended to take her niece with her to her own lodgings; for indeed, brother," says she, "these rooms are not fit to receive a Christian soul in."

"Very well, madam," quoth Western, "whatever you please. The girl can never be in better hands than yours."

"I have not the least doubt of her," answered Mrs. Western, "She hath had already an example before her eyes in the behavior of that wretch her cousin Harriet, who ruined herself by neglecting my advice. Oh, brother, what think you? You was hardly gone out of hearing, when you set out for London, when who should arrive but that impudent fellow with the odious Irish name—that Fitzpatrick. He broke in abruptly upon me without notice, or I would not have seen him. I made him very little answer, and delivered him the letter from his wife, which I bid him answer himself. I suppose the wretch will endeavor to find us out, but I beg you will not see her, for I am determined I will not."

"I zee her!" answered the squire; "you need not fear me. I'll ge no encouragement to such undutiful wenches. You zee, Sophy, what undutifulness brings volks to. You have an example in your own family."

"Brother," cries the aunt, "you need not shock my niece by such odious repetitions. Why will you not leave everything entirely to me?"

"Well, well, I wull, I wull," said the squire.

And now Mrs. Western, luckily for Sophia, put an end to the conversation by ordering chairs to be called. I say luckily, for had it continued much longer, fresh matter of dissension would, most probably, have arisen between the brother and sister; between whom education and sex made the only difference; for both were equally violent and equally positive; they had both a vast affection for Sophia, and both a soveregn contempt for each other.

III

THE arrival of Black George in town, and the good offices which that grateful fellow had promised to do for his old benefactor, greatly comforted Jones in the midst of all the anxiety and uneasiness which he had suffered on the account of Sophia; from whom, by the means of the said George, he received the following letter, which Sophia, to whom the use of pen, ink, and paper was restored with her liberty, wrote the very evening when she departed from her confinement:

"SIR—As I do not doubt your sincerity in what you write, you will be pleased to hear that some of my afflictions are at an end, by the arrival of my aunt Western, with whom I am at present, and with whom I enjoy all the liberty I can desire. One promise my aunt hath insisted on my making, which is, that I will not see or converse with any person without her knowledge and consent. This promise I have most solemnly given, and shall most inviolably keep: and you cannot expect that I shall, after this, continue to write myself or to receive letters, without her knowledge. A promise is with me a very sacred thing, and this consideration may perhaps, on reflection, afford you some comfort. But why should I mention a comfort to you of this kind; for though there is one thing in which I can never comply with the best of fathers, yet am I firmly resolved never to act in defiance of him, or to take any step of consequence without his consent. A firm persuasion of this must teach you to divert your thoughts from what fortune hath (perhaps) made impossible. This your own interest persuades you. This may reconcile, I hope, Mr. Allworthy to you; and if it will, you have my injunctions to pursue it. Fortune may perhaps be some time kinder to us both than at present. Believe this, that I shall always think of you as I think you deserve, and am, sir, your obliged humble servant,

"SOPHIA WESTERN.

"I charge you, write to me no more—at present at least; and accept this, which is now of no service to me, which I know you must want, and think you owe the trifle only to that fortune by which you found it." [1]

[1] Meaning, perhaps, the bank-bill for £100.

312

A child who hath just learned his letters would have spelled this letter out in less time than Jones took in reading it. Upon the whole he was more pleased than displeased; and indeed the reader may probably wonder that he was displeased at all; but the reader is not quite so much in love as was poor Jones; and love is a disease which, though it may, in some instances, resemble a consumption (which it sometimes causes), in others proceeds in direct opposition to it, and particularly in this, that it never flatters itself, or sees any one symptom in a favorable light.

IV

LOVE had taken too deep a root in the mind of Lord Fellamar to be plucked up by the rude hands of Mr. Western.

In the afternoon then next after the intended rape of Sophia, his lordship made a visit to Lady Bellaston, who laid open so much of the character of the squire, that his lordship plainly saw the absurdity he had been guilty of in taking any offense at his words, especially as he had those honorable designs on his daughter.

He then unbosomed the violence of his passion to Lady Bellaston, who readily undertook the cause, and encouraged him with certain assurance of a most favorable reception from all the elders of the family, and from the father himself when he should be sober, and should be made acquainted with the nature of the offer made to his daughter. The only danger, she said, lay in the fellow she had formerly mentioned, who, though a beggar and a vagabond, had, by some means or other, she knew not what, procured himself tolerable clothes, and passed for a gentleman.

"Now," says she, "as I have, for the sake of my cousin, made it my business to inquire after this fellow, I have luckily found out his lodgings"; with which she then acquainted his lordship. "I am thinking, my lord," added she, "(for this fellow is too mean for your personal resentment), whether it would not be possible for your lordship to contrive some method of having him pressed and sent on board a ship. Neither law nor conscience forbid this project: for the fellow, I promise you, however well dressed, is but a vagabond, and as proper as in any fellow in the streets to be pressed into the service; and as for the conscientious part, surely the preservation of a young lady from such ruin is a most meritorious act."

Lord Fellamar very heartily thanked her ladyship for the part which she was pleased to take in the affair, upon the success of which his whole future happiness entirely depended. He said, he saw at present no objection to the pressing scheme, and would consider of putting it in execution. He then most earnestly recommended to her ladyship to do him the honor of immediately mentioning his proposals to the family; to whom he said he offered a *carte blanche*, and would settle his fortune in almost any manner they should require.

The moment Mrs. Western was arrived at her lodgings, a card was despatched with her compliments to Lady Bellaston; who no sooner received it than, with the impatience of a lover, she flew to her cousin.

The two ladies being met, after very short previous ceremonials, fell to business, which was indeed almost as soon concluded as begun; for Mrs. Western no sooner heard the name of Lord Fellamar than her cheeks glowed with pleasure; but when she was acquainted with the eagerness of his passion, the earnestness of his proposals, and the generosity of his offer, she declared her full satisfaction in the most explicit terms.

"For indeed," added she, "I must do Sophy the justice to confess this Blifil is but a hideous kind of fellow, as you know, Bellaston, all country gentlemen are, and hath nothing but his fortune to recommend him."

"Nay," said Lady Bellaston, "I don't then so much wonder at my cousin; for I promise you this Jones is a very agreeable fellow, and hath one virtue, which the men say is a great recommendation to us. What do you think, Mrs. Western—I shall certainly make you laugh; nay, I can hardly tell you myself for laughing—will you believe that the fellow hath had the assurance to make love to me? But if you should be inclined to disbelieve, here is evidence enough, his own handwriting, I assure you." She then delivered her cousin the letter with the proposals of marriage, which, if the reader hath a desire to see, he will find already on record in the fifteenth book of this history.

"Upon my word I am astonished," said Mrs. Western; "this is, indeed, a masterpiece of assurance. With your leave I may possibly make some use of this letter."

"You have my full liberty," cries Lady Bellaston, "to apply it to what purpose you please. However, I would not have it shown to any but Miss Western, nor to her unless you find occasion."

"Well, and how did you use the fellow?" returned Mrs. Western.

"Not as a husband," said the lady; "I am not married, I promise you, my dear. You know, I have tried the comforts once already; and once, I think, is enough for any reasonable woman."

But perhaps the reader may wonder why Lady Bellaston, who in her heart hated Sophia, should be so desirous of promoting a match which was so much to the interest of the young lady. Now, I would desire such readers to look carefully into human nature, page almost the last, and there he will find, in scarce legible characters, that women, notwithstanding the preposterous behavior of mothers, aunts, etc., in matrimonial matters, do in reality think it so great a misfortune to have their inclinations in love thwarted, that they imagine they ought never to carry enmity higher than upon these disappointments; again, he will find it written much about the same place, that a woman who hath once been pleased with the possession of a man, will go above half way to the devil to prevent any other woman from enjoying the same.

If he will not be contented with these reasons, I freely confess I see no other motive to the actions of that lady, unless we will conceive she was bribed by Lord Fellamar, which for my own part I see no cause to suspect.

V

THE reader may now, perhaps, be pleased to return with us to Mr. Jones, who, at an appointed hour, attended on Mrs. Fitzpatrick; but, before we relate the conversation which now passed, it may be proper, according to our method, to return a little back, and to account for so great an alteration of behavior in this lady, that she had industriously sought this interview.

The reader must remember that he was acquainted by Mrs. Fitzpatrick, in the account she gave of her own story, with the fondness Mrs. Western had formerly shown for Mr. Fitzpatrick at Bath. She had, therefore, no doubt but that the good lady would as easily listen to the addresses of Mr. Jones as she had before done to the other; for the superiority of charms was clearly on the side of Mr. Jones; and the advance which her aunt had since made in age, she concluded (how justly I will not say), was an argument rather in favor of her project then against it.

Therefore, when Jones attended, after a previous declaration of her desire of serving him, she very explicitly mentioned her scheme to him, and advised him to make sham addresses to the older lady, in order to procure an easy access to the younger, informing him at the same time of the success which Mr. Fitzpatrick had formerly owed to the very same stratagem.

Mr. Jones expressed great gratitude to the lady for the kind intentions towards him which she had expressed, and indeed testified, by this proposal; but, besides intimating some diffidence of success from the lady's knowledge of his love to her niece, which had not been her case in regard to Mr. Fitzpatrick, he said, he was afraid Miss Western would never agree to an imposition of this kind.

"Indeed, sir," answered the lady, with some warmth, "I cannot think there is anything easier than to cheat an old woman with a profession of love, when her complexion is amorous. Can't you pretend that the despair of possessing her niece, from her being promised to Blifil, has made you turn your thoughts towards her? As to my cousin Sophia, I can't imagine her to be such a simpleton as to have the least scruple on such an account, or to conceive any harm in punishing one of these hags for the many mischiefs they bring upon families by their tragicomic passions; for which I think it is a pity they are not punishable by law."

Jones, however, persisted in declining the undertaking, which had not, indeed, the least probability of success. He said he would not deny the tender and passionate regard he had for Sophia; but was so conscious of the inequality of their situations, that he could never flatter himself so far as to hope that so divine a young lady would condescend to think on so unworthy a man; nay, he protested, he could scarce bring himself to wish she should.

When Jones had finished his exclamations, Mrs. Fitzpatrick heaved a deep sigh, and, taking her eyes off from Jones, on whom they had been some time fixed, and drooping them on the ground, she cried,

"Indeed, Mr. Jones, I pity you; but it is the curse of such tenderness to be thrown away on those who are insensible of it. I know my cousin better than you, Mr. Jones, and I must say, any woman who makes no return to such a passion, and such a person, is unworthy of both."

"Sure, madam," said Jones, "you can't mean——"

"Mean!" cries Mrs. Fitzpatrick, "I know not what I mean; there is something, I think, in true tenderness bewitching; few women ever meet with it in men, and fewer still know how to value it when they do. I never heard such truly noble sentiments, and I can't tell how it is, but you force one to believe you. Sure she must be the most contemptible of women who can overlook such merit."

The manner and look with which all this was spoke infused a

suspicion into Jones which we don't care to convey in direct words to the reader. Instead of making any answer, he said, "I am afraid, madam, I have made too tiresome a visit"; and offered to take his leave.

"Not at all, sir," answered Mrs. Fitzpatrick.——"Indeed I pity you, Mr. Jones; indeed I do: but if you are going, consider of the scheme I have mentioned—I am convinced you will approve it—and let me see you again as soon as you can.—Tomorrow morning if you will, or at least some time tomorrow. I shall be at home all day."

Jones then, after many expressions of thanks, very respectfully retired; nor could Mrs. Fitzpatrick forbear making him a present of a look at parting, by which if he had understood nothing, he must have had no understanding in the language of the eyes. In reality, it confirmed his resolution of returning to her no more; for, faulty as he hath hitherto appeared in this history, his whole thoughts were now so confined to his Sophia, that I believe no woman upon earth could have now drawn him into an act of inconstancy.

Fortune, however, who was not his friend, resolved, as he intended to give her no second opportunity, to make the best of this, and accordingly produced the tragical incident which we are now in sorrowful notes to record.

VI

Mr. Fitzpatrick having received the letter before mentioned from Mrs. Western, and being by that means acquainted with the place to which his wife was retired, returned directly to Bath, and thence the day after set forward to London.

The reader hath been already often informed of the jealous temper of this gentleman. He may likewise be pleased to remember the suspicion which he had conceived of Jones at Upton, upon his finding him in the room with Mrs. Waters; and, though sufficient reasons had afterwards appeared entirely to clear up that suspicion, yet now the reading so handsome a character of Mr. Jones from his wife, caused him to reflect that she likewise was in the inn at the same time.

And now, as he was inquiring in the street after his wife, and had just received directions to the door, unfortunately Mr. Jones was issuing from it.

Fitzpatrick did not yet recollect the face of Jones; however, seeing a young well-dressed fellow coming from his wife, he made directly up to him, and asked him what he had been doing in that house? "for

I am sure," said he, "you must have been in it, as I saw you come out of it."

Jones answered very modestly, "That he had been visiting a lady there."

To which Fitzpatrick replied, "What business have you with the lady?"

Upon which, Jones, who now perfectly remembered the voice, features, and indeed coat, of the gentleman, cried out,

"Ha, my good friend! give me your hand; I hope there is no ill blood remaining between us, upon a small mistake which happened so long ago."

"Upon my soul, sir," said Fitzpatrick, "I don't know your name nor your face."

"Indeed, sir," said Jones, "neither have I the pleasure of knowing your name, but your face I very well remember to have seen before at Upton, where a foolish quarrel happened between us, which, if it is not made up yet, we will now make up over a bottle."

"At Upton!" cried the other;——"Ha! upon my soul, I believe your name is Jones?"

"Indeed," answered he, "it is."

"Oh! upon my soul," cries Fitzpatrick, "you are the very man I wanted to meet. Upon my soul, I will drink a bottle with you presently; but first I will give you a great knock over the pate. There is for you, you rascal. Upon my soul, if you do not give me satisfaction for that blow, I will give you another." And then, drawing his sword, put himself in a posture of defense, which was the only science he understood.

Jones was a little staggered by the blow, which came somewhat unexpectedly; but presently recovering himself he also drew, and though he understood nothing of fencing, pressed on so boldly upon Fitzpatrick, that he beat down his guard, and sheathed one half of his sword in the body of the said gentleman, who had no sooner received it than he stepped backwards, dropped the point of his sword, and leaning upon it, cried, "I have satisfaction enough: I am a dead man."

"I hope not," cries Jones; "but whatever be the consequence, you must be sensible you have drawn it upon yourself." At this instant a number of fellows rushed in and seized Jones, who told them he should make no resistance, and begged some of them at least would take care of the wounded gentleman.

"Ay," cries one of the fellows, "the wounded gentleman will be taken care enough of; for I suppose he hath not many hours to live. As for you, sir, you have a month at least good yet." "D—n me, Jack," said another, "he hath prevented his voyage; he's bound to another port now"; and many other such jests was our poor Jones made the subject of by these fellows, who were indeed the gang employed by Lord Fellamar, and had dogged him into the house of Mrs. Fitzpatrick, waiting for him at the corner of the street when this unfortunate accident happened.

The officer who commanded this gang very wisely concluded that his business was now to deliver his prisoner into the hands of the civil magistrate. He ordered him, therefore, to be carried to a public-house, where, having sent for a constable, he delivered him to his custody.

The constable, seeing Mr. Jones very well dressed, and hearing that the accident had happened in a duel, treated his prisoner with great civility, and at his request despatched a messenger to inquire after the wounded gentleman, who was now at a tavern under the surgeon's hands. The report brought back was, that the wound was certainly mortal, and there were no hopes of life. Upon which the constable informed Jones that he must go before a justice. He answered, "Wherever you please; I am indifferent as to what happens to me; for though I am convinced I am not guilty of murder in the eye of the law, yet the weight of blood I find intolerable upon my mind."

Jones was now conducted before the justice, where the surgeon who dressed Mr. Fitzpatrick appeared, and deposed that he believed the wound to be mortal; upon which the prisoner was committed to the Gatehouse. It was very late at night, so that Jones would not send for Partridge till the next morning; and, as he never shut his eyes till seven, so it was near twelve before the poor fellow, who was greatly frightened at not hearing from his master so long, received a message which almost deprived him of his being when he heard it.

He went to the Gatehouse with trembling knees and a beating heart, and was no sooner arrived in the presence of Jones than he lamented the misfortune that had befallen him with many tears, looking all the while frequently about him in great terror; for, as the news now arrived that Mr. Fitzpatrick was dead, the poor fellow apprehended every minute that his ghost would enter the room. At last he delivered him a letter, which he had like to have forgot, and which came from Sophia by the hands of Black George.

Jones despatched everyone out of the room, and, having eagerly broke open the letter, read as follows:

"You owe the hearing from me again to an accident which I own surprises me. My aunt hath just now shown me a letter from you to Lady Bellaston, which contains a proposal of marriage. I am convinced it is your own hand; and what more surprises me is, that it is dated at the very time when you would have me imagine you was under such concern on my account.— I leave you to comment on this fact. All I desire is, that your name may never more be mentioned to   S. W."

Of the present situation of Mr. Jones's mind, and of the pangs with which he was now tormented, we cannot give the reader a better idea than by saying, his misery was such that even Thwackum would almost have pitied him. But, bad as it is, we shall at present leave him in it, as his good genius (if he really had any) seems to have done. And here we put an end to the sixteenth book of our history.

Book XVII

I

Mr. Allworthy and Mrs. Miller were just sat down to breakfast, when Blifil, who had gone out very early that morning, returned to make one of the company.

He had not been long seated before he began as follows:

"Good Lord! my dear uncle, what do you think hath happened? I vow I am afraid of telling it you, for fear of shocking you with the remembrance of ever having shown any kindness to such a villain."

"What is the matter, child?" said the uncle. "I fear I have shown kindness in my life to the unworthy more than once. But charity doth not adopt the vices of its objects."

"Oh, sir!" returned Blifil, "it is not without the secret direction of Providence that you mention the word adoption. Your adopted son, sir, that Jones, that wretch whom you nourished in your bosom, hath proved one of the greatest villains upon earth."

"By all that's sacred, 'tis false," cries Mrs. Miller. "Mr. Jones is no villain. He is one of the worthiest creatures breathing; and if any other person had called him villain, I would have thrown all this boiling water in his face."

Mr. Allworthy looked very much amazed at this behavior. But she did not give him leave to speak before, turning to him, she cried, "I

321

hope you will not be angry with me; I would not offend you, sir, for the world; but indeed I could not bear to hear him called so."

"I must own, madam," said Allworthy, very gravely, "I am a little surprised to hear you so warmly defend a fellow you do not know."

"Oh! I do know him, Mr. Allworthy," said she, "indeed I do; I should be the most ungrateful of all wretches if I denied it. Oh! he hath preserved me and my little family; we have all reason to bless him while we live. And I pray Heaven to bless him, and turn the hearts of his malicious enemies. I know, I find, I see, he hath such."

"You surprise me, madam, still more," said Allworthy; "sure you must mean some other. It is impossible you should have any such obligations to the man my nephew mentions."

"Too surely," answered she, "I have obligations to him of the greatest and tenderest kind. Indeed, my best of friends, he deserves a kinder appellation from you, had you heard the good, the kind, the grateful things which I have heard him utter of you. He never mentions your name but with a sort of adoration."

"I see, sir, now," said Blifil, with one of those grinning sneers with which the devil marks his best beloved, "Mrs. Miller really doth know him. I suppose you will find she is not the only one of your acquaintance to whom he hath exposed you. As for my character, I perceive, by some hints she hath thrown out, he hath been very free with it, but I forgive him."

"And the Lord forgive you, sir!" said Mrs. Miller; "we have all sins enough to stand in need of his forgiveness."

"Upon my word, Mrs. Miller," said Allworthy, "I do not take this behavior of yours to my nephew kindly; and I do assure you, as any reflections which you cast upon him must come only from that wickedest of men, they would only serve, if that were possible, to heighten my resentment against him; for I must tell you, Mrs. Miller, the young man who now stands before you hath ever been the warmest advocate for the ungrateful wretch whose cause you espouse. This, I think, when you hear it from my own mouth, will make you wonder at so much baseness and ingratitude."

"You are deceived, sir," answered Mrs. Miller; "if they were the last words which were to issue from my lips, I would say you were deceived; and I once more repeat it, the Lord forgive those who have deceived you! I do not pretend to say the young man is without faults; but they are all the faults of wildness and of youth; faults which he may, nay, which I am certain he will, relinquish, and, if he should not, they are vastly overbalanced by one of the most humane, tender, honest hearts that ever man was blest with."

"Well, madam," said Allworthy, "I shall be very glad to hear any good excuse for a behavior which, I must confess, I think wants an excuse. And now, madam, will you be pleased to let my nephew proceed in his story without interruption? He would not have introduced a matter of slight consequence with such a preface. Perhaps even this story will cure you of your mistake."

Mrs. Miller gave tokens of submission, and then Mr. Blifil began thus: "I am sure, sir, if you don't think proper to resent the ill-usage of Mrs. Miller, I shall easily forgive what affects me only. I think your goodness hath not deserved this indignity at her hands."

"Well, child," said Allworthy, "but what is this new instance? What hath he done of late?"

"What," cries Blifil, "notwithstanding all Mrs. Miller hath said, I am very sorry to relate, and what you should never have heard from me, had it not been a matter impossible to conceal from the whole world. In short he hath killed a man; I will not say murdered—for perhaps it may not be so construed in law, and I hope the best for his sake."

Allworthy looked shocked, and blessed himself; and then, turning to Mrs. Miller, he cried, "Well, madam, what say you now?"

"Why, I say, sir," answered she, "that I never was more concerned at anything in my life; but, if the fact be true, I am convinced the man, whoever he is, was in fault. Heaven knows there are many villains in this town who make it their business to provoke young gentlemen. Nothing but the greatest provocation could have tempted him; for of all the gentlemen I ever had in my house, I never saw one so gentle or so sweet-tempered. He was beloved by everyone in the house, and everyone who came near it."

While she was thus running on, a violent knocking at the door interrupted their conversation, and prevented her from proceeding further, or from receiving any answer.

II

Mrs. Miller had not long left the room when Mr. Western entered.

"There," says he, "there is fine business forwards now. The hounds have changed at last; and when we imagined we had a fox to deal with, od-rat it, it turns out to be a badger at last!"

"Pray, my good neighbor," said Allworthy, "drop your metaphors, and speak a little plainer."

"Why, then," says the squire, "to tell you plainly, we have been all this time afraid of a son of a whore of a bastard of somebody's, I don't know whose, not I. And now here's a confounded son of a whore of a lord, who may be a bastard too for what I know or care, for he shall never have a daughter of mine by my consent. They have beggared the nation, but they shall never beggar me."

"You surprise me much, my good friend," said Allworthy.

"Why, zounds! I am surprised myself," answered the squire. "I went to zee sister Western last night, according to her own appointment, and there I was had into a whole room full of women. There was my lady cousin Bellaston, and my Lady Betty, and my Lady Catherine, and my lady I don't know who; d—n me, if ever you catch me among such a kennel of hoop-petticoat b—s! if I dodged one way, one had me; if I offered to clap back, another snapped me. 'Oh! certainly one of the greatest matches in England,' says one cousin (here he attempted to mimic them). 'A very advantageous offer indeed,' cries another cousin (for you must know they be all my cousins, thof I never zeed half o' um before). 'Surely,' says that fat a—se b—, my Lady Bellaston, 'cousin, you must be out of your wits to think of refusing such an offer.' "

"Now I begin to understand," says Allworthy: "some person hath made proposals to Miss Western, which the ladies of the family approve, but is not to your liking."

"My liking!" said Western, "how the devil should it? I tell you it is a lord, and those are always volks whom you know I always resolved to have nothing to do with. Did unt I refuse a matter of vorty years' purchase now for a bit of land, which one o' um had a mind to put into a park, only because I would have no dealings with lords, and dost think I would marry my daughter zu? Besides, ben't I engaged to you, and did I ever go off any bargain when I had promised?"

"As to that point, neighbor," said Allworthy, "I entirely release you from any engagement. No contract can be binding between parties who have not a full power to make it at the time, nor ever afterwards acquire the power of fulfilling it."

"Slud! then," answered Western, "I tell you I have power, and I will fulfil it. Come along with me directly to Doctors' Commons, I will get a license; and I will go to sister and take away the wench by force, and she shall ha un, or I will lock her up, and keep her upon bread and water as long as she lives."

"Mr. Western," said Allworthy, "shall I beg you will hear my full sentiments on this matter?"

"Hear thee; ay, to be sure I will," answered he.

"Why, then, sir," cries Allworthy, "to force a woman into a marriage contrary to her consent or approbation, is an act of such injustice and oppression, that I wish the laws of our country could restrain it; but a good conscience is never lawless in the worst regulated state, and will provide those laws for itself, which the neglect of legislators hath forgotten to supply. This is surely a case of that kind; for, is it not cruel, nay, impious, to force a woman into that state against her will? I must speak very plainly here. I think parents who act in this manner are accessories to all the guilt which their children afterwards incur.

"For these reasons, my best neighbor, as I see the inclinations of this young lady are most unhappily averse to my nephew, I must decline any further thoughts of the honor you intended him, though I assure you I shall always retain the most grateful sense of it."

"Well, sir," said Western (the froth bursting forth from his lips the moment they were uncorked), "am I not to govern my own child? and if I am to govern her in other matters, surely I am to govern her in this, which concerns her most. And what am I desiring all this while? I am only desiring her to take away half my estate now, and t'other half when I die. Well, and what is it all vor? Why, is unt it to make her happy? It's enough to make one mad to hear volks talk: if I was going to marry myself, then she would ha reason to cry and to blubber; but, on the contrary, han't I offered to bind down my land in such a manner that I could not marry if I would, seeing as narro' woman upon earth would ha me. What the devil in hell can I do more? Zounds! I'd zee all the world d—n'd bevore her little vinger should be hurt."

Blifil now desired to be permitted to speak a few words. "As to using any violence on the young lady, I am sure I shall never consent to it, but yet I have read that women are seldom proof against perseverance. Why may I not hope, then, by such perseverance at last to gain those inclinations, in which for the future I shall, perhaps, have no rival; for as for this lord, Mr. Western is so kind to prefer me to him; and sure, sir, you will not deny but that a parent hath at least a negative voice in these matters; nay, I have heard this very young lady herself say so more than once. Besides, though the other ladies of the family seem to favor the pretensions of my lord, that wickedest of men remains uppermost in her heart."

"Ay, ay, so he does," cries Western.

"But surely," says Blifil, "when she hears of this murder which he hath committed, if the law should spare his life——"

"What's that?" cries Western. "Murder! hath he committed a murder, and is there any hopes of seeing him hanged?—Tol de rol, tol lol de rol." Here he fell a-singing and capering about the room.

"Lookee," says Allworthy, "you have my leave to write, to visit, if she will permit it—but I insist on no thoughts of violence. I will have no confinement, nothing of that kind attempted."

"Well, well," cries the squire, "nothing of that kind shall be attempted; we will try a little longer what fair means will effect; and if this fellow be but hanged out of the way—Tol lol de rol! I never heard better news in my life—Do, prithee, dear Allworthy, come and dine with me at the Hercules Pillars: I have bespoke a shoulder of mutton roasted, and a spare-rib of pork, and a fowl and egg-sauce."

Mr. Allworthy at last agreed to this invitation, and soon after the squire went off, singing and capering at the hopes of seeing the speedy tragical end of poor Jones.

When he was gone, Mr. Allworthy resumed the aforesaid subject with much gravity. He told his nephew, "He wished with all his heart he would endeavor to conquer a passion in which I cannot," says he, "flatter you with any hopes of succeeding. It is certainly a vulgar error, that aversion in a woman may be conquered by perseverance. Indifference may, perhaps, sometimes yield to it; but a fixed dislike, as I am afraid this is, will rather gather strength than be conquered by time."

The reader may pretty well guess Blifil's answer; but if he should be at a loss, we are not at present at leisure to satisfy him, as our history now hastens on to matters of higher importance, and we can no longer bear to be absent from Sophia.

III

THE servants were no sooner departed after dinner than Mrs. Western, who had opened the matter to Sophia, informed her, "That she expected his lordship that very afternoon, and intended to take the first opportunity of leaving her alone with him."

"If you do, madam," answered Sophia, with some spirit, "I shall take the first opportunity of leaving him by himself."

"How! madam!" cries the aunt; "is this the return you make me for my kindness in relieving you from your confinement at your father's?"

"You know, madam," said Sophia, "the cause of that confinement was a refusal to comply with my father in accepting a man I detested; and will my dear aunt, who hath relieved me from that distress, involve me in another equally bad?"

"And do you think, then, madam," answered Mrs. Western, "that there is no difference between my Lord Fellamar and Mr. Blifil?"

"Very little, in my opinion," cries Sophia; "and if I must be condemned to one, I would certainly have the merit of sacrificing myself to my father's pleasure."

"Then," said the aunt, "have you no sense of ambition? Are there no charms in the thoughts of having a coronet on your coach?"

"None, upon my honor," said Sophia. "A pin-cushion upon my coach would please me just as well."

"Never mention honor," cries the aunt. "It becomes not the mouth of such a wretch. I am sorry, niece, you force me to use these words, but I cannot bear your groveling temper; you have none of the blood of the Westerns in you. But, however mean and base your own ideas are, unless you agree to see his lordship this afternoon, I will, with my own hands, deliver you tomorrow morning to my brother, and will never henceforth interfere with you, nor see your face again."

Sophia stood a few moments silent after this speech, which was uttered in a most angry and peremptory tone; and then, bursting into tears, she cried, "Do with me, madam, whatever you please; I am the most miserable undone wretch upon earth; if my dear aunt forsakes me, where shall I look for a protector?"

"My dear niece," cries she, "you will have a very good protector in his lordship."

"Sure, madam," said Sophia, "I told you he had used me in the rudest and vilest manner."

"Indeed, child," answered she, "I never heard you, or did not understand you;—but what do you mean by this rude, vile manner?"

"Indeed, madam," said Sophia, "I am almost ashamed to tell you. He caught me in his arms, pulled me down upon the settee, and thrust his hand into my bosom, and kissed it with such violence that I have the mark upon my left breast at this moment."

"I am astonished and confounded," cries the aunt. "No woman of the name of Western hath been ever treated so since we were a family. I would have torn the eyes of a prince out, if he had attempted such freedoms with me. I have had lovers formerly, not so long ago neither; several lovers, though I never would consent to marriage, and I never encouraged the least freedom. It is a foolish custom, and what I never would agree to. No man kissed more of me than my cheek. It is as much as one can bring oneself to give lips up to a husband; and indeed, could I ever have been persuaded to marry, I believe I should not have soon been brought to endure so much."

"You will pardon me, dear madam," said Sophia, "if I make one observation: you own you have had many lovers, and the world knows it, even if you should deny it. You refused them all, and, I am convinced, one coronet at least among them."

"It is true, child," said she, "I have refused the offer of a title; but it was not so good an offer; that is, not so very, very good an offer."

"Well, madam," continued Sophia, "and why may not I expect to have a second, perhaps, better than this? You are now but a young woman, and I am convinced would not promise to yield to the first lover of fortune, nay, or of title too. I am a very young woman, and sure I need not despair."

"Well, my dear, dear Sophy," cries the aunt, "what would you have me say?"

"Why, I only beg that I may not be left alone, at least this evening; grant me that, and I will submit, if you think, after what is past, I ought to see him in your company."

"Well, I will grant it," cries the aunt. "Sophy, you know I love you, and can deny you nothing. You know the easiness of my nature; I have not always been so easy. I have been formerly thought cruel; by the men, I mean. I was called the cruel Parthenissa. I have broke many a window that has had verses to the cruel Parthenissa in it." Thus ran she on for near half an hour upon herself, and her conquests, and her cruelty, till the arrival of my lord, who, after a most tedious visit, during which Mrs. Western never once offered to leave the room, retired, not much more satisfied with the aunt than with the niece; for Sophia had brought her aunt into so excellent a temper, that she consented to almost everything her niece said, and agreed that a little distant behavior might not be improper to so forward a lover.

WHEN Mr. Allworthy and his nephew went to meet Mr. Western, Mrs. Miller set forwards to her son-in-law's lodgings, in order to acquaint him with the accident which had befallen his friend Jones; but he had known it long before from Partridge (for Jones, when he left Mrs. Miller, had been furnished with a room in the same house with Mr. Nightingale). The good woman found her daughter under great affliction on account of Mr. Jones, whom having comforted as well as she could, she set forwards to the Gatehouse, where she heard he was, and where Mr. Nightingale was arrived before her.

While Jones was expressing great satisfaction in the presence of his friends, Partridge brought an account that Mr. Fitzpatrick was still alive, though the surgeon declared that he had very little hopes. Upon which, Jones fetching a deep sigh, Nightingale said to him,

"My dear Tom, why should you afflict yourself so upon an accident, which, whatever be the consequence, can be attended with no danger to you, and in which your conscience cannot accuse you of having been the least to blame? If the fellow should die, what have you done more than taken away the life of a ruffian in your own defense? So will the coroner's inquest certainly find it; and then you will be easily admitted to bail; and though you must undergo the form of a trial, yet it is a trial which many men would stand for you for a shilling."

"Come, come, Mr. Jones," says Mrs. Miller, "cheer yourself up. I knew you could not be the aggressor, and so I told Mr. Allworthy, and so he shall acknowledge too, before I have done with him."

Jones gravely answered, "That whatever might be his fate, he should always lament the having shed the blood of one of his fellow-creatures, as one of the highest misfortunes which could have befallen him. But I have another misfortune of the tenderest kind——Oh! Mrs. Miller, I have lost what I held most dear upon earth."

"That must be a mistress," said Mrs. Miller. "But come, come; I know more than you imagine" (for indeed Partridge had blabbed all), "and I have heard more than you know. Matters go better, I promise you, than you think; and I would not give Blifil sixpence for all the chance which he hath of the lady."

"Indeed, my dear friend, indeed," answered Jones, "I apprehend no danger from Blifil. I have undone myself."

"Don't despair," replied Mrs. Miller; "you know not what a woman can do; and if anything be in my power, I promise you I will do it to serve you. Shall I go to the lady myself? I will say anything to her you would have me say."

"Thou best of women," cries Jones, taking her by the hand, "If you could contrive to deliver this (giving her a paper from his pocket), I shall forever acknowledge your goodness."

"Give it me," said Mrs. Miller. "If I see it not in her own possession before I sleep, may my next sleep be my last!"

The remainder of the conversation passed in the joint attempts of that good woman and Mr. Nightingale to cheer the dejected spirits of Mr. Jones, in which they so far succeeded as to leave him much better comforted and satisfied than they found him.

V

SOPHIA was dressing when she was acquainted that there was a gentlewoman below to wait on her. As she was neither afraid nor ashamed to see any of her own sex, Mrs. Miller was immediately admitted.

"Pray, what is your business, madam?" said Sophia, with a little emotion.

"Madam, we are not alone," replied Mrs. Miller, in a low voice.

"Go out, Betty," said Sophia.

When Betty was departed, Mrs. Miller said, "I was desired, madam, by a very unhappy young gentleman to deliver you this letter." Sophia changed color when she saw the direction, well knowing the hand, and, after some hesitation, said, "I could not conceive, madam, from your appearance, that your business had been of such a nature. —Whomever you brought this letter from, I shall not open it."

Mrs. Miller then fell upon her knees, and in the most passionate terms implored her compassion; to which Sophia answered,

"Sure, madam, it is surprising you should be so very strongly interested in the behalf of this person. I would not think, madam——"

"No, madam," says Mrs. Miller, "you shall not think anything but the truth. I will tell you all, and you will not wonder that I am interested. He is the best-natured creature that ever was born."——She then began and related the story of her cousin.——After this she cried, "This, madam, this is his goodness; but I have much more tender obligations to him. He hath preserved my child." Here, after shedding some tears, she related everything concerning that fact, suppressing only those circumstances which would have most reflected on her daughter, and concluded with saying, "Now, madam, you shall judge whether I can ever do enough for so kind, so good, so generous a young man; and sure he is the best and worthiest of all human beings."

The alterations in the countenance of Sophia had hitherto been chiefly to her disadvantage, and had inclined her complexion to too great paleness; but she now waxed redder, if possible, than vermilion, and cried, "I know not what to say; certainly what arises from gratitude cannot be blamed——But what service can my reading this letter do your friend, since I am resolved never——"

Mrs. Miller fell again to her entreaties, and begged to be forgiven, but she could not, she said, carry it back.

"Well, madam," says Sophia, "I cannot help it, if you will force it upon me.—Certainly you may leave it whether I will or no." What Sophia meant, or whether she meant anything, I will not presume to determine; but Mrs. Miller actually understood this as a hint, and presently laying the letter down on the table, took her leave, having first begged permission to wait again on Sophia; which request had neither assent nor denial.

The letter lay upon the table no longer than till Mrs. Miller was out of sight; for then Sophia opened and read it.

This letter did very little service to his cause; for it consisted of little more than confessions of his own unworthiness, and bitter lamentations of despair, together with the most solemn protestations of his unalterable fidelity to Sophia; and that he could account for the letter to Lady Bellaston in such a manner that, though it would not entitle him to her forgiveness, he hoped at least to obtain it from her mercy.

VI

MRS. MILLER had a long discourse with Mr. Allworthy, at his return from dinner, in which she acquainted him with Jones's having unfortunately lost all which he was pleased to bestow on him at their separation, and with the distresses to which that loss had subjected him; of all which she had received a full account from the faithful retailer Partridge. She then explained the obligations she had to Jones: not that she was entirely explicit with regard to her daughter; for though she had the utmost confidence in Mr. Allworthy, yet she could not prevail with herself to mention those circumstances which reflected most on the chastity of poor Nancy.

Allworthy said, there were few characters so absolutely vicious as not to have the least mixture of good in them. "However," says he, "I cannot deny but that you have some obligations to the fellow, bad as he is, and I shall therefore excuse what hath passed already; but must insist you never mention his name to me more; for, I promise you, it was upon the fullest and plainest evidence that I resolved to take the measures I have taken."

"Well, sir," says she, "I make not the least doubt but time will show all matters in their true and natural colors, and that you will be convinced this poor young man deserves better of you than some other folks that shall be nameless."

"Madam," cries Allworthy, a little ruffled, "I will not hear any reflections on my nephew; and if ever you say a word more of that kind, I will depart from your house that instant. He is the worthiest and best of men; and I once more repeat it to you, he hath carried his friendship to this man to a blamable length, by too long concealing facts of the blackest die. The ingratitude of the wretch to this good young man is what I most resent; for, madam, I have the greatest reason to imagine he had laid a plot to supplant my nephew in my favor, and to have disinherited him."

"I am sure, sir," answered Mrs. Miller, a little frightened (for, though Mr. Allworthy had the utmost sweetness and benevolence in his smiles, he had great terror in his frowns), "I shall never speak against any gentleman you are pleased to think well of. I am sure, sir, such behavior would very little become me, especially when the gentleman is your nearest relation; but, sir, you must not be angry with me, you must not indeed, for my good wishes to this poor wretch. I must, I must lament him. If you had a dagger in your hand, ready to plunge into my heart, I must lament the misery of one whom you have loved, and I shall ever love."

Allworthy was pretty much moved with this speech, but it seemed not to be with anger; for, after a short silence, taking Mrs. Miller by the hand, he said very affectionately to her,

"Come, madam, let us consider a little about your daughter. I cannot blame you for rejoicing in a match which promises to be advantageous to her, but you know this advantage, in a great measure, depends on the father's reconciliation. I know Mr. Nightingale very well, and have formerly had concerns with him; I will make him a visit, and I promise you I will do all I can for you."

Mr. Allworthy and Mrs. Miller had been above an hour together, when their conversation was put an end to by the arrival of Blifil and another person, which other person was Mr. Dowling, the attorney, who was now become a great favorite with Mr. Blifil, and whom Mr. Allworthy, at the desire of his nephew, had made his steward; and had likewise recommended him to Mr. Western, from whom the attorney received a promise of being promoted to the same office upon the first vacancy.

VII

MR. JONES passed about twenty-four melancholy hours by himself, unless when relieved by the company of Partridge, before Mr. Nightingale returned.

He had heard, upon inquiry, that the only persons who had seen the beginning of the unfortunate rencounter were a crew belonging to a man-of-war which then lay at Deptford. To Deptford, therefore, he went in search of this crew, where he was informed that the men he sought after were all gone ashore. He then traced them from place to place, till at last he found two of them, drinking together, with a third person, at a hedge-tavern near Aldersgate.

Nightingale desired to speak with Jones by himself (for Partridge was in the room when he came in). As soon as they were alone, Nightingale, taking Jones by the hand, cried,

"Come, my brave friend, be not too much dejected at what I am going to tell you——I am sorry I am the messenger of bad news; but I think it my duty to tell you."

"I guess already what that bad news is," cries Jones. "The poor gentleman, then, is dead."

"I hope not," answered Nightingale. "He was alive this morning; though I will not flatter you—I fear, from the accounts I could get, that his wound is mortal. But if the affair be exactly as you told it, your own remorse would be all you would have reason to apprehend, let what would happen; but forgive me, my dear Tom, if I entreat you to make the worst of your story to your friends. If you disguise anything to us, you will only be an enemy to yourself."

"What reason, my dear Jack, have I ever given you," said Jones, "to stab me with so cruel a suspicion?"

"Have patience," cries Nightingale, "and I will tell you all. After the most diligent inquiry I could make, I at last met with two of the fellows who were present at this unhappy accident, and I am sorry to say, they do not relate the story so much in your favor as you yourself have told it."

"Why, what do they say?" cries Jones.

"Indeed what I am sorry to repeat, as I am afraid of the consequence of it to you. They say that they were at too great a distance to overhear any words that passed between you: but they both agree that the first blow was given by you."

"Then, upon my soul," answered Jones, "they injure me. He not only struck me first, but struck me without the least provocation. What should induce those villains to accuse me falsely?"

"Nay, that I cannot guess," said Nightingale, "and if you yourself, and I, who am so heartily your friend, cannot conceive a reason why they should belie you, what reason will an indifferent court of justice be able to assign why they should not believe them?"

A very mournful scene now passed, at which, as few readers would have been pleased to be present, so few, I believe, will desire to hear it particularly related. We will therefore pass on to the entrance of the turnkey, who acquainted Jones that there was a lady without who desired to speak with him when he was at leisure.

If Jones was surprised at the news of a visit from a lady how greatly was he astonished when he discovered this lady to be no other than Mrs. Waters! In this astonishment, then, we shall leave him awhile, in order to cure the surprise of the reader, who will likewise, probably, not a little wonder at the arrival of this lady.

Who this Mrs. Waters was, the reader pretty well knows; what she was, he must be perfectly satisfied. He will therefore be pleased to remember that this lady departed from Upton in the same coach with Mr. Fitzpatrick and the other Irish gentleman, and in their company traveled to Bath.

Now there was a certain office in the gift of Mr. Fitzpatrick at that time vacant, namely, that of a wife: for the lady who had lately filled that office had resigned, or at least deserted her duty. Mr. Fitzpatrick therefore, having thoroughly examined Mrs. Waters on the road, found her extremely fit for the place, which, on their arrival at Bath, he presently conferred upon her, and she without any scruple accepted. As husband and wife this gentleman and lady continued together all the time they stayed at Bath, and as husband and wife they arrived together in town.

As Mr. Fitzpatrick had not the clearest way of telling a story at any time, and was now, perhaps a little more confused than usual, it was some time before she discovered that the gentleman who had given him this wound was the very same person from whom her heart had received a wound, which, though not of a mortal kind, was yet so deep that it had left a considerable scar behind it. But no sooner was she acquainted that Mr. Jones himself was the man who had been committed to the Gatehouse for this supposed murder, than she took the first opportunity of committing Mr. Fitzpatrick to the care of his nurse, and hastened away to visit the conqueror.

She now entered the room with an air of gaiety, which received an immediate check from the melancholy aspect of poor Jones, who started and blessed himself when he saw her.

"Indeed, madam," says Jones, "I must look upon this visit as kind; few will follow the miserable, especially to such dismal habitations."

"I protest, Mr. Jones," says she, "I can hardly persuade myself you are the same agreeable fellow I saw at Upton. Why, your face is more miserable than any dungeon in the universe. What can be the matter with you?"

"I thought, madam," said Jones, "as you knew of my being here, you knew the unhappy reason."

"Pugh!" says she, "you have pinked a man in a duel, that's all." Jones expressed some indignation at this levity, and spoke with the utmost contrition for what had happened. To which she answered,

"Well, then, sir, if you take it so much to heart, I will relieve you; the gentleman is not dead, and, I am pretty confident, is in no danger of dying. The surgeon, indeed, who first dressed him was a young fellow, and seemed desirous of representing his case to be as bad as possible, that he might have the more honor from curing him: but the king's surgeon hath seen him since, and says, unless from a fever, of which there are at present no symptoms, he apprehends not the least danger of life." Jones showed great satisfaction in his countenance at this report; upon which she affirmed the truth of it, adding, "By the most extraordinary accident in the world I lodge at the same house; and have seen the gentleman, and I promise you he doth you justice, and says, whatever be the consequence, that he was entirely the aggressor, and that you was not in the least to blame."

Jones expressed the utmost satisfaction at the account which Mrs. Waters brought him. He then told her several facts of which she was ignorant, as the adventure of the muff, and other particulars, concealing only the name of Sophia. He then lamented the follies and vices of which he had been guilty; every one of which, he said, had been attended with such ill consequences, that he should be unpardonable if he did not take warning, and quit those vicious courses for the future. He lastly concluded with assuring her of his resolution to sin no more, lest a worse thing should happen to him.

Mrs. Waters with great pleasantry ridiculed all this, as the effects of low spirits and confinement. She repeated some witticisms about the devil when he was sick, and told him, "She doubted not but shortly to see him at liberty, and as lively a fellow as ever; and then," says she, "I don't question but your conscience will be safely delivered of all these qualms that it is now so sick in breeding."

We shall suppress the rest of this conversation, and only observe that it ended at last with perfect innocence, and much more to the satisfaction of Jones than of the lady; for the former was greatly transported with the news she had brought him; but the latter was not altogether so pleased with the penitential behavior of a man whom she had, at her first interview, conceived a very different opinion of from what she now entertained of him.

Thus the melancholy occasioned by the report of Mr. Nightingale was pretty well effaced; but he made not the least doubt but that Sophia had taken a fixed resolution to abandon him. The torments this thought gave to him were to be equalled only by a piece of news which fortune had yet in store for him.

Book XVIII

CONTAINING ABOUT SIX DAYS

I

WHILE Jones was employed in those unpleasant meditations, with which we left him tormenting himself, Partridge came stumbling into the room with his face paler than ashes, his eyes fixed in his head, his hair standing on end, and every limb trembling. In short, he looked as he would have done had he seen a spectre, or had he, indeed, been a spectre himself.

Jones, who was little subject to fear, could not avoid being somewhat shocked at this sudden appearance. He did, indeed, himself change color, and his voice a little faltered while he asked him, What was the matter?

"I hope, sir," said Partridge, "you will not be angry with me. Indeed I did not listen, but I was obliged to stay in the outward room. I am sure I wish I had been a hundred miles off, rather than have heard what I have heard."

"Why, what is the matter?" said Jones.

"The matter, sir? Oh, good Heaven!" answered Partridge, "was that woman who is just gone out the woman who was with you at Upton?"

"She was, Partridge," cried Jones.

"And did you really, sir, go to bed with that woman?" said he, trembling.

"I am afraid what passed between us is no secret," said Jones.

"Why, then, the Lord have mercy upon your soul, and forgive you," cries Partridge; "but as sure as I stand here alive, you have been a-bed with your own mother."

Upon these words Jones became in a moment a greater picture of horror than Partridge himself. He was, indeed, for some time struck dumb with amazement, and both stood staring wildly at each other.

"Nay, sir," cries Partridge, "What I have said is most certainly true.—That woman who now went out is your own mother. How unlucky was it for you, sir, that I did not happen to see her at that time, to have prevented it! Sure the devil himself must have contrived to bring about this wickedness."

"Sure," cries Jones, "Fortune will never have done with me till she hath driven me to distraction. But why do I blame Fortune? I am myself the cause of all my misery. All the dreadful mischiefs which have befallen me are the consequences only of my own folly and vice. What thou hast told me, Partridge, hath almost deprived me of my senses! And was Mrs. Waters, then—but why do I ask? for thou must certainly know her——If thou hast any affection for me, nay, if thou hast any pity, let me, beseech thee to fetch this miserable woman back again to me." He then fell into the most violent and frantic agonies of grief and despair, in which Partridge declared he would not leave him; but at last, having vented the first torrent of passion, he came a little to himself; and then, having acquainted Partridge that he would find this wretched woman in the same house where the wounded gentleman was lodged, he despatched him in quest of her.

After a fruitless search of two or three hours, Partridge returned back to his master, without having seen Mrs. Waters. Jones, who was in a state of desperation at his delay, was almost raving mad when he brought him his account. He was not long, however, in this condition before he received the following letter:

"Sir—Since I left you I have seen a gentleman, from whom I have learned something concerning you which greatly surprises and affects me; but as I have not at present leisure to communicate a matter of such high importance, you must suspend your curiosity till our next meeting, which shall be the first moment I am able to see you. Oh, Mr. Jones, little did I think, when I passed that happy day at Upton, the reflection upon which is like to embitter all my future life, who it was to whom I owed

such perfect happiness.—Believe me to be ever sincerely your
unfortunate   J. WATERS.

"*P.S.*—I would have you comfort yourself as much as possible, for Mr. Fitzpatrick is in no manner of danger; so that
whatever other grievous crimes you may have to repent of, the
guilt of blood is not among the number."

Jones having read the letter, let it drop (for he was unable to hold
it, and indeed had scarce the use of any one of his faculties). Partridge took it up, and having received consent by silence, read it likewise; nor had it upon him a less sensible effect. The pencil, and not
the pen, should describe the horrors which appeared in both their
countenances.

II

THE morning after these things had happened, Mr. Allworthy went,
according to his promise, to visit old Nightingale, with whom his
authority was so great, that, after having sat with him three hours,
he at last prevailed with him to consent to see his son.

Here an accident happened of a very extraordinary kind; one indeed of those strange chances whence very good and grave men
have concluded that Providence often interposes in the discovery of
the most secret villainy, in order to caution men from quitting the
paths of honesty, however warily they tread in those of vice.

Mr. Allworthy, at his entrance into Mr. Nightingale's, saw Black
George; he took no notice of him, nor did Black George imagine he
had perceived him.

However, when their conversation on the principal point was over,
Allworthy asked Nightingale, Whether he knew one George Seagrim, and upon what business he came to his house?

"Yes," answered Nightingale, "I know him very well, and a most
extraordinary fellow he is, who, in these days, hath been able to
hoard up £500 from renting a very small estate of £30 a year."

"And is this the story which he hath told you?" cries Allworthy.

"Nay, it is true, I promise you," said Nightingale, "for I have the
money now in my own hands, in five bank-bills, which I am to lay
out either in a mortgage, or in some purchase in the north of England."

The bank-bills were no sooner produced at Allworthy's desire than he blessed himself at the strangeness of the discovery. He presently told Nightingale that these bank-bills were formerly his, and then acquainted him with the whole affair. Nightingale no sooner heard the story than he exclaimed against the fellow in terms much severer than the justice and honesty of Allworthy had bestowed on him.

Allworthy desired Nightingale to retain both the money and the secret till he should hear further from him; and if he should in the meantime see the fellow, that he would not take the least notice to him of the discovery which he had made. He then returned to his lodgings, where he found Mrs. Miller in a very dejected condition, on account of the information she had received from her son-in-law. Mr. Allworthy, with great cheerfulness, told her that he had much good news to communicate; and, with little further preface, acquainted her that he had brought Mr. Nightingale to consent to see his son, and did not in the least doubt to effect a perfect reconciliation between them.

Allworthy told her he had still something more to impart, which he believed would give her pleasure.

"I think," said he, "I have discovered a pretty considerable treasure belonging to the young gentleman, your friend; but perhaps, indeed, his present situation may be such that it will be of no service to him." The latter part of the speech gave Mrs. Miller to understand who was meant, and she answered with a sigh, "I hope not, sir."

"I hope so too," cries Allworthy, "with all my heart; but my nephew told me this morning he had heard a very bad account of the affair."

"Good Heaven! sir," said she—"Well, I must not speak, and yet it is certainly very hard to be obliged to hold one's tongue when one hears."

"Madam," said Allworthy, "you may say whatever you please, you know me too well to think I have a prejudice against anyone; and as for that young man I assure you I should be heartily pleased to find he could acquit himself of everything, and particularly of this sad affair."

Allworthy then inquired for his nephew, and was told that he had been for some time in his room with the gentleman who used to come to him, and whom Mr. Allworthy guessing rightly to be Mr. Dowling, he desired presently to speak with him.

When Mr. Dowling withdrew, Mrs. Miller introduced Mr. Nightingale the younger, to return thanks for the great kindness done him by Allworthy: but she had scarce patience to let the young gentleman finish his speech before she interrupted him, saying,

"Oh, sir! Mr. Nightingale brings great news about poor Mr. Jones: he hath been to see the wounded gentleman, who is out of all danger of death, and, what is more, declares he fell upon poor Mr. Jones himself, and beat him. I am sure, sir, you would not have Mr. Jones be a coward. If I was a man myself, I am sure, if any man was to strike me, I should draw my sword. Do pray, my dear, tell Mr. Allworthy, tell him all yourself."

Nightingale then confirmed what Mrs. Miller had said; and concluded with many handsome things of Jones, who was, he said, one of the best-natured fellows in the world, and not in the least inclined to be quarrelsome. Here Nightingale was going to cease, when Mrs. Miller again begged him to relate all the many dutiful expressions he had heard him make use of towards Mr. Allworthy. "To say the utmost good of Mr. Allworthy," cries Nightingale, "is doing no more than strict justice, and can have no merit in it: but indeed, I must say, no man can be more sensible of the obligations he hath to so good a man than is poor Jones. Indeed, sir, I am convinced the weight of your displeasure is the heaviest burthen he lies under."

"Indeed, Mr. Nightingale," answered Allworthy, "I applaud your generous friendship, and I wish he may merit it of you. I confess I am glad to hear the report you bring from this unfortunate gentleman; and if that matter should turn out to be as you represent it (and indeed I doubt nothing of what you say), I may, perhaps, in time, be brought to think better than lately I have of this young man; for this good gentlewoman here, nay, all who know me, can witness that I loved him as dearly as if he had been my own son." At which words he ceased, and the tears stood in his eyes.

We will here stop to account for the visible alteration in Mr. Allworthy's mind, and the abatement of his anger to Jones.

This alteration was occasioned by a letter he had just received from Mr. Square:

"MY WORTHY FRIEND—I informed you in my last that I was forbidden the use of the waters, as they were found by experience rather to increase than lessen the symptoms of my distemper. I must now acquaint you with a piece of news, which, I believe, will afflict my friends more than it hath afflicted me.

Dr. Harrington and Dr. Brewster have informed me that there is no hope of my recovery.

"When I reflect on the actions of my past life, I know of nothing which sits heavier upon my conscience than the injustice I have been guilty of to that poor wretch your adopted son. I have, indeed, not only connived at the villainy of others, but been myself active in injustice towards him. Believe me, my dear friend, when I tell you, on the word of a dying man, he hath been basely injured. As to the principal fact, upon the misrepresentation of which you discarded him, I solemnly assure you he is innocent. When you lay upon your supposed deathbed, he was the only person in the house who testified any real concern; and what happened afterwards arose from the wildness of his joy on your recovery; and, I am sorry to say it, from the baseness of another person (but it is my desire to justify the innocent, and to accuse none). Believe me, my friend, this young man hath the noblest generosity of heart, the most perfect capacity for friendship, the highest integrity, and indeed every virtue which can ennoble a man. He hath some faults, but among them is not to be numbered the least want of duty or gratitude towards you. On the contrary, I am satisfied, when you dismissed him from your house, his heart bled for you more than for himself.

"Worldly motives were the wicked and base reasons of my concealing this from you so long: to reveal it now I can have no inducement but the desire of serving the cause of truth, of doing right to the innocent, and of making all the amends in my power for a past offense. I hope this declaration, therefore, will have the effect desired, and will restore this deserving young man to your favor; the hearing of which, while I am yet alive, will afford the utmost consolation to—Sir, your most obliged, obedient humble servant,   "THOMAS SQUARE"

The reader will, after this, scarce wonder at the revolution so visibly appearing in Mr. Allworthy.

III

MR. ALLWORTHY, in his last speech, had recollected some tender ideas concerning Jones, which had brought tears into the good man's eyes. This Mrs. Miller observing, said,

"Yes, yes, sir, your goodness to this poor young man is known, notwithstanding all your care to conceal it; but there is not a single syllable of truth in what those villains said. Mr. Nightingale hath now discovered the whole matter. It seems these fellows were employed by a lord, who is a rival of poor Mr. Jones, to have pressed him on board a ship.——I assure them I don't know who they will press next. Mr. Nightingale here hath seen the officer himself, who is a very pretty gentleman, and hath told him all, and is very sorry for what he undertook, which he would never have done, had he known Mr. Jones to have been a gentleman; but he was told that he was a common strolling vagabond."

Allworthy stared at all this, and declared he was a stranger to every word she said.

"Yes, sir," answered she, "I believe you are.——It is a very different story, I believe, from what those fellows told the lawyer."

"What lawyer, madam? what is it you mean?" said Allworthy.

"Nay, nay," said she, "this is so like you to deny your own goodness: but Mr. Nightingale here saw him."

"Saw whom, madam?" answered he.

"Why, your lawyer, sir," said she, "that you so kindly sent to inquire into the affair."

"I am still in the dark, upon my honor," said Allworthy.

"Indeed, sir," said Nightingale, "I did see that very lawyer who went from you when I came into the room, at an ale-house in Aldersgate, in company with two of the fellows who were employed by Lord Fellamar to press Mr. Jones, and who were by that means present at the unhappy rencounter between him and Mr. Fitzpatrick."

Allworthy showed marks of astonishment in his countenance at this news, and was indeed for two or three minutes struck dumb by it. At last, addressing himself to Mr. Nightingale, he said, "I must confess myself, sir, more surprised at what you tell me than I have ever been before at anything in my whole life. Are you certain this was the gentleman?"

"I am most certain," answered Nightingale.

"At Aldersgate?" cried Allworthy. "And was you in company with this lawyer and the two fellows?"

"I was, sir," said the other, "very near half an hour."

"Well, sir," said Allworthy, "and in what manner did the lawyer behave? did you hear all that passed between him and the fellows?"

"No, sir," answered Nightingale, "they had been together before I came. In my presence the lawyer said little; but, after I had several times examined the fellows, who persisted in a story directly contrary to what I had heard from Mr. Jones, and which I find by Mr. Fitzpatrick was a rank falsehood, the lawyer then desired the fellows to say nothing but what was the truth, and seemed to speak so much in favor of Mr. Jones, that, when I saw the same person with you, I concluded your goodness had prompted you to send him thither."

"Dear madam," said Allworthy, "do me the favor to send a servant upstairs to call Mr. Dowling hither, if he be in the house, or, if not, Mr. Blifil." Mrs. Miller went out muttering something to herself, and presently returned with an answer,

"That Mr. Dowling was gone; but that the t'other," as she called him, "was coming."

Allworthy was of a cooler disposition than the good woman, whose spirits were all up in arms in the cause of her friend. He was not, however, without some suspicions which were near akin to hers. When Blifil came into the room, he asked him with a very serious countenance, and with a less friendly look than he had ever before given him, "Whether he knew anything of Mr. Dowling's having seen any of the persons who were present at the duel between Jones and another gentleman?"

There is nothing so dangerous as a question which comes by surprise on a man whose business it is to conceal truth or to defend falsehood. And such indeed were the alterations which the countenance of Blifil underwent from this sudden question, that we can scarce blame the eagerness of Mrs. Miller, who immediately cried out, "Guilty, upon my honor! guilty, upon my soul!"

Mr. Allworthy sharply rebuked her for this impetuosity; and then turning to Blifil, who seemed sinking into the earth, he said, "Why do you hesitate, sir, at giving me an answer? You certainly must have employed him; for he would not, of his own accord, I believe, have undertaken such an errand, and especially without acquainting me."

Blifil then answered, "I own, sir, I have been guilty of an offense, yet may I hope your pardon?"

"My pardon," said Allworthy, very angrily.

"Nay, sir," answered Blifil, "I knew you would be offended; yet surely my dear uncle will forgive the effects of the most amiable of human weaknesses. Compassion for those who do not deserve it, I own is a crime; and yet it is a crime from which you yourself are not entirely free. I will own I did send Mr. Dowling, not on a vain and fruitless inquiry, but to discover the witnesses, and to endeavor to soften their evidence. This, sir, is the truth; which, though I intended to conceal from you, I will not deny."

"I confess," said Nightingale, "this is the light in which it appeared to me from the gentleman's behavior."

"Now, madam," said Allworthy, "I believe you will once in your life own you have entertained a wrong suspicion, and are not so angry with my nephew as you was."

Mrs. Miller was silent; for, though she could not so hastily be pleased with Blifil, whom she looked upon to have been the ruin of Jones, yet in this particular instance he had imposed upon her as well as upon the rest.

As for Jones, the resentment of Mr. Allworthy began more and more to abate towards him. He told Blifil, "He did not only forgive the extraordinary efforts of his good-nature, but would give him the pleasure of following his example." Then, turning to Mrs. Miller with a smile which would have become an angel, he cried, "What say you, madam? shall we take a hackney-coach, and all of us together pay a visit to your friend? I promise you it is not the first visit I have made in a prison."

Few, I hope, are capable of feeling what now passed in the mind of Blifil; but those who are will acknowledge that it was impossible for him to raise any objection to this visit. Fortune, however, prevented his undergoing so great a shock; for at the very instant when the coach was sent for, Partridge arrived.

Allworthy recollected Partridge the moment he came into the room, though many years had passed since he had seen him.

"And are you," said Allworthy to Partridge, "the servant of Mr. Jones?"

"I can't say, sir," answered he, "that I am regularly a servant, but I live with him, an't please your honor, at present. *Non sum qualis eram*, as your honor very well knows."

Mr. Allworthy then asked him many questions concerning Jones, as to his health, and other matters; to all which Partridge answered, without having the least regard to what was, but considered only what he would have things appear; for a strict adherence to truth was not among the articles of this honest fellow's morality or his religion.

During this dialogue Mr. Nightingale took his leave, and presently after Mrs. Miller left the room, when Allworthy likewise despatched Blifil; for he imagined that Partridge when alone with him would be more explicit than before company. They were no sooner left in private together than Allworthy began, as in the following chapter.

IV

"SURE, friend," said the good man, "you are the strangest of all human beings. Not only to have suffered as you have formerly for obstinately persisting in a falsehood, but to persist in it thus to the last, and to pass thus upon the world for a servant of your own son! What interest can you have in all this? What can be your motive?"

"I see, sir," said Partridge, falling down upon his knees, "that your honor is prepossessed against me, and resolved not to believe anything I say, and, therefore, what signifies my protestations? but yet there is one above who knows that I am not the father of this young man."

"What am I to think of this matter?" cries Allworthy. "For what purpose should you so strongly deny a fact which I think it would be rather your interest to own?"

"Nay, sir," answered Partridge (for he could hold no longer), "if your honor will not believe me, you are like soon to have satisfaction enough. I wish you had mistaken the mother of this young man, as well as you have his father." And now being asked what he meant, with all the symptoms of horror, both in his voice and countenance, he told Allworthy the whole story.

Allworthy was almost as much shocked at this discovery as Partridge himself had been while he related it. "Good heavens!" says he, "in what miserable distresses do vice and imprudence involve men! How much beyond our designs are the effects of wickedness sometimes carried!" He had scarce uttered these words, when Mrs. Waters came hastily and abruptly into the room. Partridge no sooner saw her than he cried, "Here, sir, here is the very woman herself. This is the unfortunate mother of Mr. Jones. I am sure she will acquit me before your honor. Pray, madam——"

Mrs. Waters, without paying any regard to what Partridge said, and almost without taking any notice of him, advanced to Mr. Allworthy.

"I believe, sir, it is so long since I had the honor of seeing you, that you do not recollect me."

"Indeed," answered Allworthy, "you are so very much altered, on many accounts, that had not this man already acquainted me who you are, I should not have immediately called you to my remembrance. Have you, madam, any particular business which brings you to me?" Allworthy spoke this with great reserve; for the reader may easily believe he was not well pleased with the conduct of this lady;

neither with what he had formerly heard, nor with what Partridge had now delivered.

Mrs. Waters answered, "Indeed, sir, I have very particular business with you; and it is such as I can impart only to yourself. I must desire, therefore, the favor of a word with you alone; for I assure you what I have to tell you is of the utmost importance."

Partridge was then ordered to withdraw, but before he went, he begged the lady to satisfy Mr. Allworthy that he was perfectly innocent. To which she answered, "You need be under no apprehension, sir; I shall satisfy Mr. Allworthy very perfectly of that matter."

Then Partridge withdrew, and that passed between Mr. Allworthy and Mrs. Waters which is written in the next chapter.

V

MRS. WATERS remaining a few moments silent, Mr. Allworthy could not refrain from saying, "I am sorry, madam, to perceive, by what I have since heard, that you have made so very ill a use——"

"Mr. Allworthy," says she, interrupting him, "I know I have faults, but ingratitude to you is not one of them. I never can nor shall forget your goodness, which I own I have very little deserved; but be pleased to waive all upbraiding me at present, as I have so important an affair to communicate to you concerning this young man, to whom you have given my maiden name of Jones."

"Have I, then," said Allworthy, "ignorantly punished an innocent man, in the person of him who hath just left us? Was he not the father of the child?"

"Indeed he was not," said Mrs. Waters. "You may be pleased to remember, sir, I formerly told you, you should one day know; and I acknowledge myself to have been guilty of a cruel neglect, in not having discovered it to you before. Indeed I little knew how necessary it was."

"Well, madam," said Allworthy, "Be pleased to proceed."

"You must remember, sir," said she, "a young fellow, whose name was Summer."

"Very well," cries Allworthy; "he was the son of a clergyman of great learning and virtue, for whom I had the highest friendship."

"So it appeared, sir," answered she; "for I believe you bred the young man up, and maintained him at the university; where, I think, he had finished his studies, when he came to reside at your house. A finer man, I must say, the sun never shone upon; for, besides the handsomest person I ever saw, he was so genteel, and had so much wit and good breeding."

"Poor gentleman," said Allworthy, "he was indeed untimely snatched away; and little did I think he had any sins of this kind to answer for; for I plainly perceive you are going to tell me he was the father of your child."

"Indeed, sir," answered she, "he was not."

"How!" said Allworthy; "to what then tends all this preface?"

"To a story," said she, "which I am concerned falls to my lot to unfold to you. Oh, sir! prepare to hear something which will surprise you, will grieve you."

"Speak," said Allworthy; "I am conscious of no crime, and cannot be afraid to hear."

"Sir," said she, "that Mr. Summer, the son of your friend, educated at your expense, who, after living a year in the house as if he had been your own son, died there of the smallpox, was tenderly lamented by you, and buried as if he had been your own; that Summer, sir, was the father of this child."

"How!" said Allworthy; "you contradict yourself."

"That I do not," answered she; "he was indeed the father of this child, but not by me."

"Take care, madam," said Allworthy, "do not, to shun the imputation of any crime, be guilty of falsehood. Remember there is One from whom you can conceal nothing, and before whose tribunal falsehood will only aggravate your guilt."

"Indeed, sir," says she, "I am not his mother; nor would I now think myself so for the world."

"I know your reason," said Allworthy, "and shall rejoice as much as you to find it otherwise; yet you must remember, you yourself confessed it before me."

"So far what I confessed," said she, "was true, that these hands conveyed the infant to your bed; conveyed it thither at the command of its mother; at her commands I afterwards owned it, and thought myself, by her generosity, nobly rewarded, both for my secrecy and my shame."

"Who could this woman be?" said Allworthy.

"Indeed I tremble to name her," answered Mrs. Waters.

"By all this preparation I am to guess that she was a relation of mine," cried he.

"Indeed she was a near one." At which words Allworthy started, and she continued—"You had a sister, sir."

"A sister!" repeated he, looking aghast.

"As there is truth in heaven," cries she, "your sister was the mother of that child you found between your sheets."

"Can it be possible?" cries he. "Good heavens!"

"Have patience, sir," said Mrs. Waters, "and I will unfold to you the whole story. Just after your departure for London, Miss Bridget came one day to the house of my mother. She was pleased to say she had heard an extraordinary character of me, for my learning and superior understanding to all the young women there, so she was pleased to say. She then bid me come to her to the great house; where, when I attended, she employed me to read to her. She expressed great satisfaction in my reading, showed great kindness to me, and made me many presents. At last she began to catechize me on the subject of secrecy, to which I gave her such satisfactory answers, that, at last, having locked the door of her room, she took me into her closet, and then locking that door likewise, she said she should convince me of the vast reliance she had on my integrity, by communicating a secret in which her honor, and consequently her life, was concerned. She then stopped, and after a silence of a few minutes, during which she often wiped her eyes, she inquired of me if I thought my mother might safely be confided in. I answered, I would stake my life on her fidelity. She then imparted to me the great secret which labored in her breast, and which, I believe, was delivered with more pains than she afterwards suffered in childbirth. It was then contrived that my mother and myself only should attend at the time, and that Mrs. Wilkins should be sent out of the way, as she accordingly was, to the very farthest part of Dorsetshire, to inquire the character of a servant; for the lady had turned away her own maid near three months before; during all which time I officiated about her person upon trial, as she said, though, as she afterwards declared, I was not sufficiently handy for the place. This, and many other such things which she used to say of me, were all thrown out to prevent any suspicion which Wilkins might hereafter have, when I was to own the child; for she thought it could never be believed she would venture to hurt a young woman with whom she had entrusted such a secret. You may be assured, sir, I was well paid for all these affronts, which, together with being informed with the occasion of them, very well contented me. Then the child was born, in the presence only of myself and my mother, and was by my mother conveyed to her own house, where it was privately kept by her till the evening of your return, when I, by the command of Miss Bridget, conveyed it into the bed where you found it. And all suspicions were afterwards laid asleep by the artful conduct of your sister, in pretending ill-will to the boy, and that any regard she showed him was out of mere complaisance to you."

"I need not, madam," said Allworthy, "express my astonishment at what you have told me; and yet surely you would not, and could not, have put together so many circumstances to evidence an untruth. I confess I recollect some passages relating to that Summer, which formerly gave me a conceit that my sister had some liking to him. I mentioned it to her; for I had such a regard to the young man, as well on his own account as on his father's, that I should willingly have consented to a match between them; but she expressed the highest disdain of my unkind suspicion, as she called it; so that I never spoke more on the subject. Good heavens! Well! the Lord disposeth all things.——Yet sure it was a most unjustifiable conduct in my sister to carry this secret with her out of the world."

"I promise you, sir," said Mrs. Waters, "she always professed a contrary intention, and frequently told me she intended one day to communicate it to you. She said, indeed, she was highly rejoiced that her plot had succeeded so well, and that you had of your own accord taken such a fancy to the child, that it was yet unnecessary to make any express declaration. Oh! sir, had that lady lived to have seen this poor young man turned like a vagabond from your house: nay, sir, could she have lived to hear that you had yourself employed a lawyer to prosecute him for a murder of which he was not guilty ——Forgive me, Mr. Allworthy, I must say it was unkind. He never deserved it of you."

"Indeed, madam," said Allworthy, "I have been abused by the person, whoever he was, that told you so."

"Nay, sir," said she, "I would not be mistaken, I did not presume to say you were guilty of any wrong. The gentleman who came to me proposed no such matter; he only said, taking me for Mr. Fitzpatrick's wife, that, if Mr. Jones had murdered my husband, I should be assisted with any money I wanted to carry on the prosecution, by a very worthy gentleman, who, he said, was well apprised what a villain I had to deal with. It was by this man I found out who Mr. Jones was; and this man, whose name is Dowling, Mr. Jones tells me is your steward."

"And did this Mr. Dowling," says Allworthy, with great astonishment in his countenance, "tell you that I would assist in the prosecution?"

"No, sir," answered she, "I will not charge him wrongfully. He said I should be assisted, but he mentioned no name. Yet you must pardon me, sir, if from circumstances I thought it could be no other."

"Indeed, madam," says Allworthy, "from circumstances I am too well convinced it was another. Good Heaven! by what wonderful means is the blackest and deepest villainy sometimes discovered!— Shall I beg you, madam, to stay till the person you have mentioned comes, for I expect him every minute? nay, he may be, perhaps, already in the house."

Allworthy then stepped to the door, in order to call a servant, when in came, not Mr. Dowling, but the gentleman who will be seen in the next chapter.

VI

THE gentleman who now arrived was no other than Mr. Western. He no sooner saw Allworthy than, without considering in the least the presence of Mrs. Waters, he began to vociferate in the following manner:

"Fine doings at my house! A rare kettle of fish I have discovered at last! who the devil would be plagued with a daughter?"

"What's the matter, neighbor?" said Allworthy.

"Matter enough," answered Western: "when I thought she was just a-coming to; nay, when she had in a manner promised me to do as I would ha her, what do you think I have found out? that the little b— hath bin playing tricks with me all the while, and carrying on a correspondence with that bastard of yours. I have packed her up in chamber again, and tomorrow morning down she goes into the country, unless she consents to be married directly, and there she shall live in a garret upon bread and water all her days; and the sooner such a b— breaks her heart the better, though, d—n her, that I believe is too tough. She will live long enough to plague me."

"Mr. Western," answered Allworthy, "you know I have always protested against force, and you yourself consented that none should be used."

"Ay," cries he, "that was only upon condition that she would consent without."

"Well, neighbor," answered Allworthy, "if you will give me leave, I will undertake once to argue with the young lady."

"Will you?" said Western; "why, that is kind now, and neighborly, and mayhap you will do more than I have been able to do with her; for I promise you she hath a very good opinion of you."

"Well, sir," said Allworthy, "if you will go home, and release the young lady from her captivity, I will wait upon her within this half-hour."

"But suppose," said Western, "she should run away with un in the meantime? For lawyer Dowling tells me there is no hope of hanging the fellow at last, for that the man is alive, and like to do well, and that he thinks Jones will be out of prison again presently."

"How!" said Allworthy; "what, did you employ him, then, to inquire or to do anything in that matter?"

"Not I," answered Western; "he mentioned it to me just now of his own accord."

"Just now!" cries Allworthy; "why, where did you see him, then? I want much to see Mr. Dowling."

"Why, you may see un an you will presently at my lodgings; for there is to be a meeting of lawyers there this morning about a mortgage."

"Well, sir," said Allworthy, "I will be with you within the half-hour."

"And do for once," cries the squire, "take a fool's advice; never think of dealing with her by gentle methods, take my word for it those will never do!"

As soon as Mr. Western was gone, Allworthy was interrupted by the arrival of Mr. Dowling, who, upon his first entrance, seeing Mrs. Waters, started, and appeared in some confusion; from which he soon recovered himself as well as he could, and then said he was in the utmost haste to attend counsel at Mr. Western's lodgings.

Allworthy bolted the door, and then, advancing with a stern look to Dowling, he said,

"Whatever be your haste, sir, I must first receive an answer to some questions. Do you know this lady?"

"That lady, sir!" answered Dowling, with great hesitation.

Allworthy then, with the most solemn voice, said, "Look you, Mr. Dowling, as you value my favor, or your continuance a moment longer in my service, do not hesitate nor prevaricate; but answer faithfully and truly to every question I ask.——Do you know this lady?"

"Yes, sir," said Dowling, "I have seen the lady."

"Where, sir?"

"At her own lodgings."

"Upon what business did you go thither, sir; and who sent you?"

"I went, sir, to inquire, sir, about Mr. Jones."

"And who sent you to inquire about him?"

"Who, sir? why, sir, Mr. Blifil sent me."

"And what did you say to the lady concerning that matter?"

"Nay, sir, it is impossible to recollect every word."

"Will you please, madam, to assist the gentleman's memory?"

"He told me, sir," said Mrs. Waters, "that if Mr. Jones had murdered my husband, I should be assisted by any money I wanted to carry on the prosecution, by a very worthy gentleman, who was well apprised what a villain I had to deal with. These, I can safely swear, were the very words he spoke."

"Were these the words, sir?" said Allworthy.

"I cannot charge my memory exactly," cries Dowling, "but I believe I did speak to that purpose."

"And did Mr. Blifil order you to say so?"

"I am sure, sir, I should not have gone on my own accord, nor have willingly exceeded my authority in matters of this kind. If I said so, I must have so understood Mr. Blifil's instructions."

"Look you, Mr. Dowling," said Allworthy; "I promise you before this lady, that whatever you have done in this affair by Mr. Blifil's order I will forgive, provided you now tell me strictly the truth; for I believe what you say, that you would not have acted of your own accord and without authority in this matter.——Mr. Blifil then likewise sent you to examine the two fellows at Aldersgate?"

"He did, sir."

"Well, and what instructions did he then give you? Recollect as well as you can, and tell me, as near as possible, the very words he used."

"Why, sir, Mr. Blifil sent me to find out the persons who were eye-witnesses of this fight. He said, he feared they might be tampered with by Mr. Jones, or some of his friends. He said, blood required blood; and that not only all who concealed a murderer, but those who omitted anything in their power to bring him to justice, were sharers in his guilt. He said, he found you was very desirous of having the villain brought to justice, though it was not proper you should appear in it."

"He did so?" says Allworthy.

"Yes, sir," cries Dowling; "I should not, I am sure, have proceeded such lengths for the sake of any other persons living but your worship."

"What lengths, sir?" said Allworthy.

"Nay, sir," cries Dowling, "I would not have your worship think I would, on any account, be guilty of subornation of perjury; but there are two ways of delivering evidence. I told them, therefore, that if any offers should be made them on the other side, they should refuse them, and that they might be assured they should lose nothing by being honest men, and telling the truth. I said, we were told that Mr. Jones had assaulted the gentleman first, and that, if that was the truth, they should declare it; and I did give them some hints that they should be no losers."

"I think you went lengths indeed," cries Allworthy.

"Nay, sir," answered Dowling, "I am sure I did not desire them to tell an untruth;——nor should I have said what I did, unless it had been to oblige you."

"You would not have thought, I believe," says Allworthy, "to have obliged me, had you known that this Mr. Jones was my own nephew."

"I am sure, sir," answered he, "it did not become me to take any notice of what I thought you desired to conceal."

"How!" cries Allworthy, "and did you know it then?"

"Nay, sir," answered Dowling, "if your worship bids me speak the truth, I am sure I shall do it. Indeed, sir, I did know it; for they were almost the last words which Madam Blifil ever spoke, which she mentioned to me as I stood alone by her bedside, when she delivered me the letter I brought your worship from her."

"What letter?" cries Allworthy.

"The letter, sir," answered Dowling, "which I brought from Salisbury, and which I delivered into the hands of Mr. Blifil."

"Oh, heavens!" cries Allworthy. "Well, and what were the words? What did my sister say to you?"

"She took me by the hand," answered he, "and, as she delivered me the letter, said, 'I scarce know what I have written. Tell my brother, Mr. Jones is his nephew—He is my son.—Bless him,' says she, and then fell backward, as if dying away. I presently called in the people, and she never spoke more to me, and died within a few minutes afterwards."

Allworthy stood a minute silent, lifting up his eyes; and then, turning to Dowling, said, "How came you, sir, not to deliver me this message?"

"Your worship," answered he, "must remember that you was at that time ill in bed; and, being in a violent hurry, as indeed I always am, I delivered the letter and message to Mr. Blifil, who told me he would carry them both to you, which he hath since told me he did, and that your worship, partly out of friendship to Mr. Jones, and partly out of regard to your sister, would never have it mentioned, and did intend to conceal it from the world; and therefore, sir, if you had not mentioned it to me first, I am certain I should never have thought it belonged to me to say anything of the matter, either to your worship or any other person."

We have remarked somewhere already, that it is possible for a man to convey a lie in the words of truth; this was the case at present; for Blifil had, in fact, told Dowling what he now related, but had not imposed upon him, nor indeed had imagined he was able so to do. In reality, the promises which Blifil had made to Dowling were the motives which had induced him to secrecy; and, as he now very plainly saw Blifil would not be able to keep them, he thought proper now to make this confession, which the promises of forgiveness, joined to the threats, the voice, the looks of Allworthy, and the discoveries he had made before, extorted from him, who was besides taken unawares, and had no time to consider of evasions.

Allworthy appeared well satisfied with this relation, and, having enjoined on Dowling strict silence as to what had passed, conducted that gentleman himself to the door, lest he should see Blifil, who was returned to his chamber, where he exulted in the thoughts of his last deceit on his uncle, and little suspected what had since passed below-stairs.

As Allworthy was returning to his room he met Mrs. Miller in the entry, who, with a face all pale and full of terror, said to him, "Oh! sir, I find this wicked woman hath been with you, and you know all; yet do not on this account abandon the poor young man. Consider, sir, he was ignorant it was his own mother; and the discovery itself will most probably break his heart, without your unkindness."

"Madam," says Allworthy, "I am under such an astonishment at what I have heard, that I am really unable to satisfy you; but come with me into my room. Indeed, Mrs. Miller, I have made surprising discoveries, and you shall soon know them."

The poor woman followed him, trembling; and now Allworthy, going up to Mrs. Waters, took her by the hand, and then, turning to Mrs. Miller, said, "What reward shall I bestow upon this gentlewoman for the services she hath done me?—Oh! Mrs. Miller, you have a thousand times heard me call the young man to whom you are so faithful a friend, my son. Little did I then think he was indeed related to me at all.—Your friend, madam, is my nephew; he is the brother of that wicked viper which I have so long nourished in my bosom.—She will herself tell you the whole story, and how the youth came to pass for her son. Indeed, Mrs. Miller, I am convinced that he hath been wronged, and that I have been abused—abused by one whom you too justly suspected of being a villain. He is, in truth, the worst of villains."

The joy which Mrs. Miller now felt bereft her of the power of speech, and might perhaps have deprived her of her senses, if not of life, had not a friendly shower of tears come seasonably to her relief. At length, recovering so far from her transport as to be able to speak, she cried, "And is my dear Mr. Jones, then, your nephew, sir, and not the son of this lady? And are your eyes opened to him at last? And shall I live to see him as happy as he deserves?"

"He certainly is my nephew," says Allworthy, "and I hope all the rest."

"And is this the dear good woman, the person," cries she, "to whom all this discovery is owing?"

"She is indeed," says Allworthy.

"Why, then," cried Mrs. Miller, upon her knees, "may Heaven shower down its choicest blessings upon her head, and for this one good action forgive her all her sins, be they never so many!"

Mrs. Waters then informed them that she believed Jones would very shortly be released; for that the surgeon was gone, in company with a nobleman, to the justice who committed him, in order to certify that Mr. Fitzpatrick was out of all manner of danger, and to procure his prisoner his liberty.

Allworthy said he should be glad to find his nephew there at his return home; but that he was then obliged to go on some business of consequence. He then called to a servant to fetch him a chair, and presently left the two ladies together.

Mr. Blifil, hearing the chair ordered, came downstairs to attend upon his uncle; for he never was deficient in such arts of duty. He asked his uncle if he was going out, which is a civil way of asking a man whither he is going: to which the other making no answer, he again desired to know when he would be pleased to return. Allworthy made no answer to this neither, till he was just going into his chair, and then, turning about, he said,

"Harkee, sir, do you find out, before my return, the letter which your mother sent me on her death-bed." Allworthy then departed, and left Blifil in a situation to be envied only by a man who is just going to be hanged.

VII

ALLWORTHY took an opportunity, whilst he was in the chair, of reading the letter from Jones to Sophia, which Western delivered him; and there were some expressions in it concerning himself which drew tears from his eyes. At length he arrived at Mr. Western's, and was introduced to Sophia.

Allworthy, who was himself a little disconcerted, began thus:

"I am afraid, Miss Western, my family hath been the occasion of giving you some uneasiness; to which, I fear, I have innocently become more instrumental than I intended. Be assured, madam, had I at first known how disagreeable the proposals had been, I should not have suffered you to have been so long persecuted."

"Sir," said Sophia, with a little modest hesitation, "I am convinced you are too good and generous to resent my refusal of your nephew. Our inclinations are not in our own power; and whatever may be his merit, I cannot force them in his favor."

"I sincerely believe you, madam," replied Allworthy, "and I heartily congratulate you on your prudent foresight, since by so justifiable a resistance you have avoided misery indeed!"

"You speak now, Mr. Allworthy," cries she, "with a delicacy which few men are capable of feeling! If I had married Mr. Blifil——"

"Pardon my interrupting you, madam," answered Allworthy, "but I cannot bear the supposition.—Believe me, Miss Western, I rejoice from my heart, I rejoice in your escape.——I have discovered the wretch for whom you have suffered all this cruel violence from your father to be a villain!"

"How, sir!" cries Sophia—"you must believe this surprises me."

"It hath surprised me, madam," answered Allworthy, "and so it will the world. I have another matter of a very serious nature to propose. Oh! Miss Western, I know your vast worth, nor can I so easily part with the ambition of being allied to it.—I have a near relation, madam, a young man whose character is, I am convinced, the very opposite to that of this wretch, and whose fortune I will make equal to what his was to have been. Could I, madam, hope you would admit a visit from him?"

Sophia, after a minute's silence, answered, "I will deal with the utmost sincerity with Mr. Allworthy. His character, and the obligation I have just received from him, demand it. I have determined at present to listen to no such proposals from any person. My only desire is to be restored to the affection of my father, and to be again the mistress of his family. This, sir, I hope to owe to your good offices. Let me beseech you, let me conjure you, by all the goodness which I, and all who know you, have experienced, do not, the very moment when you have released me from one persecution, do not engage me in another as miserable and as fruitless."

"Indeed, Miss Western," replied Allworthy, "I am capable of no such conduct; and if this be your resolution, he must submit to the disappointment, whatever torments he may suffer under it."

"I must smile now, Mr. Allworthy," answered Sophia, "when you mention the torments of a man whom I do not know, and who can consequently have so little acquaintance with me."

"Pardon me, dear young lady," cries Allworthy, "I begin now to be afraid he hath had too much acquaintance for the repose of his future days; since, if ever man was capable of a sincere, violent, and noble passion, such, I am convinced, is my unhappy nephew's for Miss Western."

"A nephew of yours, Mr. Allworthy!" answered Sophia. "It is surely strange I never heard of him before."

"Indeed, madam," cries Allworthy, "it is only the circumstance of his being my nephew to which you are a stranger, and which, till this day, was a secret to me.—Mr. Jones, who has long loved you, he! he is my nephew!"

"Mr. Jones your nephew, sir!" cries Sophia; "can it be possible?"

"He is indeed, madam," answered Allworthy; "he is my own sister's son—as such I shall always own him; nor am I ashamed of owning him. I am much more ashamed of my past behavior to him; but I was as ignorant of his merit as of his birth. Indeed, Miss Western, I have used him cruelly——Indeed I have." Here he stopped, seeming to expect an answer, which he presently received from Sophia, after she had a little recovered herself from the hurry of spirits into which so strange and sudden information had thrown her:

"I sincerely wish you joy, sir, of a discovery in which you seem to have such satisfaction. I doubt not but you will have all the comfort you can promise yourself from it. The young gentleman hath certainly a thousand good qualities, which makes it impossible he should not behave well to such an uncle."

"I hope, madam," said Allworthy, "he hath those good qualities which must make him a good husband.—He must, I am sure, be of all men the most abandoned, if a lady of your merit should condescend——"

"You must pardon me, Mr. Allworthy," answered Sophia; "I cannot listen to a proposal of this kind. Mr. Jones, I am convinced, hath much merit; but I shall never receive Mr. Jones as one who is to be my husband—Upon my honor I never will."

"Pardon me, madam," cries Allworthy, "if I am a little surprised, after what I had heard from Mr. Western. I am cautious of offending you, young lady; but am I to look on all which I have hitherto heard or seen as a dream only? And have you suffered so much cruelty from your father on the account of a man to whom you have been always absolutely indifferent?"

"I beg, Mr. Allworthy," answered Sophia, "you will not insist on my reasons;—yes, I have suffered indeed; I will not, Mr. Allworthy, conceal——I will be very sincere with you—I own I had a great opinion of Mr. Jones—I believe—I know I have suffered for my opinion—I have been treated cruelly by my aunt, as well as by my father; but that is now past—I beg I may not be further pressed; for, whatever hath been, my resolution is now fixed. At present there is not a man upon earth whom I would more resolutely reject than Mr. Jones; nor would the addresses of Mr. Blifil himself be less agreeable to me."

Western had been long impatient for the event of this conference, and was just now arrived at the door to listen; when, having heard the last sentiments of his daughter's heart, he lost all temper, and, bursting open the door in a rage, cried out—"It is a lie! It is a d—n'd lie! It is all owing to that d—n'd rascal Jones; and if she could get at un, she'd ha' un any hour of the day."

"Indeed, my good friend," answered Allworthy, "you yourself are the cause of all the trouble you complain of. Place that confidence in the young lady which she so well deserves, and I am certain you will be the happiest father on earth."

"I confidence in her?" cries the squire. " 'Sblood! what confidence can I place in her, when she won't do as I would ha' her?"

"You have no right, neighbor," answered Allworthy, "to insist on any such consent. A negative voice your daughter allows you, and God and nature have thought proper to allow you no more."

"A negative voice!" cries the squire—"Ay! ay! I'll show you what a negative voice I ha'. Go along, go into your chamber, go, you stubborn——See here, sir, here is a letter from my cousin, my Lady Bellaston, in which she is so kind to gi' me to understand that the fellow is got out of prison again; and here she advises me to take all the care I can o' the wench."

The squire ended his speech with some compliments to his own sagacity; and then Allworthy, after a formal preface, acquainted him with the whole discovery which he had made concerning Jones, with his anger to Blifil.

Men overviolent in their dispositions are, for the most part, as changeable in them. No sooner, then, was Western informed of Mr. Allworthy's intention to make Jones his heir, than he joined heartily with the uncle in every commendation of the nephew, and became as eager for her marriage with Jones as he had before been to couple her to Blifil.

Here Mr. Allworthy was again forced to interpose, and to relate what had passed between him and Sophia, at which he testified great surprise.

The squire was silent a moment, and looked wild with astonishment at this account. At last he cried out, "Why, what can be the meaning of this, neighbor Allworthy? Vond o' un she was, that I'll be sworn to.——Odzookers! I have hit o't. The girl hath goth a hankering after this son of a whore of a lord. He hath turned the head o' her, that's certain—but d—n me if he shall ha' her—I'll ha' no lords nor courtiers in my vamily."

Allworthy now made a long speech, in which he repeated his resolution to avoid all violent measures, and very earnestly recommended gentle methods to Mr. Western, as those by which he might be assured of succeeding best with his daughter. He then took his leave, and returned back to Mrs. Miller, but was forced to comply with the earnest entreaties of the squire, in promising to bring Mr. Jones to visit him that afternoon, that he might, as he said, "make all matters up with the young gentleman."

VIII

WHEN Allworthy returned to his lodgings, he heard Mr. Jones was just arrived before him. He hurried therefore instantly into an empty chamber, whither he ordered that Mr. Jones be brought to him alone.

It is impossible to conceive a more tender or moving scene than the meeting between the uncle and nephew (for Mrs. Waters, as the reader may well suppose, had at her last visit discovered to him the secret of his birth). After Allworthy had raised Jones from his feet, where he had prostrated himself, and received him into his arms, "Oh, my child!" he cried, "how have I been to blame! how have I injured you! What amends can I ever make you for those unkind, those unjust suspicions which I have entertained, and for all the sufferings they have occasioned you?"

"Am I not now made amends?" cries Jones. "Would not my sufferings, if they had been ten times greater, have been now richly repaid? Oh, my dear uncle, this goodness, this tenderness overpowers, unmans, destroys me. I cannot bear the transports which flow so fast upon me. To be again restored to your presence, to your favor; to be once more thus kindly received by my great, my noble, my generous benefactor."

"Indeed, child," cries Allworthy, "I have used you cruelly."—— He then explained to him all the treachery of Blifil, and again repeated expressions of the utmost concern, for having been induced by that treachery to use him so ill.

"Oh, talk not so!" answered Jones; "indeed, sir, you have used me nobly. The wisest man might be deceived as you were; and, under such a deception, the best must have acted just as you did. Alas! sir, I have not been punished more than I have deserved; I thank Heaven, I have had time to reflect on my past life, where I can discern follies and vices more than enough to repent and to be ashamed of."

"I am rejoiced, my dear child," answered Allworthy, "to hear you talk thus sensibly. You now see, Tom, to what dangers imprudence alone may subject virtue (for virtue, I am now convinced, you love in a great degree). You say, however, you have seen your errors, and will reform them. I firmly believe you; and therefore, from this moment, you shall never be reminded of them by me."

At these words Jones fetched a deep sigh; upon which, when Allworthy remonstrated, he said, "Sir, I will conceal nothing from you: I fear there is one consequence of my vices I shall never be able to retrieve. Oh, my dear uncle! I have lost a treasure."

"You need say no more," answered Allworthy; "I have seen the young lady, and have discoursed with her concerning you. This I must insist on, that you abide entirely by the determination of the young lady, whether it shall be in your favor or no. I know her father will be as ready to torment her now on your account as he hath formerly been on another's; but I am determined she shall suffer no more confinement, no more violence, no more uneasy hours."

"Oh, my dear uncle!" answered Jones. "Believe me, sir, the only instance in which I could disobey you would be to give an uneasy moment to my Sophia. No, sir, if I am so miserable to have incurred her displeasure beyond all hope of forgiveness, that alone, with the dreadful reflection of causing her misery, will be sufficient to over-power me."

"I will not flatter you, child," cries Allworthy; "I fear your case is desperate: I never saw stronger marks of an unalterable resolution in any person than appeared in her vehement declarations against receiving your addresses; for which, perhaps, you can account better than myself."

"Oh, sir! I can account too well," answered Jones; "I have sinned against her beyond all hope of pardon; and guilty as I am, my guilt unfortunately appears to her in ten times blacker than the real colors."

A servant now acquainted them that Mr. Western was below-stairs; for his eagerness to see Jones could not wait till the afternoon. Upon which Jones, whose eyes were full of tears, begged his uncle to entertain Western a few minutes, till he a little recovered himself.

Mrs. Miller no sooner heard that Jones was alone (for she had not yet seen him since his release from prison) than she came eagerly into the room, and, advancing towards Jones, wished him heartily joy of his new-found uncle and his happy reconciliation; adding, "I wish I could give you joy on another account, my dear child; but anything so inexorable I never saw."

Jones, with some appearance of surprise, asked her what she meant. "Why, then," says she, "I have been with your young lady, and have explained all matters to her, as they were told to me by my son Nightingale. She can have no longer any doubt about the letter; of that I am certain; for I told her my son Nightingale was ready to take his oath, if she pleased, that it was all his own invention, and the letter of his inditing. I told her the very reason of sending the letter ought to recommend you to her the more, as it was all upon her account, and a plain proof that you was resolved to quit all your profligacy for the future; that you had never been guilty of a single instance of infidelity to her since your seeing her in town: I am afraid I went too far there; but Heaven forgive me! I hope your future behavior will be my justification. I am sure I have said all I can; but all to no purpose. She remains inflexible."

"Oh, Mrs. Miller!" answered Jones, "can I bear to think I have lost such an angel?"

"Lost! no," cries Mrs. Miller; "I hope you have not lost her yet. Resolve to leave such vicious courses, and you may yet have hopes."

Here the conversation was interrupted by the arrival of Western, who could no longer be kept out of the room even by the authority of Allworthy himself; though this, as we have often seen, had a wonderful power over him.

Western immediately went up to Jones, crying out, "My old friend Tom, I am glad to see thee with all my heart! all past must be forgotten; I could not intend any affront to thee, because, as Allworthy here knows, nay, dost know it thyself, I took thee for another person; and where a body means no harm, what signifies a hasty word or two? One Christian must forget and forgive another."

"I hope, sir," said Jones, "I shall never forget the many obligations I have had to you; but as for any offense towards me, I declare I am an utter stranger."

"A't," says Western, "then give me thy fist; a't as hearty an honest cock as any in the kingdom. Come along with me; I'll carry thee to thy mistress this moment." Here Allworthy interposed; and the squire, being unable to prevail either with the uncle or nephew, was obliged to consent to delay introducing Jones to Sophia till the afternoon; at which time Allworthy, as well in compassion to Jones as in compliance with the eager desires of Western, was prevailed upon to promise to attend at the tea-table.

And now a message was brought from Mr. Blifil, desiring to know if his uncle was at leisure that he might wait upon him. Allworthy started and turned pale, and then in a more passionate tone than I believe he had ever used before, bid the servant tell Blifil he knew him not.

"Consider, dear sir," cried Jones, in a trembling voice.

"I have considered," answered Allworthy, "and you yourself shall carry my message to the villain. No one can carry him the sentence of his own ruin so properly as the man whose ruin he hath so villainously contrived."

"Pardon me, dear sir," said Jones; "a moment's reflection will, I am sure, convince you of the contrary. What might perhaps be but justice from another tongue, would from mine be insult; and to whom?—my own brother and your nephew. Nor did he use me so barbarously—indeed that would have been more inexcusable than anything he hath done. Fortune may tempt men of no very bad dispositions to injustice; but insults proceed only from black and rancorous minds, and have no temptations to excuse them. Let me beseech you, sir, to do nothing by him in the present height of your anger. Consider, my dear uncle, I was not myself condemned unheard."

Allworthy stood silent a moment, and then, embracing Jones, he said, with tears gushing from his eyes, "Oh, my child! to what goodness have I been so long blind!"

Mrs. Miller entering the room at that moment asked what was to be done with Blifil? "for indeed," says she, "I cannot be easy while such a villain is in my house."

Allworthy answered, "He was as uneasy as herself on the same account."

"Oh!" cries she, "if that be the case, leave the matter to me, I'll soon show him the outside out of my doors, I warrant you. Here are two or three lusty fellows below-stairs."

"There will be no need of any violence," cries Allworthy; "if you will carry him a message from me, he will, I am convinced, depart of his own accord."

"Will I?" said Mrs. Miller; "I never did anything in my life with a better will."

Here Jones interfered, and said, "He had considered the matter better, and would, if Mr. Allworthy pleased, be himself the messenger. I know," says he, "already enough of your pleasure, sir, and I beg leave to acquaint him with it by my own words. Let me beseech you, sir," added he, "to reflect on the dreadful consequences of driving him to violent and sudden despair. How unfit, alas! is this poor man to die in his present situation."

This suggestion had not the least effect on Mrs. Miller. She left the room, crying,

"You are too good, Mr. Jones, infinitely too good to live in this world." But it made a deeper impression on Allworthy.

"My good child," said he, "I am equally astonished at the goodness of your heart, and the quickness of your understanding. Heaven indeed forbid that this wretch should be deprived of any means or time for repentance! That would be a shocking consideration indeed. Go to him, therefore, and use your own discretion; yet do not flatter him with any hopes of my forgiveness; for I shall never forgive villainy further than my religion obliges me, and that extends not either to our bounty or our conversation."

Jones went up to Blifil's room, whom he found in a situation which moved his pity, though it would have raised a less amiable passion in many beholders. He cast himself on his bed, where he lay abandoning himself to despair, and drowned in tears; not in such tears as flow from contrition; no, these tears were such as the frighted thief sheds in his cart, and are indeed the effects of that concern which the most savage natures are seldom deficient in feeling for themselves.

It would be unpleasant and tedious to paint this scene in full length. Let it suffice to say, that the behavior of Jones was kind to excess. He omitted nothing which his invention could supply, to raise and comfort the drooping spirits of Blifil, before he communicated to him the resolution of his uncle that he must quit the house that evening. He offered to furnish him with any money he wanted, assured him of his hearty forgiveness of all he had done against him, that he would endeavor to live with him hereafter as a brother, and would leave nothing unattempted to effectuate a reconciliation with his uncle.

Blifil was at first sullen and silent, balancing in his mind whether he should yet deny all; but, finding at last the evidence too strong against him, he betook himself at last to confession.

He then asked pardon of his brother in the most vehement manner, prostrated himself on the ground, and kissed his feet; in short, he was now as remarkably mean as he had been before remarkably wicked.

Jones could not so far check his disdain, but that it a little discovered itself in his countenance at this extreme servility. He raised his brother the moment he could from the ground, and advised him to bear his afflictions more like a man; repeating, at the same time, his promises, that he would do all in his power to lessen them; for which Blifil, making many professions of his unworthiness, poured forth a profusion of thanks; and then, he having declared he would immediately depart to another lodging, Jones returned to his uncle.

Among other matters, Allworthy now acquainted Jones with the discovery which he had made concerning the £500 bank-notes. "I have," said he, "already consulted a lawyer, who tells me, to my great astonishment, that there is no punishment for a fraud of this kind. Indeed, when I consider the black ingratitude of this fellow toward you, I think a highwayman, compared to him, is an innocent person."

"Good Heaven!" says Jones, "is it possible?—I am shocked beyond measure at this news. I thought there was not an honester fellow in the world.——The temptation of such a sum was too great for him to withstand; for smaller matters have come safe to me through his hand. Indeed, my dear uncle, you must suffer me to call it weakness rather than ingratitude; for I am convinced the poor fellow loves me, and hath done me some kindnesses, which I can never forget. Consider, sir, what a temptation to a man who hath tasted such bitter distress, it must be, to have a sum in his possession which must put him and his family beyond any future possibility of suffering the like."

"Child," cries Allworthy, "you carry this forgiving temper too far. Such mistaken mercy is not only weakness, but borders on injustice, and is very pernicious to society, as it encourages vice. I am convinced the fellow is a villain, and he shall be punished; at least as far as I can punish him."

This was spoken with so stern a voice, that Jones did not think proper to make any reply; besides, the hour appointed by Mr. Western now drew so near, that he had barely time left to dress himself. Here therefore ended the present dialogue, and Jones retired to another room, where Partridge attended, according to order, with his clothes.

Partridge had scarce seen his master since the happy discovery. The poor fellow was unable either to contain or express his transports. He behaved like one frantic, and made almost as many mistakes while he was dressing Jones as I have seen made by Harlequin in dressing himself on the stage.

His memory, however, was not in the least deficient. He recollected how many omens and presages of this happy event, some of which he had remarked at the time, but many more he now remembered; nor did he omit the dreams he had dreamt the evening before his meeting with Jones; and concluded with saying, "I always told your honor something boded in my mind that you would one time or other have it in your power to make my fortune." Jones assured him that this boding should as certainly be verified with regard to him as all the other omens had been to himself; which did not a little add to all the raptures which the poor fellow had already conceived on account of his master.

IX

JONES, being now completely dressed, attended his uncle to Mr. Western's. He was, indeed, one of the finest figures ever beheld, and his person alone would have charmed the greater part of womankind; but we hope it hath already appeared in this history that Nature, when she formed him, did not totally rely, as she sometimes doth, on this merit only, to recommend her work.

Sophia, who, angry as she was, was likewise set forth to the best advantage, for which I leave my female readers to account, appeared so extremely beautiful, that even Allworthy, when he saw her, could not forbear whispering to Western, that he believed she was the finest creature in the world. To which Western answered, in a whisper, overheard by all present, "So much the better for Tom; for d—n me if he shan't ha the tousling her." Sophia was all over scarlet at these words, while Tom's countenance was altogether as pale, and he was almost ready to sink from his chair.

The tea-table was scarce removed before Western lugged Allworthy out of the room, telling him he had business of consequence to impart, and must speak to him that instant in private, before he forgot it.

The lovers were now alone, and it will, I question not, appear strange to many readers, that those who had so much to say to one another when danger and difficulty attended their conversation, and who seemed so eager to rush into each other's arms when so many bars lay in their way, now that with safety they were at liberty to say or do whatever they pleased, should both remain for some time silent and motionless; both sat with their eyes downwards on the ground, and for some minutes continued in perfect silence.

Mr. Jones during this interval attempted once or twice to speak, but was absolutely incapable, muttering only, or rather sighing out, some broken words; when Sophia at length, partly out of pity to him, and partly to turn the discourse from the subject which she knew well enough he was endeavoring to open, said—

"Sure, sir, you are the most fortunate man in the world in this discovery."

"And can you really, madam, think me so fortunate," said Jones, sighing, "while I have incurred your displeasure?"

"Nay, sir," says she, "as to that you best know whether you have deserved it."

"Indeed, madam," answered he, "you yourself are as well apprised of all my demerits. Mrs. Miller hath acquainted you with the whole truth. Oh! my Sophia, am I never to hope for forgiveness?"

"I think, Mr. Jones," said she, "I may almost depend on your own justice, and leave it to yourself to pass sentence on your own conduct."

"Alas! madam," answered he, "it is mercy, and not justice, which I implore at your hands. Justice I know must condemn me.—Yet not for the letter I sent to Lady Bellaston. Of that I most solemnly declare you have had a true account."

"I do not, I cannot," says she, "believe otherwise of that letter than you would have me. And yet, Mr. Jones, have I not enough to resent? After what passed at Upton, so soon to engage in a new amour with another woman, while I fancied, and you pretended, your heart was bleeding for me? What happiness can I assure myself of with a man capable of so much inconstancy?"

"Oh! my Sophia," cries he, "do not doubt the sincerity of the purest passion that ever inflamed a human breast. Inconstancy to you! Oh, Sophia! if you can have goodness enough to pardon what is past, do not let any cruel future apprehensions shut your mercy against me. No repentance was ever more sincere!"

"Sincere repentance, Mr. Jones," answered she, "will obtain the pardon of a sinner, but it is from one who is a perfect judge of that sincerity. You must expect, however, that if I can be prevailed on by your repentance to pardon you, I will at least insist on the strongest proof of its sincerity."

"Name any proof in my power," answered Jones eagerly.

"Time," replied she; "time alone, Mr. Jones, can convince me that you are a true penitent, and have resolved to abandon these vicious courses, which I should detest you for, if I imagined you capable of persevering in them."

"Do not imagine it," cries Jones. "On my knees I entreat, I implore your confidence, a confidence which it shall be the business of my life to deserve."

"Well," says Sophia, "the proof of this must be from time. Your situation, Mr. Jones, is now altered, and I assure you I have great satisfaction in the alteration. You will now want no opportunity of being near me, and convincing me that your mind is altered too."

"Oh! my angel," cries Jones, "I will be all obedience to your commands. I will not dare to press anything further than you permit me. Yet let me entreat you to appoint a short trial. Oh! tell me when I may expect you will be convinced of what is most solemnly true."

"When I have gone voluntarily thus far, Mr. Jones," said she, "I expect not to be pressed. Nay, I will not."

"Oh! don't look unkindly thus, my Sophia," cries he. "I do not, I dare not press you.—Yet permit me at least once more to beg you would fix the period. Oh! consider the impatience of love."

"A twelvemonth, perhaps," said she.

"Oh! my Sophia," cries he, "you have named an eternity."

"Perhaps it may be something sooner," says she; "I will not be teased. If your passion for me be what I would have it, I think you may now be easy."

"Easy! Sophia, call not such an exulting happiness as mine by so cold a name.——Oh! transporting thought! am I not assured that the blessed day will come, when I shall call you mine; when fears shall be no more; when I shall have that dear, that vast, that exquisite, ecstatic delight of making my Sophia happy?"

"Indeed, sir," said she, "that day is in your own power."

"Oh! my dear, my divine angel," cried he, "these words have made me mad with joy.——But I must, I will thank those dear lips which have so sweetly pronounced my bliss." He then caught her in his arms, and kissed her with an ardor he had never ventured before.

At this instant Western, who had stood some time listening, burst into the room, and, with his hunting voice and phrase, cried out, "To her, boy, to her, go to her.——That's it, little honeys; oh, that's it! Well! what, is it all over? Hath she appointed the day, boy? What, shall it be tomorrow or next day? It shan't be put off a minute longer than next day, I am resolved."

"Let me beseech you, sir," says Jones, "don't let me be the occasion——"

"Beseech mine a——," cries Western. "I thought thou hadst been a lad of higher mettle than to give way to a parcel of maidenish tricks.——I tell thee 'tis all flimflam. Zoodikers! she'd have the wedding tonight with all her heart. Would'st not, Sophy? Come, confess, and be an honest girl for once. What, art dumb? Why dost not speak?"

"Why should I confess, sir," says Sophia, "since it seems you are so well acquainted with my thoughts?"

"That's a good girl," cries he, "and dost consent, then?"

"No, indeed, sir," says Sophia, "I have given no such consent."

"And wunt not ha' un, then, tomorrow, nor next day?" says Western.

"Indeed, sir," says she, "I have no such intention."

"But I can tell thee," replied he, "why hast nut; only because thou dost love to be disobedient, and to plague and vex thy father."

"Pray, sir," said Jones, interfering——

"I tell thee thou art a puppy," cries he. "When I vorbid her, then it was all nothing but sighing and whining, and languishing and writing; now I am vor thee, she is against thee. All the spirit of contrary, that's all. She is above being guided and governed by her father, that is the whole truth on't. It is only to disoblige and contradict me."

"What would my papa have me do?" cries Sophia.

"What would I ha' thee do?" says he; "why, gi' un thy hand this moment."

"Well, sir," says Sophia, "I will obey you.—There is my hand, Mr. Jones."

"Well, and will you consent to ha' un tomorrow morning?" says Western.

"I will be obedient to you, sir," cries she.

"Why, then, tomorrow morning be the day," cries he.

"Why, then, tomorrow morning shall be the day, papa, since you will have it so," says Sophia. Jones then fell upon his knees, and kissed her hand in an agony of joy, while Western began to caper and dance about the room, presently crying out—"Where the devil is Allworthy? He is without now, a-talking with that d——d lawyer Dowling, when he should be minding other matters." He then sallied out in quest of him, and very opportunely left the lovers to enjoy a few tender minutes alone.

But he soon returned with Allworthy, saying, "if you won't believe me, you may ask her yourself. Hast nut gin thy consent, Sophy, to be married tomorrow?"

"Such are your commands, sir," cries Sophia, "and I dare not be guilty of disobedience."

"I hope, madam," cries Allworthy, "my nephew will merit so much goodness, and will be always as sensible as myself of the great honor you have done my family. An alliance with so charming and so excellent a young lady would indeed be an honor to the greatest in England."

"Yes," cries Western, "but if I had suffered her to stand shill I shall I, dilly dally, you might not have had that honor yet a while; I was forced to use a little fatherly authority to bring her to."

"I hope not, sir," cries Allworthy, "I hope there is not the least constraint."

"Why, there," cries Western, "you may bid her unsay all again if you will.—Dost repent heartily of thy promise, dost not, Sophia?"

"Indeed, papa," cries she, "I do not repent, nor do I believe I ever shall, of any promise in favor of Mr. Jones."

"Then, nephew," cries Allworthy, "I felicitate you most heartily; for I think you are the happiest of men.—And, madam, you will give me leave to congratulate you on this joyful occasion: indeed I am convinced you have bestowed yourself on one who will be sensible of your great merit, and who will at least use his best endeavors to deserve it."

"His best endeavors!" cries Western; "that he will, I warrant un. ——Harkee, Allworthy, I'll bet thee five pounds to a crown we have a boy tomorrow nine months; but prithee tell me what wut ha'! Wut ha' Burgundy, Champagne, or what? for, please Jupiter, we'll make a night on't."

"Indeed, sir," said Allworthy, "you must excuse me; both my nephew and I were engaged before I suspected this near approach of his happiness."

"Odzookers!" answered the squire, "I will go with thee, and so shall Sophy! for I won't part with thee tonight; and it would be barbarous to part Tom and the girl." This offer was presently embraced by Allworthy, and Sophia consented, having first obtained a private promise from her father that he would not mention a syllable concerning her marriage.

X

YOUNG Nightingale had been that afternoon, by appointment, to wait on his father, who received him much more kindly than he expected.

In this situation were affairs when Mr. Allworthy and his company arrived to complete the happiness of Mrs. Miller, who no sooner saw Sophia than she guessed everything that had happened; and so great was her friendship to Jones, that it added not a few transports to those she felt on the happiness of her own daughter.

There have not, I believe, been many instances of a number of people met together where every one was so perfectly happy as in this company. Amongst whom the father of young Nightingale enjoyed the least perfect content; for, notwithstanding his affection for his son, notwithstanding the authority and the arguments of Allworthy, he could not so entirely be satisfied with his son's choice; and perhaps the presence of Sophia herself tended a little to aggravate and heighten his concern, as a thought now and then suggested itself that his son might have had that lady, or some other such. Not that any of the charms which adorned either the person or mind of Sophia created the uneasiness; it was the contents of her father's coffers which set his heart alonging. These were the charms which he could not bear to think his son had sacrificed to the daughter of Mrs. Miller.

The evening was spent in much true mirth. Yet, as great joy, especially after a sudden change and revolution of circumstances, is apt to be silent, and dwells rather in the heart than on the tongue, Jones and Sophia appeared the least merry of the whole company; which Western observed with great impatience, often crying out to them, "Why dost not talk, boy? Why dost look so grave? Hast lost thy tongue, girl? Drink another glass of wine; sha't drink another glass." And, the more to enliven her, he would sometimes sing a merry song, which bore some relation to matrimony. Nay, he would have proceeded so far on that topic as to have driven her out of the room, if Mr. Allworthy had not checked him.

Notwithstanding this little restraint, he was so pleased with the cheerfulness and good-humor of the company, that he insisted on their meeting the next day at his lodgings. They all did so; and the lovely Sophia, who was now in private become a bride too, officiated as the mistress of the ceremonies, or, in the polite phrase, did the honors of the table. She had that morning given her hand to Jones, in the chapel at Doctors' Commons, where Mr. Allworthy, Mr. Western, and Mrs. Miller were the only persons present.

Thus, reader, we have at length brought our history to a conclusion, in which, to our great pleasure, though contrary, perhaps, to thy expectation, Mr. Jones appears to be the happiest of all humankind; for what happiness this world affords equal to the possession of such a woman as Sophia, I sincerely own I have never yet discovered.

As to the other persons who have made any considerable figure in this history, as some may desire to know a little more concerning them, we will proceed, in as few words as possible, to satisfy their curiosity.

Allworthy hath never yet been prevailed upon to see Blifil, but he hath yielded to the importunity of Jones, backed by Sophia, to settle £200 a-year upon him; to which Jones hath privately added a third. Upon this income he lives in one of the northern counties, about 200 miles distant from London, and lays up £200 a-year out of it, in order to purchase a seat in the next parliament from a neighboring borough, which he has bargained for with an attorney there. He is also lately turned Methodist, in hopes of marrying a very rich widow of that sect, whose estate lies in that part of the kingdom.

Square died soon after he wrote the before-mentioned letter; and as to Thwackum, he continues at his vicarage. He hath made many fruitless attempts to regain the confidence of Allworthy, or to ingratiate himself with Jones, both of whom he flatters to their faces, and abuses behind their backs.

Mrs. Fitzpatrick is separated from her husband, and retains the little remains of her fortune. She lives in reputation at the polite end of the town, and is so good an economist, that she spends three times the income of her fortune, without running in debt. She maintains a perfect intimacy with the lady of the Irish peer; and in acts of friendship to her repays all the obligations she owes to her husband.

Mrs. Western was soon reconciled to her niece Sophia, and hath spent two months together with her in the country. Lady Bellaston made the latter a formal visit at her return to town, where she behaved to Jones as to a perfect stranger, and, with great civility, wished him joy on his marriage.

Mr. Nightingale hath purchased an estate for his son in the neighborhood of Jones, where the young gentleman, his lady, Mrs. Miller, and her little daughter reside, and the most agreeable intercourse subsists between the two families.

As to those of lower account, Mrs. Waters returned into the country, had a pension of £60 a-year settled upon her by Mr. Allworthy, and is married to Parson Supple, on whom, at the instance of Sophia, Western hath bestowed a considerable living.

Black George, hearing the discovery that had been made, ran away, and was never since heard of; and Jones bestowed the money on his family, but not in equal proportions, for Molly had much the greatest share.

As for Partridge, Jones had settled £50 a-year on him; and he hath again set up a school, in which he meets with much better encouragement than formerly, and there is now a treaty of marriage on foot between him and Miss Molly Seagrim, which through the mediation of Sophia is likely to take effect.

We now return to take leave of Mr. Jones and Sophia, who, within two days after their marriage, attended Mr. Western and Mr. Allworthy into the country. Western hath resigned his family seat, and the greater part of his estate, to his son-in-law, and hath retired to a lesser house of his in another part of the country, which is better for hunting. Indeed he is often as a visitant with Mr. Jones, who, as well as his daughter, hath an infinite delight in doing everything in their power to please him. And this desire of theirs is attended with such success, that the old gentleman declares he was never happy in his life till now. He hath here a parlor and antechamber to himself, where he gets drunk with whom he pleases; and his daughter is still as ready as formerly to play to him whenever he desires it; for Jones hath assured her that, as, next to pleasing her, one of his highest satisfactions is to contribute to the happiness of the old man, so the great duty which she expresses and performs to her father renders her almost equally dear to him with the love which she bestows on himself.

Sophia hath already produced him two fine children, a boy and a girl, of whom the old gentleman is so fond, that he spends much of his time in the nursery, where he declares the tattling of his little granddaughter, who is above a year and a half old, is sweeter music than the finest cry of dogs in England.

Allworthy was likewise greatly liberal to Jones on the marriage, and hath omitted no instance of showing his affection to him and his lady, who love him as a father. Whatever in the nature of Jones had a tendency to vice, has been corrected by continual conversation with this good man, and by his union with the lovely and virtuous Sophia. He hath also, by reflection on his past follies, acquired a discretion and prudence very uncommon in one of his lively parts.

To conclude, as there are not to be found a worthier man and woman than this fond couple, so neither can any be imagined more happy. They preserve the purest and tenderest affection for each other, an affection daily increased and confirmed by mutual endearments and mutual esteem. Nor is their conduct towards their relations and friends less amiable than towards one another. And such is their condescension, their indulgence, and their beneficence to those below them, that there is not a neighbor, a tenant, or a servant, who doth not most gratefully bless the day when Mr. Jones was married to his Sophia.